FOR YOU, TH
A SPECIAL IN

Come journey with us to the wildest frontiers of the heart...

Diamond Wildflower Romance

A breathtaking new line of searing romance novels

...where destiny meets desire
in the untamed fury of the
American West.

...where passionate men
and women dare to embrace their
boldest dreams.

...where the heated rapture
of love runs free and wild
as the wind!

Invitation to Temptation

"Miss Cassie," Shane greeted her, the expression in his eyes unbelievably sensual.

"Mr. Lancer," she replied, equally polite, intensely aware of the score of eyes trained in their direction—and intensely aware of his eyes perusing more than the smile on her face.

"Right nice evenin', isn't it, ma'am?" he parried, his gaze focusing on the lips she nervously moistened.

"Yes, Mr. Lancer, it is," Cassie answered, uncomfortably aware of the townspeople's scrutiny, uncomfortably aware of the heat his presence evoked. His gaze raked the form-fitting bodice of her taffeta dress, his appreciation evident in the smile slowly touching his lips.

"May I have the next dance, ma'am?"

She lowered her eyes, hoping to control the sudden throbbing in her veins she felt must be visible, trying to remember she must not lose control with this man . . .

This book also contains a preview of the newest Diamond Wildflower Romance, *OUTLAW HEART by Catherine Palmer.*

Summer Rose

Bonnie K. Winn

DIAMOND BOOKS, NEW YORK

This book is a Diamond original edition, and has never
been previously published.

SUMMER ROSE

A Diamond Book / published by arrangement with
the author

PRINTING HISTORY
Diamond edition / July 1992

ISBN: 1-55773-734-7

Diamond Books are published by The Berkley Publishing Group,
200 Madison Avenue, New York, New York 10016.

PRINTED IN THE UNITED STATES OF AMERICA

10 9 8 7 6 5 4 3 2 1

Dedicated to my real-life heroes—

my husband, Howard . . .
and son, Brian.

I love you.

Acknowledgments

With love and gratitude to the Yedlovskys: my father who spent hours with me in the nooks and crannies of the library, instilling in me the love of reading—along with the belief that I could do anything I dared try. My mother, whose cache of books, along with her love, shaped my destiny. To both of you and Gary—you always believed. You made me believe.

A special thanks to my editor, Judith Stern, for your encouragement, guidance, and creative direction throughout the development of this novel. You unfolded the "rose."

With warm appreciation to my agent, Jane Jordan Browne, for your persistence, unwavering support, and wisdom. I couldn't have done it without you.

To Jean, Karen, and Lisa: without you there would be no "legacy."

Thanks, Marita, for always being there; Max and Eunice, for your unflagging support.

To Caren McCurdy: your friendship has touched my soul, your humor has brightened my life, and your courage has surpassed our dreams.

And to Donna. For all you do.

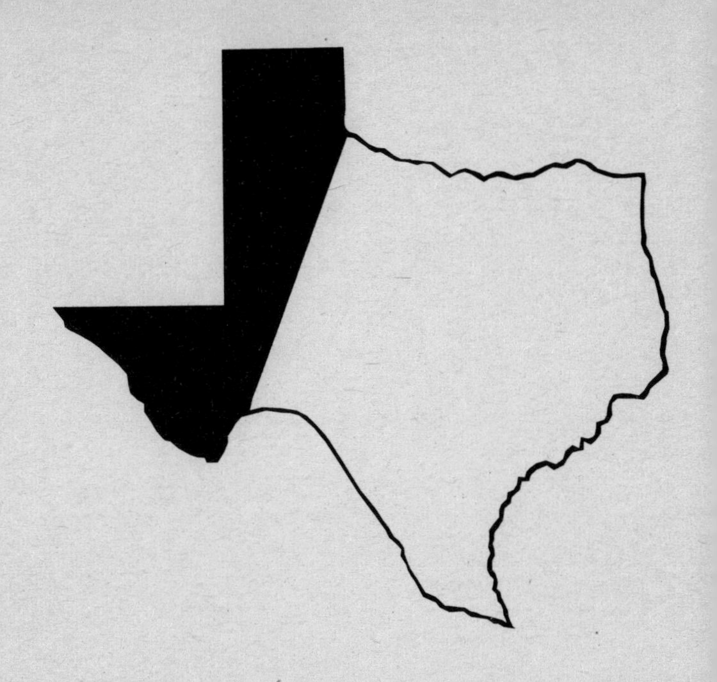

Chiluahuan Province

The Chiluahuan province of Texas is a meeting place of the flora and fauna associated with the southwestern deserts, central plains, and eastern forests. This province includes all of the Trans Pecos and has a greater diversity of land features than any province in Texas. The highest peak in the Chiluahuan province is Mount Livermore in the Davis Mountains with an elevation of 8,000 feet. It encompasses mountain ranges, desert basins, arid plains, and river valleys which support more biological diversity than anywhere else in the continental United States.

Prologue

Boston, Spring 1879

Cassandra Dalton's hands trembled with barely suppressed fury as she reread the letter. The words *I strongly advise you to sell the property at a fair price agreed upon by the solicitors of both parties* leaped out at her. Her lips curled in contempt.

Cassie knew all about the "fairness" of solicitors. She and her twelve-year-old half brother were now living in virtual poverty because of the "fairness" of a solicitor after their father's death. She looked again at the ridiculous price quoted. Even the tenements surrounding her brought twice that amount.

This Shane Lancer—a land baron, no doubt—expected her to sign away her legacy without even seeing the property. Cassie's violet eyes hardened in determination. He was not dealing with a fool. She hadn't quit her job and thrown away their security only to be cheated by yet another solicitor.

Resolutely she squared her jaw, determined to claim the property that her Uncle Luke had willed to her. No dishonest robber baron was going to frighten her away. Especially not with a barely veiled threat that she would be better off staying in Boston.

Cassie remembered the ridiculous explanation they had provided for her uncle's death. A chill raced through her as she wondered what was being concealed.

Raising her head, Cassie stared out the murky window at the tenements crowding about her. *No, Mr. Lancer, I won't be cowed by your threats. I'm fighting for what's mine, no matter what it costs.*

1

Texas, Summer 1879

Shane Lancer cantered across the cactus-laden plain, the weariness of the week's trail ride eating into his bones. Shifting in the creaking saddle, he glanced at the land that led to his home. As he ran a callused hand across the rough stubble on his face, all he could think of was a hot bath and a soft bed.

He blinked his dry, dust-filled eyes, thinking he was seeing a mirage. No, it was a prairie schooner, all right. The distinctive white canvas covering stood out on the deserted plain as though it were a white flag waving surrender.

Approaching cautiously, Shane wondered if the innocent-seeming vehicle was an ambush. Memories of Indian wars that had plagued the land assaulted him while his horse's ears pricked forward, its flared nostrils twitching. The horse had definitely picked up a scent. Either another beast or a human. With each step forward, Shane expected an assault. But no shots rang out. Silently he slid from the dapple-gray horse, unsheathing the rifle from its scabbard and checking the low-slung holster strapped to his leg.

It was hard to say who was more surprised when three scared-looking faces peered from around the side of the wagon. The raven-haired younger woman tried to shove a teen-age boy behind her, but he took a defensive stance in front of her. The red-haired woman smoothed capable hands over her calico skirt, but her face had paled considerably, causing her freckles to stand out in the hollows of her unlined face.

The dark-haired woman stepped aside, refusing to hide behind the boy. Her hands shook, but nonetheless she faced Shane bravely, holding a snub-nosed derringer tightly in those same shaking fingers. The red-haired woman swung her gaze between her friend's ridiculous weapon and Shane's long rifle.

Shane bit back a snort of contempt as the delicate woman still challenged him with that bit of useless metal. He looked her up and down, his compelling green eyes narrowing during the inspection. What was a beautiful creature like her doing out in the brush? he wondered.

"Where are your husbands?" he asked them. Both women were beyond marriageable age. If he had to guess, he'd say the dark-haired one was over twenty-five while the red-haired woman appeared to be at least in her early thirties. They certainly shouldn't be out on the range alone with only a boy for protection.

The younger woman seemed to draw her diminutive height up even further. "And what concern is that of yours?"

"I want to know who the hell might be sneaking up on me," he returned, moving even nearer to her. She was a bitty thing, he thought. Looking down at her, he could tell she was a good foot shorter than he was—putting her only a few inches over five feet tall. His well-muscled build seemed bulky next to her petite frame. Even closer proximity provided him a view that had him dry-mouthed in moments. She was a looker, all right.

She held the pistol out a bit as though expecting him to back off. He advanced even closer.

"If you have honorable intentions, sir, ambush would hardly be on your mind." The woman's voice shook only slightly, he noticed. Sure sounded like a priss, though.

"The hell it wouldn't. Only a fool would come out here by himself and not expect trouble." He gazed around the wagon, seeing only their furniture and supplies scattered on the ground. No one was in sight. But that didn't mean someone wasn't hidden somewhere close by. Perhaps in the ungainly wagon. "You mean to tell me you three are out here alone?"

The older of the two women answered. "I'm afraid so."

"Millicent!" The voice of the woman holding the gun filled with distress. Shane noticed her finger slipping toward the trigger of the pistol. While he didn't think much of her sissy weapon, he didn't want to test its merit on his hide.

"Well, you tell me what we're going to do out here without some help, Cassie. I believe this gentleman will rescue us."

Cassie emitted an unladylike snort of disbelief while she inched the derringer higher.

"Unless you plan to shoot the top off that cactus, you're way off aim, lady."

Cassie jerked the gun downward, ivory cheeks flaming as Shane continued to glare at her.

"What the hell are you doing out here?" he asked, hoping he wasn't stepping into the best-set trap he'd seen in years. Shane approached the wagon, and cautiously opened the flaps with the barrel of his rifle. Satisfied that no one was hiding inside, he turned back to them.

"We left the wagon train a few days back and we're heading southwest," Millicent explained after a moment.

Shane watched in amusement as Cassie sent the red-haired Millicent a look filled with warning. It was apparent she thought he was a ruthless bandito. He didn't mind baiting them. Especially the one with the flashing violet eyes and midnight-colored hair. But he didn't want to push her into actually taking a shot at him.

"So, what's the trouble, ladies?" He nodded at the dark-haired boy, who stared with guarded curiosity, his deep blue eyes resting on Shane's low-slung holster. At closer inspection the boy appeared to be around twelve or thirteen years old. They sure as hell were an odd trio.

Millicent pushed past Cassie and led Shane toward the rear of the wagon. "We believe the wheel's broken." Cassie kept the derringer trained on Shane as he moved along beside Millicent, who continued speaking. "I'm Millicent Groden. This is my friend Cassandra and her brother, Andrew Da—"

Shane interrupted. "You know, I might be tempted to fix the wheel, but not if you keep that gun pointed at my back." Shane turned around quickly, deftly taking the gun out of the surprised woman's hands before she could react. Holding Cassie's small hand a moment longer than necessary, he palmed the small gun.

"Silly little thing," he remarked. Glancing at Cassie's scared face, he continued, "But it could go off and hurt somebody. And the way you had it pointed, that somebody would probably have been me."

Cassie jerked her hand from his grasp, glaring when he smiled easily. Shane leaned into the wagon and put the derringer up out of reach, noting her embarrassment at being so easily outmaneuvered. Silently she watched him turn back to the wheel.

Pushing his hat up on his forehead, Shane squatted down to inspect the damage. "Wheel's not all that's broken. Your axle's busted too."

He swung around as Cassie made a moue of disappointment. "You can fix it, can't you?"

Didn't expect much, did she? He pulled off his Stetson and scratched his shaggy head of chestnut hair.

"No, ma'am. I don't generally carry an extra axle in my saddlebags." She looked ready to puff up again. "But I can get my buckboard and take your stuff to town. We're only a couple of hours from there."

She seemed to wrestle with an answer, and he wondered if it was that hard for her to come up with a simple thank you. 'Course he hadn't done much to gain her confidence. Maybe he'd been on the trail too long—seemed his manners had deserted him. Hell, he hadn't even introduced himself.

"Where you headin'?" he asked, noting their wagon had been packed to overflowing before they'd unloaded it.

"To my uncle's ranch," Cassie finally replied.

Puzzled, he stared at her. He knew all the ranches around. If anyone was expecting an Easterner to show up, the news would have been all over the range by now.

"Who's your uncle?"

"Luke Dalton."

The corner of his mouth, which had turned upward a fraction, tightened abruptly.

"Dalton . . . ?" he repeated almost inaudibly.

"Yes," Cassie replied. "You probably knew him. He died not too long ago. His place—"

"I know the place. Are you here to sell the land?"

"Why, no. We're going to try ranching," Cassie replied uncertainly. "Mister . . . ?"

"Lancer. Shane Lancer."

Cassie's mouth opened in what seemed to be shock.

At least she'd reacted to his name. So, this was Dalton's niece who'd written back and told him to take his offer to the devil. He had an urge to leave her to that very fate. Would he never be free of the curse of the Daltons?

Shane unhooked a canteen from his pack and tossed it to the boy. "I'll send my buckboard. I expect you'll be all right till then." He had to leave before his temper blew. Mounting the horse, Shane dug his heels into the stallion and galloped away across the changing countryside.

Shane wondered what had possessed the Dalton woman to refuse his offer to buy her out. Why would she travel thousands of miles with only another woman and a young boy as companions?

Shane felt the knot in his craw grow. What was it about the Daltons that made them want to deny the natural order of things? This land had been settled and tamed by Lancers. But did that stop the Daltons from thinking they belonged here? Hell, no. They reminded him of a dog gnawing on a month-old bone, still hoping for a morsel.

Shane couldn't believe she was related to Luke Dalton. But a lifetime of hate would never be forgotten. Or forgiven. The deathbed promise he'd made to his father rang in Shane's head with unending clarity. He would get the Dalton land back for his father no matter what he had to do. He'd been the head of his family for the better part of his thirty-four years, far too long to let the sight of a pretty woman sway him from protecting the interests of the Lazy H.

Straightening in his saddle, Shane followed the line of the mesa that started sloping upward toward his own land. He planned to make sure no more Daltons desecrated his land, and certainly not at the whim of a mere woman, even if she did have eyes the color of ransomed jewels.

Cassie kicked the broken wagon wheel for the second time. "Damn," she swore under her breath. When her efforts produced only more choking dust, she wished for a more effective expletive. Watching Millicent's concerned face, Cassie expected some censure for her language.

"Where's a good sailor's curse when you need one?"

Cassie lifted one side of her mouth in a half smile. Then she stared at the receding dust of Shane's horse, her smile turning into a frown. "Of all the men in Texas to ride to our rescue, why did it have to be Shane Lancer?"

"I don't know, but as long as he gets us out of this heat, he can spit cactus spurs."

"I'm surprised he didn't offer us the use of his buckboard in exchange for the deed to our ranch," Cassie muttered.

"You need to have a little more faith in your fellowman," Millicent cautioned, not for the first time in their ten-year friendship.

"Do you think he's coming back?" Cassie tasted the ever-present bite of dust that caked her lips and choked off her breath. She had a frightening thought. Maybe he'd decided to leave them there to die. Then he'd get her land without a fight.

"He didn't seem any too happy at having us here, but he didn't look like the sort to abandon us." Millicent mopped her perspiring neck with a crumpled hankie. "But, then, my training at Miss Harrington's School for Young Ladies didn't cover this situation."

Cassie smiled wryly, shooting a worried glance at her younger brother, Andrew, who was propped against the rear of the wagon. His raven-haired head was thrown back, eyelids screwed shut, while a deep flush of heat had settled over his features. His fair skin, much like hers, told of his battle against the elements.

Cassie didn't think any of them could make it very far in the crippling heat. But with precious little water left, the choices were few. If this Lancer man had been involved in her uncle's death, she doubted he'd draw the line at leaving them to die. He certainly appeared the desperado she'd imagined him to be.

"He did say we're fairly close to town. Maybe we should try walking. Unless he was lying about that, too."

Millicent shot her a reproachful glance.

The hours passed slowly. Millicent and Cassie watched the position of the sun, trying to discern how much time had passed.

"I'm hungry," Andrew announced.

"There's some jerky and hardtack . . ."

Andrew accepted a piece of jerky, biting down and tearing off a chunk. "I'm never gonna eat any more of this as long as I live. When we get to town, I want steak. And apple pie. And milk." The last was said with longing. "Do you think it'll be much longer, Sis?" he asked Cassie.

She shot Millicent a worried, questioning glance. What if Lancer had deserted them? Andrew's excited voice interrupted her fearful thoughts.

"Look, Cassie!" Andrew whooped, pointing into the distance.

Peering intently they could see a cloud of dust amidst the scrub brush that covered the low-rising foothills. Almost afraid to hope, the women watched in silence while Andrew chattered excitedly as the cloud approached and the shape of a wagon could be seen. It moved closer until it reached them.

A white-haired man, almost hidden by the explosion of whiskers on his wrinkled face, pulled up in a curtain of dust. He hollered "Whoa" in a dry voice that seemed to protest its use. A much younger man sat beside him surveying them with uncontained curiosity.

"Hello, sir. Mr. Lancer must have sent you," Cassie began, uncertain of her reception.

"Yes'm." The older man doled out the single word as he dismounted, eyeing their crippled wagon. He bent to inspect the axle.

"I'm afraid it's broken," Cassie offered hesitantly.

"Yes'm." Once again the bewhiskered fellow bit out the single word.

"Well, I . . ." Cassie felt at a loss with the taciturn man.

"Best get your things in the wagon," he finally allowed, jerking a thumb over his shoulder toward the buckboard.

"Yes, thank you. I'm Cassandra Dalton." He nodded his round-brimmed hat in her direction. "And this is Millicent Groden and my younger brother, Andrew."

"They call me Cookie." He addressed them all. "I 'spect that's 'cause I do the cooking. And this here's Matt—my swamper."

Matt shyly tipped his hat in greeting. As though aware that he'd used far more words than necessary, Cookie turned toward their wagon. He produced a canteen, which they gratefully shared.

Matt jumped down and examined the broken axle as the threesome drank thirstily of the stale water, warm from the hot canteen.

"Let's get 'er loaded up," Cookie ordered his helper as he picked up a heavy trunk.

Thinking they'd traveled so far to meet such a sorry end, Cassie stared at the pathetic reminders of their former lives, littered about the dusty ground as though they were yesterday's trash. Their trunks and barrels stood like uprooted scrub amidst the desolate countryside. And her mother's treasured spinet piano lay sprawled against a boulder, its hand-carved rosewood now sadly scratched, one leg twisted irreparably into the granitelike earth.

But in a short time everything was loaded, and the draft horses were tied to the rear of the wagon. The buckboard lurched forward, sinking into the foot-deep ruts in the clay road, raising a sandy storm of dust. The wagon moved upward, rapidly gaining altitude. It was hard to believe they were in the same territory as they left behind the flat land decorated only with bleak tumbleweed and cacti, and rode upward into the wooded thicket of juniper and pinyon pines that melted into the mountains.

The wind tousled Cassie's ebony hair and skipped through the grass, furrowing the clustered blades against rock-hard earth while prairie clover, virgin bower, and foxfire battled the elements, poking their gold and scarlet heads skyward.

After the long bumpy ride, they were all relieved when Cookie pulled up to the Dalton ranch. A whitewashed frame house and red-planked barn sat on the rise of a gently sloping hill. It was almost exactly as Cassie had pictured it.

She remembered the countless nights she'd lain awake trying to decide whether or not to accept her uncle's legacy. Night after night she'd told herself the reasons why she shouldn't give up her teaching job to pursue a wild dream. Each night had been spent listening to her neighbors quarrel through paper-thin walls. Coupling that with the disturbing sounds of crime from the streets below, Cassie was convinced they had to leave the slums.

Since their father's death, she and Andrew had been forced to move to a dreary tenement in a dismal section of Boston. It was all she could afford after the solicitor had absconded with their inheritance, but she'd always envisioned life where home was more than a cramped one-room flat. A life where fear didn't rule. She wanted so much more for Andrew than she could provide on her meager wages, so the inheritance from Uncle Luke had seemed like a godsend.

Now there was no turning back, no job to return to. She had escaped the suffocating life they'd led since her father's death, and nothing would make her give up this chance to make a new start.

Slowly she climbed down from the wagon, surveying the first true home they'd had in years. She paused at the front porch, running her hand along the smooth wood of the well-used swing. Hesitantly she turned the handle on the front door, feeling as though she were intruding as she stepped into the neat keeping room.

The massive hearth and dusty, man-sized furniture dominated the room. Sunshine poured in the curtainless windows, spilling over the black cooking stove and onto the worn trestle dining table. Cassie's sturdy traveling shoes echoed against the bare wooden floor as she moved to the oak sideboard, lightly touching the humidor and pipe that sat neatly to one side. She felt a sharp pang of regret for her uncle as she stared at the evidence of his solitary existence.

Cassie gazed around the sun-filled room and felt her heart catching as she realized she was truly home. Remembering the wagon outside still to be unloaded, she reluctantly left the house, pausing once more to savor the rightness of her decision in coming here.

"Cookie, where are the animals?" Cassie asked, nearing the wagon. Not one chicken scratched about the deserted henhouse, and the corrals were empty except for the horses that had brought the Daltons west. Only a few ornery ducks waddled past. They glared at her, intent on reaching the water trough.

"I reckon the Basque's got 'em," he answered, not pausing as he rolled a distended barrel to the rear end of the wagon.

"The Basque?"

"Yep." This time the single word would not suffice.

"What's a Basque?"

"Sheepherder—name's Manuelo. He was a friend of your uncle's," Cookie replied.

"But why does he have my sheep?" Cassie persisted.

Disgust was written in Cookie's faded blue eyes. " 'Cause the critters are too stupid to even graze on their own."

Cassie tried to digest this information, wondering who and where this Basque person was. Voicing her doubts, she asked, "Where do I find him?"

Cookie shifted his eyes toward the low, greenish-brown hills to the north. "Up there."

"Oh." The quiet rejoinder was issued as Cassie tried to imagine finding a lone sheepherder in the vast landscape. There wouldn't be any street signs to guide her here, she thought ruefully, remembering how easily she'd navigated the twisted streets of Boston.

"How will I know him?" Cassie questioned.

"He's more garbed up than a saloon gal on Saturday night. . . . Sorry 'bout that, ma'am. Forgot I was speakin' to a lady."

Cassie nodded to show his choice of words hadn't offended her. "What do you mean by 'garbed up'?"

"Wears purple and red doodads around his middle where his belt should be. Black hat with silver geegaws all over it—crown big enough to take a bath in. And them pants."

Cookie rolled his eyes. "Him and a couple of friends could fit in 'em, they're so baggy."

"And this Manuelo was a good friend of my uncle's?"

"Yep. His best one, I'd say."

"And he has my sheep?"

"Yep. He'd probably buy the lot of 'em off you," Cookie answered, busying himself with a leatherbound trunk that contained her carefully selected books on sheep ranching.

"But why would I sell my stock? Without the sheep we can't keep the ranch."

Cookie stood still and looked her in the eye. "You'll save yerself a mess of grief if'n you sell the stock and the land."

"Why does Mr. Lancer want my land so badly?"

Cookie decided to let that pass. If she was lucky, she'd get her fill and leave before she found out the truth. He mumbled a noncommittal reply.

Cassie visibly stiffened, her resolve apparent. "I appreciate the advice, but we're staying. This is our home now." As she spoke, she turned to the whitewashed house nestled snugly on the hillside. The determination in her face was clear.

Cookie grunted in exasperation and bent to retrieve another fully loaded trunk.

Cassie studied his shaded face and made one last attempt. "I do thank you for your help. I don't know what we'd have done without you."

"Yes'm. We don't hold to Dal . . . to sheepherders," he corrected himself hastily, "but we don't hold to leaving women and children in the brush, neither." He pulled the trunk forward with a kerplunk and lowered it over the rear board of the wagon.

Cassie faced him as he straightened up, and she held out her hand. "Nonetheless, we're grateful to you, and I hope we can repay the kindness."

Grudging respect crept into his wizened eyes as he accepted her handshake with his own weathered paw. "Mebbe so, ma'am. I'd best be gettin' the rest of yer trunks down," he replied, gesturing to the half-filled wagon.

Cassie turned slightly toward the oversized barn. Cookie watched her, thinking she seemed forlorn for all her pluckiness. "I'll send Matt over tomorrow or the next day."

Turning back to face him, Cassie gazed at Cookie inquisitively. He flushed a bit under her intense regard. "You ladies and the boy might be needing a man's help." He'd better make damn sure Shane didn't find out he was helping a Dalton. What'd possessed him to offer a fool thing like that?

Her lips parted in a tremulous smile. Flustered, he turned back to the wagon, busying himself with the remaining cargo. Either he'd had too much of the Texas sun, or it had been a far sight too long since he'd seen such a pretty filly.

Suspecting further thanks would only embarrass Cookie, Cassie walked past her uncle's sturdy wagon. She glanced at the vehicle, glad to see Luke's reliable wagon, considering the sorry state of theirs, and then continued into the barn. The rafters secured the giant beams in place, while the loft still held bales of sweet-smelling hay. Cassie breathed in the fecund smell of horses redolent in the closed stalls and remembered her dreams of land as far as the eye could see. And a home of their own after living in bleak, ugly rented rooms since her father's death.

Straightening her shoulders, Cassie firmed her resolve. This *was* her dream, and no robber baron was going to scare her away. She wandered back to the double doors, fingering an oil lamp hung on a wooden peg and a bridle tossed on a bench as though waiting for a rider that had never returned. *I know you can't come back, Uncle Luke. But I'm here now. And the fight's only begun.*

2

Cassie swiped the back of her gritty forearm across her temples, pushing away the straggly hair that clung to the sheen of sweat she'd worked up. Expelling a deep breath, she rubbed the small of her protesting back and glanced down at her trouser-encased legs with a rueful grin. Andrew and Millicent had been shocked when she'd appeared in them that morning. But it took only one day for her to decide that a skirt was no garment in which to tend sheep.

Ignoring her aching back, she bent to the task at hand. She glanced at the diagram in the book that outlined a perfectly formed corral. The bent and twisted frame she was trying to repair held little resemblance to the one pictured in the book. Glancing at the other text spread out before her, however, she knew she had no choice. Reinforcing the corral was her first priority.

Trying to read the book at the same time, Cassie pulled a ten-penny nail from the edge of her mouth where it rested with several others. Wielding the heavy hammer, she concentrated on the placement of the nail. Recent experience had taught her that pounding one of the nails in the wrong place meant a lot of hard work removing it. As Cassie strained to study the diagram, the wind kept teasing the pages of the book, making the task of reading the book and hammering at the same time nearly impossible.

Engrossed in her work, Cassie didn't hear Shane as he rode up to the corral. He reined in his horse, studying the provocative derriere that greeted him. The trousers had thrown him. But there was no doubt in his mind that the form they clearly outlined was female. She sure didn't look like a priss in that outfit. Studying her with a grin, he ignored all the reasons why he shouldn't be eyeing Cassie's trim curves. His horse inopportunely whinnied, and Cassie swung around, straightening up as she saw him.

If the first view had been pleasing, the second was damnably breathtaking. Dressed in what appeared to be her brother's shirt and pants, the material clung to her like the skin of an overripe fruit. He found himself swallowing a gathering lump as he gazed at the straining material stretched taut against her full breasts. Forcing his eyes upward, he paused at the droplets that enveloped her neck and slid maddeningly into the gap of her too-tight shirt. Her skin had darkened slightly to the shade of light honey, enhanced by the slick sheen from her labors.

His eyes drifted upward to the dewy mouth and flushed cheeks that were framed by wisps of raven curls. And, finally, her eyes. Those startling violet eyes that looked as if they were stolen from a jeweler's case and framed with spiky dark lashes.

Cassie's unfriendly voice jarred him back to earth. To reason, he hoped. "Afternoon, Mr. Lancer. Can I help you with something?"

He forced the hardness in his tone, knowing it should come naturally, resenting that it didn't. Looks aside, she was still a Dalton. "Some of your sheep wandered onto my range."

"I'm not surprised. This corral has more posts missing than in place." Shane watched her hands flutter gracefully in the air as she gestured to the hammer and nails. A tiny bead of perspiration gathered and rolled into the vee of her shirt, disappearing in the valley between her breasts. He tore his eyes from the elusive drop and tried to remember what she'd said.

Cassie rushed on defensively. "Andrew and I will round

them up as soon as we can." Her hands moved nervously to the tendrils of hair escaping about her face.

"There's no hurry," Shane surprised himself by saying. He stared spellbound as her hands moved from the escaping curls to rest near her legs. He should be telling her to leave, not giving her more time to get entrenched here, he thought.

She seemed to weigh his words and then said reluctantly, "I appreciate that. We're a little green, and this is taking longer than we thought. None of the books mentioned fixing corrals."

"Books?" He couldn't believe what he'd heard. "You're using books to figure out"—he made a sweeping motion with his hand as he twisted around in his saddle—"this?"

"Well, yes. I realize it may not always be exactly like what I've studied . . ."

He harrumphed in the middle of her words as he glanced down at her feet to the manuals spread around her like primers on the first day of school. Books! An Easterner trying to run a sheep ranch based on a bunch of books. They were probably written by some dude who had never set foot outside of the city. Momentarily forgetting his mission, he tipped his hat forward to hide a growing smile. Green, hell. They were as helpless as the sheep running loose over half the countryside.

"Excuse me, Miss Dalton. I didn't realize you were so learned."

He read the wariness in her eyes as she replied, "I am—was—a schoolteacher."

A schoolteacher! She sure didn't look like a schoolmarm to him. Every schoolteacher he'd ever had looked as though they'd had every shred of femininity removed when they'd taken the job. His memories were of starched, dull black, high-necked dresses that primly covered every inch of skin. Not an alluring open-necked man's shirt, breeches. . . . He jerked his mind back with a snap. *Remember who she is!*

"That explains it, then."

Cassie glared at him as though she'd read his thoughts. Shane was certain she was about to retort when Millicent neared the corral.

"Good afternoon, Mr. Lancer," Millicent greeted him with her usual good cheer.

"Miss Millicent," he replied politely, unable to dislike Cassie's friend.

Millicent turned toward Cassie. "I found these letters in the back of the cupboard. What do you want me to do with them?"

Cassie, who wasn't thinking at all of the letters, answered absently, "Put them back in the cupboard, I guess."

Millicent nodded in agreement, turning to Shane. "Won't you join us in some refreshment?" she asked, smoothing the starched white apron over her calico skirt.

Shane glanced at Cassie's irate face and realized the only refreshment she'd like to serve him would be arsenic-laced. He started to refuse, but the chance to goad her was too tempting.

Then again, maybe there was more than one way to get her to sell the land. Maybe he should try a little honey instead of vinegar. If she hadn't found a husband by now, she might be susceptible to a little well-placed charm.

"Thanks, that sounds mighty good." Dismounting, Shane led his horse to the hitching rail and looped the reins around the rough wood. Following Cassie through the open door, he focused involuntarily on the gentle swing of her hips. He gazed about the house he'd never set foot in before and recognized the signs of a woman's touch.

Shane had never thought he'd find himself in this house. Old wounds seeped as he stared around the neat room. Bringing himself back to the present, he realized the embroidered pillows and lace runners covering the furniture must be new additions. New additions that needed to be stopped now.

Tapping down buried emotions, he searched for something civil to say, allowing his gaze to roam about the comfortable keeping room. Millicent's chatter saved him.

"Let me see if I can find one of those sweet rolls I baked this morning," Millicent said as she walked toward the oak sideboard. Not waiting for a reply, she turned to the immaculate kitchen where Cassie resentfully picked up an enameled coffee pot simmering on the stove.

Shane eyed the laden tray Millicent carried into the room a few moments later. Accepting a steaming mug of coffee, he settled stiffly into an oversized leather chair.

He watched with veiled interest as Cassie sullenly perched on the edge of the horsehair settee that faced him. Continuing his study, Shane found to his annoyance that he liked the way her ebony hair curled about her face as though it had a will of its own. Glancing at her breeches again, he wondered what the women in town would say if they saw her in them. As if another Dalton back in the valley wasn't bad enough. Seeing Cassie in form-fitting trousers made him think, and he stifled a smile, that they were previously a highly underrated garment. He felt his breath coming a bit shorter. Was it suddenly a lot warmer in the room?

"Won't you have a roll, Mr. Lancer?" Cassie offered, hoping he'd choke on it.

"Just Shane—my *father* was Mr. Lancer."

Cassie wondered at Shane's emphasis as he chose a sticky bun from its resting place. Her hand grazed his as he accepted the tray, and she almost drew back from the startling contact. Stuff and nonsense! He was, after all, only a man.

"Hmmm," she tried to reply noncommittally. Handing him a dainty saucer for his sweet roll, she thought of all the unsavory things she'd rather call him.

He accepted the plate while Cassie secretly studied the planes of his face. Now clean-shaven, except for a well-trimmed mustache, he no longer looked like a desperado.

In fact . . . Her stomach tightened abruptly when she spotted the tufts of chestnut hair escaping from the open neck of his chambray work shirt. She glanced at his well-muscled arms. There she saw an equal measure of alluringly silky hair covering the bronze skin of his forearms. Swallowing, she wished her suddenly rapid breathing would return to normal.

Abruptly she wondered what Mrs. Lancer was like, if there was a Mrs. Lancer. But surely there was. He appeared older than her own twenty-eight years, and she'd already learned people married uncommonly young here in the West. Cassie pushed aside her traitorous thoughts. She should feel pity for the woman who was stuck with this crook.

"How'd you and the boy come to be living on your own?" he asked, disturbing her uncomfortable musings.

As she grudgingly explained, Cassie felt her bitterness surfacing. "Andrew's mother—my stepmother—died when he was born. Our father died when Andrew was four." Her mouth tightened abruptly. And that was when her parents' solicitor had stolen their inheritance and left them penniless.

Misinterpreting her angry expression, he wondered if Cassie resented the fact that she'd had to care for a younger half brother. But then what did he expect from a Dalton?

Shane decided to get to the point. The less time he spent in this house the better. "Your reply to my letter wasn't what I was expecting. I was hoping to save you a hard trip out here. Why don't you reconsider and sell your grazing land to me and your critters to the Basque? This spread was hard enough for your uncle to handle when he was alive. It's all too much for a couple of women and a boy."

While still clutching the remains of his cinnamon bun, Shane gestured vaguely about the room as though they stood outside in the midst of her land.

He bit into the sweet roll, but forgot to chew when he saw Cassie's flushed cheeks and overly bright eyes. It was apparent she wasn't buying his benevolent-neighbor act. So much for charm.

"How very generous of you. Does your wife share your enlightened views, *Mister* Lancer?" She unfolded her body and rose to her full height. Shane choked on the mouthful of sweet roll as he found himself staring upward into her furious face. Cassie crossed the short distance between them, her flush deepening. "Or do you just keep her penned up with the rest of the cattle?"

He tried to break into her tirade. "I'm only thinking of your welfare. My intentions—"

"Your intentions are quite clear, sir. You intend to steal my land, and the devil with my welfare!"

Listening to her, Shane could not draw his eyes from her heaving breasts. Cassie's expression was steely when his gaze finally returned to her face. If possible, an even brighter light of fury flashed from her eyes as she stepped back abruptly.

Caught ogling her, he bit out a quick "Good day, ladies," raising his voice for Millicent's benefit, and left before Cassie could utter another word.

Cassie was speechless with fury. Her decision to come West after her uncle's sudden death was a momentous undertaking. And now to have her rich, highfalutin neighbor try to convince her to sell out on the pretense of concern! Concern, hell. Robbery was more like it. Where was his concern when Uncle Luke had been killed? Maybe that was why he was trying so hard to get rid of her—so she wouldn't question his death.

Everything, *everything* depended on their success with the sheep ranch. So, he thought they couldn't run the ranch on their own. Maybe he was right. She only hoped he'd see the irony of his words when she hired his own men away from him. If she was lucky, Cookie's swamper, Matt, would be around for more than a few days. He'd be a permanent addition.

* * *

Shane mounted the dapple gray quickly and rode out with a sharp snap of the reins. He passed the mewling sheep, their distasteful odor assailing his nostrils. He quickened the horse's gait, approaching the sagebrush flats that bordered his land and fell away from the gently sloping mesas. Riding over the ridge into the evergreen thicket of ponderosa pine and red cedar, he breathed deeply of their clean, spicy scent, ridding himself of the sheep's smell.

He regretted Cassie's fury, knowing it would only get worse, but after the disaster Luke Dalton had wreaked on this valley, Shane had little sympathy for anyone related to the man. He knew Cassie had no idea what she'd gotten into. But if she were wise, she'd get out before past mistakes forced her out.

Shane had no tolerance for Daltons, free rangers, or anyone else who desecrated the land. Lancer land. Past promises pulled at him. Prodding his horse up the steep rise, he paused at the top, surveying his domain. No checkerboard restraints hampered the lay of the land. Fallow grass carpeted the plain, and his cattle grazed the rich foliage.

A deep surge of pride surfaced as he remembered his father, seated on a massive sorrel, surveying the land from this very point. *Son, someday this will be yours to shape and rule, but above all respect. The land's like a woman. Tame her gently, treat her good, and you'll never be without her. Strip her bare, and she'll be colder than a whore's heart.*

Shane shook off his memories and slapped the reins, sending the horse down the other side of the rise. Approaching the sprawling ranch house with its pillared veranda, he spotted a rented rig clearly belonging to the livery stable in town.

Now what?

He cantered up to the corral, dismounted, and handed the reins to a young Mexican boy who offered him a bright-toothed smile when Shane ruffled his thick, shaggy hair.

Shane's long-legged stride carried him up the wide steps to the front porch and through the massive double-door entryway. Hanging his hat on the oak hall tree, he searched the well-appointed front parlor for an unexpected guest, but the room stood empty. One of the tall library doors stood ajar. Shane moved toward it cautiously, wondering what kind of stranger would invade the privacy of a man's study. Quietly, he loosened his holster and eased the pistol from his side.

The high-backed leather chair behind the mahogany desk was swiveled toward the bookcases lining the rear wall. Over the back of the chair, Shane could see the top of a sandy-haired head.

Gun in hand, he entered the room, and just as abruptly the chair swiveled around. Shane's angry words dissolved, and he yelped in excitement. "Michael! What the hell are you doing here? God, it's good to see you, boy."

Shane quickly sheathed the gun, clasped Michael's outstretched hand, and then pulled him closer with a fierce bear hug. When they stepped apart, they grinned at each other with matching smiles.

It had been almost two years since Shane had seen his younger brother. All of the mixed emotions that tore at him when he thought of Michael assailed him now. Pride was foremost as he saw that Michael had matured from a gangling boy to a strapping young man. Looking into Michael's shining blue eyes, Shane could see their mother all over again. Even his sandy blond hair was hers. Only hers. Age-old memories assailed him. Now as then, protective urges came to the fore.

Shane eyed Michael from head to toe, suddenly fearful of the reason for his unexplained visit. Michael seemed healthy, if looking a bit like a dude. He wore a conservative gray wool suit and a starched white shirt with a rigid boiled collar. Shane noticed that his equally drab black bowler lay on the desk. Shane felt his own neck itch just watching him.

"There's nothing wrong with me, Shane. Just hadn't been home in too long." Despite his positive words, Michael's face was filled with ill-concealed anxiety.

Shane heaved a sigh of relief and dropped into the nearest wing chair. "You're not having trouble at school, are you?" Worry etched a frown of concern on Shane's normally cheerful face. He'd felt like a father to Michael for too long to abandon the role now. It was apparent something was worrying the boy, and everything that concerned Michael had always been a priority to Shane.

"No, nothing like that. The term's up, and I didn't want to clerk for Judge Yarborough this summer. I needed to come home for a while."

Shane expelled a sigh of relief. Law school had been Michael's dream for as long as they both could remember. As a young boy, he'd been more content dragging heavy volumes of law around Judge McCracken's law office than he had been roping cattle and riding the range. It had been another bittersweet mixed blessing.

"So, you needed to see the old homestead again?" Shane prodded, falling easily into his role of protector and father figure.

"Maybe for more than a visit."

Shane's eyebrows rose in surprise.

"I'm just not sure I made the right choice." Michael got up and paced restlessly across the length of the room, raking his hands impatiently through well-groomed blond hair. "Do you know how cramped it is in the city? One tenement after another, squeezed together tighter than two bulls after one cow."

Michael paused briefly to gaze longingly out the window. Then he turned back to face Shane. "I miss riding for miles, knowing the land's ours. I'm tired of breathing filthy air that's thicker than a duststorm. I miss the heat of the sun on my face." He sank noisily into the desk chair. "Hell, I even miss the smell of the cattle. Don't see too many longhorns in Philadelphia," Michael finished with a mirthless laugh.

Shane studied him with concern. While he'd never held with leaving the land himself, his brother's dreams had always been wrapped up in the law. Had he just been homesick or was his problem more serious? Shane wondered briefly if there was a woman in the East that Michael was avoiding. But he wasn't planning on making any accusations or asking too many questions. What the boy needed now was an unqualified welcome back into the fold.

"Well, it's damn good having you home, little brother." Shane slapped Michael's knee good-naturedly. "Let's go put some meat on those bones. After that we'll get you out of those duds." Shane made a face as he surveyed Michael's suit. "Cookie'll have a fit seeing you home."

Michael's face filled with relief, and Shane realized he had indeed expected either a tongue-lashing or to be packed back off to school.

Wouldn't do any good to force the boy. He'd have to make his own decision. But a summer of hot, backbreaking labor ought to make that law school look mighty good.

Entering Cookie's domain, they were greeted by the smell of hearty stew, mouth-watering biscuits, and chicory-flavored coffee. Cookie spotted Michael and let out a huge roar. Michael answered in kind, and Shane stepped back to watch and enjoy.

The two circled each other as though stepping off a fight. Cookie advanced. Michael feinted and drew closer. Just when it seemed as if they were coming to blows, Cookie made a grab for Michael. His bear hug made Shane's look weak in comparison. Then he set Michael back on his feet, stepped back, and looked at him carefully through squinted eyes.

Finished with his scrutiny, Cookie finally allowed, "Looks like you came home just in time, boy. Another few weeks, come a big storm, you'da blowed plumb off the ground."

Michael laughed heartily in response. "I just needed another dose of your poison," he retorted, sniffing the pot of stew.

"Looks like poison's all they been feedin' you since you left," Cookie responded tartly, unable to disguise the pride in his eyes as he gazed at Michael.

Torrents of confused emotions pulled at Shane as he and Cookie shared a rush of fatherly pride, knowing they'd shaped the fine young man standing before them.

"Not poison, but I haven't had a decent steak since I left. I want one about a foot thick," Michael declared.

"Might be we're havin' mutton for dinner," Cookie answered slyly without looking at Shane.

"Sheep?" Michael glanced from Shane to Cookie in puzzlement. "On old man Dalton's spread?" Shane felt a familiar wrenching in his gut. "I thought you had that problem almost licked. You got a new bunch of sheepherders giving you trouble?"

"A lady sheepherder, no less. Shane went over to send her packin' this morning. But from the expression on his face, I'd say she sent him packin'," Cookie informed Michael, unable to keep his crusty smile in check.

Michael turned to Shane in amazement. "A lady sheepherder? She must be some old buzzard."

Cookie couldn't contain his laughter. Shane wanted to reach out and choke him. Michael searched both faces for an explanation.

"She's not exactly an old buzzard," Shane finally admitted.

"Hell, she's a looker, boy. Don't know why she wanted to take up where her uncle left off, but she's the best-lookin' thing to come along this range."

Shane knew Cookie was enjoying making him squirm. Michael clasped his arm around Shane's shoulder. "Give me a chance to put some food in my belly, and you can introduce me to the good-lookin' lady sheepherder."

The irony of Michael's words washed over Shane as he watched Michael walk back to where Cookie stood at the stove. Raising a cool drink to his lips, he wondered how much longer the truth would stay hidden.

3

Cassie entered the mercantile, hearing the creak of wooden floorboards beneath her feet, her nose twitching at the vinegary smell of pickles resting in casks of brine. She stepped further inside, scanning the walls that seemed to contain a wealth of goods. Canned and dry goods were stacked neatly in some spots on shelves and rather haphazardly on the floor in others.

The walls were covered with overalls, bits, scrubboards, rope, and every tool imaginable. Scarcely an inch of space was left uncovered. Cassie fingered a bolt of soft blue material but regretfully passed it by. Uncle Luke's inheritance was dwindling quickly, and she'd have to show a profit before indulging in material for new dresses.

As Cassie approached the counter, one by one the customers noticed her. All conversation ceased as they turned to stare. Even the children were still as the unhealthy silence hung in the air. Cassie smiled tentatively at the proprietor. But her smile faded as he stared at her sternly, grim eyes narrowed, lips pursed in disapproval.

Puzzling over what she'd done to anger the man sight unseen, Cassie cleared her throat and spoke, hearing her voice sounding scratchy and uncertain. "I'm Cassandra Dal—"

He interrupted abruptly. "We know who you are."

Surprised that he knew of her, she tried to regain her composure, attempting a second smile. The proprietor remained unsmiling, while Cassie glanced around at the other customers. Glares of hate and suspicion emanated from all their faces. Uncertainly, Cassie turned back to the proprietor, holding up her list as though it were a shield. Swallowing nervously, she began, "I'll need fifty pounds of flour—"

"Don't have none."

Cassie glanced up in surprise. Flour was a basic necessity. But then perhaps they were expecting a shipment soon, and she was buying for the future. She'd wanted to make sure they didn't deplete the two-month supply she had set in.

She asked for the next item on her list and got the same response. Tentatively she tried the next two items, only to get identical responses. Frustrated, Cassie shoved the list over to the man.

"Perhaps you could tell me when you'll be getting in some of these things."

The man let the list lie on the counter, untouched. His eyes didn't even stray near the precise lines of writing.

"Won't be."

"But . . ." Cassie gazed at the circle of people around her. "I don't understand."

"I ain't got no supplies for a Dalton." The man almost spit out the words, and Cassie stepped back involuntarily, feeling as though he'd struck her. She glanced around at the people in the store for support. One by one they looked her over, turned around, and marched out the door.

As the floorboards creaked behind the last one, Cassie turned back to the proprietor. He had folded back the flap of the curtain to his storeroom, but paused before he departed.

"And if you got any sense, you'll get out while you can."

"I . . . why?"

But the curtain had already flapped shut behind him, and Cassie stared about the deserted room. A cold chill of misery settled around her heart as she tried to guess what had caused such animosity. Why didn't he have any supplies for a Dalton? She shook her head uncertainly. It just didn't make any sense.

Disheartened, she walked slowly out of the store, her eyes sweeping the boardwalk. The two women heading toward Cassie raked her with scathing glares and then purposefully crossed the street to avoid her.

Cassie stared after the women for a moment and then walked toward her wagon, shaking inwardly. Just as she reached the wagon and began to step up, she heard an unfamiliar masculine voice.

"Miss Dalton?"

Cassie turned and nodded as the man bowed over her hand. Taken aback at the unaccustomed gesture, she studied the handsome stranger. The expensively tailored woolen suit spoke of Boston or New York, and the thick gold chain looped beneath his watch pronounced his wealth. His mane of blond hair under a dashing black bowler was meticulously groomed, while his even teeth were impossibly white.

It was a relief to have someone speak to her. "How do you do, Mister . . ."

"Fredericks. Karl Fredericks." His incredibly smooth voice flowed over Cassie like cool water. She couldn't place the accent. "I'm delighted to meet you, my dear. Have you settled into your new home?"

Cassie tried to relax as she answered, "We're still trying to get acclimated." Her words held an undertone of irony. If today was any indication, fitting into this community could prove impossible.

"Ah, you mean the fine folk of Keenonburg." He shrugged his elegantly slim shoulders. "Small-minded buffoons for the most part. I've lived here for years, and they still treat me like an outsider—being a foreigner, you know." Fredericks's aristocratic face mirrored his belief that to look down on him was ridiculous. "The people of this town have no vision. They can't see the potential of this vast land." His face held a longing, faraway expression. He brought himself back to the present with a shake. "Don't let the people here disturb you. A beautiful woman like you need not worry about such things."

Cassie let the compliment pass, cocking her head as she studied him. "Germany?" she guessed.

He laughed, emitting little sound—as though laughter was a seldom-used tool. "Austria, my dear. Much more civilized."

She had to hide a small smile of disbelief. He'd certainly traveled to the opposite end of the spectrum for civilization. "Of course," she answered, wondering why he was showing an interest in her.

"If you need any assistance in selling your land, I'd be pleased to help you."

Her mouth tightened abruptly. Was this another one of Shane's henchmen? "Since I don't intend to sell, I hardly think I'll need that sort of help. You can tell Mr. Lancer to keep his offer."

His composure slipped for a fleeting moment and then he recovered. "Apparently I was misinformed. I apologize for speaking out of turn. But I assure you I'd be the last person Lancer would send."

"You aren't in business with him?"

He laughed aloud. "Hardly. We both want the same thing. And unfortunately there'll be only one winner—and I don't intend for it to be Shane Lancer."

Cassie thawed slightly. So Fredericks was in league against Lancer. That alone gave her every reason to like him. Coupled with his explanation about selling her land, things made more sense. No doubt everyone had expected her to sell. That alone might have accounted for the greeting she'd received, although she couldn't see how her land could affect so many people. Unless her uncle's death was being covered up and her presence was a sore reminder. But she was still grateful for his friendliness.

"Apology accepted. Evidently you weren't the only one who thought I was selling."

Fredericks smiled, lifting his eyebrows in reply. Offering her a hand up to the wagon, his cultivated voice shed one last comment.

"If I can be of service, don't hesitate to call on me." With that, he tipped his hat and effected a courtly bow. Cassie smiled politely. As he left, however, her smile faded. She hoped he wasn't the only person in town who would befriend them.

The following day dawned hot and clear. The sky was cloudless and blue. Cassie pulled up on the reins of her horse, pausing at the top of the mesa. Shading her eyes with an upraised hand, she searched for strays.

Unable to pick out any of the woolly creatures between the sagebrush and bordering cedars, she leaned down and uncapped her canteen. She drank thirstily and bathed her face with a few precious drops. Replacing the canteen, she pulled her horse about, heading west where her land bordered with Shane's.

She'd saved those acres for last. After his visit she had avoided any contact with him. But Cassie knew she'd have to search for the remaining sheep or be faced with yet another confrontation. Urging her horse forward, she sighed mightily in the hot, dry wind whipping about her face.

Cassie searched the juniper and pine thicket as she rode on but saw no sheep. As she approached Shane's bordering land, Cassie felt her stomach quiver and questioned if it were with dread or anticipation.

Continuing forward, she gazed at the rich grasslands and was forced to admit he did have an impressive spread. It was apparent he didn't need her land, she thought resentfully. Riding further, she heard the bellowing of an animal in pain. She dug in her heels, quickening the horse's gait, grateful for the riding experience she'd gained in the last few weeks. Manuel had been a good teacher.

Rounding the mesa at a gallop, she pulled sharply back on the reins when she almost plowed into Shane. He was bent over the swollen belly of a cow while his horse grazed obediently, its reins trailing along the grass.

Shane barely glanced up and bent back to his task. Cassie dismounted, approaching him as she led her horse behind. She hesitated as she neared him. He turned his head to the side, briefly explaining, "Downer."

Cassie wasn't sure what that meant but sensed there was trouble. Even her animosity toward Shane couldn't override her concern for the helpless animal.

"Can I do something? Or would you like me to ride for help?"

"No time for that. Could you hand me my canteen?" He gestured toward his dapple gray, and Cassie approached the horse cautiously. The brute stood a full two hands higher than her own mount. Nearing him, she saw his ears prick up and his massive nostrils flare. Cassie edged closer, leaving her own horse to graze behind her. Thinking of her own canteen, resting on less ferocious territory, she turned.

"I'll need my saddlebags and rope, too," Shane tossed over his shoulder.

She swallowed, nibbling on her lower lip, and turned back to face the animal. He seemed even larger now that she was close to him. Cassie was almost within touching distance, speculating how long it would take him to turn her into mincemeat, when he turned his huge head, indolently gazed at her, and bent back to the fragrant grass wisping about his oversized hooves.

"Nice boy," she murmured quietly, timidly grasping the canteen looped about the saddle. He remained perfectly still while she removed the canteen and rope and then gently uncinched the saddlebags, dragging them down. Heaving a sigh of relief, she hurried back to Shane.

She bent beside him, offering the canteen to him first. He accepted the canteen without comment, whipped the bandanna from around his neck, and moistened the reddish material. Cassie grudgingly marveled at the gentleness of his hands as he ministered to the agonized animal. The cow quieted under his soothing voice. Cassie strained to hear his words and found them to be lulling.

When he raised his voice back to a normal tone, she nearly tipped over backward. Then scrambling to regain her balance, she almost fell in his lap. Seared by the contact, she flushed heatedly and realized she hadn't heard what he said.

"I . . . I didn't hear you."

He seemed not to notice her confusion and embarrassment. "I said I thought you might not want to watch the rest of this," he answered, gesturing to the animal at his feet.

"I'm not going to swoon, if that's what you mean."

"I should hope not. You'll have a lambing season yourself."

His words brought her up short. She hadn't really thought that far ahead. Each day she discovered she had more to learn than she'd ever thought possible. Far more than the books had revealed. Swallowing her growing nervousness, she replied with a bravado she didn't feel, "Just tell me what to do and I'll help."

"Nothing . . . yet."

Millicent dumped the soapy water out of the chipped enameled washbasin and over the side of the front porch. They needed to plant some flowers, she thought, critically studying the barren strip of dirt that surrounded the house.

She gazed out over the rolling foothills, still taken with the enormity of the country and the endless range. Spotting a rising cloud of dust, she shaded her eyes with an upraised hand and peered into the distance. She wondered if Cassie had found the strays. Privately she shared Cookie's opinion. Sheep were not the brightest creatures in God's kingdom.

As the rider came into clear view, Millicent realized it was a stranger. Automatically she smoothed back her coppery hair and ran a restless hand over her starched apron.

The rider slowed his horse as he approached the house. Millicent looked him over critically. His worn but clean denims, work boots, and dusty Stetson were the familiar trappings of a cow hand. His blunt-featured face was well tanned. Millicent hid her nervousness at being alone as he pulled up his mount and tugged at the brim of his hat.

"Ma'am."

"Good day," she replied, noting the kindness in his eyes and feeling her own fear disappear.

"Howdy. Would you mind if I watered my horse, ma'am?"

His intense blue eyes met hers, and she found herself surprisingly weak-kneed under his regard.

"No. Go right ahead. Would you like a cool drink, Mister . . . ?" She paused.

"Bond," he supplied, leading his horse to the trough. Turning to her with a small smile, he continued, "A drink for me sounds right nice, ma'am."

His gaze held hers, and she swallowed nervously, tearing her eyes away. "I'll just be a moment," she murmured, turning to go inside.

"Thank you," he answered, his smile growing a bit.

She hustled into the house, castigating herself. *Old fool. Going all giddy just 'cause a man smiles at you. Land sakes, he's probably got a half-dozen kids at home waiting for him. And you're older than Methusela!*

Continuing her silent, one-sided conversation, Millicent took the cider out of the larder and impulsively piled a plate with a few slices of the fresh bread she'd baked that morning. Quickly Millicent turned back to the door before she could change her mind.

Stepping onto the porch, she put the tray on the small receiving table in front of the swing. She had been half-tempted to invite him in, but propriety had to be observed, even if they were on the frontier. She gestured to the swing.

"Please have a seat."

"Thank you, ma'am." He waited for her to be seated, then doffed his hat, revealing thick black hair. Gingerly he eased his tall, lanky frame down on the far side of the swing.

"Cider?" she asked, pouring him a generous glass. He accepted the drink and she offered him a slice of bread.

Taking the proffered bread, he settled back in the swing, inhaling the fresh-baked aroma.

"So you're the lady sheeprancher?" he asked calmly, taking another bite.

Millicent nearly choked on her cider. Swallowing the unladylike sputter, she gasped out, "Why, no. That is, this is my friend's ranch. I'm Millicent Groden," she offered by way of explanation.

"Pleased to meet you, Millicent Groden," he replied, and she almost blushed as he used her full name. It didn't sound quite so spinsterish when he said it.

"And yourself, Mr. Bond. Are you a neighbor?"

"I'm your closest neighbor to the east," he replied, holding her glance with his own once again.

Flustered, she cast her moss-green eyes downward, picking at an invisible thread on her apron. "I'm happy to make your acquaintance, Mr. Bond. Cassie will be, too, when she gets back." At his unspoken question she continued, "She's out rounding up strays."

"So there really is a lady sheepherder." His even, calm tone made it impossible to take offense.

"Yes, there really is," she responded, gauging the kindness in his weathered blue eyes. If asked to judge, she'd have guessed him to be nearly forty.

"Well, that should liven things up." He bent to take another sip of cider, and Millicent detected a smile of amusement lurking behind the glass of amber liquid.

"Undoubtedly." Her single rejoinder was rewarded with a full-fledged smile.

She returned his smile and found herself wondering about the lucky woman who could lay claim to that smile.

"Cassie and I would love to meet your family, too. Why don't you bring them by sometime soon?"

His smile faded, and white lines of tension replaced the earlier laugh lines. "Don't have a family. Anymore."

Millicent could have bitten off her tongue. "I didn't know," she replied softly, surprised at her urge to smooth away the tense lines etched in his face.

"Of course not." He seemed to mentally shake himself. "But I would be pleased to meet your family."

"My family are my friends—Cassie Dalton and her brother, Andrew."

"Dalton?" His surprise was clear.

Millicent nodded in acknowledgment and watched his eyes as his thoughts seemed to chase rapidly, one after another. He looked as though he were carefully weighing his words, deciding what to say. "Then you have your work cut out for you," he finally stated.

"That we do," she answered, wondering if he would also advise them to sell out.

"Like I said, I'm just the next ranch over. When you need help, I expect you to ask."

Millicent noted that he had said "when," not "if." She found her heart warming as she realized he didn't expect them to turn tail and run.

Milly remembered self-consciously that it had been a great many years since she'd sat on a front porch swing with a man. Years since Papa's stroke and the dreams of marriage to a handsome young beau. And now years had passed since

Papa died, and she was alone. She shook her head to stop her woolgathering.

"I expect we will," she answered, a smile lighting her even features.

Cassie wiped the rivulets of sweat from Shane's forehead with her own bandanna. She doubted he even noticed. His concentration was on the calf he hoped to extricate from its mother. She'd watched in amazement as Shane had reached in to turn the calf and had begun the harrowing process of bringing the calf's stubborn leg into position.

"I'll need to get its head," he explained, searching through his saddlebags. Disappointment loomed in his eyes. "I guess I'll have to use that rope."

"What do you need? Maybe I have it in my saddlebags."

"Something soft and flat I can wrap around the head so I don't damage the calf when I bring him out."

"Soft and flat," Cassie murmured. She knew without looking she didn't have anything fitting that description in her saddlebags. But . . .

Taking a deep breath, Cassie slipped off her boots and began to roll up the legs of her trousers. She swallowed convulsively and tried to ignore the amazement and fascination on Shane's face as she slipped her fingers beneath her garter and began peeling off her first stocking.

Her face colored in embarrassment as creamy flesh glistened in the sunlight when the first soft cotton stocking slipped off. Cassie wondered if she imagined the hiss of Shane's indrawn breath.

Blushing hotly, Cassie fumbled with the second garter and slowly peeled off the remaining stocking. The second stocking, still carrying the shape of her exposed leg, joined the first in the soft grass by her feet.

Cassie tried to control the surge of fire that singed her veins as she handed the silky, still-warm garments to Shane and encountered the hot blaze of his eyes. His jagged breath matched hers as she asked, "Will these do?"

Shane's eyes locked with hers, refusing to relinquish their hold. For a long moment he didn't speak but instead seemed to search her face. The harshness in his expression had momentarily disappeared. His voice was low and husky when he finally answered.

"They'll do."

Once again he reached in to reposition the calf, looping the stockings around its head. "The leg's doubled back," he bit out briefly, panting lightly in exertion. "I hope to hell the calf doesn't put its hoof right through the cow."

Cassie gulped, realizing the plight of the animal, and wondered how she'd have coped if one of her sheep . . .

"I've got his nose!" Shane's voice was threaded with excitement. "Come on, girl. We're almost there," he murmured to the heifer.

Shane studied Cassie's fascinated gaze. "I think I can get his head into position now," he explained. Cassie nodded in agreement and wonder at his expertise. Shane winced as the cow bore down, and she wondered that it didn't break his arm.

"Thatta girl. I see his legs." He continued comforting the animal as first the legs and then the head emerged.

Cassie gazed in wonder as the shoulders emerged and the calf slid into the wild grass at its mother's feet. Shane examined the calf, making sure its nose and throat were clear and then turned his attention to the mother.

"I knew you could do it, girl," he murmured, stroking the cow's back and rump.

Cassie felt an unexpected surge of camaraderie with him after sharing the miracle of birth. What a complex man he was, she thought, studying his face as he hunkered down by the newborn animal. She'd have thought a man who owned half the territory wouldn't be bothered by the plight of one of his thousands of cattle.

Because of her help Shane called a silent truce for the moment, letting his bitterness slip aside as he dropped lightly onto the grass at her side. There was plenty of time later to resurrect the past.

Having retrieved the canteen, Shane poured a generous amount of water in his hands and over his arms, washing away the afterbirth. Without asking permission, he picked up her hands, trickled water over them, and gently rubbed them clean with his own.

"What brings you out here?" he questioned.

Cassie purposely kept her eyes on the tottering calf, watching as the mother tenderly licked her new baby.

"Looking for my sheep," she explained briefly, trying to still the sudden breathlessness she felt at his touch.

Releasing her hands, Shane reached out to pull up a blade of weathered grass. Feeling suddenly bereft at the loss of his touch, she tucked her hands at her sides.

"Best I can remember, your uncle always had several dogs helping him, and even then he could have used another," Shane commented, sticking the blade of grass between his teeth and stretching his legs out. "Dogs keep the strays rounded up."

Cassie watched his long legs unfold as her heartbeat irrationally accelerated. His nearness unnerved her now that their shared task was completed. It was hard to remember that she needed to keep him at a distance for more than one reason. She felt her breath catch when he fastened his green eyes on hers.

He plucked another blade of grass, and Cassie tried not to stare as he pushed it past his mustache-covered lip.

Pulling her eyes away from his mouth, she tried to remember what he'd said. Oh, yes, the dogs. She answered shortly, "One of Uncle Luke's dogs died with him—went off the ledge at the same time. Manuelo kept old Pal alive—guess he was grieving pretty bad. I hate to take Pal back now because he's finally getting used to Manuelo, and I do have the other three dogs Manuelo's been taking care of. For now, I'll make do with them. And me."

"And you," he repeated softly as her stomach flip-flopped.

She studied the now dangling blade of grass that was carelessly tucked into the corner of his mouth. He eased the blade to the center of his firm lips. She swallowed, jerking her eyes away.

To her dismay, her gaze landed on his darkening green eyes. She couldn't control the sensations in her stomach that were creeping higher, threatening to cut off her breath. He'd pushed his Stetson back, revealing warm chestnut hair that shone in the sunlight. Cassie nibbled on her lower lip, staring at him.

Unaware of the beguiling picture she made, sitting in the meadow in her rolled-up trousers, hatless with her ebony tresses blowing gently in the breeze, she wondered if he sensed the unwilling attraction she was battling to overcome. The calf bawled, tottering about on unsteady legs. Cassie laughed in delight.

"I'm kind of looking forward to my new lambs now."

But Shane didn't seem to hear. She listened distractedly as her own laughter floated away on the wind. A myriad of conflicting emotions crossed Shane's face as ever so slowly he closed the distance between them.

Cassie watched breathlessly as Shane's strong, tanned hands began to unroll her pushed-up trouser leg. Swallowing hard, she stared in fascination at the darker skin of his hands contrasting sharply with the ivory skin of her legs. As he smoothed the material down over Cassie's bare flesh, his hands lingered, caressing the curve of her leg, tantalizing her ankle and sensitive instep.

Her breath caught as he bent to retrieve her boot and slipped it over her tingling foot. Trembling now, Cassie knew he must surely feel her erratic pulse as it threatened to pound out of control.

Shane twisted around to retrieve the second boot, and Cassie tried to swallow past the large lump in her throat. When he straightened up, Cassie caught his gaze. His eyes didn't waver, and she felt the message that emanated from them as surely as the strong hands that now grasped her other leg. Never releasing her from his scrutiny, Shane unfolded the material of her other pant leg with excruciating care.

As his hand purposely caressed her leg, Cassie thought she'd melt from the exquisite ache he was igniting. She sat perfectly still, holding her breath as he finally slipped the second boot over her foot. His hand lingered on the sensitive flesh of her ankle, the touch of his skillful fingers almost unbearable. Slowly he picked up her garters, still holding her rapt gaze with his own. He held out one to her while boldly slipping the other in his pocket.

Gazing into her delicately carved face, Shane felt a sharp pang of regret that this vulnerable-looking woman was related to the man he'd sworn to avenge. He knew she had unwittingly stepped into a fight that had dominated a generation and torn apart a community. But he also knew he could not let past promises go unfulfilled.

One thing had set him on his heels: a woman who would peel off her stockings in the middle of a meadow just to help a cow. As though they shared a moment suspended out of time—out of reach with the past—he grasped her face in his hands.

As his lips captured hers, Cassie thought inanely that the lines near his eyes were even more fascinating up close than they'd been at a distance. The warm fullness of his lips, coupled with the incredible teasing of his mustache, launched Cassie into a world of sensation she wondered if she'd forgotten or had never really known.

It seemed perfectly natural to melt against the solidity of his body. As Shane gently grasped the long tresses of hair that flowed about her shoulders, Cassie felt a tingling response ricochet through her body. When his other hand massaged the tender flesh of her neck and exposed throat, Cassie felt her own fire build.

As the kiss deepened, Cassie shivered at the feelings his touch created. At the first thrust of his tongue, Cassie felt momentary alarm, but she quickly discarded it in the persistent rush of emotion that followed.

And, if possible, she entered even closer into his embrace. His tongue washed over hers, seeking, finding. Each thrust sent a bolt of liquid desire. Feeling his tongue stroking the recesses of her mouth, she weakened, feeling the heat searing a path through her body. One hand rested of its own accord on the thick expanse of corded muscle on his shoulder. The other wound itself through the thick locks of his shaggy chestnut hair.

When Shane pressed even closer, she felt the unfamiliar hardness of his male body. Gulping, she swallowed the ache that filled her throat and traveled downward at an alarming rate. An unexpected tingle between her thighs ignited as he ground himself even closer. Heavy dregs of honeylike warmth weighted down her limbs.

When Cassie thought she'd die of the exquisite agony he was causing, he pulled away abruptly. She searched his eyes for the reason and saw a blaze of desire tinged with undisguised regret. Then his eyes hardened into the flinty coals she'd remembered from the day before.

Cassie flushed hotly. What must he think of her? That she was a frustrated old maid ready to literally throw herself at the first available man?

"Cassie, you don't belong here. Most women would see that and sell out."

Unaware of the demons chasing him, Cassie flinched at his words. The warmth in her limbs was replaced by a slow chilling wash of reality. Their kiss had meant nothing. He was still trying to run her off—and she could never let herself slip and forget it.

Shakily she rose to her feet, unable to banish her own regret. Her emotion-filled voice was as soft as the breeze that whispered about them.

"You're right, but then I'm not most women."

4

Cassie tried to demur, but Karl Fredericks was insistent. "You need the help, and I have the extra manpower." Fredericks shrugged his shoulders as he spoke. They both glanced over at Jim Fowler, the cowhand Fredericks had brought along.

Jim Fowler ducked his face, then peered up, his dull brown hair falling into his eyes. His black eyes shifted nervously about the barn.

"But I really can't accept such a generous gesture," Cassie argued. While pleased at his neighborly overture, she was uneasy about accepting his help. She didn't want to be obligated to Fredericks, knowing he wanted to buy her land. The situation made her distinctly uncomfortable—especially when Fredericks stared at her with that gleam in his eye. She didn't feel a flicker of interest.

"There's no reason for you to attempt to run this ranch alone when I have an extra hand."

Fredericks's voice was as smooth as she remembered. It glided over her, making it difficult to resist without appearing ungracious.

Her attention focused again on Jim Fowler. A bright gleam of perspiration had settled over his gaunt face while his hand gripped a quirt so tightly it was a wonder the whip didn't tear in two.

Cassie didn't like the look of him, from the top of his greasy head to the tips of his scuffed, muddy boots. But she needed the help. Judging from what she'd witnessed in town, hiring someone else would not be easy. She debated, glancing from Fredericks's self-assured, expectant face to Fowler's nervous-looking one.

"Won't nobody in town work for you," Fowler bit out, voicing Cassie's thoughts.

She stared silently at him, distaste and more than a little curiosity washing over her face.

Seeing her reaction, Fowler added with a sneer, "Not after what your uncle did."

Both Cassie and Fredericks responded to Fowler with varying degrees of surprise: Cassie with interest, hoping for an answer to the puzzling reaction of the townspeople, and Fredericks with ill-concealed anger.

"What do you mean?"

"He didn't mean anything, my dear. He's just—"

"I want to hear what he has to say."

The ranch hand squirmed uneasily when he sensed Fredericks's anger. Shrugging one shoulder, he mumbled, "Just the water thing."

"*What* water thing?"

Fowler's voice dropped lower. "Your uncle cut off enough water to kill half the valley."

"I don't believe you!"

"Of course you don't. There's no need to. Now I insist that you accept my help," Karl pressed.

All three of them fell into startled silence when Shane filled the doorway, his voice booming into the barn.

"Insist on what, Fredericks?"

Shane had watched the hunger in Fredericks's too-pretty face. And he didn't like it. He wasn't quite sure why, but he had the urge to shove Fredericks's immaculately groomed form into the nearest pile of manure.

"Insist on what, Fredericks?" Shane repeated.

"That's between the lady and myself." Fredericks's voice

sounded as smooth as ever, but he couldn't completely suppress the anger he was feeling.

"Why don't I decide about that?" Shane countered.

Cassie viewed the two of them in astonishment. "Does anybody here remember that the question was directed to me? And that I'm still here?"

All three heads swung in her direction, and Cassie suddenly felt uncomfortable under their scrutiny.

"Since you won't be staying around long, you won't be needing Fowler's help," Shane stated as though her decision had already been made. The hold on her temper dropped like whipped cream in the sun.

"Is that so, Mr. Lancer?" she demanded angrily. "Well, for your information, I plan to accept Mr. Fowler's help."

Fredericks's face radiated victory while Shane's features grew thunderous. His cheek twitched with the effort to keep his temper under control. Fowler reminded Cassie of a prize hog at the county fair. He'd won, but now he was going to the slaughterhouse for first-place honors.

Then, forgetting Fredericks and Fowler, Shane stepped close to Cassie. "That's not a very smart choice, lady. I came over here today to tell you I'd double my offer."

Their eyes locked, the air between them nearly crackling with tension. "But it's *my* choice, Mr. Lancer—not yours! And you can keep your blasted offer!" Cassie held her ground, trying not to remember how his closeness had affected her the day before.

"It won't be your choice for long," he growled back, looking as though he remembered exactly how she'd affected him.

"Is that a threat, *Mister* Lancer?" she taunted, wishing she weren't so aware of his lean form near hers.

"If that's what it takes," he responded, his eyes darkening, his voice stern as he worked to maintain control. She was close enough for him to see the flush under her dewy skin, the softness of her hair as it framed her face, and the fire in those extraordinary eyes.

"Is that any way to talk to a lady, Shane?" Fredericks's irritated voice interrupted them. They both stared at him, having forgotten anyone else was there.

Shane stared down from his superior height at Fredericks. "Don't get in my way, Karl," he warned.

Shane turned once again and held Cassie's eyes. "We'll finish this later." He glanced pointedly at Fredericks as though challenging him to interfere again. "When we're alone."

Shane walked away, and Cassie tried to still the sudden excitement she felt at the thought of being alone again with him. Knowing it was ridiculous, she coveted the liquid fire he'd ignited, and stared at his retreating figure until it disappeared from sight.

When Karl Fredericks cleared his throat to get her attention, she blushed hotly and, meeting Fredericks's cool gray eyes, knew her reactions to Shane had not gone unnoticed.

"I'll help Fowler settle in, my dear. I'm sorry if my offer of help caused more harm than good."

"Of course not. I appreciate your concern."

"Think nothing of it. I'll say good day to you now. Come along, Fowler."

Fowler followed reluctantly after Fredericks. Cassie sighed and turned toward the house.

Fredericks waited until Cassie was out of sight. "Why the hell did you tell her about Luke Dalton?"

"I didn't tell her half of what I could've," Fowler answered sullenly.

"No doubt, you buffoon. But I don't want her to find out the extent of the damage her uncle caused."

"Hell, why not? Maybe if she knew he'd cut off everybody's water till half of 'em died, she'd turn tail and run."

"Your perception, as usual, is totally wrong. If I can convince her there's no just cause for her neighbors' actions,

Cassie will sell out without a fuss. If the woman thinks she has to clear her uncle's reputation, she'll dig in forever."

"Won't do her no good no how. Folks know what ol' man Dalton did—they ain't gonna forget."

"Let's be sure of that."

"Milly, how much flour is left in the pantry?" Cassie's voice was muffled as she dug around the larder, checking their supplies.

"None. I need to get out another sack for today's baking."

Cassie tried to stifle her alarm. A cursory inventory told her what she'd feared: they'd never make it through the winter on the meager supplies that remained. Her mind searched the possibilities. She imagined she could order the supplies, but knew it would be months before the shipment arrived. And since Mr. Peabody controlled the shipping office, she wondered if trying to order the goods would simply be another futile gesture.

"Milly, where's the seed we brought along?"

Millicent stopped at the doorway of the larder, drying her hands on her apron. "It's in there somewhere."

"I think we'd better put a garden in."

"But it's so late in the season," Millicent protested. "And with this heat—"

"I know, Milly!" Cassie realized her tone sounded short, and gentled her voice, wishing for patience that wasn't forthcoming. "But I think it would be wise to set in some canned goods for the winter."

Millicent's face still mirrored puzzlement, and Cassie rushed on. "We don't know how the fleece sales will go. I'd feel better if we could conserve our supplies and make sure we have a good stock of canned food for the winter."

Millicent shrugged in agreement, seeming to see the wisdom in Cassie's logic. "Fine by me. I'll work the soil tomorrow."

Cassie breathed a silent sigh of relief. But she knew a garden was only a temporary measure. She had to find a solution for their survival, or social ostracism would be the least of their problems. Starvation was a horrifying possibility.

5

Evening star, mountain snowberry, and foxfire painted the canvas of the meadow in colors more startling than any artist's brush could create. The rugged wildflowers pushed past coarse native grass to decorate the untamed landscape.

Tying the mare's reins to a sturdy sapling, Cassie walked slowly through the wild grass. Breathing deeply, she wondered if she could ever get enough of the sweet-smelling air. How different this land was from her native Boston! But this particular meadow somehow embodied the differences most starkly. Here was beauty, grandeur, and, most importantly, peace—something she needed rather desperately right now.

She lamented her lack of wisdom in accepting Fredericks's help. Admittedly, she'd been pushed into the decision by Shane's interference. Still, it had been her choice. A choice she didn't feel right about.

Cassie took several deep breaths. Each one filled her with the serenity that had deserted her when she'd met Shane. Reluctantly, she acknowledged that her feelings had cascaded like the great falls of Niagara since their first encounter.

When she thought of Shane's high-handed methods with Karl Fredericks and Jim Fowler, she wanted to lash out and assert her independence. But when she remembered the day on Shane's land when they'd birthed the calf, she wished she were still in his arms.

Shivering in the light breeze of the field, Cassie knew the

goose bumps chasing up and down her flesh had nothing to do with the cool wind.

No, her emotions had taken over her body and were out of control. She had retreated to this, her favorite piece of land, to reflect on the past days. She also needed to determine how Shane had managed to destroy a lifetime of rigid self-control.

Never before had she reacted so shamelessly to a kiss, to a touch. Never before had she wanted both to continue, but to what end she did not know.

Tipping her head back, Cassie studied the cloudless sky, seeking answers in the endless field of blue. Instead of answers, her mind centered on the tender feelings that cropped up as she thought of Shane.

Each nuance and glance conjured up a conflict she despaired of resolving. The logical part of Cassie's brain told her that Shane wanted the land at any cost, and that most likely he was involved in Uncle Luke's murder.

But her illogical heart recalled his gentle ministrations, the beguiling laugh lines etched on his face, and the kindness he had shown to both Millicent and Andrew. Milly had only high praise for Shane, while Andrew tried to imitate his every action, pleased by the adult male companionship. Cassie knew Shane could scarcely spare the time he devoted to Andrew, which made his kindness even more compelling. She could scarcely believe that her initial feelings had changed so drastically. Dislike had turned to attraction. Suspicion was replaced with a growing trust. Trust that made her want the feel of his arms around her again. The taste of his lips . . .

Dropping lightly to the grass, Cassie pulled her knees upward and tucked her chin against them. She could deny none of the contradictions Shane embodied.

Cassie plucked a stalk of prairieclover and twirled the stem, watching the breeze lift the gentle blossoms. No, she couldn't deny the spectrum of emotions Shane had unleashed in her, least of all her desire.

Trailing one hand over the tangybush that flanked the meadow, Cassie tried to recapture the serenity she'd sought in this treasured part of her land. Instead she stilled her hand and glanced upward at the unending sky. As long as her heart yearned for a tall cowboy named Lancer, she knew with utter conviction that there would be no peace.

Hooking his arms over the top rail of the corral, Shane leaned against the splintery bark. For the past week he'd given Michael all the dust-eating, backbreaking chores he could find, and Michael had yet to complain. Worse, he'd seemed to enjoy the lowliest tasks. Shane glanced at the pawing stallion restrained in the breaking chute and hoped the ornery horse would end Michael's love affair with ranching. Not that his brother shouldn't respect his heritage, but hell, Michael was meant to be a lawyer. And staying back East meant he'd be safe.

Shane ran his eyes over the stallion's sleek lines as it bucked off the saddle for the fourth time. Dodging flying hooves, a cowhand rescued the saddle and made another attempt at saddling him. The horse would make fine breed stock, Shane thought, watching the beast rear his massive head.

"He's a beauty," Michael stated, joining Shane at the railing.

"That he is," Shane replied, wondering if Michael would still think the horse a beauty after he'd been bucked off a few times.

"Who's breaking him? Petey?"

Shane turned his head in Michael's direction. "No, I thought I'd give you a crack at him."

"I see." Apparently he did, Shane thought. So Michael *had* realized he'd been given a greenhorn's work.

"Tell you what, big brother. If I break him, you have to

introduce me to the lady sheepherder."

Shane stiffened. Ever since Cookie had raved about Cassie's beauty, Michael had been pestering him to meet her, and Shane had doggedly put him off. Hell, Michael was just a pup, still . . .

After Shane's own words in the meadow, he wondered if Cassie thought any more of him than of the cowpies littering the prairie. Not that it mattered. He'd lost his head and gone against his better judgment by kissing her. He wondered what had possessed him to lose sight of what was important. She was only a woman, albeit an intriguing one.

But it wouldn't happen again. Not when so much was at stake. Shane had promised his father he'd get the Dalton land back, and he wasn't going to let a pair of violet eyes and velvety lips sway him.

Hearing the stallion snorting and bucking about the chute, Shane made up his mind. He would be there to take control. As he always had.

"It's a deal."

Hooting his acceptance, Michael loped to the chute. "He's mine, boys."

Petey and George looked at Shane for confirmation. He nodded his head, wondering how many times the boy would be thrown before he gave up.

Michael mounted gingerly as the horse reared and thrashed about the stall. Wrapping the reins tightly over his hand, he gave the signal to open the stall. Petey swung the gate open and leaped up onto the railing, out of the way of the enraged horse.

One . . . two—Shane mentally counted the seconds, wondering if Michael would go down in two or three. To his amazement, Michael hung on. The stallion bucked ferociously, and Shane could see the sweat flying from Michael's face as he held on, gripping desperately with hands, legs, and body. Petey and George shouted encouragement as the stallion flung Michael forward and back, whipping his body mercilessly.

Shane winced, almost able to feel the rawhide cutting into Michael's hands, the bones crunching under the horse's impact, the strained muscles screaming. The stallion bucked violently, circling the corral, flinging Michael about like a rag doll.

Still he hung on.

Stepping up onto the bottom rung of the railing, Shane leaned into the corral. He felt an immense pride build to the point of bursting. Lost bet or not, he wanted Michael to conquer the beast. Michael wasn't a boy anymore, but a man to be reckoned with.

The stallion's bucking built to a frenzy, and Shane gripped the railing, afraid that if Michael fell now he'd be crushed under the horse's hooves. The worst of its frenzy finally spent, the horse ceased its bucking. Snorting, but under control, it cantered around the corral. And Michael was in control. Breathing as hard as the animal, Michael pulled the horse to a stop and dismounted, handing the reins to a grinning Petey.

Shane's face split into a wide grin as he scaled the railing, leaped over the fence, and gripped his brother's hand. "You won fair and square. And damned if I'm not proud of you for doing it." He ignored the niggling reminders of the consequences.

Michael slipped off his bandanna and wiped his sweat-covered brow. He weaved a bit as they headed for the house. "I'll keep you to your promise, Shane." Michael rubbed his bruised posterior. "But I may have to wait a few weeks before I get in the saddle again. But when I can, I get to meet the sheep lady."

Roaring with laughter, Shane slapped Michael on the back. Michael flinched, nursing his bruises. "Easy, big brother. You don't know your own strength."

Shane clasped his arm about his brother's shoulders and guided him up the front porch steps. "And you, little brother, are just beginning to learn yours."

6

Shane approached Cassie's corral with trepidation. He glanced over at Michael's cheerful face and fought back the urge to turn his horse around and head home. Michael hadn't forgotten their bet in the ensuing weeks after he'd broken the horse, much to Shane's regret.

He scanned the near-empty pens and barnyard but didn't see any signs of life. Approaching the house, Shane swung down from his saddle and looped the reins over the rail near the front porch. Michael followed suit while Shane strode across the wooden planks and knocked determinedly on the oak door. The pungent smell of fresh coffee wafted through the open window, but no voices stirred the easy silence.

"Let's try the barn," Shane said shortly, hoping Cassie was out with her flock. He wished he'd never agreed to this introduction.

The hazy, sun-filled barn was empty. Shane noticed the orderly interior and neatly stacked bales of sweet-smelling hay. *No slacking off here,* he thought, wishing there was. He needed a reason to dislike her—since she hadn't provided any of her own, other then being a Dalton. A muffled thud hit the side of the barn, and they backed out, searching for the source.

"How about in there?" Michael questioned, pointing to a small, unpainted wooden shed adjacent to the barn and pen that held a few bleating sheep.

"Tarnation! Hold still! Do you want me to cut off your hide, too?" The exasperated female voice stopped them at the entrance to the shed. Whatever they had expected couldn't have prepared them for the sight of a five-foot-two-inch, hundred-and-five-pound woman wrestling with a two-hundred-pound sheep.

What fleece wasn't lying in shreds about the sheep was plastered to Cassie's clothes and skin. Shane and Michael watched in stunned silence as Cassie grappled the ewe to the floor and gripped her shears determinedly.

"Trust me. This is hurting me more than you," she panted as the spooked sheep tried to escape her shears. The sheep bawled its protest, still struggling.

"Guess you could use some help." Shane's strong voice reverberated through the shed, startling Cassie and sending her tumbling backward as she loosened her grip on the sheep, who promptly bolted.

Shane bent to help Cassie up, and his gaze collided with her dark purple eyes. He was startled at the mixture of anger, frustration, and embarrassment he saw there. He extended his hand, again surprised by the jolt he felt holding her delicate hand in his. She grudgingly accepted his help, brushing ineffectually at the fleece clinging to her trousers.

"Didn't mean to startle you," he began, unaccountably touched by the flush that colored her cheeks. He called on his reserve of strength to ignore the feeling.

"It's all right," she muttered, ducking her head and biting her lip. Shane had noted the characteristic before and realized she nibbled on those delightful pink lips when she was scared, uncertain, or embarrassed. Right now he suspected she was all three.

Michael cleared his throat noisily, and Shane wheeled around, having forgotten him. "This is my younger brother, Michael. He's home from law school and wanted to meet you."

"I'm pleased to meet you, Michael," Cassie replied stiffly, having regained her dignity and standing as poised as if she were in her sitting room, dressed for afternoon tea.

Michael bent over her extended hand, and Shane had to restrain himself from asking where Michael had learned such tomfoolery. Studying the expression on Cassie's face, Shane saw that she appeared to enjoy Michael's formal manners. Natty manners, Shane corrected himself. Shane considered shoving Michael's half-bent form all the way to the dirt floor.

"We don't want to keep you from your work," Shane interjected, motioning to the littered floor where they stood. Cassie's dog-eared books lay almost hidden under the white piles. He had to hide an unexpected smile. How many women would actually try to shear a sheep guided only by a diagram in a book?

"You mean from the butchering," Cassie said disgustedly, studying Michael's face. So this was the family solicitor. She had little doubt what had prompted him to meet her. Shane must be bringing out fresh troops to try and bully her into selling the land.

"Is it supposed to turn out like this?" Michael asked, tactfully pointing to the fractured heaps of fleece scattered about the floor.

"It's supposed to be all in one piece. That's the only way the buyers will take it. If the shearers don't get here soon, I'm afraid all my profits will be lost," Cassie responded, thrusting a booted toe into the mangled pile of wool.

"What are the chances of the shearers getting through?" Michael questioned, surprising Cassie with his frank admiration. He was hardly the sinister solicitor she'd envisioned; he was a handsome, blond version of his brother, but much younger, and not yet harsh like Shane.

"Perhaps you should ask your brother," Cassie challenged, unable to repress her feeling that the shearers had been waylaid.

Michael shot a questioning glance at Shane who deigned not to answer. Cassie suspected he wasn't pleased with the admiring glances Michael continued to send her way.

Michael's next words drove the point home. "If you need a man's help, you can depend on me," he offered, his eyes full of a puppylike adoration.

What a tempting offer, Cassie thought. Her eyes cut briefly to Shane's. Maybe it was time he saw how it felt to be on the outside looking in.

7

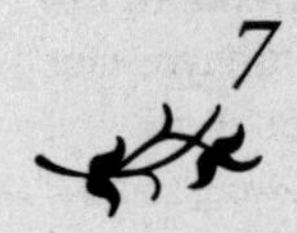

Cassie threw the broken shears to the barn floor in disgust. Not only were the sheep long overdue for shearing, but now her shears were conveniently ruined. She felt sure they were in one piece the last time she'd used them. Manuelo kept waiting for the shearers to pass their way, but no one had shown up. She wondered if the townspeople had kept the shearers away, along with the blockade on her supplies. A shadow darkened the oversized doorway of the barn.

"Find the shears?" Millicent questioned, peering into the hazy barn.

"Yes. Not that they'll do us any good." Millicent followed Cassie's eyes to the damaged shears.

"I don't suppose we could buy another pair in town?" Millicent half questioned, half stated.

Stalling, Cassie paused, not wanting to tell Millicent they wouldn't be getting anything from town. She'd kept the worrisome secret to herself, still not knowing how to solve the problem. She decided to stretch the truth a bit. "They have to come through the mail order catalogue. And we can't wait that long. I'll have to try and borrow Manuelo's."

"Maybe we could help shear his flock in return," Millicent suggested. "Manuelo's been teaching Andrew, and we could probably learn too."

Cassie brightened. "I hadn't thought of that." A sudden frown replaced her smile. "I don't know if he'll let us get near them, though. Maybe we could keep trying to shear ours first till we know what we're doing."

"You really think we're going to know what we're doing by then?"

Letting out a noisy sigh, Cassie nibbled on her bottom lip. "Probably not. I counted on the shearers getting through. Our fleece won't be worth much if we butcher it up."

"It'll be worth even less if we don't get it sheared at all." Millicent's no-nonsense tone penetrated Cassie's gloom.

"You're right. I'll get the shearing shed in order."

"I'll go borrow the shears if you like," Millicent offered. "And I bet I'll be back before you get the sheep rounded up."

"Don't remind me!" Cassie rolled her expressive eyes.

Millicent answered her with a laugh and headed for the wagon, pulling off her apron as she went.

Opening her book, Cassie found the right chapter and studied the pages. She couldn't quite control the grimace on her face. The shed was a filthy mess. Had schoolteaching in the city really been all that bad? Yes, worse. She sighed again and took a deep breath. Facing the dirty shed, she rolled up her flannel shirt sleeves and set to work. An hour later, the shed looked transformed with the floor shoveled out and fresh hay covering the packed dirt.

She propped her manual on the railing, studying the pictures. Satisfied she was following the right procedure, Cassie found the wide leather belting used for the shearing. Glancing up, she realized the hook to hang it on was out of her reach. She searched for something to stand on and found a rickety stool. Gingerly she climbed up, secured her footing, and looped the heavy leather over the hook. Just as she was about to fasten the belt to the hook, a deep voice boomed near the front of the shed. Cassie grasped the hook, almost losing her balance.

"Well, missy, looks like you've grabbed on to more than you can handle."

Cassie stood still and silent. She didn't recognize the voice, but the mocking undertone sent prickles flying up and down her spine. The hulking form filled the doorway, blocking the sunlight and shading his face.

"I thought you Daltons always had plenty to say." His voice curled maliciously, and Cassie's heart flew to her throat. Andrew was in the summer pasture, and Millicent wouldn't be back for some time.

"I don't believe we've been introduced." Cassie tried to sound calm, but even to her own ears her voice was high-pitched and wavering.

"That's right, little lady." His voice paused over the last word, and he almost spit it out. The man stepped out of the shadows, and Cassie found herself recoiling as he fastened his menacing gaze on her. She gulped, stunned by his thick face, muscular arms, and barrel-shaped body. He seemed to bare his teeth at her from his fully fleshed face.

"I'm Cassandra Dalton," she began in her most formal tone, hoping to still the growing fright in the pit of her stomach.

"I ain't saying I'm pleased to meet you,'cause I'm not. We don't want your kind 'round here. We didn't want your uncle and we don't want you." The chills chasing up her spine multiplied and spread to her weakening limbs.

"I . . ." Her words were drowned out as a wagon pulled to a stop in the yard, and a female voice called out, "Whoa!"

The man filling her doorway doffed his hat as Cassie heard a reserved voice greet him. "Mr. Robertson."

"Miss Sarah." So the bear could be polite when he wanted to, Cassie thought, still gripping the stool she was perched upon.

A slim, brown-haired young woman, dressed in calico, stood in the doorway of the shed. Cassie watched as the woman glanced from the hulking man to Cassie and back again. The woman he'd called Sarah addressed Cassie in a confident manner.

"How do you do? You must be Mr. Dalton's niece."

Cassie scrambled off the creaking stool. "Yes, I am. I'm Cassandra Dalton."

Sarah stepped forward, directing her vivid green-eyed gaze pointedly at the man. "I hope I'm not interrupting anything."

"I have to be gettin' on," the man mumbled, edging uneasily out of the shed.

After he left, Sarah eyed Cassie knowingly. "Was this a timely interruption?"

"Yes, thank you, most opportune. Evidently Mr. . . ."

"Robertson," Sarah supplied.

"Mr. Robertson came by to inform me I'm not wanted around here."

"Charming, isn't he?"

"Very. I was beginning to feel like a trapped rat."

"I thought as much. I'd say ignore him, but that probably won't be possible. But I wouldn't let him corner you again."

"I'll try not to." Cassie felt relief wash through her, and she sat down abruptly on the stool.

"You're shaking!" Sarah's concerned voice swept over Cassie in a warming wave. Seeing Cassie's fear, Sarah's normal caution deserted her. She swept aside years of hurtful memories and clasped Cassie's work-worn hands in her own, rubbing them vigorously. Sarah thought of Shane's reaction to her befriending Cassie, but she reached out to the frightened young woman regardless. Sarah refused to accept that another generation of hate was beginning with this vulnerable woman.

"I'm being silly," Cassie protested, embarrassed by her dusty hands in comparison to the immaculate white-gloved ones that had captured hers.

"I'd hardly call reasonable fear silly. Jacob Robertson is an overbearing hulk of a man, and I honestly don't know how seriously you should take him. He's been bitter for so many years it's become his nature. Jacob's a widower with one boy—Zack. They live alone in a broken-down ranch that borders your land. Shane thinks Jacob's full of overheated air, but I'm not sure."

"Shane?" Cassie felt her heart sink and cursed her own weakness. They'd only shared a kiss, after all. Something he no doubt did far more often than she. Cassie hadn't really thought Shane was married, but . . . "Then you're Mrs. Lancer?"

A look of puzzlement settled over Sarah's even features. "No, I'm Sarah Adams, Shane's sister. There isn't a Mrs. Lancer."

"Oh." The quiet one-word answer was expressive.

"Not from lack of trying. Shane's been chased by the best, but he just hasn't been caught yet. Sometimes I think it's because it's too easy for him." Cassie saw the concern in eyes that were so like Shane's, and instantly liked her.

"Well, I haven't joined the race," Cassie intoned, dismissing her own treacherous attraction to Shane.

"So I've heard."

Cassie's face jerked upward, and her eyes widened in an unspoken question.

"It doesn't take two shakes of a cow's tail for news to travel on the range. We chew over the same old gossip for so long that when we have something new to tell, it travels fast."

"But there's nothing to tell," Cassie protested.

"Nothing to tell!" Sarah's voice was incredulous. "A single woman takes on the territory's most eligible bachelor, and there's nothing to tell?"

Cassie felt herself blushing. "I wouldn't say I took on Shane—"

"That's not the way I heard it. Didn't you have Matt, his swamper, herding your sheep?"

Swallowing, Cassie nodded.

"And didn't you send Shane scooting back home when he told you to sell out?"

Cassie nodded again. "But how . . . ?"

Sarah chuckled. "It's a big, lonely country out here. And news—any news—gets around faster than you can blink. Don't worry about what people say or think. I like your spunk." Sarah stared down her pert nose and pursed her heart-shaped lips. "Don't know about the trousers, though."

Glancing down at her brother's well-worn trousers, Cassie ran a self-conscious hand across her knees.

"Don't be embarrassed. Just warning you that some of the *ladies* around these parts won't take to them. But the men surely will."

Cassie looked slightly askance at Sarah's last comment. Then she felt her lips curve upward a bit as she considered Sarah's words.

"It's just that with fence mending and herding and shoveling out pens . . ." Cassie shrugged as she motioned about her.

"You'd look a darn sight worse doing your chores in a dress. But don't you have any men to help you?"

"My brother—but he's only twelve. And it's a full-time job watching the flock. I can barely find enough time for him to do his lessons." Cassie paused. "And Jim Fowler. I haven't found any other help yet."

Sarah's eyes shone with sympathy. "That won't be easy," Sarah said frankly, covering her distaste at the mention of Fowler's name. "At least you're making your brother do his lessons. A lot of frontier women give up on educating their children."

"What about you?"

"Mine wishes I'd forget his lessons," Sarah answered with a laugh. "I have a boy who's eight—Timmy." Her lips pursed speculatively for a moment. "I guess he'd be too young to be friends with your brother. And Timmy can be a handful." Sarah's expression conveyed that Timmy was much more than a mere handful. Cassie found herself laughing along with Sarah. "And there's my baby," Sarah continued softly. "Little

Megan—she's two. For a long time we didn't think there'd be another baby." Sarah's voice was thoughtful, but her face brightened suddenly. "But there was—and she's a joy."

Cassie smiled at the expression of gentle happiness on Sarah's face. "I'm glad for you."

"Me, too."

"Do you live close by?" Cassie asked, hoping she did. It would be comforting to have one friendly neighbor close by, even if she were related to Shane.

"Close for out here. Not close by city standards. I live in that direction." Sarah pointed out the shed toward the east. "Just headed by to see Shane. I hear our younger brother's home. Since he's supposed to be in law school, I want to find out why he's at the ranch. And if I know my big brother, he's going to be hopping mad."

"Really?"

"I'm afraid so. Ever since Pa died, Shane's been the self-appointed head of the family. I'm surprised he hasn't packed Michael back off to school yet."

"Don't any of you object to his taking charge?" Cassie didn't think Sarah appeared to be a timid female ready and willing to obey Shane's bidding.

"I think I'm giving you the wrong idea. Shane didn't decide Michael should go to law school. That's been Michael's dream for as long as I can remember. And Shane's been like a father to Michael. Michael was only eight when Pa died. Since Shane took charge and kept the ranch going, we all pretty much accepted him as head of the family."

For some reason, Cassie doubted Shane's role in placing Michael in law school was that innocent. But since Shane's situation as head of the family was uncomfortably close to her own, Cassie decided to steer away from the subject.

"I met Michael the other day."

"You did?" The surprise was evident on Sarah's face.

"Shane brought him by."

Surprise turned into shock. “Well, well.”

Cassie glanced up a bit shyly. “I do hope we can be friends, in spite of my sheep and my tangles with Shane.”

Sarah burst into unladylike laughter, momentarily forgetting the past. “I don’t give a whit about the sheep,” she finally managed. “It’s the tangles with Shane.”

Uncomfortably aware that Sarah was Shane’s sister, Cassie said stiffly, “I can understand if my tangles with Shane might cause you to be uncomfortable, making friendship difficult . . .”

“Nonsense. Don’t you dare ruin all my fun! I’m counting on you to give Shane a run for his money. And I want a front-row seat!”

8

"How've you been, Fowler?" Shane asked lazily, glancing around Cassie's corral in apparent disinterest.

"Just fine, Mr. Lancer. Just fine." Fowler's nervousness increased. Beads of sweat popped out on his forehead while his eyes darted about the yard.

"Like working for Miss Dalton?"

The ranch hand nodded nervously and shrugged his shoulders at the same time. "Sure—it's all right."

Remembering the poisoned water discovered on Cassie's land a few days earlier, Shane studied the man's perspiring face before he asked softly, "Been pissing in any water holes lately, Fowler?"

Fowler's head jerked up, and anxiety engulfed his face.

"Make sure you're not." Shane's voice was soft, but an unmistakable thread of steel laced through his words.

"Harassing my help?" Cassie's voice was nearby, and she sounded mad.

"I'll leave that to you." His gaze raked her face and body, his expression once again detached, cool.

Exasperation flooded Cassie as she willed her stomach to stop tightening in anticipation. It was one thing to plan to stay in control when he was away, but at this proximity her head whirled treacherously. She thought with disgust that she'd laid all those sorts of feelings to rest years before. It was even more annoying to find them resurrecting themselves for an unprincipled man like Lancer.

"Are you implying I don't know how to treat my hired help?"

Shane took Cassie's arm unceremoniously and led her out of Fowler's earshot. She refused to acknowledge the tingle she felt at his touch. The strength in his long, lean fingers both irritated and unnerved her.

"I tried to tell you before. You don't need someone like Fowler working for you."

"And I suppose you know who should be working for me?"

His eyes were hard again. She must have imagined the softness she'd seen in them that day in the meadow. Every other time she'd seen him, his eyes appeared flinty, emotionless.

"Sell out and you won't need anyone working for you."

"Save your breath," she answered shortly, wishing she were standing further away from him. But to back up would show cowardice. She dug in her heels.

"How long do you think you'll get along without any supplies?" Shane had to remember why he'd come here. It wasn't to admire the way her eyes flashed or to fantasize about the curves beneath her form-fitting breeches.

The surprise in her face almost made him regret his words. Almost. The townspeople were justified in their actions, and he had to remember he had good reason too.

"So you were the one behind my supplies being cut off," she accused softly, disbelieving. Shaken by his revelation, she refused to let him see her reaction. Had he convinced the townspeople of some horrible story about her uncle?

"Believe that if it'll make you feel better. But I warned you to sell out."

"And if I don't, you'll see that I'm starved into selling?"

"I won't rest till I have this land, Cassie." His warning reverberated in the air already thick with tension. She swallowed, the mix of emotions she felt impaling her, choking her.

When Cassie finally spoke, her voice grew husky with repressed feelings. "And I won't sell," she said with finality.

He watched the emotions chasing over her face—disappointment, anger, regret, and then stubbornness. He clenched his jaws together, the pocket of his cheek twitching with the effort. Shane wanted to erase the regret. But the past could not be denied.

"You'll sell. You just don't know it yet. In the meantime, keep on eye on Fowler unless you want to be murdered in your sleep."

She blanched. Was he saying Fowler had been involved in her uncle's murder? She pressed her knuckles to her lips. And did that mean Shane had orchestrated his death?

Unable to reply, she stared sightlessly into the dust following in his wake as Shane rode away. Remembering his kisses, her body fought the accusation, but her mind whirled as she turned to stare at Jim Fowler. He hastily averted his gaze, and Cassie swallowed her growing horror. The vast plains seemed to close in as despair engulfed her. If what Shane had implied was true, she might well have set the stage for her own murder.

9

Days had passed slowly while Cassie waited for Fowler to set some trap in motion. When none materialized, she finally relaxed. Picking up the feed bucket, Cassie patiently tossed a few pieces of grain on the ground, glancing backward as she did so.

Apparently it worked. The books had said that in order to establish a leader, you worked to get the sheep accustomed to following a particular person. It seemed that sheep had good memories, even if they weren't able to reason very well.

Cassie grinned back at the flock of sheep that followed contentedly behind, feeling a bit like Mary with her little lambs. She stopped tossing the grain to see if the animals would still follow her. The faithful group continued shadowing her lead.

Pleased that it had worked, Cassie turned toward her horse to return home. It always seemed she had thousands of chores waiting. No matter how hard she worked, or the long hours she spent on the books, she never felt caught up.

But as Cassie moved forward, she heard the hooves of the sheep close behind. Craning her neck backward, she saw the flock moving steadily behind her. She stopped and turned toward the group.

"Go back. Go on." Cassie took a few steps forward. The flock pranced forward as though on cue.

"I really mean it. I have to go home now. Shoo!" Cassie began walking hurriedly toward her horse. The woolly creatures moved quickly in her wake.

"Hey, I have to leave now. And you have to stay here." Cassie broke into a run. The sheep hurried along, keeping step with her.

Exasperated, she tried to plead with them. "You don't want to come with me." Cassie pointed at the grassy pasture in which the animals stood. "See, this is much nicer than where I'm going." She backed away slowly and then turned toward her horse. The sheep moved along behind her, keeping rank.

"I'll just get on my horse and outrun you!" she finally shouted, then stopped still. No she couldn't. Running sheep on a warm day would kill them. Wonderful. She'd trained the little beasties so well, she was going to be stuck out in the pasture with them.

Disgusted, she flopped onto the grass, cradling her knees with her arms. The confused sheep crowded closer. Unable to believe what she'd created, Cassie got to her feet. Gazing to the east, she realized that Andrew was only about two miles over the crest. She mounted the horse, but the skittish mare refused to walk slowly enough to accommodate the sheep. Knowing what would happen to the sheep if they ran on the hot summer day, she stared at them in dismay. Exasperated, Cassie dismounted, tying the horse to a nearby oak tree. With a sigh, she glanced at her maddeningly obedient flock and started walking.

A few blisters later, Cassie rested on a crested butte, wondering where Andrew was. She checked again and saw what seemed to be patches of sunlight under the trees. Then some of the patches moved. All at once the whole side of the hill seemed to be moving, and Cassie realized she was watching the sheep, breast high in the brush.

Walking down the crest, she spotted the odd-shaped canvas-topped wagon. Smoke billowed from the stovepipe that jutted upward in the center of the wagon. Near the wagon tongue, Andrew sat by the door on a collection of different-sized boxes that served as steps. Cassie waved and hollered a greeting.

When they were close enough to hear one another, Andrew yelled at her in disgust. "Why'd you bring them back over here? I just got 'em moved to the other pasture this morning."

"I didn't exactly plan on bringing them over here."

"You were just out taking a walk, and they followed you here, I guess."

"Well . . ."

"Have you been training them to follow you again?"

"I thought it'd be a good idea."

"Except now you can't get away."

"I hadn't counted on that happening."

Andrew rolled his eyes. "There's only one cure."

"I don't care what it is. I'm not sleeping with this pack of overgrown babies."

"We're going to have to lead them down to the next pasture," Andrew warned.

Cassie wiggled her protesting toes. Then she glanced back at the white, woolly faces waiting for her.

"Let's go," she agreed with a sigh.

"Lead on," Andrew replied, snickering.

"Funny, Andrew. Really funny."

It took better than an hour, but they finally reached Manuelo's corral area. Andrew pointed to a series of gates that had been built between each corral and pen.

Cassie glanced at Andrew inquisitively.

"You'll see." Andrew headed toward the corrals. Cassie and her group followed. When they neared the gates, Andrew paused.

"Move to the side, Cass."

She moved, and Andrew waited while the sheep crowded around. Then he opened the gate. As though on fire, the sheep rushed forward. Cassie watched in amazement as they clambered to get through the gate.

"But . . . why?" Cassie asked.

"They love gates, any kind of gates. Even Manuelo doesn't know why. But give 'em a gate, and they go crazy. Can't wait to get in there."

Cassie shook her head in wonder.

Andrew smiled. "Wait till you see this." He jumped into the next holding pen, which emptied into the large corral. Winking at Cassie, he put his hand on the gate latch. The sheep immediately crowded close. When they were all pawing at the ground, Andrew opened the gate and they bolted through, running madly into the large corral area.

Hooting, Andrew ran back to Cassie. "Now watch," he said with a giggle. After all the sheep had rushed through the open gate, they stopped and gazed back, puzzled. The poor beasts acted as though they wondered what all the rush had been about.

"Problem's solved, Cass. Just carry a gate with you wherever you go and—"

"You're so funny I think I'll double your lessons," Cassie retorted.

"I could let them back out before you get away—"

Cassie broke in hastily. "You'll glide by this time, little brother, but—"

"Yep, I think they're about ready to break out."

Her voice held a mixture of frustration, amusement, and acceptance. "Don't get too big for your britches, young man."

"Uh-oh. I see them nearing the gate leading out now . . ."

"I'm going." Cassie slammed her hat on and limped away on blistered feet. After she was out of Andrew's line of sight, she allowed a smile to surface. Wouldn't do to let him know she'd given up the struggle for authority without concern.

Glancing behind her, seeing the sheep securely penned, she issued a sigh of blessed relief. Favoring her painful feet, she hobbled forward with a grimace. No wonder they called dudes "tenderfeet," she thought with disgust. By the time Cassie reached her mare, she'd be lucky if she had any feet left.

Hearing a rumble in the distance, she hoped fervently it wasn't Shane. Spotting Cookie's wagon, she raised a hand in greeting, a smile lighting her face.

But when the wagon pulled up, her smile dissolved into a frown of embarrassment.

"Out for a walk?" Shane asked pleasantly, slowing the wagon to accommodate her pace.

Shooting him a murderous glare, Cassie continued walking. He continued to hold the wagon in a slow, even gait.

"It's been a fine day to take a ride. You can see the most interesting sights from up on the bluff," he continued.

"I didn't know you were reduced to hauling supplies," she responded nastily, gesturing to Cookie's wagon. Did the man have some sort of sixth sense that beckoned when she was making a fool of herself?

"I'm not proud. Just do what needs to be done—even if it means hauling piece goods from town."

She merely nodded in reply, trying not to limp as she strode forward.

"One thing about these wagons, though . . ."

He paused, and she answered through gritted teeth, "And what might that be?"

"Just that they're kind of lonely. All this room and only one body to fill it." He shrugged his shoulders expressively.

Peering at him suspiciously, she doubted that he'd been lonely one second of his life.

" 'Course, you could help me out of my predicament."

She tried not to concentrate on how many blisters had no doubt formed by then as she placed one painful foot in front of the other.

"So you won't be *lonely,* I suppose?" She would walk all the way to Boston before she admitted she needed a ride.

"No, so I don't have to visit my sister by myself."

"Sarah?" Cassie halted abruptly.

"She talked me into getting her shipment while I was in town, so now I have to go out to her place."

Cassie thought briefly of Sarah's visit and about her friendliness and good humor.

"I would like to see Sarah," she replied hesitantly.

Shane set the brake, jumped down, and lifted her into the wagon before she could protest.

"We can tie your mare to the back of the wagon," he began.

"How do you know my horse is out here?" she asked warily.

"I'm sure you didn't get all the way out here by yourself," he answered innocently, his eyes carefully blank.

"Not exactly," she admitted, thinking of the flock that had cheerfully accompanied her.

He flicked the reins, increasing their speed. He spared her one glance filled with both understanding and amusement. "I didn't think so."

She kept her silence, realizing that he was merely being kind. He hadn't offered her a ride because he needed company or, more importantly, to humiliate her. He'd saved her from a painful walk—and from an even more painful embarrassment.

Gazing into his face, Cassie saw more than handsome features and Lancer pride. She saw kindness that bespoke a good heart. And with a start she realized this quality attracted her as much as the desire he'd aroused within her.

As the wagon bumped over the rough ground leading away from the hillside, Cassie enjoyed the companionable silence, listening as Shane whistled to the horses. The hills receded, sloping downward to a sprawling house. Cassie gasped when she saw the sleek lines of the home; its elegance befitted Beacon Hill. Rather than seeming out of place, however, the home lent grace to an incomparable setting.

Cassie's face lit with pleasure when Sarah swept out of the tall double doors. Cassie returned Sarah's wave and smile, relieved to see a friendly face.

But instead of stopping to speak, Sarah rushed to the bed of the wagon. "Did my material come in?" She continued digging until she unearthed the treasure she'd been searching for. Holding up a bolt of piece goods, Sarah squealed in delight. "Look, Cassie. For the dress I'm going to wear to the annual cookout. What do you think?" Twirling slightly with the material held in front of her, Sarah preened while she waited for an answer.

"I'm sure it'll be fine," Cassie answered quietly, aware she hadn't been invited to the event. In fact, she'd never heard a word about it.

"What are you planning to wear?" Sarah continued, admiring the fabric.

Cassie's chin lifted a fraction. "I haven't been invited." Her voice was quiet, calm, laced with hurt.

"Of course you are. Everyone is." She turned to her brother. "You told her about the Lancer cookout for July fourth, didn't you?"

Shane gazed up toward the sky. "Not yet."

"Shame on you! Well, of course you're invited, Cassie. You and Millicent and Andrew. I don't know where my brother's manners are." This was said with a heated look directed toward Shane.

"Maybe I didn't have a chance to ask her yet, Sarah."

"What better time is there?"

"When you're not around, for one. I was figuring on a long ride home alone with Cassie—seems like that would have been a good time, Miss Nosey Pants."

Cassie glanced at Shane in surprise. The indignation on his face seemed real.

"Sarah won't be happy till I'm on bended knee, I suppose," Shane muttered. "I had planned on asking you later . . ." He glanced aside to glare at his sister who promptly stuck her tongue out at him. "Would you like to go to the cookout we have every year—that is—you and Millicent and Andrew?"

"I've never been to a Western cookout," Cassie replied hesitantly, remembering her neighbors' hostile behavior. She wasn't sure she wanted to be cast inside a hornets' nest.

"Then you have a treat in store." Sarah took Cassie's arm and led her toward the house. "We'll have some dinner, and I'll tell you all about—"

"But I don't want to impose," Cassie tried to protest.

"You're not imposing. 'Sides, Shane doesn't have to get back for a while. Let me show you the picture in the fashion magazine of the dress I'm going to make with this material. I have the newest *Godey's Lady's Book* my aunt sent me. Of course, it hasn't been the same since Godey sold out, but this style's still way ahead of anything I have hanging in my chifforobe. You know, I've been thinking about trying one of those new graded patterns through Godey's shopping service. What do you think? I bet we could . . ."

Sarah's voice trailed off as she continued into the house. Shane shook his head in a mixture of amusement and exasperation. His sister not only took the cake, she diced it up and threw it to the hogs. Expelling a gusty sigh, he climbed the steps into his sister's house, trying to fix a smile on his face while he listened to what he knew would be hours of talk on fashions. He'd have had more luck getting Cassie alone in the middle of town hall. And Cassie thought she lived in an isolated territory. Hah!

10

Millicent guided the wagon down the dusty road. Fire-red clay rose in choking waves, and she was beginning to regret her rash decision. She had watched Cassie try the shearing for the last two weeks with a pair of clippers borrowed from Manuelo and realized they were fighting a losing battle. So Millicent decided to learn how to shear a sheep. It had seemed like a very sensible idea that morning, but now, a few hours later, she had yet to find Manuelo. She squinted through the orange haze of dust and thought she spotted a horseman.

Elated, she snapped the reins smartly and headed his way. As she neared the chestnut bay, she realized the rider was not Manuelo. Millicent felt a warmth spreading through her limbs as she recognized her neighbor. She slowed the wagon, easing to a stop.

He tilted his hat, a smile transforming his face.

"Miss Groden. So you've found my place."

Millicent hated to dash cold water on his pleasure. "Actually, Mr. Bond, I was trying to find Manuelo but I seem to have lost the proper direction." Millicent wondered if she imagined the disappointment that flickered briefly in his eyes. "It is a pleasure to see you, though," she added hastily.

His smile widened. "Ringer, please."

"I beg your pardon?"

"Would you call me Ringer, ma'am?"

"If you wish," she responded cautiously. "Is Ringer your Christian name?"

He laughed heartily in response. "No, ma'am, but that's what I go by."

"I see." But it was apparent she didn't. "Would you mind my asking why?"

"When I was a kid, some of the older cowpokes set me up with a horse that nobody'd ever been able to break. They told me he was an old horse we'd already put out to pasture. Fact was he was a dead ringer for the horse in the pasture. I was too embarrassed to admit the horse was killing me, so I kept getting back on till I broke him. The boys started calling me Ringer, and it stuck."

The humor of his story struck Millicent, and she tried to restrain the laughter that bubbled to the surface. But when she gazed into his mischievous eyes, she was lost. The laugh grew, erupted, and multiplied as Ringer joined in.

"I'm sorry," she finally gasped.

"Nothing to be sorry about, ma'am. Guess I've had that handle for so long that it just sounded natural. Took somebody new to remind me how funny it is."

"I don't mean to poke fun at your name," Millicent replied. "And please call me Millicent, not ma'am."

"I'd be pleased to, Millicent." She met his eyes and felt an odd catch in her throat as he spoke her name. He made it seem almost lovely.

Millicent started to reply and found that the breeze snatched away the beginning of her answer, tossing it skyward and leaving her breathless. She searched the gentle creases of his weathered face and wondered at the pain that had caused them. And wondered at the floating sensation that seemed to possess her limbs. *You're too old to be getting fanciful,* she scolded herself. *Much too old.*

She cleared her throat, hoping her head would clear also. "I don't suppose you'd know where the Basque's pasture would be?" she questioned.

His easy smile split his face. "Yes'm. Just over the next

rise. You were almost there."

"I was lucky to have seen you, then. I was heading down the road and I . . ." Her words trailed off as his impossibly wide smile grew even wider.

"If you don't mind my saying, ma'am, I'm the lucky one."

Millicent found herself doing something she hadn't done in more years than she cared to count. She blushed. From the top of her ginger hair to the lace collar of her calico dress, she flushed. "Well, I . . ." Millicent stuttered, hopelessly realizing that flirtation was a lost art she'd never really mastered.

Ringer tipped his Stetson. "I'd best let you get on your way, Millicent."

She willed the revealing heat to leave her burning cheeks, wondering if she sounded as rattled as she no doubt looked. "Yes, I need to see the Basque." She picked up the reins to signal the horses, hesitated, and stared straight ahead, avoiding Ringer's face as she spoke. "I'd be pleased to have you stop by for coffee." She fervently hoped her face hadn't taken on the hue of a ripe tomato.

"That'd be right nice, ma'am."

Daring a quick glance at him, she relaxed a bit at the pleasure showing on his face. "Well, then, I'll be on my way."

"Yes'm." He gaited his horse back as she flicked her reins. "I'll be seeing you soon, Millicent."

She nodded her head in reply, inwardly glowing as he said her name. Millicent felt as foolish as an old maid at a wedding, but the dreamer locked inside her melted as she thought of his blue eyes and winsome smile.

The warmth of that smile carried her through the dandelion-laden meadow and over the gentle rise to the abundant summer pasture. She spotted the Basque and opened her mouth to call a greeting. Instead her smile froze and the warmth in her stomach cooled and battled with the bile rising in her throat. Oh, God, no!

11

Cassie forced the cup of hot tea into Millicent's shaking hands.

"You'll feel better with something warm in you," Cassie insisted gently, shaken more than she'd cared to admit by Millicent's discovery.

More than a dozen of their spring lambs had been slaughtered horribly. Their decapitated, mutilated carcasses had been strewn over the south end of the pasture, and their heads floated grotesquely in the water barrels.

Millicent shivered uncontrollably despite the warm tea in her hands and the shawl Cassie had wrapped around her knees.

"Andrew!" Cassie blurted out, suddenly worried about his safety.

"I sent Michael to find him," Shane replied.

Suspicion overwhelmed Cassie, and she observed Shane closely.

"I figured you'd want the boy close to home."

Cassie didn't answer. Had Shane purposely planned his visit so that he would be free of suspicion when the sheep were discovered?

Glancing at the top of Shane's gleaming head as he leaned toward Millicent, Cassie wanted urgently to believe they didn't need protection from Shane. She stilled her shaking hands. Suddenly she encountered Shane's intense regard and felt her stomach constricting. Could she stand knowing the answer?

* * *

"Milly." Cassie shook her friend's shoulder gently, and Millicent's eyelids slowly fluttered open. "I'm sorry to wake you, but you have a visitor, and he's very insistent. He says he has to see you."

Millicent shook her head groggily and raised herself up on her elbows. "Who could it be, Cass?" Millicent didn't know how long she'd been asleep. Cassie had insisted she go to bed after she'd fixed her a liberally laced hot toddy, and Cassie had drawn the curtains so the room had remained darkened. It was hard to tell if it were still afternoon, evening, or the next morning.

"A Mr. Bond. I tried to send him away but he wouldn't budge."

Ringer! Millicent felt a sudden rush of warmth. "Tell him I'll see him in a moment. I have to freshen up."

Cassie's jaw dropped in amazement.

"He's perfectly respectable. I met him one day when you were out rounding up strays."

"You didn't mention it." Millicent could hear the gentle reproach in Cassie's voice.

"It must have slipped my mind, Cassie," Millicent fibbed. She hadn't wanted to share the pleasant encounter with anyone. She'd been afraid it wouldn't be repeated, and she'd wanted to treasure the surprisingly pleasant feelings his visit had evoked.

"If you're certain." Cassie's face was wreathed in concern, and Millicent didn't want to cause her any more worry.

"Ringer came by to meet you. He offered to help us out since he's our nearest neighbor." Millicent could see some of the worry falling from Cassie's brow.

"Ringer?" Cassie said curiously, then smiled and shook her head. "Oh, well, I trust your good judgment . . . I'll offer him coffee while you're getting ready if he can settle in one place long enough. The man's about worn a hole in the rug already."

Millicent rapidly discarded her rumpled dress and pulled a fresh Wedgwood-blue day dress from the oversized pine wardrobe. She fastened the long row of cloth-colored buttons up the bodice of her dress and crossed to the full-length mirror. One glance at her puffy eyes was enough. Wishing she had a bottle of witch hazel, Millicent instead poured a generous amount of water from the pitcher into the bowl and dipped a linen cloth in the liquid. She laid the cool cloth against her swollen eyes and bathed her cheeks and forehead.

Another critical examination in the cheval glass assured her that her red hair was still wound into a respectable coil. She knew she didn't look her best, but only time would improve her puffy eyes.

Taking a deep breath, Millicent grasped the door handle and pulled the door open. She hesitated as she entered the front room, studying Ringer's back as he paced toward the window. He held his hat in his hand, turning it around continually. Just as abruptly, he turned toward her. Without a word he covered the room in a few immense strides.

"Are you really all right, Millicent?" The agitation in his voice was clear.

"Yes, Ringer. I was upset, but I'm all right." She cocked her head in puzzlement. "How did you know what happened?" It seemed unlikely that Cassie would have revealed to a perfect stranger what her friend had discovered.

"You didn't come back, and after a few hours I rode to the Basque's pasture and I saw . . . Hell, I didn't know what to think!"

Millicent felt her heart catch in her throat at his concern. "Manuelo took me home over the eastern crest. I'm sorry if you were worried."

"Worried doesn't begin . . ." Ringer reached out and grasped her shoulders. "I'm just glad you weren't hurt." As though realizing he was overstepping the bounds of propriety, Ringer dropped his hands to his sides. "What are you going to do now?"

"Do? Well, I guess we'll group our flock with Manuelo's and—"

"You don't mean you're going through with this tomfoolery?"

Millicent's head jerked upright. "Tomfoolery?" She kept her voice deceptively quiet.

"Whoever butchered your sheep was playing for keeps. What makes you think it won't be you or one of your friends instead of a sheep next time?"

His concern was touching, but she'd thought he was different. She'd thought he understood. "Do you expect us to just pack up and leave? That's what this despicable person is hoping for."

"It isn't safe for you here. Not while you're tied in with the Daltons. You just don't realize—" He broke off abruptly, pain filling his face as it had when he'd told her he no longer had a family.

"We aren't running." Millicent heard the determination in her voice and realized she felt as strongly as Cassie did about their new start in the West. It might not be her legacy, but it was a chance for a life she couldn't have even dreamed of in Boston.

Ringer sighed deeply, then lifted his head and locked her autumn-green eyes with his own deep blue ones. "Then you're being as foolish as your friend."

"I appreciate your concern, Ringer." Millicent's voice was soft in the growing shadows of twilight that shrouded the house. She wondered absently where Cassie had gone.

Ringer's eyes seemed to narrow in determination. "You may be seeing more of me than you counted on, ma'am."

"Oh?" Millicent questioned almost breathlessly.

"Yes'm. If I can't talk you into leaving for your own safety, then I'm going to be around here a lot more often."

Millicent nodded her acceptance. "I'll agree to that, Ringer. But make no mistake: we're neither faint-hearted nor feather-brained. We'll not be scared off by cowards that sneak in, destroy, and then flee."

Ringer's grim eyes flickered with untold pain as they met and held hers. "That's what I'm afraid of, ma'am."

12

"It's been almost two weeks, Sis! You can't keep me hidden behind your skirts forever doing lessons!" Andrew's changing voice cracked on the last word, rising in high-pitched anxiety.

Cassie placed a worried hand on his still smooth cheek. "I know, Button." She hadn't called him that in years. Not since he'd told her it embarrassed him in front of his friends. She understood his frustration; he was no longer a child, but not yet a man. It tore at her when he tried to grow up faster than she could accept.

And now she felt equally torn. She'd taken a stand that they would remain, yet she was too fearful to let Andrew return to the flock.

Shane repeated his offer daily to buy her out, and his bullying tactics chipped away at her. His attempts grew more insistent, more relentless.

"Oh, Cassie!" Andrew's adolescent voice broke with a cry between disgust and frustration.

"What if there's trouble?" she questioned, wishing she hadn't placed him in such a dangerous situation, wishing she'd realized all the pitfalls before impulsively bringing them all here.

"Do you want to lose the ranch?"

"Of course not. I just want to make sure you're safe."

"I'll be careful, Sis. If we group together and keep all of the dogs with the flock, we'll be safe."

"If I say yes . . ."

"I knew you'd come to your senses."

"I did say 'if,' " she reminded him. "I want you to have a plan of watch."

"Anything you say. Between Matt, Jim, and me, we'll be covered."

Cassie tried to keep a frown from forming on her face. She still didn't trust Jim Fowler. His constantly shifting eyes and stealthy ways bothered her. But she hadn't been able to get anyone else besides Matt, Cookie's swamper, to work for her. And it galled Cassie that Shane had wanted her to get rid of Fowler. What made the situation even more intolerable was that Shane had planted those seeds of distrust about Fowler.

"Andrew's right, you know." Cassie swung around at the sound of Millicent's voice, and they both watched Andrew tear off to the barn.

"I suppose so. It doesn't make letting him go any easier, though." Cassie leaned against the corral railing as she spoke.

"So, what's on the agenda for today?"

"Flushing."

"I beg your pardon?"

"Flushing. It's to get ready for breeding."

Millicent backed away. "Don't count on me."

"We're stretched pretty thin right now, Milly. I could really use your help."

"I don't know . . ."

"We don't have to do very much. Right now, we just have to put one ram in with the ewes. Oh, and check to make sure their feed's up."

"Why?"

"Geez, Milly. You know."

"You mean so they can . . ."

"Uh-huh."

"Oh."

"Besides, haven't you noticed the rams lately?"

"Running the house keeps me pretty busy, Cass. What do you mean?"

"Come on."

They walked beyond the barn, over to the far side of the yard to a pen that held breeding rams. The pen was, unfortunately, next to the one holding the ewes in heat. The groups were intensely aware of one another. The bleats of the ewes filled the air, like a symphony gone wrong. The anxious rams kept butting horns. Some attempted to slip between the rails to get into the ewes' pen. One who'd tried that stunt was now stuck neatly between the rails.

Millicent rolled her eyes at Cassie. "Well, it's easy to see which of the sexes has the brains."

"One of the easier problems to fix," Cassie replied nonchalantly. She walked up to the ram, grabbed his back leg, and pulled. He popped out as though she'd greased him with lard.

Millicent clapped her hands appreciatively. "Got any more tricks up your sleeve?" she asked, pointing toward the pen. Cassie's glance followed in the direction Millicent indicated.

One randy male was sniffing at one of the ewes, much like a wine lover inhaling a fragrant cork. The other two were in a fight that was threatening to become dangerous. If they were injured seriously, they would be useless for the coming season.

The one ram stopped sniffing and began to "talk" to the ewe, making throaty sounds of enticement. Cassie and Millicent watched in amusement as the poor beast gargled at the ewe, his tongue hanging out in desperation.

Startled, their glances were drawn toward the other pen as one of the ewes started calling out with exceptionally loud bleats. A moment later, the same ewe started running wildly about as though in intense pain. Her loud, pitiful baas filled the air.

"I think I know just how she feels," Millicent muttered.

Cassie stared at Millicent in surprise and then clapped one hand over her mouth to stop the laugh threatening to erupt.

"Well, I do," Millicent reiterated belligerently.

At that moment, the barn cat wandered into the ewes' pen. The agitated ewe followed the cat, bleating frantically when the cat jumped up on the railing.

"The book did say a desperate ewe will follow most anything or anybody," Cassie whispered in a horrified tone.

"And you want us to go into that pen?"

"We could try to bring the ram into the ewes' pen." Cassie glanced over at the amorous ram. "I have a feeling he'll be glad to go."

"I'd say his dance card was full," Millicent answered, her eyes widening in fascination as the "talk" between the ewe and the ram escalated.

"It does beat all, doesn't it?" Cassie commented, equally uneasy about cutting the ram from his pen.

The desperate-sounding ewe cried more piteously. "Maybe people would be better off if they could be as honest," Millicent replied.

"Let's get her fella in the chute. I'll herd him. You pull the gate shut behind him."

Working together, they herded the eager ram into the waiting chute. Cassie peered down first at him and then at Millicent. "Here goes." Releasing the chute latch, the ram burst into the pen of ewes.

As soon as the male entered the ewes' pen, all of the females crowded around him, scarcely allowing him to move. Each time he changed direction, the females followed him in a pack, refusing to let him move more than a foot at a time.

"Looks like a church social," Millicent commented.

"The ratio of men to women is about right," Cassie agreed, still staring.

When the ram finally broke through the group of ewes, he ran from female to female. He tried to mount one. Failing, he ran to the next. And the next. And the next.

Cassie and Millicent gave in to the hilarity of the situation. Finally, wiping her eyes, Cassie turned to Millicent. "And back home we thought old Mr. Gandy was bad. Remember how he chased anything in skirts? And he must have been about ninety years old!"

Millicent gasped out, "Randy Gandy."

They were both lost to laughter again. The ram finally settled on one ewe, but neither woman noticed. Laughing until they were weak, each looked to the other for a measure of propriety. Finding none, they escaped instead into trills of laughter. Somehow, it seemed a fitting release for all.

13

Cassie tossed the wicking to Millicent, eyes widening as she watched a wagon come into clear view. Since the slaughter of their lambs, they'd been suspicious of anything out of the ordinary. And visitors were glaringly out of the ordinary. When the wagon neared the barnyard, the squawking and smell of chickens filled the air.

Millicent and Cassie cautiously stepped closer as the rattletrap conveyance shuddered to a stop, raining a scraggly cloud of feathers and dust in its wake. They looked up simultaneously as the broad-featured, heavyset woman driver yelled "Whoa!" in a voice loud enough to be heard in the south pasture.

She jumped down from the rickety seat, landing on her heavy leather men's boots while her drab brown skirt billowed with a will of its own. The bonnet, looped around her neck and pushed back on her shoulders, jiggled as well. Cassie and Millicent regarded the woman wordlessly.

"You must be the Dalton gal," the woman announced.

Cassie nodded in acknowledgment as the woman turned and marched toward the rear of the wagon, not giving Cassie time to answer. The woman's masculine stride didn't break until she reached the rear board, which she unfastened with ease. Leaning her burly arms forward, the woman grasped one of the makeshift cages filled with protesting chickens and pulled it forward.

"Want to give me a hand?" It was more of an order than a request.

"Why, yes. Of course." Cassie and Millicent hurried toward the wagon, exchanging questioning glances. The crusty woman continued unloading the chickens, handing each close-to-bursting cage to either Cassie or Millicent without benefit of explanation. When the wagon was empty, and the barnyard littered with chicken wire and flying feathers, the woman stood back, hands on hips, and surveyed Cassie and Millicent.

"You don't look crazy," she finally allowed.

Cassie and Millicent swung their heads toward one another simultaneously as their eyebrows rose in surprise and bewilderment.

"Hold on," the woman continued, not allowing them to answer as she lifted one of her beefy hands from her ample hips. "I'm Maude O'Leary. I live a few miles over thataway." She pointed a bulky arm to the south. "These here are your chickens, and I don't give a hoot if you are crazy."

"Well, thank you, I guess," Cassie managed, trying to decide what to make of their visitor.

Maude's eyes flicked over Millicent and then traveled down Cassie's trouser-clad legs. "Meant to get over here sooner with them chickens, but the young'uns has been laid up with croup. 'Course, I never really 'spected another Dalton back in these parts—that's how come I took the chickens. I ain't no thief, but I couldn't see lettin' them good layers go to waste."

"Won't . . ." Cassie tried to gather her voice and manners, both of which seemed to have disappeared. "Won't you come in and have some refreshment?"

"Never was one to turn down an invite," Maude answered. She stomped up the porch steps behind Cassie and Millicent.

"Won't you have a seat, Mrs. O'Leary?" Millicent offered, gesturing to the chairs flanking the settee.

"Maude, just plain Maude. Never get to sit in my own chairs. Young'uns," she explained succinctly, her eyes roaming around the pleasant room.

"I see. Please make yourself comfortable," Millicent replied, moving toward the cookstove.

"How many children do you have?" Cassie asked, gathering cups as Millicent sliced the fresh strudel she'd baked early that morning.

"Nine."

Cassie gasped before she could catch herself, then started to apologize. Maude interrupted before she could speak, waving a hand in dismissal. "Sight more than I counted on myself. Just can't resist havin' a new baby in the house."

"Babies are wonderful," Millicent agreed, bringing in the strudel.

"Don't that look tasty." Maude almost licked her lips when she eyed the dessert. Cassie and Millicent exchanged amused glances as they settled into the settee opposite Maude.

Three slices of strudel later, Maude leaned back in her chair with a look of contentment. "Didn't mean to make a pig of myself," she stated, not looking especially remorseful.

"I'm glad you enjoyed it," Millicent answered, glancing at the demolished strudel.

"Young'uns eat up all the sweets at home. Does a body good to go visiting. I don't 'spect you get too many visitors," she remarked sagely.

Cassie caught her eye and answered truthfully. "Not too many."

"Yer not missin' much. There's some good folks. But there's plenty of no good, too. Carry grudges too far apiece. Me, I don't got no ax to grind. Can't say the same for most everybody else."

Cassie and Millicent remained silent, uncertain how to answer her plainspoken observation.

"Thanks for the strudel and the loan of the chickens. I 'spect I'll see you again Saturday night." At their blank expressions she continued. "Barn dance in town Saturday night. Be good for you to get out. Your boy can meet the other young'uns." She rose heavily to her feet. "Have to head home. It's pert time to get the feedbag on for my clan." She stared down her broad nose at them. "I'll expect to see you both at the dance. If not, I'll have to come round you up."

Cassie and Millicent walked Maude to her wagon, both protesting—Millicent because of her natural shyness, and Cassie because she wasn't ready to face the townspeople again.

"Won't do no good to make no excuses. I'll see ya Saturday." Maude heaved herself up and shouted a command to the horses. Cassie and Millicent glanced at one another helplessly and stepped back, nearly deafened by Maude's shouting as she guided the lurching wagon out of the barnyard.

Cassie and Millicent waved good-bye, finally dropping their arms limply to their sides.

"Whew! I feel like a storm just blew in, stirred us around, and blew back out," Millicent said, still staring at the disappearing wagon.

Cassie murmured her agreement, puzzling over Maude's odd choice of words. What grudge was she having to pay for?

Cassie, Millicent, and Andrew hesitantly entered the decorated barn, pausing to watch the dancers whirling by. Andrew spotted some boys his own age and disappeared, while the women stood uneasily near the entrance. Cassie tugged nervously at her taffeta dress, hoping she'd chosen the right clothing. Everything out West was so different from Boston.

Relieved, she noticed the other women were wearing their Sunday best too. Millicent's brown dress was properly starched, but tonight she'd added a cascade of wildflowers to the lapel. Repressing a grin, Cassie wondered if the flowers were for Ringer's benefit. The beginning of her smile faded, though, as she faced the crowd. Cassie had reluctantly told Millicent what to expect tonight. Millicent had been horrified when Cassie told her she'd been refused supplies, though neither of them believed Luke Dalton had caused as much damage as Fowler claimed.

Cassie had sounded confident when telling Millicent she was sure they'd find a solution. But she wasn't sure at all. While she was convinced the townspeople were overreacting to her uncle's actions, Cassie also knew she had no other source for supplies.

By its own volition, Cassie's toe started to tap to the music. A tentative smile formed on her face as she searched the crowd. Abruptly the music stopped, the fiddle screeching to a squeaky halt. Simultaneously the heads of the dancers swung in their direction. Each closed face, each hostile glare, split the eerie silence. Cassie swallowed and almost stepped back. Pride alone kept her in place. The hostility was a palpable force, rippling through the people, filling the air. The silence seemed to shimmer in the enclosed space.

"What the hell happened to the music?" Maude's booming voice seemed to ricochet off the rafters and bellow through the crowd. Followed by her noisy brood of children and a small skinny man Cassie assumed was her husband, Maude stomped into the room.

"Best get to playin' before my young'uns start hollerin'," she ordered the fiddler.

Hesitantly he picked up the instrument and laid the bow against the strings. A weak tune emerged as better than half the crowd swept their spouses and children to the far side of the room, glaring at Cassie as they passed.

Maude watched their rude behavior, her good cheer never wavering. "Good riddance. More room over here for us," she announced without concern. She moved onto the dance floor, her family straggling noisily in her wake.

Cassie stared at the people, unable to believe that an old grudge could still bear so much hostility. She heard Ringer's voice behind them.

"Evenin', ladies." His voice was directed to them both, but his eyes were on Millicent.

"Mr. Bond," Cassie answered, watching in surprise as Millicent blushed prettily when Ringer moved to her side. Cassie realized with a start that she'd never known how lovely Milly could look when they'd lived in the harsh tenements of Boston.

Ringer claimed Millicent for that dance, leaving Cassie on the sidelines where she continued to collect hostile stares.

Trying to blend into the background, Cassie walked over to the punch bowl, but as soon as she neared the table, the ladle was deliberately dropped into the middle of the bowl with a loud clang. The people standing nearby turned their backs. With a sigh, Cassie took a glass of punch and walked over to a bale of hay, hoping to appear inconspicuous. Maude whirled by, offering encouragement. Once she enthusiastically clapped Cassie on the back, nearly knocking the glass out of her hand.

Cassie found herself shrinking further into the background, hoping to avoid the open hostility. After the first set, Ringer had delivered a breathless Millicent and brought them both glasses of punch. Millicent wanted to stay and keep her company, but Cassie had insisted she enjoy the dance with Ringer. Occasionally Cassie spotted Maude squiring her pint-sized husband around the floor and waved when Maude aimed them in her direction.

Unable to cling to the timber wall any longer, Cassie decided to brave the punch table once again. It was deserted as she reached for the ladle.

"Allow me," Karl Fredericks's smoothly modulated voice spoke next to her ear. She drew back, feeling the warmth of his breath close to her neck. Swallowing an unreasonable feeling of distaste, Cassie backed away slightly as she held out her punch glass. His cool fingers brushed hers as he took the glass, and Cassie noted with an almost detached interest that his touch had no effect upon her.

Not sure what to say to him, Cassie stalled by sipping her punch and studying him over the rim of her glass. Fredericks took control of the conversation.

"I hope Mr. Fowler is working out to your satisfaction, my dear."

Cassie paused, not wanting to sound ungracious. Fowler really hadn't given her any reason to complain. "He is, thank you."

"Excellent. I understand things are still difficult for you." At her puzzlement he continued, "Financially, that is."

"What?" Cassie blinked in astonishment.

He went on smoothly, "This is a very isolated community, Miss Dalton. News travels incredibly fast. A word here, a word there." He shrugged his shoulders.

Cassie remembered Sarah saying the same thing.

"If you'll allow me to suggest something that could help your solvency problem . . ." He paused, and she nodded silently, listening. "You have a large parcel of land—much larger than you need to graze your flock. I know your uncle never fully utilized the entire amount. If you'd consider selling a portion of it, you could still remain in business yet have the cash you'll need for winter feed. I don't really need the entire piece—just enough for extra grazing area."

She mulled over his proposition. It sounded logical on the surface. But why did he want to help her? Cassie studied him, but his cool gray eyes hid any revealing emotion. Whatever she decided, it wouldn't be tonight.

Putting on her best party smile, Cassie replied, "I appreciate your offer, but I'll have to think it over. We're not quite in the poorhouse yet."

Fredericks bowed over her hand, but not before Cassie caught the disappointment crossing his face.

"Of course, you may call on me anytime, my dear." As he straightened up, Cassie saw that his face had changed. She read an unmistakable invitation in his eyes and speculated on why it left her so unmoved. He offered her a courtly bow. "Perhaps you'll save me a dance?"

She nodded and he moved away. Gazing around the lantern-lit dance area, Cassie sensed a stirring among the females. Mothers leaned over to pinch their daughters' cheeks, and lips were pressed together and bitten to redden in the lamplight. Countless hands ran over newly coiffed hairstyles while a sudden nervous energy permeated the air. Cassie followed all those female glances toward the entrance to the barn.

Shane, followed by Michael, stepped through the oversized double doors and into the soft lantern light. Cassie could see why the unattached females were striving to look their best. Shane had replaced his denims with a well-fitting woolen suit, neatly arranged string tie, and a stiffly starched white shirt that set off his bronze skin and rugged features. He held an uncreased felt Stetson in his hand as he appraised the gathering. Michael, a younger blond version of his brother, garnered his share of feminine attention too.

Cassie watched Shane's eyes skip over the crowd as hopeful mothers eagerly pushed their daughters forward. She noted with amusement that almost all the unattached females managed to direct their glances his way, their invitations easily read. And easily ignored, she saw, as he bypassed pasty-faced, overeager young women. She felt more than saw his eyes move in her direction.

Cassie felt suddenly conspicuous as he avoided the rush of girls straining toward him. Absently he returned their greetings, adroitly sidestepping their invitations while heading straight for her. Her throat tightened when he neared, and she felt a visible wave of wrath from those he'd passed by.

"Miss Cassie," he greeted her, the expression in his eyes unbelievably sensual.

"Mr. Lancer," she replied, equally polite, intensely aware of the score of eyes trained in their direction—and intensely aware of his eyes perusing more than the smile on her face.

"Right nice evenin', isn't it, ma'am?" he parried, his gaze focusing on the lips she nervously moistened.

"Yes, Mr. Lancer, it is," Cassie answered, uncomfortably aware of the townspeople's scrutiny, uncomfortably aware of the heat his presence evoked. His gaze raked the form-fitting bodice of her taffeta dress, his appreciation evident in the smile slowly touching his lips.

"May I have the next dance, ma'am?"

"Sounds like more fun than shearing sheep," she replied tartly, wishing his nearness wouldn't make her feel as though she were about to melt into a puddle.

"Try not to sound *too* excited," he murmured.

They swept onto the dance floor. Cassie wasn't surprised at the natural grace Shane displayed as he led them around the makeshift dance floor. She tried unsuccessfully to squelch the jolt of feeling that ignited when he grasped her hand and they weaved to the music. How could his simple touch alone cause such a flood of emotion?

She lowered her eyes, hoping to control the sudden throbbing in her veins she felt must be visible, trying to remember she must not lose control with this man. Cassie wondered when he'd decided to try this tack of persuasion. Since threats, the friendly-neighbor act, and killing her sheep hadn't worked, he must have decided to overwhelm a poor spinster with his flirting. She ignored the niggling jabs of a guilty conscience that reminded her Shane was not the sort of man to do any of those things.

"You're almost as fetching in a dress as in trousers," he commented, whirling her about the dance floor, pulling her so close the tips of her breasts grazed his chest. Her eyes widened in reproach as well as pleasure when he leaned closer to reassure her. "Everyone will just think I'm whispering sweet nothings in your ear."

"That's what I'm afraid of," she whispered back, deciding to play his game, trying to find the detachment that seemed to come so naturally to him. Whirling with him to avoid another couple, she continued, "If looks could kill, I'd have a quiver of arrows in my back right now."

"Oh?" he said, rounding the corner of the dance floor and expertly avoiding the better lit areas of the room.

"Such well-acted surprise. You know as well as I do that every unattached female in the room, not to mention their mothers, would like to run me out of town on a rail."

"Then I guess we'll have to keep you off the tracks," he replied evenly as they whirled to the music.

She looked at him in disbelief because he'd be the first in line to get rid of her in order to control the Dalton land. "I haven't even met these people yet and I've already given reason for half the population—the female half—to dislike me," she chided him.

"In that case, we'll have to introduce you before they misjudge you," Shane replied as the tune ended. He grasped her hand before she could reply and led her off the dance floor to the nearest group of indignant women.

"Ladies, let me introduce my neighbor, Miss Cassandra Dalton," he began as the women visibly puffed up. "Mrs. Jenkins, you get prettier every time I see you." The scrawny, washed-out woman blushed unbecomingly as he turned to her companion. "And Mrs. Underwood, that Laura Mae of yours is going to steal the young men's hearts tonight."

Practicing his easy charm on all the women, Shane wheedled smiles out of even the grumpiest ones. Cassie watched, silently amused despite herself, as he cajoled the women out of their immediate anger.

Shane finally turned to Cassie. "I don't know about you, but I'm right parched. Would you care for a glass of punch, ma'am?" Cassie agreed to the refreshment, and he turned to the still somewhat peeved group of women. "Ladies?" They declined his offer, and Shane led Cassie to the punch bowl on a table in the corner of the barn.

"I suppose you know they'd still like to snatch me bald-headed," Cassie said pleasantly, smiling over her punch glass at the women who were watching them intently. She still wondered what Shane's game really was.

"Their daughters have been after me for years," he replied, "and I wouldn't be caught within ten miles of any of them," he finished, nodding and smiling at Mrs. Jenkins.

"They seem like such nice girls," Cassie protested, thinking of all the younger women she'd seen that night. Women much younger than she. "Much nicer than you," she finished with a wicked smile, as Mrs. Underwood seemed to visibly strain closer.

"Spare me," Shane answered as he refilled her punch glass and surveyed the room.

"Perhaps it's the girls who've been spared," she retorted, spying one of the matrons advancing toward them.

"Perhaps," he agreed too readily, grasping her punch glass in one hand and depositing it on the table. He used his other hand to pull her onto the dance floor, without asking permission. So he'd seen the dowager too.

"And am I supposed to spare you from all of your admirers and their mothers?" Cassie taunted carelessly, tilting her heart-shaped face upward, wondering how she could stick him with the plainest of the lot.

He laughed as though remembering a private joke. "If only you knew."

"You could try convincing me," she offered, following his tack, her midnight-blue taffeta dress rustling as they circled the floor.

"I suppose I could. Just remember—you asked. First, there's the lovely Laura Mae. That's her over there by her mother, the one who distinctly resembles a scarecrow." Cassie and Shane smiled in Laura's direction as they glided by.

"If you overlook her buckteeth and perpetual desperation, you discover the true vixen she tries so hard to conceal," Shane continued.

Cassie stifled an unexpected giggle and tried to appear appropriately serious. She did her best to give him a glare of disapproving reproach but instead found herself swallowing her amusement. "Go on."

"And then there's Herminnie." Cassie's eyes widened in disbelief. "Yes, that's really her name. I don't want to be unkind, but I've met more sincere girls in the saloon. She can't see past my money, a ring on her finger, and one through my nose."

"You flatter yourself," Cassie countered, trying to remember who she was dancing with and why she shouldn't let down her guard, even for a moment. "When I'm no longer the new attraction in town, you'll squire another woman around the dance floor while amusing her with tales of the crazy lady sheepherder who wears trousers and shears sheep for fun."

The glib answer she'd expected didn't emerge. Cassie's mouth opened slightly, and her eyes widened, meeting his chameleon-green eyes that deepened in color as they held her captive in their depths. This game of his was becoming increasingly dangerous. Cassie felt a fear that reached into her soul. She was afraid he was a master at this artifice. As a novice, she might lose not only her land but her heart as well to a man who cared not a whit for her.

"Circle 'round!" the caller shouted. "Alamand left, swing your lady. All join hands, circle to the right."

Cassie stumbled into position as Shane released his hold. She tried to pour her concentration into the dance. But she found herself dwelling on Shane instead of the caller, stepping on more than one partner's booted toes. When the round ended, Cassie felt an overwhelming sense of relief as she escaped the dance floor after a perfunctory thank you to a surprised Shane. Spotting Millicent standing under a rafter, Cassie approached her, dropping lightly onto one of the bales of hay that served as chairs.

"Oh, Cass. Isn't it a lovely dance?"

Cassie smiled softly at her friend. Millicent hadn't acted so young and happy in years. "Yes, it is, Milly. Your Mr. Bond seems quite taken with you."

Millicent blushed, bringing a rosy glow to her already happy face. "I wouldn't say that," she protested. "I'm simply new in town, and he's being neighborly."

Too bad the same thing couldn't be said for Shane. But Cassie knew his attention wasn't prompted by true interest. Her value lay in the land that bordered his. Why was that suddenly the most distasteful thought in the world?

Lost in her musings, she was startled by the voice she heard over her shoulder.

"Didn't mean to sneak up on you," Michael apologized as she rose to her feet.

"I was woolgathering, to use an unpopular pun," she explained with a laugh. "It's nice to see you again, Michael."

"You, too, ma'am." Cassie easily recognized his interest in her and wondered how to direct his enthusiasm to one of the younger ladies at the dance. His attention was flattering, but, she realized with a start, her feelings were already tied in knots by Shane.

"May I have this dance, ma'am?"

She started to refuse, but didn't want to crush his eagerness. Perhaps one dance wouldn't encourage him too much. She held out her hand to him as the music changed. She almost groaned aloud when she realized it was a romantic waltz.

Forcing a smile on her face, Cassie swirled about the room to Michael's graceful lead.

When they advanced across the floor, Cassie spotted Shane's thunderous face glaring at them. Apparently he didn't want her to taint his precious baby brother. Still, his anger seemed out of proportion to the circumstances. She might not be a master at his game, but she could learn as she played. Still smiling, she turned her attention to Michael.

As the music faded, Michael held out his hand, hoping for a second dance. Unable to resist the temptation, Cassie accepted and deliberately kept her complete attention on Michael while she floated across the room.

Afraid she would give Michael the wrong idea, she refused a third dance, insisting she needed a breather. Cassie's eyes swept the room, wondering where Shane was and who he was entertaining. She'd noticed a bevy of girls at least ten years her junior, at the height of their appeal. Girls that were very marriageable. Girls that a handsome, wealthy man like Shane could have in a moment. Girls that a man like him would certainly choose over a twenty-eight-year-old spinster. He'd all but said he'd move heaven and earth to get rid of her.

Unable to spot him, she felt an unexpected twinge of disappointment and mentally kicked herself for the unwelcome feeling. She headed toward the punch bowl when his deep voice startled her.

"Allow me." Shane's voice washed over her as she spun around. She glanced at the two punch glasses in his hand and wordlessly accepted one, hoping the cool liquid would ease the sudden burning in her cheeks. She searched for the hard, relentless glare in his eyes that she'd come to expect. Instead his eyes were cool, unrevealing.

Finally, she raised her amethyst eyes and managed to smile at him, holding up her punch glass. "Just what I needed. Thank you."

"My pleasure. Perhaps we could step out for a bit of air. I have a surprise for you."

Cassie glanced around at the collection of dowagers and their charges and decided they wouldn't approve of her, regardless of her actions, and threw caution to the wind. "Thank you. That would be nice."

They slipped into the inky darkness, and Cassie breathed deeply of the cleansing air that greeted them. The cool night breeze stirred the long tresses she'd left loosened down her back. Cassie shivered deliciously as the same wind whispered against her skin. Tilting her head backward, she studied the profusion of stars that danced across the moonlit sky.

To forestall the emotions she knew he could cause, Cassie mused dreamily, "When I was small, my father would sit with me on the balcony of our house and tell me the name of each star. See that one?" She pointed to the north as Shane's eyes moved with hers. "That one was my special star. He told me that as long as that star shone, I would shine too. When I was sad, he'd tell me to cheer up. 'Look at how bright your star is,' he would say. 'Can you be any less?' " Gazing into Shane's eyes, she smiled in memory. "And I believed him. I thought that explained why there were so many stars in the sky, because there were so many people they belonged to."

"He sounds like a special man," Shane offered quietly.

"He was, Shane. He always believed in me. He'd expect no less from me. And see there—despite everything—my star's still shining bright." She was startled by the unexpected gentleness in his eyes before he shuttered the telltale emotion, reminded for a fleeting moment of the kindness that always shone in her father's eyes.

"I have a feeling that your star will always shine, Cassie girl."

Cassie heard his endearment with amusement, as if at her age she could ever be considered a girl.

She was unable to disguise her curiosity when Shane reached into his pocket and pulled out his "surprise." Cassie's eyes widened as he unfolded the light pink stockings in his hand. She gasped. They were the most beautiful stockings she'd ever seen. Since all she could afford were practical cotton hose, she'd never let herself dream of unmentionables so fine, so elegant, so irresistible. These must have been confected by elves. She'd never seen such delicate clocking embracing the sides: scrolled ivy and roses had been embroidered at the ankles and tapered up to the knee. Her breath caught as she reached out to touch them reverently. Silk! They were actually silk.

Just when she thought she'd surpassed her limit of incredulousness, Shane reached his other hand into his pocket. Her eyes were riveted on the satin garter centered in the palm of his tanned hand. As he held it up, the delicate rose-colored ribbons unfolded gently against the pearl beading and wine-colored tassels surrounding the edging.

Cassie swallowed against the conflicting emotions she was experiencing. Shane had overstepped all bounds of propriety. She shouldn't even be *looking* at the marvelous creations he offered, much less touching them as though she wanted to keep them. She opened her mouth to refuse his gift indignantly and then snapped her lips back together. Damn, she wanted them!

She lifted her gaze from the delicate pink of the stockings to rest on his face. When she saw his mouth twitch with ill-concealed amusement, she knew she ought to be angered by his blatant disregard for convention. Instead, his shared knowledge of her quandary made her want the blasted things that much more.

Even as she tried to form the words of refusal, she reached out again to touch the silk and satin—and was lost. Worse, he knew it.

Just as she started to sputter out a reply, he reached back into his pocket. Holding up the garter he'd taken that day in the meadow, he leaned closer, his eyes dancing devilishly. "Trust me, it's more than a fair trade."

"But I can't . . ."

"Yes, you can. Don't forget. I owe you a pair."

"But not ones like these." Cassie's eyes clung to the proffered luxuries. "And you know I shouldn't even be discussing unmentionables—"

Shane held a finger to her lips. "Then don't."

Cassie battled her conscience for another agonizing moment before she snatched them away from his grasp. Ignoring the significance of her action, Cassie stuffed the delightful concoctions in the pocket of her skirt before she could change her mind. If her mother could see her now. . . .

Shane felt a bittersweet moment of regret as he tried to read the messages hidden in the depths of Cassie's eyes. It was a foolhardy game he was playing. But the stakes were high, he reminded himself, high enough to warrant his actions. If he couldn't convince her to sell any other way, maybe she'd do it for love.

But even as he tried to justify the reasons, his hand gently touched the satin of her cheek, edging ever so sweetly to her lips. Just one touch, one taste before he drew away. Only to convince her, he told himself.

He ran his roughened thumb over her full lower lip, surprised at the trembling it caused. He wondered if the ragged breaths he heard being drawn were his own or hers. Cassie's shallow breathing had brought her trembling body even closer to his. The air seemed too heavy to breathe; the fluidity of his thoughts seemed to turn to slow-moving molasses. Each minuscule step closer seemed to bring him nearer to the whisper of her hair in the breeze, to the pliant flesh he remembered so well.

With agonizing slowness he lowered his lips to hers, and she felt the sudden heat rushing through her veins. One hand crept up to embrace his neck. His skin when she touched it was not rough as she expected; rather it was surprisingly silky. Surprisingly sensual. Her fingertips grazed the pulse point of his throat, feeling a ragged beat that matched hers.

Shane deepened his kiss, and Cassie moved her head back, allowing him access, accepting his seeking tongue with shudders of pleasure. She tasted the cleanliness of him and breathed in the lingering aroma of cheroots, fresh soap, and an unidentifiable maleness that assaulted her already quaking senses. She knew only that she wanted the sensations to continue on and on. . . . She felt his hands clasp her shoulders and pull her away, and first she felt only disappointment. Then reality returned, and her cheeks burned in humiliation. He'd had to wrest her away again.

"Cassie," he whispered urgently.

She lifted her head reluctantly, unable to bear the censure she supposed was in his eyes—as if accepting his gifts and forgetting he represented everything she was fighting wasn't bad enough.

"I think there's trouble."

Only then did she hear the scuffling and shouts. She looked into his face and saw the reluctant flush of desire still reflected in his eyes.

"I'd best go see what it is," he continued, his voice still husky with the seeds of unwanted passion.

He headed toward the noise. She followed him as he shouldered his way through the group of youngsters who formed a circle near the side of the barn. Searching through the faces, Cassie didn't see Andrew. Filled with unnamed dread, she pushed her way through the group and gasped in shock when she saw Andrew's bloodied face. Shane grasped Andrew and another boy by their collars and pulled them apart. Cassie rushed up to Andrew, horrified by his battered face.

"Andrew! Zack! What's going on, boys?" Shane demanded.

Andrew remained silent. Shane turned toward his opponent. "What's the story, fellas?"

"He started it!" the other boy accused, kicking to get away from Shane's ironclad grip.

Cassie stared at the youngster in disbelief. "Is that true, Andrew?"

Andrew glared at her through purpling eyes. "Only after he called me a dirty, worthless Dalton," he spat out. Cassie saw the trembling under his bravado and wanted to wipe the hurt away.

"Well, he is!" the other one shouted.

"Enough, young man," Shane admonished. "That'll do, Zack Robertson, unless you'd like your other end paddled off."

Cassie gasped before she could complete the question in her mind. Zack Robertson? Jacob Robertson's boy? The man who had scared and threatened her that afternoon in the shearing shed? Sickened, she stared at the two boys. Like father, like son?

Zack closed his mouth but sent Andrew a threatening look. Shane loosened his hold on both boys, and they stepped back sullenly. Cassie wanted to gather Andrew in her arms but knew it would only add to his humiliation.

"I suppose I could let you two slug it out until one of you is out cold," Shane drawled. "Someone'll probably end up with a broken nose, a split lip, or a missing tooth . . ." Cassie's head shot up in disbelief and horror. Surely he wouldn't take out his vendetta on a couple of young boys. Cassie opened her mouth, but Shane shot her a look over the boys' heads that warned her not to speak.

The boys glared at one another warily. Neither one looked very eager to carry out Shane's suggestion.

"You could always work out your problem and then you wouldn't have to kill each other."

Gazing first at one another, then down at the ground, Andrew and Zack remained silent. Both of them stubbed their booted feet into the dirt, kicking up dust swirls as they debated Shane's words.

"Of course, when your folks find out you can't get along and take you home before the games begin . . ."

The pair looked at each other and Shane in dismay.

"To my way of thinking, only fools win by using their fists. What do you say, boys? You want to fight or be friends?"

With heads ducked, they simultaneously mumbled, "Friends."

"Good choice. Now shake on it." The two hesitantly reached out to shake as Shane's large hand covered both smaller ones, pulling them together. "Now, hurry and get cleaned up or you'll miss the Indian wrestling and the apple bob."

Both heads shot up and peered back toward the tub of water resting beneath a canopy of trees to the north of the barn. They took off at a dead run and disappeared before Cassie could open her mouth.

Shane took her arm to lead her back to the dance. She twisted around, trying to get one final glimpse of the boys who were no longer in sight.

An unexpected smile twitched at the corners of Shane's mouth. "Boys will be boys."

Cassie met the unusual teasing gold flecks of his eyes, and sighed in mock resignation. "And then they grow into men who know how to handle these situations."

"And I thought from all those books you were a slow learner . . ."

14

"I must've been crazy to let you talk me into this," Millicent complained.

"Don't give up, Aunt Milly," Andrew urged.

"He's right, Mill. You can do it," Cassie encouraged, shaking her head in amusement.

Instead of lessons, Andrew had been reading books on sheep ranching, most recently on the training of herding dogs. He was convinced that a border collie could herd anything. The quacking of disgruntled ducks underfoot proved he truly meant *anything*.

Manuelo had sold them two young herding dogs that were scarcely more than large puppies. Playful and rambunctious, they weren't trained yet, but Andrew was convinced that the three of them could handle something that simple.

Trained dogs would provide immeasurable help, but none of the city-bred trio had ever owned, much less trained, a dog. They were going to now, however.

"Close the gate, Aunt Milly!" Andrew's voice was shrill. Millicent jumped to latch the offending gate, and Cassie had to turn away to hide a smile. Far from the prim picture she usually presented, Millicent was a disheveled mess.

Although initially reluctant to take on what she'd called a harebrained scheme, Milly had nonetheless thrown herself into the project. Cassie had a feeling that if Millicent put her mind to it, the dogs wouldn't have a chance of growing up without their diplomas in herding.

Cassie turned back toward their training pen, a smile still tugging at her lips. Her smile rapidly disappeared, however. All the blasted animals were charging toward her.

Shrieking, Cassie ran as the two half-grown dogs, chasing a flock of errant ducks, raced toward her. She almost escaped. Almost.

First the ducks tripped her—quacking furiously, wings flapping, feathers flying. Before she could get to her knees, both dogs romped over her prone body. Barking happily, they continued their mad dash after the noisy, disgruntled ducks. Cassie sat up slowly, spitting dust and feathers.

"He's right," Millicent mimicked. "You can do it."

"Oh, shut up." Cassie plucked more feathers from her hair and shirt.

Millicent reached out a hand to help Cassie up. "Come on. If we can cross the plains, we can outwit two puppies and a flock of dim-witted ducks."

With renewed fervor, the threesome shooed the ducks back into the confining pens. The border collies panted happily, their tongues lolling—even though Andrew glared at them in a stern, commanding manner. The pups obviously thought this was a fine game.

"The book said these dogs are born knowing how to herd," Andrew began.

"Sure they are," Cassie muttered, as one of the dogs attacked the cuff of her pants, chewing the material ecstatically.

Andrew shot her a withering gaze. "As I was saying, they'll herd anything—chickens, geese, small children, cats, *ducks* . . ."

"All right, Andrew. What now?" Cassie asked. She wanted this to work for more than just Andrew's sake. They needed the additional dogs.

Andrew gave directions. Cassie and Millicent carried them out. After a few more disastrous misstarts, the dogs actually began to get the idea.

"Hey, they really are herding the little beauties!" Millicent whooped, not seeming to care as the dust settled over her once starched dress.

Cassie hid another smile. She wished their former faculty members could see Millicent now. Their prune-faced headmistress would be in a full-blown swoon.

"See, Cass? I told you this would work!"

"You're right, Andrew. Guess I'll have to start listening to you more often."

He struck a pose, holding one hand against his heart. "Be still, my heart."

Cassie thumped him affectionately on the shoulder. They both climbed up on the corral railing, watching the incredible process. The dogs were now earnestly herding the ducks from the larger area into the small confining pens. When one tried to escape, the dogs nipped it smartly and sent it flapping back to the pen.

"Well, fellow ranchers, I think we can congratulate ourselves," Cassie commented, pleased at their success.

"You can say that again!" Millicent agreed, carelessly sliding onto a tree stump with a whoosh, her skirts flying.

Cassie and Andrew stared at one another and burst into laughter. What *had* gotten into Millicent?

She looked up unconcernedly from her unlikely perch.

"Go ahead and laugh." Millicent waved a hand pointedly at Cassie's rumpled appearance. "I'm not the one wearing a feather boa."

Cassie and Andrew just laughed harder. It didn't take long for Millicent to join in. While the dogs efficiently herded the agitated ducks into a neat row, the three tired city slickers collapsed on the ground. It was a small victory, to be sure, but it was a victory.

15

The Fourth of July had always conjured up memories of fireworks and ice cream, but today nostalgia had been replaced by nausea. Cassie's stomach warred with the hordes of butterflies crowding the small space. Turning her head, she saw Andrew greeting his new friend, Zack. Only moments later, Shane ruffled Andrew's hair, and they exchanged good-natured pokes. Angling her head in another direction, Cassie could see Millicent basking in Ringer's attention.

"They're not going to roast you on a spit," Sarah chided, taking Cassie's arm firmly and drawing her closer into the group. "I didn't ride all the way over to get you just to have you stand on the sidelines."

Cassie knew without question that had Sarah not come personally to drag her to the Lancer cookout, she would be safely at home. When Sarah and Shane had talked about the annual cookout weeks before, it had sounded like fun. But after she'd been shunned at the dance, Cassie knew she'd rather shovel out dirty pens than try to socialize with those same people.

"There's Karl Fredericks—our own royal Hapsburg," Sarah said in a mock whisper.

Cassie's head swiveled as though attached to a hook. "Is he actually related to the royal family?"

"No, and I think that's what's wrong with him. I'm not sure just why he left Austria, but I suspect it wasn't under good circumstances."

"You mean he's on the run?"

Sarah laughed. "I don't think it's anything quite that dramatic. But ever since the day he got to Keenonburg, he's bought every available acre of land he could. It's as though he's trying to rebuild something he lost back in Austria."

Cassie's mind clicked, registering this piece of information. Was that why he wanted the Dalton ranch?

"His own little kingdom?"

Sarah shrugged. "Something like that."

A rumble of male voices filled the air. Sarah shook her head. "Grown men—all ready to act like little boys again."

Cassie quickly saw what Sarah meant. The men were all lined up for arm wrestling. Cassie and Sarah strolled forward to join the other women who stood in the shade and watched, some with pride and some with disappointment, as their men won or lost each bout. Gasping, Cassie saw that Shane, who had easily won every round, was now pitted against Andrew. Her brother's face was screwed up in determination, and she could see his still developing muscles try to expand even further. Hand held to her chest, Cassie waited for the boy's inevitable defeat, knowing how crushed he'd be. The seconds ticked by like hours, then both arms started to waver. The slamming sound of one arm slapping down against the table was heard. Cassie blinked her eyes in disbelief. Andrew couldn't have won! But Shane, Michael, and Zack crowded around him offering congratulations. It was all Cassie could do to restrain herself from rushing forward to where the men were gathered. Instead she remained in the shadows, silently cheering for Andrew.

Rubbing his arm ruefully, Shane shook Andrew's hand. "Taught me not to mess with the young bucks."

"Aw, you coulda licked me if you'd tried harder."

"If I'd tried any harder, you'd have wrenched my arm clear out of the socket. Nope, I've learned my lesson."

Andrew beamed, strutted a bit, and then swaggered off with Zack.

Shane moved away from the crowd to Cassie's side as Sarah drifted over to the crowded tables. "If my recollection's about right, Andrew's just a tad stronger than me. I guess that means I can beat you up."

"We could slip away from here, and you could try."

Cassie smiled at the casual flirtation. "Thanks for being so nice to Andrew. He hasn't had many men in his life as an example. Our father died when he was so young."

"No thanks needed. He's a good boy."

She glanced over at the collection of neighbors and townsfolk, some sampling the food, others talking casually. Nibbling on her lower lip, she took a deep breath, wishing she didn't have to mingle with them.

"There's nothing to be nervous about, Cassie. They're just people."

"People who hate me enough to slaughter my sheep."

"My father never let anything interfere with this annual cookout. Not droughts, Indian raids, or cattle rustling. Those didn't matter. He insisted on this cookout, and we had a damn good time or else. Don't want to break tradition, do you?"

"I'd like to be home in bed with the covers over my head."

"Can't eat much that way. Let's go get some of that food." Taking her arm, Shane led Cassie from the shadows beneath the outstretched oak tree over to the large pits that had been dug to accommodate huge sides of beef that roasted slowly on hand-turned spits. The tangy aroma of burning mesquite chips and slow-cooked beef hit Cassie's nostrils at the same time as she heard the sizzle and hiss of juices dripping onto the coals.

"It does smell good," she admitted.

Picking up a wicked-looking carving knife, Shane hacked off two good-sized portions and loaded them onto the plates Cookie held out.

"Afternoon, Cookie," Cassie greeted the grizzled man.

"Miss Cassie." His eyes twinkled, and he seemed to straighten up a bit. "Glad you could make it. You sure pretty up a party."

Touched, she replied, "Thank you, Cookie. You're looking mighty slicked-up yourself."

He glanced down self-consciously at the immaculately starched shirt and new string tie. "Just same ol' duds," he muttered.

"Well, you look very nice. I'm sure the other ladies think so too."

Cookie straightened up a bit, running a hand over his wiry beard. "Nah."

"Be sure you save me a dance later," Cassie warned. "I don't want to find out I can't get even one dance because you've turned all the ladies' heads."

Cookie managed to laugh and duck his head at the same time. Shane guided Cassie away from the roasting pit to a table nestled beneath spreading limbs that provided some refreshing shade.

"You planning on charming all the men here?" he asked with a half smile, as though sharing a joke.

"Cookie deserves to be charmed. He's a very nice man."

"Yeah. You're not too awful yourself."

"Please, please. Such flattery may make me swoon. I'll scarcely be able to take a nibble of this"—she looked down at her plate, eyes widening—"pound or two of beef."

"Thought you might be hungry."

Considering the state her stomach was in, Cassie doubted she could do justice to a few bites. But she discovered the tender beef too delicious to refuse. Still, she could scarcely eat all he'd piled on her plate.

Ruefully she glanced at Shane's clean plate. "Looks like your eyes were bigger than my stomach."

"Then let's go meet some people."

Cassie's now full stomach plummeted as though she'd eaten lead rather than beef. "I'd rather not."

"Remember, it's against the rules to spoil the Lancer annual cookout."

Sighing, she rose to her feet. "I don't see Manuelo," Cassie commented, glancing around.

"He never comes—no one to watch his flock. 'Sides, he seems kind of fond of mutton."

Cassie pointedly ignored his comment, her stomach knotting as they approached the others. When Shane walked over to Sarah, Cassie was relieved. She'd briefly met Sarah's husband, Patrick, when their carriage had come to collect her, Andrew, and Millicent for the cookout, and she'd noted then that Patrick's attention remained focused on his wife, as it was now. Heads close together, they glanced up in unison when Shane spoke.

"You two lovebirds at it again?" Shane teased. "You've been married too long to still like each other."

"And you've been single too long to know what you're missing," Sarah retorted with easy camaraderie. "Right, Patrick?"

"You two leave me out of your squabbles." Patrick gazed directly at Cassie, still smiling. "They keep forgetting they're grown-ups now."

"That's why we have you to remind us," Sarah replied, her hand still entwined in her husband's.

Timmy, Sarah's eight-year-old, rushed up to his mother, his baby sister trailing yards behind him, her unsteady steps slowing her down. "Mother, Mother!" he shouted.

"I'm right here," Sarah replied calmly, trying to slick back Timmy's mussed hair. He evaded her hand, wriggling away to launch himself at his father's knee.

"Can I? Can I?"

"Can you what?" Patrick replied, also remaining calm while Timmy hopped from foot to foot.

"Be in the rodeo? Please?"

"Oh, I don't think so . . ." Sarah started to answer.

"Mother!" Timmy wailed.

Shane's deep voice rumbled, and Timmy quieted for a moment. "How 'bout the calf run, Sis? He can't get hurt. Some of the older boys'll be out there. Cassie's brother for one—he's a responsible boy."

"Yeah, Mother. Could I please? Please?" Timmy turned to his father. "Please?"

"If your father and Uncle Shane promise to watch out for you, I guess so," Sarah agreed reluctantly.

Patrick rose and scooped Timmy up, putting him on his shoulders. "Guess we'd better go pick out the calf you want to catch."

Little Megan finally reached her mother's skirts on chubby legs. Shane bent and twirled the toddler around, eliciting squeals of delight. "Guess this one's too little for most of the rodeo events," Shane mused.

"Unhand my baby," Sarah demanded with mock severity, shaking her head. "Come on, Megan, let's get away from your uncle and hope none of his lunacy is hereditary." The blond-haired little girl, who resembled a beautiful porcelain doll, smiled adoringly at Shane and her mother.

"Maybe next year," Shane continued, teasing his sister.

Sarah muttered something under her breath as she walked over to watch her husband and son in the calf corral.

Before Cassie could catch her breath, Shane led her from person to person. Maude, her husband, and their children were warm, effusive. Most of the others were civil while Shane stood at her side, but their expressions while staring at Cassie were cold. Only Jacob Robertson made a rude comment, but before many words could be exchanged, Robertson turned and stomped off. Karl Fredericks was unfailingly polite, although his dislike of Shane was only thinly veiled.

"Why did he come to your cookout if you dislike one another?" Cassie questioned.

Shane shrugged. "I'm not sure. But I haven't been sure of him since the day he first turned up in town."

"Why do you suppose he came way out here?"

"Maybe back home nobody took much notice of him. Probably thought he could be a pretty big man in a little town like ours."

Cassie turned toward the house, dismissing Karl. "You have a beautiful home." The pillared veranda was long and sweeping while the huge columns flowed upward as though capable of holding up the vast Texas sky. Huge old oaks shaded the house; outbuildings and well-tended corrals surrounded the barn.

"My family's proud of what they built," he admitted, gazing at the graceful structure.

They should be, Cassie thought. The structure rose up amidst thousands of acres of isolation with as much grace as the Parthenon. The wide double doors were flung open, and Cassie could see the curving banister and steps of a huge stairway. She itched to tour the house and peek into all the grand rooms, but unfortunately an outside cookout was outside.

Turning away slightly, Cassie spotted Millicent. "I believe I'll talk to Millicent for a moment."

Instead of walking away to join his friends, Shane fell into step beside her, watching Ringer and Millicent as they faced one another talking. "I guess Ringer's pretty sweet on her."

Cassie glanced at Shane in surprise. "Is there anything in this place that's not public knowledge?"

"Nope," he answered companionably.

Sighing, Cassie continued forward. At the same time, Millicent moved to sit down. Apparently wrapped up in Ringer's words, she failed to judge the distance to the tree stump. Cassie's hand flew to her mouth. Proper, dignified

Milly was about to land on her derriere in front of Ringer and all the townspeople. Cassie started to rush forward, but Shane beat her to it. Running forward, he sat on the tree stump, reached forward, and pulled Millicent onto his lap.

Blushing, she sputtered in surprise.

"Sorry, old man," Shane said to Ringer. "But with two such lovely ladies around . . ."

Millicent unseated herself from Shane's lap, realizing she'd been about to make a fool of herself. But before she could verbalize her realization, Shane spoke again. "I guess she really does prefer you to me. My loss. I guess I'm stuck with the ornery one."

Taking Cassie's arm, Shane led her away from a still crimson Millicent. But the embarrassment in Millicent's eyes had faded, replaced by gratitude.

"It seems you've a habit of rescuing all of us. Does that mean I'm next?" Cassie asked.

Shane scratched his chin in consternation. "Don't know about that. Might be kind of interesting to watch you land with your skirts flying."

16

The days after Shane's cookout seemed to pass in a whirlwind of activity. Cassie and Andrew had to retrain the flock to follow their most dependable dog, Pepe, instead of Cassie. Her blisters had been a week-long reminder of the ridiculous hike with the flock. In addition, Millicent found herself battling an onslaught of locusts in her garden, so she, Cassie, and Andrew all pitched in to build tentlike covers to protect the tender seedlings. At the same time, it seemed every sheep in the flock individually wandered off and got lost. Long days of riding and searching left Cassie exhausted.

When she was finally able to breathe a sigh of relief, she longed again for the peace of her meadow. Slipping away from the ranch, she rode to her sanctuary, relishing the serenity that eased over her like the mist from a gentle tropical rain.

Reckless with abandon, she pulled the boots from her aching feet and tugged at her cotton stockings. Barefoot, she sank into the cool grass. With her toes curled deliciously in the green carpet, Cassie gazed at the endless panorama. For the first time since she'd discovered her hideaway, she sensed a restlessness.

Glancing around the flowery expanse, Cassie wondered what seemed different. *She had no one to share her joy in the meadow*. It hit her with force. Before, she'd automatically shared what little she had with Andrew and Millicent.

But Andrew was growing away from her, and Millicent now had Ringer to share her special moments. A picture of Shane's crinkling smile surfaced in her thoughts. Her mouth curved upward—it was Shane she wanted to share her happiness with.

Her smile lingered as she remembered Shane's deft handling of the boys at the barn dance. And those incredible stockings and the garter he had presented to her! Softening, she realized her trust in him was growing. When she pictured his face in her mind, she thought of his kindness when he'd taken her to visit Sarah, saving her pride and aching feet. What a complex man he was.

Unexpectedly, her mind skipped back to her last exchange with Shane at his cookout. A slow smile enveloped her face when she thought of his last comment to her. She felt the beginning of a blush tinge her cheeks, wondering what might have happened if they'd had a moment alone together. But they hadn't. Suddenly she sat upright.

Gazing around, Cassie realized she had the perfect spot to bring Shane to, one that wouldn't be invaded by Millicent, Andrew, or any one of the dozens of people on the Lancer ranch. But could she control her emotions once she had the privacy that beckoned her? Caution fled. It was time she dared to find out.

"This is it," Cassie stated softly, reining her horse into the wildflower-filled meadow.

Shane didn't answer, instead dismounting and walking over to her horse to help her down.

Surprised, Cassie caught her breath as she slid against the hard contours of his body. Laughing shakily, she moved away quickly, hoping to put some distance between them.

Despite being drawn to Shane, Cassie had lectured herself against any sort of relationship with Shane other than friendship. She must have been crazy bringing him here. If she'd melted like a late-winter storm when they were surrounded by a barn full of people, why had she expected to be able to remain in control when they were alone?

Belatedly realizing her folly, Cassie bent her head to inhale the pungent aroma of pricklepoppy.

"Careful, they smell fine but they've got a powerful kick."

"Kick?"

Shane picked one of the podlike seeds. "There's enough narcotic in one of these to make you do most anything."

"Anything?" Her question was tinged with a devastating mixture of naïveté and flirtation.

"Almost," he responded briefly, as one of his hands reached up to remove her hat and allow her hair to tumble out in breathtaking disarray.

Cassie reached up to refasten the errant locks, but Shane's other hand grasped her arm before she could do so.

"Leave it." His voice was low, commanding. She stilled her arm, leaving it in Shane's grasp. Dropping her hat to the grass, Shane used both arms to pull her close. She thought for the briefest of moments of resisting. But somewhere in the back of her mind she was prompted by the realization that this was what she'd hoped would happen.

For a moment Shane simply savored her closeness and inhaled the sweet smell of violets wafting from her ebony hair. He knew what dangerous ground lay ahead. It was now devilishly hard to remember that his pursuit was only to gain Cassie's land. As he held her in his arms, Shane knew he'd veered off his vengeful course. It was time to turn back, to protect himself against the emotions she stirred within him.

But first, one last kiss. One last touch. Gently, he smoothed the hair that wisped about her face, savoring the softness of her skin. The kiss, which he intended to be light and meaningless, instead deepened. Her lips, soft and pliant, met his lovingly. Holding her close, heart to heart, he could feel the ragged beat that matched his. Expecting her to pull back,

Shane was amazed when instead she willingly and naturally returned his embrace.

Unprepared for her response, Shane couldn't pull away. He meant to, had fully intended to. Instead he lifted her into his arms and laid her gently amidst the profusion of wildflowers that carpeted the meadow.

She offered no resistance when Shane outlined the contours of her face with a gentle hand. The once ivory skin had darkened becomingly to a light honey from hours spent outdoors. The vivid color of her eyes and the redness of her lips beckoned as he kissed each enchanting feature.

He felt as much as heard her sigh with pleasure. Emboldened, Shane unfastened the buttons of her shirt, exposing the lace of her chemise. Cassie didn't stop him as he continued to seek out each pleasure spot. When his lips dared to light on her nipples, still covered by the chemise, Cassie's eyes flew open in shock.

Replacing his mouth on hers, Shane instead used a gentle hand to massage the breast in his hand. He imagined what their tips must look like. Were they soft and dusky or rosy pink and full?

Cassie moaned softly beneath him, and Shane knew he didn't want to guess anymore. He unfastened the remaining buttons on her shirt, slid it carefully off her shoulders and down her arms, and tossed it aside. The chemise held his attention now. His mouth suddenly dry, Shane grasped the lace ties holding the flimsy garment together. With a few tugs the chemise parted.

Shane almost gasped aloud. Here her skin was still ivory, crowned with dusky peaks. When the air reached her bared skin, the nipples stood up proudly. He couldn't resist their urging. Slowly, reverently, he kissed the throbbing flesh, his hands roaming down her sides and over the breeches that still separated their bodies. He felt Cassie pull away, her hands flailing to cover her exposed flesh. Capturing her shaking hands, he kissed each finger, lingering as he turned her palms upward, caressing the sensitive lines of each hand.

"You're beautiful, Cassie. More beautiful than I ever expected."

Cassie's body seemed to relax, and her hands, no longer trembling, now rested on the grass by her sides. Then, feeling her shudders of unexpected desire, Shane slid one hand over the mound still protected by barriers of cloth. Cassie's legs tightened abruptly, effectively blocking his advances.

"Do you want me to stop, Cassie?" Shane's hands had halted their exploration.

She shook her head, finally emitting one word: "No."

"Are you sure?"

She nodded, barely breathing.

Shane reached for her, and she moaned when his hands began to massage her through the breeches. Suddenly impatient, Shane itched to unfasten the line of buttons that stood between them. Ever so carefully he eased off her boots and cotton hose.

Then with great care he reached for the fastening of her breeches. Cassie's eyes flew open, and her expression was a mixture of fear and longing as she fought with herself to trust him.

"Cassie, we can stop now . . ." His hands stilled immediately, but she realized that his assurances dissolved her uncertainty, and she no longer wanted to protest. Reaching for him, Cassie kissed away his words. She thrilled to his touch as he threaded his fingers in the masses of hair that spilled into his hands.

Still, the fear of what she was allowing to happen surfaced momentarily. What would her mother have thought of her, lying wanton, nearly naked in a field of wildflowers? What had happened to years of rigid self-control and restraint? Shane quickly erased those thoughts as he skillfully stroked her bare skin.

His hands unfastened the final buttons to her breeches, and when he pulled her hips close to his, she was breathless with anticipation. Shane quickly shed his clothes and pulled her length next to his.

Struggling to remember that she was crossing a line that could not be reconstructed, she almost reached out to stop him. But with a will of their own, her hands instead fastened on the rippling muscles that corded his lean torso.

Dimly she felt his hands grasping the fastenings to her pantalets. Only the ivory linen garment remained, and suddenly she couldn't wait for it to be removed so that she could feel Shane's naked skin upon hers.

A sudden apprehension gripped her. What if he didn't find her attractive? Her doubts vanished when she read the desire in his eyes and felt the quickening of his breath as he surveyed her body. The past months of hard work had left her body hard and muscled instead of softly voluptuous. But Cassie knew, as she gazed into his eyes, that she pleased him.

When his mouth descended upon hers, she felt his desire and his pleasure. He probed her mouth gently, tasting greedily of all she offered. Gradually, he trailed kisses down her neck, tantalizing her with their softness and fire. As he once again reached her breast, she found her own breath quickening as he tasted hungrily first of one and then the other nipple.

The grass pushed against her back while his hands roamed over her body, as though memorizing each plane and curve. Cassie felt his hands stroke her inner thighs, and she trembled, lost in the sensations he created. When Shane reached the tousled curls at the joining of her legs, she felt another moment of panic and clamped her thighs together. Remembering horror stories of the incredible pain that should accompany the act, she tried to twist away. But his mouth claimed hers as he gently but insistently probed between the folds of that sweet flesh. Soon she unclenched her legs and gave in to the incredible sensations his hands offered her. She felt a sudden unfamiliar dampness and an instant overwhelming sense of embarrassment.

As though sensing her exact feeling, he reassured her, "This is how it should be, Cassie. It means I've pleased you, and that pleases me."

Shane reveled in the sweetness of her sigh of acceptance. He'd longed for this moment—even dreamed of her surrender—but suddenly he drew back. This moment had to be freely given, knowingly offered. With a light touch he cupped her face in his broad hands.

"Are you sure, Cassie girl?" He probed the velvety depths of her amethyst eyes until he found the answer he sought.

"Very sure." Suddenly the reasons were no longer important. Neither moral decadence, pain, nor threat of shame mattered now. Her body felt as though it had waited a lifetime for what he offered. She could wait no longer to discover this final mystery.

Words escaped her as desire took control. Shane remained poised above her, searching her face as though memorizing every detail for eternity. Then, when each moment seemed suspended endlessly, Shane broke that final barrier, filling her completely, joyously.

Cassie gasped briefly at the sudden pain, but the wonder surpassed the pain, and the joy surpassed the wonder.

Every stroke, each movement brought an aching level of pleasure. As Cassie shyly then proudly moved in tune with Shane's lead, it was an orchestration of spirit, of soul, of love.

Drenched in a love-soaked sheen, Cassie found herself spiraling upward, as though searching, seeking. With Shane's every movement, every stroke, Cassie found herself reaching closer to the vortex she'd never known. She gazed into the gold flecks of Shane's eyes, and he seemed to be searching her face for something. . . .

At the brilliant shattering she gasped in wondrous delight, and they both soared as the diamonds of creation floated earthward.

Shane tried to remember the purpose of his actions. Instead he rolled over to tell Cassie not to have regrets. The passion in her eyes stopped him. Her sultry gaze of pleasure pierced him, and his body responded immediately. He watched as Cassie's eyes fell on the evidence and then widened, staring back at him.

"Can we do that again?" she asked hesitantly. "So soon?"

He chuckled at her naïveté. Her sweetness unnerved him. Sobered, he realized she had given her most precious gift. Yet there were no recriminations, and seemingly no regrets. A protectiveness surged within him as he gazed down at the softness of her trusting eyes. Violet pools of unsullied desire beckoned him.

"Again and again," he whispered, caught in the web of her exposed emotions.

Nuzzling her fragrant hair, he stroked her silky skin. Regret tore at him like the icy shards of a killing blizzard. Once again, he'd been able to set aside the past. But for how long?

Pulling back a moment, he gazed into her loving face and slammed the doors on his tormented thoughts.

"Again, Cassie girl. Again."

17

Cassie's stomach clenched in anticipation when she heard the sound of a wagon rumbling over the hill toward their pasture. Although three weeks had passed almost uneventfully since their day in the meadow, she had expected to see Shane at any time.

She'd been shocked but grateful when Michael had come by to offer his help. At first she'd refused. But at his insistence he'd reinforced the corral and helped her with the shearing shed. She knew Michael split his time between her place and the Lazy H and wondered when the issue would come to a head with Shane.

It was apparent that Michael was sweet on her, but her gentle attempts to discourage him had been unheeded. In many ways he was so like Shane, yet so different. Still, she knew from past experience that a crush was harmless—and temporary.

The disappointment she felt at Shane's absence had overshadowed her other problems. Cassie had thought that after their lovemaking she would have seen him sooner. She ached to see him again, to feel his touch. But as each day rolled around with no visit from him, she'd come to realize that perhaps even he had tired of his game. Common sense told her she was lucky. The pretense was past. But her damned heart couldn't seem to grasp the idea, much less her traitorous body.

Did he think she was tarnished now? A woman who gave away her favors without even a promise of love, much less marriage? Her heart ached at the thought. But what else was keeping him away?

Apparently Shane hadn't known before their special day that she'd hired Matt away. But she hadn't had any repercussions because of his defection. Cassie also knew Shane wouldn't have stayed away because she'd hired one of his hands. He was more likely to confront her than back away. She didn't delude herself into thinking he'd just forget the matter, however. Hiring away a borrowed hand no doubt violated another part of that mysterious unwritten code she faced every day.

Straightening up, Cassie abandoned the dipping mixture while she watched the wagon roll into sight. She tried to squelch her disappointment at the sight of Sarah's unbonneted head and perky face. If it couldn't be Shane, however, Cassie couldn't think of anyone she'd rather see.

"Hello, there," Sarah called out, pulling up on the reins and reaching for the hand brake.

Cassie replied with a smile of her own as Sarah dismounted.

"I haven't forgotten you. We took a short trip to El Paso. How've you been?"

Cassie was tempted to blurt out the truth. Instead she answered with a noncommittal shrug of her shoulders. "Just the usual amount of work."

Sarah grimaced at the foul-smelling mixture at Cassie's feet and wrinkled her nose in distaste. "Do you suppose I could drag you away from all this?"

"Gladly. Let's get out of this heat," Cassie replied, gesturing to the well-worn swing resting in the shade of the porch. As they settled on the glider, Sarah pulled a small package from her reticule.

"Just a little something for you and Millicent," she said breezily.

Touched, Cassie stared at the pale, lemon-colored tissue.

"Go ahead and open it," Sarah urged.

Cassie opened the package with trembling fingers. She was unaccustomed to surprise gifts. Since her father's death, there had never been money for such luxuries. Peeling away the tissue paper, she revealed two rose-colored soaps and a midnight-blue tin. Lifting one of the soaps, she breathed in the fragrant scent and closed her eyes in delight.

"Heavenly," she murmured.

Unable to resist, she pried open the tin and discovered an equally fragrant skin cream. To her dismay, tears prickled behind her eyelids.

"Why, whatever is the matter, Cassie?" Sarah's concerned voice only weakened Cassie's resolve.

"It's just that things have been so difficult." Cassie looked into Sarah's normally cheerful face. She wished it were possible to confide her disappointment in not seeing Shane and to guess aloud if their lovemaking had meant so little to him.

Instead she contented herself with pouring out her other troubles. "I never dreamed it would be so hard," she began.

Cassie thought of the outbreak of mange that had threatened the flock and forced them to put down four of their best ewes. Periodically they found sheep killed in the pastures. And each time Cassie wondered when her neighbors would tire of killing animals and turn on them—especially since she'd been receiving poison pen letters warning her to leave before it was too late.

She still hadn't found a solution to getting supplies. She checked her dwindling larder every day, horribly worried as their rations continued to shrink. And Andrew's growing friendship with Jacob Robertson's son, Zack, disturbed her. Since the night of the dance, the boys had decided not to fight and had become friends. Cassie remembered clearly the day Jacob Robertson had threatened her. She hoped Zack and Andrew's friendship wouldn't turn ugly. Cassie thought of the calm of her life in Boston; the comparison was stark.

"Are you ready to give up?" Sarah questioned quietly.

Cassie swallowed the growing lump in her throat. "Well, no. I just didn't know we'd have to fight for every single thing," Cassie replied, forcing back her tears.

"Texas is different from the East, I'll grant you that. But I think you'll find it worth fighting for. I can't see you trading your independence to spend your life closeted in a classroom."

Cassie smiled at the mental picture Sarah had conjured up for her. Sarah was right, of course, even though Cassie missed teaching more than she'd expected. She just felt so awfully weary at times. She'd had no idea the work would be so grueling.

"I can't either," Cassie replied. "But it would be a refreshing change to have *something* go right."

Sarah laughed at the woebegone note in Cassie's voice. "Tell me what's happened the last few weeks."

Cassie recounted their trials, and Sarah let out an understanding sigh. "No wonder you feel like last week's cowchips." Cassie laughed weakly at Sarah's puckish humor.

Searching Cassie's face, Sarah wondered what role Shane was playing in her troubles. Sarah knew he wouldn't give up easily or, for that matter, at all.

"How about that big brother of mine? Has he been making your life miserable too?"

Cassie's laughter died. "No, I haven't seen him in weeks. Apparently he thinks he has plenty of time to convince me to sell out."

Sarah sensed something more than Cassie admitted. "Hmm. Well, be glad for one thing that hasn't gone wrong!"

Continuing her cheering small talk, Sarah left Cassie with more of a smile on her face than when she'd arrived. As Sarah left, she watched Cassie waving wanly and vowed to talk to Shane and get to the bottom of the problem.

* * *

"Move 'em out!" Shane's voice could be heard thundering through the valley, and Michael shook his head in mock fear.

"Hell, Cookie. I don't know which is more likely to stampede—the cattle or Shane!"

"He's got a burr under his saddle, and no amount of work's gonna shake it loose." Cookie scratched his wiry beard as Shane's horse pounded toward him. "He's got it bad, all right."

"I've seen him happier when he was bucked off under the hooves of a longhorn bull," Michael agreed.

"Might be this time he didn't get bucked off," Cookie intoned.

"What's that, Cookie?" Shane pulled his horse up and gaited backward impatiently as he watched Michael retreat to the other side of the valley.

"I came to see if I can get my swamper back before roundup," Cookie replied, watching Shane's face.

Shane took off his work-worn hat and wiped his perspiring brow. "Well, where is Matt?"

"I hear tell he's hired on with the Dalton woman."

Shane shifted forward in his saddle, the leather creaking with his movement. "Nah."

"You sure?"

"As sure as I need to be. Can you ride into town for me, Cookie?" Shane asked, changing the subject.

"I 'spect so, if you need me to."

"I'm waiting for something that's coming in by stagecoach." Shane avoided Cookie's eyes as he scanned the outlying hills. No sheep on his range for almost a month. Cassie must have bundled herself and the critters up. Good thing, what with the brush fires that had sprung up in the dry lightning storms the past few weeks. Good thing for him, too. He'd been torturing himself about their lovemaking with the same intensity as those fires.

"Then I'll head on to town. Sounds like something mighty important," Cookie probed.

Shane lowered his head momentarily and then pulled his horse about. "Just take care of it, will you, Cookie?"

"Whatever you say, son," Cookie said obligingly, appearing as though he wanted to say more. Instead he glanced toward the thatch of ponderosa pine bordering the valley. "From the frown on Sarah's face, I'd say trouble's acomin'."

Shane followed the direction of Cookie's glance and saw the determined face of his younger sister as she guided her wagon over rocky clumps of wild grass and weeds. Shane craned his head toward Cookie in silent appeal. He didn't know what had set her off, but Sarah could be formidable when riled.

Cookie, knowing the same thing, pulled his mount about and rode off, leaving only gritty dust in his wake. Shane moved toward Sarah, meeting her halfway as her wagon climbed the low-rising hill.

"Hot day for you to be out, little sister," Shane greeted her. From the fire in her expression, he knew he wouldn't get by with pleasantries. He wondered what her cause was today.

"I'm not here to chitchat, Shane. I'll get right to the point. What have you done to Cassie?"

Shane rolled his eyes upward, realizing Sarah was in the mood to meddle. "What makes you so sure *I've* done something?"

"Because I know you, big brother. Cassie's crying her eyes out, and I know you're the reason."

"Why, what's wrong?" Shane was dismayed when he felt his midsection tighten with concern. Deliberately he threw off the feeling, steeling himself to act unconcerned.

"I don't know, but I can bet you're at the bottom of the problem."

"Thanks for your faith in me," he replied dryly. His own deceit ate at him, making him short-tempered and curt.

"Faith has nothing to do with it. Cassie's simply the first girl you've met who doesn't swoon every time she sees you, and she's not reduced to a simpering idiot by your inescapable charm. And to top it off, she's a Dalton." Sarah's rage finally conveyed itself to Shane.

"Stay out of it, Sarah. This doesn't have anything to do with you."

"Our feelings have never counted in your eyes. Your own private war, General Lancer. You're a real dolt, do you know that?" Her voice softened for a moment. "She's not her uncle, Shane."

"I know that, Sarah." That fact had haunted him night and day since their time in the meadow. "But you're wrong about me making her cry. I haven't even seen her for weeks."

"And you don't see anything wrong with that, I suppose?"

Wasn't she ever going to let up? "Dagnabit, Sis. You're getting too big for your britches. If I need you to tell me how to run my life, I'll let you know."

"Oooh!" Sarah fairly spit with frustration. "You obviously need someone to tell you how!"

They glared at each other for a few moments in crackling silence.

Shane broke the silent contest of wills. "I have cattle to tend to. Don't you have a family you should be seeing about?" He whirled his mount, heading for the top of the rise.

"Don't think you've heard the last of this," Sarah hollered after him. "You can run, but you can't hide!"

18

Cassie eased the paddle out of the sheep-dip solution and pushed the curling tendrils of hair away from her face. This was the second straight day of trying to dip the sheep, and she was sick to death of the chore. She was about ready to let the animals take their chances with getting ticks. Thumbing to the next page, she eased her marker back into the book and rechecked the formula. When reading about the mixture, it hadn't seemed nearly as smelly as it had turned out to be. She glanced around, hearing the pounding hooves of an approaching horse.

Straightening up, she unconsciously rubbed the small of her back, trying to ease the now perpetual ache. Cassie shaded her eyes from the glaring midday sun with her hand. A single glance told her the massive gray sorrel was Shane's.

Unobserved, her eyes traveled over the horse and then to Shane and lingered there while he rode toward her. The smallest detail did not escape her attention, from his tight-fitting denims to his bronzed face, but she was determined to summon her reserve of discipline to resist him. The loneliness and disappointment of the past few weeks had taught her the pitfalls of succumbing to his false charm. Trying to second-guess Shane's game and to understand why everyone in the territory hated her sight unseen had drained her emotionally. Her spirit felt as if it were tied to a whipping post.

Cassie was leery as she watched Shane pull to a stop at the railing and dismount. She stared at him, wondering what he hugged to his side. Thank heaven whatever he held was too small to be one of her lambs. Curiosity battled with the butterflies threatening to fill her stomach. She watched as he looped his reins over the hitching post and finally turned toward her. As he approached, Cassie could see that he held a small animal. When he stopped a few feet from her, she stared first at his booted feet and then finally raised her eyes to meet his.

"Cassie," he greeted her.

"Shane," she returned, volumes unspoken between them.

"Here," he said, fumbling with his armload. He thrust his bundle forward.

It was a puppy! A wriggling, cuddly puppy.

"This is for you," he insisted, dumping the squirming white creature into her arms. She accepted the warm, furry little animal and was rewarded with a series of licks.

Dumbfounded, Cassie stared at Shane. "Yours?" she questioned.

"No, yours." She gasped, and he continued rapidly. "What with no help, and not enough dogs, I figured he'd come in handy. When he grows up, that is." He'd felt such unreasonable and unexpected guilt, he'd impulsively ordered the dog. Shane knew that once he'd bought Cassie's land, there would be no place in the territory for the Daltons: he would, in effect, be denying her a home. And regardless of his growing feelings for her, he knew he wouldn't give up his mission.

But despite his resolve, hurting her was not in his plan. She'd simply gotten in the way. Regret and guilt prompted him to buy the puppy. If his plan worked out, the puppy wouldn't have time to grow to adulthood while Cassie needed him. She'd be long gone before the puppy was old enough to herd sheep. He hardened his heart to the thought. It was unfortunate but necessary.

Cassie's smile broke through the mist of tears that suddenly clouded her vision. Why did the man have to confuse her by being so *nice*! Burying her face in the puppy's fur, she tried to summon her control.

"Where in the world did you get a Komondor?" Cassie questioned, recognizing the breed from her reference books.

Shane ducked his head slightly, unaccustomed embarrassment washing over his features. "Ordered him from Denver."

Cassie was overwhelmed. Shane must have spent a great deal of time and energy to get the dog, not to mention money.

"He must have cost a fortune. I'm not sure I can afford—"

"He's a gift," Shane said stiffly.

Cassie wondered how she could ever accept such an expensive gift, especially from him. True, she'd broken every rule of etiquette since her arrival, not to mention her code of morals, but . . .

"I've never received such a lovely gift, Shane." Cassie spoke softly, stroking the generous folds of skin wrapped in puppy fur.

Apparently mollified, Shane replied, "Thought maybe he could make up for some of the bad that's happened since you got here." Shane reached over to scratch the pup's ears and was rewarded with a full-bodied wriggle. "You can be a new start, can't you, boy?"

"My good luck piece," Cassie added softly, searching Shane's eyes, unguarded for once. She glanced away for a moment, then down at the puppy. "I think I'll call you Star. After my lucky star. What do you think of that, boy?"

Despite his determination not to think about it, Shane hadn't been able to shake the vision Sarah had created by telling him of Cassie's tears.

"Have you had any trouble lately?"

Cassie glanced up from the puppy, still stroking his downy fur. "Some. The shearers never got through, and we had a touch of mange." She left out the worry, frustration, despair, and loneliness she'd felt.

"That all?"

Cassie lifted her head from its hiding place and searched his face, which had closed again. She wondered what he would say if she dumped her troubles in his lap and then cried in frustration. She shook the fantasy away.

"It's not easy being the object of everyone's hate," she finally answered, glancing away.

He stepped closer, the puppy the only barrier between them. Shane clasped her arm, feeling her slenderness anew. Her fragility had always been underlined with a sense of substance and strength. Now he was uncomfortably aware that it seemed as though she were slipping away, bit by bit.

He'd been shocked when he'd first ridden in. Her violet eyes were smudged with weariness, and her slender form now seemed dangerously delicate. Even worse, he sensed the vulnerability lying just beneath the surface. He could deal with the anger, their mismatched purposes, but her need wasn't easily dismissed. He could understand Sarah's concern, and he could feel Cassie's despair. A small portion of his heart thawed, but he locked the restraints firmly back in place.

The puppy yipped, demanding to be put down. Shane stepped back as Cassie knelt and released him. Intending only to offer a friendly hand, Shane joined her, recapturing her arms and pulling her up with him.

Her eyes flickered shut briefly, translucent lids tipped with coal-black lashes. Her heart-shaped face, tinged in palest rose, tipped back, her lips opening briefly.

Shane felt a surge of desire mingled with an equally powerful need to protect. To protect this woman whose strength and stamina amazed him, and whose vulnerability now grasped him, pulling him closer than he'd ever dared. Protect a Dalton? Never.

Unable to control himself, however, he moved toward her. Like a drunk thirsting after drink he knew would kill him, Shane hungered for her touch.

He was close enough to see the faint moisture on lips that opened into a well of sweetness he wanted to taste again. And close enough to feel the whisper of her breath, the warmth of her skin. The air seemed to crackle when she lifted her eyes to his. It was apparent that she, too, was feeling the intensity, the heat that seemed to emanate from them both.

He followed the direction of her tongue as it flicked over her mouth, barely wetting the pink lips. His breath grew short. He stood so near he could not only see, he could feel the way her breathing intensified, making her breasts strain upward against the confining fabric of her shirt. He felt himself growing hard just at the sight of her. But the sight of her was no longer enough.

When his lips touched hers, his mind sent off warning signals. Where was the hint of detachment he'd always felt, the need to stay in control? Instead he turned a deaf ear to the bells of warning and let himself taste her freshness, first exploring, then plundering.

When she abandoned herself to his embrace, he felt her nipples harden as her firm breasts pushed into his chest. He wanted to rip off her shirt and feel their heat against his skin. Instead he plunged his hands into her silky, raven hair, loosening the pins and entangling the strands in his fingers. He felt her shiver with pleasure, and giving in to desire, he caressed her breasts, feeling her nipples respond. He remembered what their areolas looked like, soft and dusky.

He heard her draw in her breath quickly and felt her start to pull away, but he held her tightly, denying all sense of propriety. His hands roamed over the tight breeches she wore, arousing him even further as he imagined the scant barrier they provided. He strained against the fabric of his denims, filling the suddenly insufficient space as he ground his hips against hers.

Lost in the magic Shane created, Cassie could scarcely control herself, much less attempt to stop him. Instead she found herself burying her hands in his chestnut locks. Then her hands roved over his muscled shoulders and glided down to rest in the silky thatch of hair on his chest. She felt his lips take hers and she drank deeply of his taste, the freshness of the woodsy scent that clung to his skin and seemed to pour into her own.

Accepting his searching tongue, she reciprocated, amazed at her boldness, and unnerved by the sensations it created. Surges of heat flowing through her veins made her aware of every nuance, every change in her body. Feeling her nipples pucker and harden, she willed him to touch her breasts again, igniting the fire between her thighs. Her limbs felt both weightless and leaden at the same time, as though a thousand pinpricks of sensation had enveloped her.

What was it about this man that made her throw caution skittering to the skies, along with her own innate sense of propriety? Instead of denying his touch, she wanted to continue on. Even if it meant he would think less of her. The loneliness and despair of the past few weeks disappeared under his caresses. The frustration faded with his touch. He had loosened feelings she'd not known existed. She felt the dam burst, and the cascade of feeling rushed heedlessly forward.

"Cass, are you out here?" Milly's voice seemed to come from a great distance, pulling her unwillingly back to the present.

Cassie felt Shane pull away and caught her breath shakily as she gazed at the desire etched in his eyes. But her heart plummeted when his expression became guarded once again.

"I'll be there in a minute, Milly," Cassie called out, her breath ragged, her body still flushed with the heat of his touch.

They stared across the scant space that separated them, each remembering the other's touch, the destination they both craved. Shane was the first to turn away. He took another shaky breath, remembering who he was with, trying to compose himself. "Cookie has some ridiculous notion that you've hired Matt."

"Does he?" Cassie's still husky voice held a note Shane could only describe as regret.

"Told him even a Dalton wouldn't steal away a hand." Shane deliberately made his voice flat.

Cassie didn't meet his eyes as she hid the hurt his words caused, pretending instead to see the early-evening sun trailing its fan of colors over the mesa. "That's unfortunate."

"What do you mean?"

"I've hired Matt to work for me."

Shane raked an impatient hand through his hair. "You're stealing away a hand I lent you?"

"I wouldn't call it stealing . . ." Cassie's pain escalated when she saw the raw anger etched in Shane's rugged face.

"What *would* you call it? Just playing fair? Out here, lady, you get back the kind of treatment you give. And from what I see, you'd better expect your fair ration."

"I'm just playing by your rules."

"I don't know what game you're playing, but I hope you don't outfox yourself." Refusing to admit to himself that his game was much worse, Shane angrily mounted his horse and galloped away.

A whimper at Cassie's feet reminded her she wasn't completely alone, but the dog's cuddly warmth remained a poor substitute for the man who now disappeared over the mesa.

A few hours later, Cassie still dwelled on Shane's words. But she'd scarcely had time to let the hurt sink in. Millicent had been searching for her so they could start the shearing. There was one advantage to the exhausting physical work: it left little time for self-pity.

"You've got her, Andrew!" Cassie yelled in encouragement as Andrew drove the ewe into the shearing shed.

Gazing through the shadows of the shed, Cassie saw Millicent, hooked up to the shearing belt and bent over a ewe, holding the beast firmly in place.

So far they'd completely destroyed three fleeces, but they were getting better at the task each time. The last few fleeces looked encouraging. If they could keep up the quality, they might see a profit after all.

The sheep Andrew drove toward her was bawling its head off; some of the beasts acted as if they would never see the rest of the flock again. They were certainly strange animals, Cassie thought, with a shake of her head. Timid, skittish. If you merely ran them too hard, they'd die. They certainly appeared a lot sturdier than they really were.

Cassie angled her head and laughed wryly as she peered through the air filled with dust, wool, and noise. Who would have thought the green trio from Boston could have conquered shearing?

Fowler and Matt were out on the ranges, keeping track of the rest of the flock. They had volunteered readily to do anything except the shearing.

Watching Andrew and Millicent, Cassie couldn't help but smile as she remembered how little the three of them had known when they came West. Millicent's face was a study in determination as she gripped the sheep and managed to cut the fleece in one piece. Her red hair had escaped its neat chignon to straggle about her face. She had completely abandoned her normally meticulous appearance. Tufts of wool stuck to her perspiring skin, while her starched dress wrinkled in a thousand places. Back in Boston, Cassie would never have believed that the prim Miss Groden would be bending over a dirt floor grappling with a sheep.

"Are you just going to stand there?" Millicent's tired voice cut through Cassie's reverie.

"No. Is this fleece ready?" Cassie asked, indicating the wool Millicent had neatly shorn.

"Sure is. I'm ready for my next victim," Millicent answered, lowering the shears to the bench.

"Andrew, this sheep's ready to go back to the pen," Cassie yelled while bundling the wool with paper twine. Careful not to allow any hay to mix in with the fleece, rendering it worthless, Cassie dropped the wool into the huge gunny sack hanging from the ceiling.

"I'll pound the sack down as soon as we get your next customer ready," Cassie commented.

"Oh, goody. Another one." Millicent's face was flushed, but she picked up the shears with energy.

"I'll shear for a while if you'd like, Milly. We can trade."

"No, thanks. I just learned how to do this part without killing the sheep or myself. Just send me another beastie."

Cassie cornered the bawling sheep and drove it over to Millicent who secured the sheep in position with little trouble. Millicent really was getting good at this, Cassie thought with surprise.

"I still think we should have built chutes," Andrew grumbled as he entered the shed.

"We didn't have time," Cassie patiently explained, pleased that Andrew had taken so efficiently to the tasks she'd given him.

"I guess, but it would've made the job a lot easier." He shrugged his thin shoulders, and Cassie noted that he was a head taller than she was. When had he grown so tall?

"You're doing a good job of driving them in, Andrew. At the rate we're going we should be able to shear a sheep in twenty minutes or less," Cassie encouraged him.

"How about ten?" Millicent asked, indicating the half-shorn sheep at her feet.

Andrew let out a whoop of enthusiasm. "You keep that up and we'll be through in no time."

Millicent and Cassie rolled their eyes at one another. With the rest of the flock waiting to be sheared, it was going to be a long, tiring job. But they were all proud that they had tackled it.

Cassie thought of Shane's words. Perhaps she hadn't played by his rules, but she had a family to provide for. And watching Millicent's and Andrew's beaming faces, Cassie knew they would succeed. No matter what the cost.

19

Cassie riffled through the dusty stack of papers she'd unearthed in her uncle's desk. She'd read his carefully lettered journal entries that showed the hardships he had faced in keeping the ranch going. But instead of discouraging her, his struggles told of a kindred spirit. It was as though she weren't alone in her battle.

Absently she patted Star's wriggling head as he battled fiercely with the end of her belt. Gently she pushed aside the puppy's moist nose when he nuzzled the book in her lap; she stroked his ears while she searched the desk with her other hand.

Refusing to be distracted, Cassie continued searching the desk. She was hunting for the shearing receipts from last season. She'd spent hours the night before trying to determine whether they would survive the winter. Cassie knew if she could estimate their potential earnings, she'd have a better idea of their chances.

Cassie attacked the last pigeonhole in the desk. A quick glance at the first few papers was disappointing. She glanced at a third paper, started to put it aside, and then reached for it again. She read and reread its contents. Finally she pushed herself back into the creaky desk chair.

Could it be? Had Uncle Luke controlled the water rights to nearly two dozen ranches? The enormity of what she held in her hand stunned her.

According to this paper, her uncle had purchased the water

rights along with his land from the cattle rancher who'd owned both. The river that snaked through her property and watered the cattle of her neighbors was only one of two in the area. The second one belonged to Shane.

She suddenly remembered Karl Fredericks's offer to buy her land. Was he after this? No, she decided quickly, that didn't make any sense. He didn't have any adjoining property. Besides, he probably assumed she knew about her ownership of the water rights—and therefore wouldn't sell that parcel.

Curious at what else the desk might contain, Cassie continued digging. She discarded piles of receipts and notes. Then she found it—another paper that puzzled her even more than the first. It was a document deeding a large portion of the Lazy H to Luke Dalton. The name on the deed glared up at her: John Lancer. This was no coincidence. The man who had deeded the biggest parcel of her ranch to Uncle Luke was a Lancer, which made even less sense. If the Lancers were that territorial about their property, why would they carve a section from the middle and deed it to her uncle?

Studying the first document again, she wondered what her mighty neighbors would do if she dammed up the whole works. *Probably shoot me in my sleep*, Cassie answered herself with a shudder. She remembered Fowler's words: "Your uncle cut off enough water to kill half the valley." She had assumed the man was only exaggerating. According to the lay of the land, it hadn't seemed possible that her uncle could have done enough damage to warrant the hate she'd experienced. Now she wasn't so sure.

Cassie perched back in her chair, silently studying the portent of the documents. Who else knew about these? she wondered as her mind flew over the consequences. She felt a cold flicker of suspicion prick her with doubts. Had Shane known all along about the controlling water rights? Was that the major reason he wanted to purchase her land? To control all the water in the area? Or did he just want back the portion that used to belong to the Lancers?

When buying her out hadn't worked, he'd no doubt figured he'd pursue her—make an old maid happy and keep her content so she wouldn't jerk the water rights away from his friends. But that still didn't explain the deed from his father to her uncle.

And, she reminded herself, if the ranchers meant to pacify her, their methods weren't showing it. *Unless they meant to frighten her away before she could discover the truth.* A chilling finger of fear chased up her spine as her mind turned to her uncle. Had his death been the only way to finally rid them of his control over the water?

While she'd never fully accepted his "accidental" death, she had nothing but intuition to warrant her suspicions. What she needed was proof.

The paper rustled in her hand as she gazed out the window of the keeping room. Uncle Luke's death should have meant an end to his control over the water. But what had it really meant?

Cassie dangled both revealing scraps of paper in her hand. Her first instinct was to confront Shane and find out if he'd known all along. An unwelcome premonition still bothered her, however. Who would profit the most from her uncle's death?

If Shane could have bought her land for next to nothing, it would have been him. The letter from Shane's solicitor to her in Boston was proof that he would have profited enormously. She spread both documents in front of her, an arsenal of destruction in the right hands. Resting her aching head momentarily against her steepled fingers, Cassie wished she could unlock the secrets that had plagued her since the day she'd arrived. But with a stab of dismay, she realized she might not want to know the answer.

* * *

Cassie strode into Peabody's General Store, not pausing this time to admire the dry goods or to take in her quaint surroundings. Trying to ignore the sudden silence that greeted her when she entered the store, Cassie marched up to the counter. The unsmiling proprietor stared at her sternly, without compromise. Having made up her mind before she entered the store to try one more time, Cassie looked him squarely in the eye and asked for a fifty-pound sack of flour. She wasn't surprised, only saddened, to hear the familiar reply.

"Don't have none."

Cassie took a deep breath to fortify herself. "That's unfortunate, Mr. Peabody. I understand your family has some land directly south of mine."

His eyes narrowed suspiciously. "That's right."

"Well, I'm afraid that until you can locate the supplies on my list, I'll be forced to cut off your water supply."

A collective gasp rose among the crowd. Cassie ignored them as she slapped the list on the counter.

"Tomorrow, Mr. Peabody. I'll expect my supplies by then, or I'll be forced to act." She didn't acknowledge the people who now stared with open hatred, but instead turned to leave. "Good day, Mr. Peabody."

Total silence accompanied her out the door. Cassie looked neither left nor right, but climbed into her wagon, picked up the reins, and headed home. Only after she was out of town did she pull over to the side of the road, trying to control the shaking of her hands.

Her reserve of courage was depleted now that she'd faced her neighbors' hostility. She rested her flushed face against the palms of her hands, wishing she hadn't had to force Mr. Peabody into selling her supplies, wishing she knew why he was so determined not to do so. The past was just that, and she refused to acknowledge the ridiculous grudge her neighbors still carried.

Hearing a wagon rumbling toward her, she wiped her clammy hands against her skirt and willed her strength to return. She smiled feebly when she recognized Cookie's grizzled face coming toward her. Shane rode close to the wagon, his massive dapple-gray horse walking slowly to accommodate the wagon's pace.

Cassie tried to straighten up and appear composed, but the trembling in her hands hadn't ceased, and the moisture in her eyes made them unnaturally bright. Shane was off his horse in an instant, closing the distance between them.

"What's wrong, Cassie?" he asked, reaching up and helping her down from the wagon seat. "Are you hurt?"

She protested for a moment, then sank gratefully against him. He allowed her to rest against him for a tantalizingly painful moment. Slowly he pulled back, examining her face as he did so.

"What is it?"

She told him what had happened, and the dam of reserve behind which he normally hid exploded with a vengeance as her story unfolded.

"You did what?" he growled.

"What else could I do?" she cried, unable to believe he, too, agreed with the townspeople. "No one seemed to care that we were going to be cut off from our supplies!"

"Did you ever stop to think they had reason to feel like they do?" He replayed his own painful memories—his father, Luke Dalton, his mother. All the years of hate and frustration boiled over.

"Whatever happened with my uncle is over, done. What reason do they have to keep refusing me supplies?"

"Because they remember what Luke Dalton did. It cost them friends and family. There's not a person in the valley that wasn't affected by what he did. And now you're starting it all over again."

"Simply by cutting off someone's water? I don't—"

"What do you think cutting off water does to people, Cassie?" His face was close, his eyes narrowed and hard. "First the cattle get sick. You ride your land, watching them go down by the dozen. Then they die, and the stench fills the air." Cassie tried to shrink away, but Shane's grip was like an iron vise as he held her close. "You can't get it out of your nostrils. The stink of it stays with you even in your sleep. And if you're one of the small ranchers, you watch until all your stock's dead, your kids have empty bellies, and then you give up. Or die. Like half the people in this valley did when your uncle cut off their water during the drought." Shane paused, his jaws clenching tightly together, thinking of all the other damage her uncle had caused. "When you're tossing out threats, you'd better know you're baiting the trap. And you're the one who's going to get snapped in two."

She stared at him in horror and disbelief, unable to believe his hateful words. But seeds of suspicion assailed her as she remembered the townspeople's reactions.

"If you know what's good for you, you'll sell now. Because I wouldn't give you two cents for what your life'll be worth if you dam up the water."

Swallowing the sudden tears clogging her throat, she watched Shane mount his horse and ride toward town. Cookie studied her quietly for a few moments, as though he wanted to speak. Finally he sighed, picking up the reins and slapping the horse as he, too, moved toward town.

Knowing she couldn't go back to her old life, and wondering what she'd do now, Cassie stared at their retreating figures. Trapped like a rat, she thought desperately. And she'd set the bait herself.

20

Millicent slapped a wet linen shirt over the taut rope that served as her laundry line. A pair of trousers followed, slapped even more fiercely against the line. She ignored the sweat trickling past her temples and the rivulets that formed and collected between her breasts. It wasn't as though anyone would see her, she thought resentfully, putting even more force into the next piece of laundry she slung over the line. It had been two weeks since she'd seen Ringer.

At first his absence hadn't concerned her. She knew his ranch kept him fully occupied. Then she started to worry. What if he were sick and alone? Or hurt? But a casual inquiry to Matt had assured her he was not sick or hurt. As the days turned into weeks, her concern turned into anger.

Apparently he's forgotten all about me. Millicent viciously snapped the dish cloth before adding it to the line. *Ought to have more sense than to believe a man's interested in me. My time for courting's long past.*

But even while reprimanding herself, she couldn't still the sharp pang of hurt that sliced through her at the thought of her barren life. She leaned her head wearily against the railing that supported the laundry line. Sometimes it seemed intolerably unfair. She thought about her sacrificed youth, her lost romance, and the babies she'd never had.

Millicent's mother had died when she was a child, and her dear papa had always tried to be both mother and father to her. And he'd made her childhood remarkably happy. It was only when she was eighteen and he'd had his stroke that their roles had been reversed.

She would never forget the stricken look on his face when he'd realized he couldn't move or speak—or the panic that ensued with his helplessness. She'd refused to leave his side, gentling his fears and seeing to his needs.

At first her suitors still came to call, but as the weeks turned into months and months turned into years, her suitors married others, others who didn't have a father to care for. Her father hadn't wanted her to make the sacrifice. He'd made that painfully clear. But she couldn't abandon him any more than he could have abandoned her when her mother died. And Millicent told herself that it didn't matter, that she didn't miss the dances and parties. As each girlhood chum became engaged and married, she donned her "best wishes" smile and almost convinced them she wasn't desperately yearning for a husband and family of her own.

But as the years passed, she was no longer greeted with looks of sympathy, because by then she was an established spinster with no hope of marriage in her future. And then Papa died, quietly in his sleep, causing little more trouble in death than he had in life. And with his death she'd resigned herself to a solitary life.

A single tear escaped and cascaded down her cheek. Angrily she wiped it away. Millicent refused to cry over a thick-headed cowhand.

With renewed vigor she clutched the red-checked tablecloth in the basket at her feet and pitched it over the line. As she straightened the folds of cloth, her hands stilled. A cloud of dust signaled an approaching rider.

She felt an uncontrollable quickening of her heart as she wondered if it could be Ringer and then flushed with renewed anger. She bent down and grasped another piece of laundry, determined to ignore the incoming rider. As the hooves beat closer, Millicent relentlessly attacked the remaining laundry.

Ringer pulled up near the wash lines and dismounted eagerly. He walked up to her confidently, doffing his hat as he approached.

"Milly. You're a sight for sore eyes. Damned if you're not the prettiest thing I've laid eyes on in—well, I don't know when."

Millicent leveled a furious glare at him. The nerve of the man! To not show up for weeks and then to appear when she was looking her absolute worst—and to add insult to injury by blatantly complimenting her. She could feel her already wilted, sweat-stained dress crumple further in the heat. And she knew her hair was straggling in helpless disrepair about her face.

"How dare you?" she hissed.

"How . . . ?" Ringer's face was a study in confusion. Finally he lowered his hat to his side. "I don't know what it is, but I can tell you seem to be riled up about something . . ."

"Oh, can you now?" Millicent's fury was barely restrained.

"Yes'm. But for the life of me, I can't figure out what it is. I ride in and tell you how pretty you are and—"

"Ooohh!" Millicent's face flushed, and her eyes flashed fire as if she were ready to explode. Ringer took an involuntary step backward.

"Now, Milly," he pleaded as she looked first at him and then at the laundry surrounding them.

"Don't you 'Now, Milly' me!" she fairly shouted, reaching into the wicker basket at her feet.

Before Ringer could reply, he felt the cold, wet, stinging slap of laundry across his face. Stunned, he stood stock-still for a minute before finally pulling the offending garment from his face. When he did, Millicent threw another well-aimed cannonball of laundry at him. The second one only grazed his shoulder.

Jehoshaphat! She must be plumb crazy from the heat. He approached her cautiously, ducking the fusillade of laundry she was hurling at him. As she bent to grasp still more, he captured her arms and pulled her close.

"Millicent!" he pleaded.

"Don't touch me, you cad!"

"Cad?"

"You ride in here after I haven't seen you in weeks and you have the nerve to call me *pretty*!"

The reason for her anger finally dawned on him. "*Pretty* dastardly calling you *pretty*, eh?"

Millicent could see the laughter in his eyes, and it only renewed her fury. It was all right for him to laugh. He hadn't lain awake nights worrying and crying only to be caught looking worse than sheep dip.

Infuriated, she struggled to break his hold. As she struggled, he held her closer. Suddenly realizing the proximity of his body to hers, she ceased her struggle. And meeting his eyes, she felt her rage evaporate only to be replaced by a simmering heat that had nothing to do with the blazing midday sun.

Millicent noticed from a great distance that the laughter in his eyes had faded only to be replaced by something darker, more promising, more frightening. His face almost touched hers, and she could taste the freshness of his breath, the clean smell of horses and masculine aroma that clung to him.

Hesitantly, she reached up to touch his face as she'd dreamed of doing a thousand times. A stubble greeted her work-roughened hands, and somewhere she registered the fact that he'd come to see her in such a hurry that he hadn't shaved. At her touch, his eyes darkened further—an unfathomable blue that captured hers, holding her helpless in their gaze. When his lips touched hers, she experienced both the thrill and fulfillment of finally kissing him in reality as she had in her dreams.

Her lips parted under his searching tongue, and she felt a bolt of sheer pleasure race up her spine at his touch.

Hesitantly she responded and felt a similar shudder shake his body. Suddenly Millicent's confidence bloomed with the thought that she could make him feel the same heat.

Her heart swelled when he gently grasped the back of her neck and loosened the chignon of carrot-red hair she always tried so desperately to hide. As their bodies melded together, she felt his rough hands gently caress her hair.

When he reluctantly released her lips, he gathered handfuls of her hair and pulled her closer. "If I'd have known a bout of bloating would've caused this, I'd have fed my cattle clover a long time ago."

"Your cattle were bloated?"

"What else would have kept me away?"

Millicent dropped her gaze and shook her head self-consciously as she tried to gather her free-flowing hair.

"This awful hair," Millicent began to mutter.

He silenced her with another kiss. "See it shine in the sunlight, Milly? It's the color of the sunset—blazing and proud."

She looked with wonder now at the hair she had hated for so many years. It did shine in the sunlight. Normally she covered it with a hat or a bonnet, and never had such lengths of it shone unbound in the sun.

Ringer gently pulled her chin upward. "It's beautiful, Milly—like you."

The simple sincerity of his compliment struck her heart with a crashing intensity. She glanced downward quickly, afraid the mist of tears suddenly clouding her vision would fall unchecked.

Ringer tucked her head into his shoulder and stroked her blazing length of hair. It had been so long since he'd tenderly held a woman. His wife had been dead for over ten years, and he'd never expected to feel the same way again. After his family had died during the big drought he'd closed his heart, he'd thought forever. But as he stroked the head of the gentle woman at his side, he wondered.

21

An unfamiliar wagon jounced over the dirt road leading to the Dalton house. Putting down the shearing belt, Cassie stepped into the yard, watching as Mr. Peabody brought his wagon to a halt. A boy in his early teens rode with him. Barely waiting for the wagon to stop, the boy jumped down and walked quickly to the back of the wagon.

Mr. Peabody stayed firmly in his seat, staring straight ahead. Cassie watched in silence as the boy unceremoniously dumped her supplies on the ground, raising a cloud of dust. When the boy climbed back on board, Mr. Peabody snapped the reins sharply, but not before he'd sent Cassie a venomous glare. The entire exchange was silent, but what hadn't been said was obvious.

After the wagon left, Cassie stared at the dust-covered sacks of flour and other staples. Her shoulders slumped in discouragement. Such hatred to overcome for a few foodstuffs. She dragged one of the sacks toward the larder, groaning a bit as the heavy weight dragged her down.

Retrieving a second sack, she tugged at the cumbersome flour sack, finally dumping it in the larder. The heavy sack raised a wave of gritty dust. She sneezed and was startled by Shane's voice just behind her. Defensively, she stood among the disarray.

He handed her a handkerchief. She debated and then accepted the white cloth.

"I came to see if Peabody was going to hold up his end of the deal. I see he did." Shane glanced at the sacks that had been heaped on the ground without care.

She nodded in agreement, watching his face.

"And I see you've not dammed up the water."

"I keep my end of a bargain."

"So I see." His eyes searched hers as though trying to see through to her soul. Cookie had given Shane hell about the tongue-lashing he'd delivered to Cassie the day before. Cookie had pointed out none too gently that Cassie wasn't responsible for the past, and she didn't understand yet what she'd gotten into.

Cookie had gone on to inform Shane that he wasn't too old to have his rear end kicked into the next state. Shane had grown up under Cookie's rule, as well as his father's. That guidance and force of habit had made him stop and take stock of what Cookie said about Cassie. Cookie was right. Cassie was the victim of what had taken place before her arrival.

Respect for Cookie's good sense made Shane agree to come and apologize to Cassie. It would be a hell of a lot better to reason her out of the land rather than scare her away. He took the heavy sack from her hands and lifted it effortlessly to his shoulder.

"Want to go on a picnic?"

"I beg your pardon?"

His request seemed to take her aback, but her response didn't surprise him; his own invitation did.

"You've got the food now," he responded, hefting another sack onto his shoulder and depositing it in the larder.

"A picnic?" she questioned in a disbelieving voice.

"You know—that's where you bring wonderful food and I provide a buggy, a blanket, and a hearty appetite."

Her lips twitched without warning. Even if he was playing her the way a virtuoso mastered a violin, his teasing was a welcome relief from the strain of the past few days. With a handsome man like Shane offering a respite, she was tempted to forget he was the one she should be running away from. For the moment she gave in to that temptation.

The breeze ruffled through the changing grass and danced through the resisting wildflowers. Pricklepoppy, Indian paintbrush, and Apache plume battled with the thistle that ranged the meadow and eclipsed the pygmy forests of pinyon pine and juniper.

Cassie breathed in the incredibly sweet aroma of dewy grass and crushed pine boughs. Gazing across the precise design of the dutch doll quilt that covered the small space between the wicker picnic basket and Shane's long, outstretched legs, she breathed a silent prayer of thanks for the perfect day.

"Don't suppose there's any food in that basket?" Shane questioned lazily as he contemplated the cloud-scattered blue sky overhead.

"Perhaps," she answered, whisking the fresh white napkin off the top. "But no help, no food."

"Oh, no, you don't! I've done unspeakable things for you so you would take a day off."

Cassie grinned to herself as she thought of Shane helping her dip the last of her sheep. He'd taken one disgusted look at her trying to dip the sheep with one hand while holding a book in the other, and had stepped in and taken over. Fortunately he hadn't run into Michael, who'd also been helping her earlier. She still didn't understand why Shane was so touchy about his brother's crush on her. Couldn't he see that it was just puppy love?

"And that, madam, is all I'm going to do. I'm going to lie here and let you cater to my every whim," he finished, pushing his hat over his eyes and resting his folded hands across his stomach.

"How gallant," Cassie responded, uncapping the jar of lemonade.

"Uh-huh," he answered lazily, refusing to move.

Cassie smiled as she laid out the fried chicken and feather-light biscuits. She didn't mind a bit. She had always resisted taking even an hour away from the never-ending chores at her ranch, but she'd finally weakened. And now, enjoying the peaceful trees swaying to the orchestration of the mild wind, and the handsome man stretched out beside her, she was inordinately glad—even though she knew he planned to try to sweet-talk her out of her land.

Refusing to dwell on what she knew was his true purpose, Cassie arranged their meal invitingly on the precious china plates she'd packed in the basket. Watching Shane relax, she plucked a long, feather-tipped wildflower from amidst the grass and crept over to his side. Whisking the errant bud beneath his nose, she announced, "Dinner is served."

Shane opened a lazy eye. "Is this how you always announce your dinners, Miss Dalton? Remind me not to ask you to host my next formal affair."

"I'm not accustomed to hosting a gentleman's *affair,* Mr. Lancer," she replied.

"Perhaps we should change that," he suggested, his eyes heating in a familiar fashion.

She whacked his knuckles lightly with the wooden spoon she'd used to stir the lemonade. "Now, now, Mr. Lancer. You wouldn't be trying to lead me astray, sir?"

"I'm trying, but I don't think I'm succeeding," he muttered, rubbing his offended knuckles as he rose to a sitting position.

Cassie offered him a dazzling smile, gleefully aware she was gloating. "That's right."

He bit into the mouth-watering chicken and was glad he did. Content to sit by her side, Shane finished off his lunch, surprised that he enjoyed their quiet rapport as much as their blazes of passion. He felt a continual need to remind himself that it was all for a purpose.

She squinted at the clouds, and Shane smiled lazily at her intense concentration.

"Hoping to conjure up some rain?"

"No, I was trying to read the cloud formations. The cirrus and cumulus—"

"Whoa—don't tell me. More book learning."

Two dots of bright pink stained Cassie's cheeks. "Book learning isn't all that awful. Perhaps there'd be more law and order if—"

"Hold on—there's nothing wrong with book learning. Tell me about something else, though. I already know how to read the weather."

Cassie searched his face to see if he was making fun of her. He seemed to be serious. Mollified, Cassie continued.

"I've been reading an interesting book on rotation grazing."

Shane cocked his eyebrows inquisitively.

"According to the studies I've read, ranchers have had a lot of success in areas with limited water resources by grazing cattle first, then sheep. Then they rest the land and repeat the whole process. It allows the grass to restore itself so that both species can benefit from the same land."

"What? You don't mean to tell me somebody's fool enough to believe cattle and sheep can graze the same patch of land?"

Her exasperation grew. "I just said," she repeated slowly, "the studies I've read indicate—"

"Studies by dried-up old kernels who've never set a foot out of their laboratories, you mean. Cattle won't drink out of water that sheep have used."

"Not according to Dr. Warren's study. He says it's a common folk legend with no basis. Cattle will drink from the same water."

"Not in this part of the country they won't."

"Well, they have to have the opportunity to prove—"

"Speaking of opportunities . . ."

"Would you, by any chance, be trying to change the subject?"

"Yes, ma'am. I certainly am. I don't plan to ruin a perfect day with an argument about whether cattle and sheep will drink . . ." He shook his head in mock horror.

Cassie laughed in spite of herself. But her laughter died, and she found herself trying to stay calm as she read the desire in his eyes. It was the first time they'd been alone since his touch had revealed desires she'd not known she possessed.

Remembering the way his hands had moved over her, she found her throat growing dry, her breathing deepening. She looked at his strong hands, remembering the feel of them on her skin, the taste of his mouth on hers. Her skin flushed as the heat she read in his eyes transmitted itself to her.

She should pack up the food and dishes, laugh lightly, and ask to be taken home. Instead she found herself wondering if the touch of his skin against hers would make her as fevered as she remembered, and if the hair she could see at the opening of his shirt was as silky as she remembered.

Blood seemed to thunder through her veins, filling her head with an echo, weighing down her limbs with a thickness that refused to allow her to move. She lowered her gaze to his throat where she spotted his pulse beating as rapidly as her own.

When he pulled her closer, the feelings were even more intense than she remembered. Caution fled as she melted against the heat of his chest, savoring the feel of him. Violet eyes locked with golden-green ones and darkened as their passion spoke silently, eloquently. Their lips met in mutual accord, mutual delight.

Shane might have expected surrender, but not this. Not the giving, the wanting, the passion. He read her desire, felt her quiver of anticipation, and found himself drowning in her sweetness as she sighed his name. He promised himself that he would remain in control.

But at her growing boldness, he found himself plundering that same sweetness, tasting, feeling, drowning. His hands seemed to move with a will of their own, caressing her silken tresses as he pulled them free of their confining pins, while his lips recaptured hers and then trailed down her neck.

He found himself lost in the fragile hollows of her throat as he pushed aside the confining buttons of her bodice, seeking her proud, uplifted breasts. Through the thin, silken confines of her chemise she responded to his touch, arching upward with a small moan as he tantalized the flesh beneath his fingers.

Six tiny fastenings stood between him and the hot flesh beneath the flimsy garment. One by one, he slipped each small button free, hearing her tiny gasps of pleasure as each opened and the air nipped her exposed skin. Almost reverently he laid back the delicate material, his fantasies materializing as he gazed at the creamy flesh that glowed in the afternoon sun. His fingers reached out to touch the tips—dusky pink as he'd remembered them—and she responded immediately.

He ground his lips against hers, his tongue spearing into her mouth, demanding and receiving an immediate response. Each thrust triggered a new onslaught of intensity. Then with a passion he couldn't restrain, his mouth left hers to kiss her exposed flesh, finally tugging gently at the soft nipples, feeling them harden beneath his tongue. His own hardness nestled against the juncture of her legs, urging the heated mound of her flesh to respond.

She writhed under his touch, her face flushed with pleasure. And as never before, he found himself trembling with the wanting of her. It seared his mind as he held her captive in his arms. As reason fled, he wondered if the wanting scorched his heart and if he could stand the consequences.

When he finally drew back, Cassie read the uncertainty that clashed with desire in Shane's eyes. She knew she had already transgressed all bounds with him, but somehow it hadn't mattered. The fire he'd created refused to be doused. The center of her womanhood throbbed with a longing she wanted him to satisfy.

Breathing raggedly and still only inches apart from her, Shane took her face in his hands and looked deeply into her eyes. She could see the searching, the unspoken questions, but as she opened her lips to ask, Shane silenced her effectively.

Suddenly impatient, Cassie pulled open Shane's shirt, burying her hands in the silky hair matting his chest, thrilled as his naked skin came into contact with hers.

Her impatience transferred itself to Shane. Urgency replaced the gentle discovery they'd both felt the first time. Cassie shuddered as Shane grasped her skirts, bunching them out of the way. Impatiently he tore loose the fastening that closed her pantalets. Cassie kicked away the restraining garment, as eager for his touch as he was.

Pulling at his denims, she ran her hands over the sleek flanks of his hips. Soon his clothing, too, was shed.

She arched upward when his hands grasped her buttocks, massaging them firmly as he positioned himself above her.

This time there was no hesitation, no question. Shane took possession like a warrior on a quest. Her response was to wrap her legs around his, reveling in the primal dance. The grass and wildflowers blanketed their glistening bodies as each thrust was met, parried, returned.

Cassie felt Shane shudder as her own body shimmered in a volcano of tremors. Only the sound of their gasping breaths filled the air. Cassie gulped the sweet air, wondering at her own abandon. Wondering, too, if Shane's feelings matched hers. As they eased away from one another, she felt no regret for her desire.

Like wary gladiators, each appraised the other. Skin damp, chests heaving, they waited. Ever so slowly, Shane skimmed his hand over the contours of her face. His hand cupped the back of her neck, bringing her close. The kiss was both brief and bittersweet.

As Shane shakily refastened the buttons on her bodice, Cassie studied the man beside her, swallowing a growing lump in her throat.

He'd not asked her to decide between her land and him. She was grateful because, gazing into his mercurial eyes, she had little doubt what her decision might have been.

22

Cassie strolled down the dusty, wooden boardwalk of Keenonburg's main street, surveying the scant selection of merchandise in the windows of the half-dozen stores the town boasted. The saddlery displayed hand-tooled Mexican saddles and buckskin chaps that didn't hold her interest. The grain store wasn't any more alluring with its collection of cattle and chicken feed.

Strolling further down the road, Cassie barely paused at the barbershop, but she did peek into the windows of the apothecary. One glance at the dusty, jewel-toned bottles was sufficient. She looked up as the family coming toward her crossed to the other side of the street to avoid her. She took a deep breath and tried to ignore the spurt of pain that the continued rejection caused.

Knowing she couldn't avoid seeing people any longer, Cassie picked up the hem of her calico skirt, crossed the dust-filled street, and entered the mercantile, inhaling its unique aroma of vinegar, beeswax, and packing crates. Since the day Mr. Peabody had delivered her supplies, Cassie hadn't been given any trouble about buying what she needed, but no one was any friendlier.

When she entered the store, Cassie noted with amusement that Millicent was fingering a bolt of ivory satin material that she couldn't possibly be considering for curtains. Cassie wondered, with an inner smile, about Millicent's protests that her relationship with Ringer was one of friendship only.

Cassie picked up a bolt of emerald-green silk, knowing she couldn't afford to buy it, yet picturing herself in a sweeping gown of the luxurious fabric. Closing her eyes, she could picture Shane's reaction. She could almost see Shane's face, his eyes darkening in appreciation, his . . .

"Thinking of making breeches out of silk, Miz Dalton?"

Jacob Robertson's mocking voice penetrated her fantasy, and Cassie's eyes flew open in shock.

"Or were you thinking of Mr. Lancer?"

The truth sent a burning wave of humiliation through Cassie's body, visibly staining her cheeks, while her anger asserted itself.

Jacob's dark eyes glittered with rage. Cassie felt a renewed quiver of fear dart through her as she remembered how menacing he'd seemed that day in her barn. He glanced around at the three men who lounged behind him, and seemed to gain encouragement from their presence.

"Mebbe you could come to the saloon and gimme a taste of what you been sharin' with Lancer," Robertson suggested with a leer.

A bolt of revulsion shot through her, and Cassie took an involuntary step backward. Had Shane been boasting about the frustrated spinster who'd tumbled into his arms?

"Maybe you ought to go home and share some of your ideas with your wife, Robertson. Or has she already thrown you out of her bed?" Maude's booming voice came from over Cassie's shoulder.

The men behind Robertson snickered, and he flushed heatedly. Before turning away, he sent Cassie a glare of pure hatred.

"Don't think this'll be the last of it, missy. Your uncle thought he'd be around a while too. Guess you Daltons still have a lot to learn."

Robertson's words sent prickles of fear up her spine. *Your uncle thought he'd be around a while too.* What did he know?

Cassie shook fearfully as Jacob left, his supporters trailing behind him. Turning to Maude, Cassie tried to convey her thanks.

"Think nothin' of it, child. Robertson's all mouth and then only when he's got his friends backing him up." Maude landed an affectionate thwack behind Cassie's shoulders. "Buck up. You're not gonna let the likes of him take the wind out of you, are you?"

Cassie swallowed hard, appreciating Maude's support. She wished she could dismiss the fear as easily.

"No, Maude. I'm not." Cassie held up the bolt of green silk, hoping to disguise her inward shaking. "Besides, this might make rather fetching breeches."

Maude laughed in return. "That's the spirit, girl!"

Millicent hovered nearby, and Cassie could sense the tangible pull of her concern.

"Come on, Milly," Cassie said, gathering her courage and trying to shut out the ugly suspicions Robertson's words had raised. "I'd like to see that satin you were looking at. Although it certainly would make peculiar curtains," she teased.

Millicent blushed crimson in response, and Cassie knew she'd been diverted for the moment. They spent more than an hour gathering their supplies before emerging from the store into the bright sunlight of the boardwalk.

Millicent adjusted her ribbon-trimmed hat and spotless white gloves. "Shall we head for home, Cassie?"

"I'm ready if—" Her last words were cut off as a man's resonant voice overrode her murmur.

"Good day, ladies." Michael Lancer tipped his Stetson politely to them both, but his eyes remained fixed on Cassie's, his interest evident.

They nodded in return and greeted him in unison. "Good day, Michael."

"Let me carry those packages for you, ladies," he offered,

taking the neatly wrapped, string-tied bundles before the women could protest.

"That's very kind of you, sir," Millicent murmured.

"And now, ladies, your carriage?"

"I'm afraid that our 'carriage' is still a buckboard," Cassie answered, leading the way along the dusty walkway. She'd been trying to discourage Michael's interest, but he was still a frequent visitor to the ranch, having taken Andrew under his wing. Whenever possible, Michael took both Andrew and Zack Robertson fishing, a diversion all three seemed to enjoy.

Cassie knew Michael's crush was harmless, but she sensed that Shane would not be pleased to have him following her around like a well-trained lap dog.

Not hurting Shane was becoming increasingly important, she realized with an uncomfortable start. When had she begun to feel this ridiculously protective urge? She'd grudgingly realized the attraction, reluctantly recognized her own treacherous need, and blushingly acknowledged the passion, but when had they melded to a point beyond?

The trio reached the buckboard, and Michael loaded their parcels into the back, then assisted Cassie and Millicent onto the high planked seat.

"Thank you for your help, Michael," Cassie began.

Michael whisked his hat off and held it nervously between both hands. "No trouble a'tall, ma'am." He seemed to hesitate and then blurted out, "I was wondering if you might be coming to Charles and Effie Lou's engagement dance next Saturday night?"

Cassie smiled at his slightly flushed face. "I'm not sure, Michael, but if we do, I'll be looking forward to seeing you."

She then rewarded him with a dazzling smile. Before he realized that she'd not agreed to let him be her escort, Cassie slapped the reins smartly, urging the team of horses forward.

As they moved forward, Cassie allowed herself a glance at Millicent. She expected at least a sly wink and a chuckle but was surprised to see a gentle smile on Millicent's face. "You handled that real well, partner."

23

Millicent stood next to the bawling sheep as Cassie read aloud from one of her texts:

" 'Proper castration promotes less disease and fighting for supremacy in non-breeding stock. It also insures a more profitable flock if only the more desirable rams are used for breeding.' "

As Cassie finished, Millicent leveled a look that would have stopped one of her former students dead in his tracks from fifty feet away.

"If you think I'm going to do that, you *are* crazy."

"Well, one of us has to," Cassie answered, paling as she studied the explicit diagram.

"Don't look at me."

"I don't want to do it, either." Cassie turned the pages, hoping for better news that wasn't forthcoming.

"If you think I'm going to touch . . ." Millicent began.

"Milly!"

"Did you think they'd just fall off on their own?"

"Well, no . . ." Cassie gazed doubtfully at the sheep.

"Count me out." Millicent started to back away.

"Milly, it says—"

"Well, how do we know he'll feel better? It doesn't *sound* like he'd feel better."

Cassie's stomach turned at the thought. If possible, her skin turned an even more sickly shade of green. "It doesn't say that—just that he's less likely to get sick."

"Maybe he'd rather get sick and live a *full* life. What's to say he won't get lovesick instead?"

"We're supposed to be concerned with breeding a flock that—"

"And what if we do it wrong?"

Cassie blanched. She'd never thought of that. None of this had seemed so graphic back in Boston when she was reading about it.

Millicent continued. "I say let him keep what God gave him."

They both stared at the spooked ram. His eyes *did* seem to be pleading. . . .

"Oh, geez, Milly. I guess we'll have to let him go." Cassie laid down her opened book. "Even if his lambs turn out to be purple, I guess I can live better with that than—"

Cassie stopped abruptly as she and Millicent froze. They'd both heard the unmistakable sound of approaching hooves—close. Too close. The last thing they needed to be was the talk of the range because they were too faint-hearted to carry out normal ranching duties.

Cassie scrambled to untie the sheep, but she wasn't fast enough. Shane's chuckle told her he'd seen enough. Too much.

"You ladies planning on doing some branding?" he asked in mock innocence, his eyes sweeping the corral. Cassie was painfully aware that no branding tools were in sight.

Cassie and Millicent glanced at one another, and between them could only manage a splutter.

Shane dismounted and leaned over the lassoed animal. Squatting, he retrieved the book that was turned to the incriminating pages.

Cassie tried to grab the book, but he held it up out of her reach. He looked at the book, then at the bound sheep, and shook his head.

"Problems, ladies?"

Cassie tried to appear nonchalant. "Of course not."

"Then why were you untying him?"

Both women stared around the corral, but neither could think of a reply.

"Couldn't be you're scared?"

"What's there to be scared of?" Cassie bluffed, while Millicent rolled her eyes.

"Then it was too indelicate . . ."

Cassie knew she could hardly call herself a rancher and then be too squeamish to perform the necessary duties. Whatever had truly riled the townspeople, she didn't intend to add to their disapproval.

"We just hadn't decided on a method," Cassie improvised.

"Ah—the methods. Which ones were you considering?"

Damn him! He knew she didn't know any methods. If she could just get her hands on that book. . . . Was there more than one? "Oh, the usual ones," Cassie finally answered, hoping her lame answer would end this interrogation.

Shane lifted his eyebrows a fraction and controlled the twitching that threatened to shape his lips into a full-blown grin.

"You want to tell me which ones those are?"

No, dammit. I don't! "Oh, you know."

"You mean cutting, tying . . ." He paused. "Biting."

She turned the alternatives over in her mind. Cutting, tying, biting. *Biting!* Surely he didn't, couldn't mean . . . She turned to Millicent, whose eyes were now even rounder than the sheep's. Both women visibly paled.

Cassie opened her mouth to reply and, for one of the few times in her life, found herself completely speechless. She turned again to Millicent, whose prickly humor seemed to have disappeared with Shane's announcement.

"Like me to give you a hand with the job?" Shane questioned.

She thought of the methods he'd just suggested and wanted to gag. Millicent's greenish hue told Cassie she was in agreement.

"Oh, that's all right. We really have a lot of other things that need to be done instead. We—"

Before she could finish, Shane burst into unrestrained laughter. Cassie spluttered, flushed, and then spluttered some more. Finally she stood with hands on hips until he finished.

Cassie's eyes narrowed as she accused, "You made that all up!"

"You sure? I thought you knew all the *methods*."

"You, you . . . You *man*!"

"You're sure? You don't have your books mixed up? You been reading all those ones on sheep . . ."

"Oohh!" Cassie advanced toward him as he backed off in simulated terror. "You did that on purpose! For your information, we can do the job perfectly well without you."

"Hmmpft!" Millicent issued loudly as both Cassie and Shane's heads swung in her direction. "I don't know about you, Cassie, but you can count me out. If I listen to any more of this, you'll have to peel me off the ground."

Feeling a little deflated, Cassie watched as a very pale Millicent turned toward the house.

"You were saying?" Shane questioned.

"I'm perfectly capable of doing it on my own," she responded, nibbling furiously on her bottom lip.

Shane's eyes softened in spite of himself at her reaction. "Probably so, Cassie. Come on, you get me what I need, and I'll take care of it."

She opened her mouth to protest, and he held up a hand.

"I'm not doing this for nothing," he warned. She stopped, watching him thoughtfully. "In exchange, you go with me to the dance Saturday."

He'd done it again, she thought ruefully as a slow smile

enveloped her features. Ignoring the warning bells, she agreed.

He'd ignored those same warnings when he decided to ask her to the dance, telling himself his reason was worth the lies. But as he gazed at her soft smile, he knew it wasn't Cassie he was lying to.

24

Entering the decorated barn, Cassie heard the lingering strains of fiddle music and smelled the fragrant aroma of newly baled hay, ripe apple cider, and freshly baked cinnamon cakes and molasses cookies. How different it felt to enter the dance tonight, she thought.

At the first dance she'd felt every inch the hated stranger she was. But now, with Shane as her escort, she shared the confidence that emanated from him as naturally as he breathed. A quick glance assured her that Jacob Robertson wasn't anywhere in sight, and Cassie let out a silent sigh of relief.

Gazing around the lantern-lit room, Cassie saw the same bevy of matrons and their overeager daughters. Fortunately, tonight's dance was in honor of Effie Lou Newton's engagement. Cassie was relieved that the party hadn't come to a halt with her arrival. Either because she was on Shane's arm or because of a tacit agreement not to ruin Effie Lou's party, the merriment continued uninterrupted.

Cassie glanced up at Shane's smiling face. His possessiveness was subtle but distinct as he held her arm firmly tucked in his. Perhaps he still didn't think she realized the reason for his acting as though she were the most irresistible female to come West. But even though it was her land he was after, she couldn't disguise the pleasure she felt in being escorted by the town catch.

Lifting her chin, she met the twinkle in his eyes and found

she could no longer prevent a smile of her own. It felt devilishly hard to remember that he was the one she needed to watch out for when he was acting as a buffer between her and the animosity of the townspeople.

Shane's head dipped closer to hers. "Prepare for battle," he whispered, laughter coating his words.

Startled, Cassie glanced up and saw a militia of women bearing down on them. Stopping short in front of them, Cassie offered the ladies a tentative smile.

They nodded their heads toward her in one collective movement. Only a few quivering feathers on their hats remained of their greeting as they ignored Cassie and turned to Shane.

"Alan Tinsdale's sick," Mrs. Humphries announced with an important air. Cassie turned to Shane with a questioning glance.

"The caller for the square dances," he explained.

"You'll simply have to replace him," Edna Simmons continued.

Shane raised his eyebrows quizzically. "I'm flattered, ladies. But why me?"

With a victorious gleam in her eye, Mrs. Humphries answered, "Because the other young men are in Effie Lou and Charles's wedding party and should be celebrating, not doing the calling."

The intentional slight was not lost on Cassie. So they'd thought of a way to remind her she was an unwanted outsider and to separate her from Shane for the evening. Refusing to let them see they'd hurt her, Cassie simply lifted her chin higher and remained quietly at Shane's side.

"Guess you have a point, ladies. It is an engagement celebration—you might say a romantic evening." The ladies nodded their flower- and feather-bedecked hats in unison, gloating as they surveyed Cassie. "So I propose that we dispense with the square dancing and have the boys play only waltzes tonight. Much more romantic, don't you think?"

Cassie had to restrain the laughter that mingled with her relief when the ladies found themselves muttering in Shane and Cassie's wake as he led her to the dance floor. She'd felt a bleak moment of despair when she'd thought he was going to blithely desert her.

She gave herself a mental shake. She'd attended enough dances in her days as a spinster to take care of herself. But she couldn't deny the delightful sensation of being cosseted and protected by Shane's interest. *You'd better stop this,* she warned herself. *You'll get used to his attention, and then what will happen when he grows tired of the game*?

Savoring the feeling of his arm firmly encircling her waist as he led her onto the dance floor, Cassie chose to ignore the warning signals.

The lilting strains of a waltz tune filtered through her consciousness, and Cassie effortlessly followed Shane's lead. The disapproving stares and hastily concealed animosity faded into a dimming background as she found herself lost in Shane's compelling gaze. For all she knew or cared, they could have been surrounded by howling wolves and irate grizzlies, yet Cassie drifted away from reality and into the fantasy Shane's arms created.

Searching the gold-flecked green of his eyes, Cassie wished for the moment that he, too, could let the rest of the world slip away as they floated around the makeshift dance floor, weaving past the other couples and seeking the corners that held little of the dim lantern light.

Shane cursed himself as the amethyst hue of Cassie's expressive eyes mesmerized him. Eyes that sucked him in like a whirlpool until he felt like flotsam in a swollen river, his emotions tossing about at the whim of a raging current. For a moment he forgot she was a Dalton.

He shook his head as though to clear it. He had far too much at stake to allow Cassie to sway him. Past promises called to him. *I won't forget, Pa*—a deathbed oath that was more sacred to him than anything he now lived for.

Yet his hand spanned her incredibly tiny waist, and he drew her even closer. He tipped his head down, breathing deeply of the teasingly fresh smell of lavender lingering in her raven curls that perched over one shoulder. He had an insane desire to rip the confining ribbon from her hair and bury his face in her luxuriant ebony tresses.

But even as he squelched the thought, the fiddles screeched to a halt, and the dancers drew apart. Reluctantly, as though loosening his hold on a lifeline, Shane relinquished his grip on Cassie, and they stepped away from one another. Her flushed face seemed to mirror his own feelings, and Shane tactfully drew her aside to the punch table. Scooping up a ladle of cider, Shane passed the glass to Cassie. She accepted it with trembling hands, and Shane found himself gulping his own cider—only to realize he was holding an empty glass and wondering where the contents had gone.

He was no gawky schoolboy to get worked up over a woman at a dance, he told himself. But this was not just some woman. This was Cassie. Cassie of the captivating eyes. Of the incredible courage. And of the open heart. He felt a sliver of his own heart melt at the realization—and an equal sliver of fear slice up his spine.

Shane had been his own man all his life. He'd never wanted the shackles that other men seemed to need and accept. Instead, he had openly ridiculed those he'd claimed were led around by an apron and chained to a skirt. And here he was making calf-eyes at a public dance—and at a Dalton, no less. Maybe it was time he backed off and sampled some of the other women he'd ignored since Cassie had come to town.

Maybe it was time to make sure she didn't have a strangle-hold on his life. She continued to turn the tables on him, and it was time to reverse the process. His interest in her was because of her land, he reminded himself fiercely. He refused to acknowledge the fear that caring for Cassie would somehow weaken him, because Lancer men felt no fear.

He was startled when Herminnie sidled up to him and awarded him a toothy smile.

"Evenin', Shane," she drawled in her magnolia-thick voice.

"Evening, Herminnie," he replied, mustering a heart-catching smile for her benefit. Might as well start with Herminnie. She'd been openly chasing him for years. It was time Cassie was reminded that he was his own man. After all, he'd forgotten easily enough.

"Would you honor me with this dance, Herminnie?" he asked, his smile suggesting more than just a dance.

Herminnie flushed, and poured even more sugar into her drawl. "Why, of course, Shane."

"You'll excuse us, won't you, Cassie?" Not waiting for a reply, Shane led Herminnie to the dance floor. Her arm entwined with Shane's, Herminnie cast a maliciously triumphant glance at Cassie.

Cassie tried to smile and appear pleasantly amused as Shane spent the next three dances in the arms of various young ladies in the room. By the fourth dance, the strain of smiling was becoming unbearable. She'd danced twice with Karl Fredericks but hadn't wanted to encourage him by accepting any more dances.

Cassie wondered what had gone so desperately wrong. Could she have imagined the desire in Shane's eyes as they'd danced? Perhaps he'd planned this all along. Maybe he'd gotten tired of his farcical game of pursuing her and had decided public humiliation would work better. Feeling her throat constrict, she tried to quell her rebellious thoughts. But it was difficult as she stood on the sidelines, feeling like a deserted wallflower.

Turning back to the punch bowl yet again, she found herself side by side with Michael.

"Hello, pretty lady," he greeted her softly. She was aware

from the sympathy in his eyes that he'd witnessed her abandonment.

Steadying her voice, unwilling to have it quiver with the emotions she couldn't deny, Cassie replied, "Good evening, Michael. Are you having a good time?" She tried to plaster on a bright smile but could see she hadn't fooled him.

"Not up till now. But if my brother's the fool I'm beginning to think he is, my evening's going to improve considerably."

Cassie sent him an uncertain smile.

"That's the spirit. Now, how about this dance?"

Without waiting for a reply, Michael led her onto the dance floor. She felt herself being drawn uncomfortably close in his arms. She started to protest when he interrupted her.

"We want to make this look good, don't we?"

She murmured an inaudible reply into his shoulder as he spun her around the floor. She could sense a hundred pairs of unfriendly eyes trained on her back. She wished suddenly that she were tucked safely in her home, away from the scrutiny of these people who so blatantly disliked her. And away from the incredible, unreasonable hurt of Shane's desertion.

Michael led her around the dance floor to a haunting melody. As the tune ended, he drew away and bent his head toward hers. To the casual observer, Michael seemed to be whispering an endearment.

Instead, as his lips grazed her ear, he said, "Buck up. Don't let them see how you really feel." Drawing back, he slipped a casual arm under her elbow and guided her to the edge of the dance floor.

Glancing up at the strong, young face so much like Shane's, Cassie murmured to him, "Thank you, Michael."

"There's no need for thanks."

"Oh, yes, there is. You've salvaged my pride."

"My brother's a fool," Michael stated bluntly. "Maybe he's beginning to realize just how much of a fool."

Cassie followed Michael's gaze until her eyes rested on Shane's angry face. She felt an immediate sense of relief, followed by a giddy sense of power. So he wasn't immune to her after all.

"Let's give him a run for his money, shall we?" Michael whispered in her ear. Not allowing her a chance to reply, he led Cassie onto the dance floor. Michael purposely swirled her in Shane's direction as much as possible. Shane's only reaction was his furious expression and the whitened knuckles that clenched a punch glass, threatening to break it.

Refusing to release her, Michael claimed the next three dances as Shane's fury grew. Having abandoned any pretense of dancing with other women, Shane merely simmered until his temper was a visible roiling boil. Cassie glanced in his direction and unconsciously tightened her hold on Michael when she countered Shane's scathing glare only inches from her face.

She started to speak, but the words froze in her throat at the murderous expression she found on Shane's face. His anger seemed completely out of proportion to the situation.

"Be glad you're my little brother, or I'd whip you where you stand," he ground out at Michael before dragging Cassie off the dance floor, through the oversized doors, and into the night air.

"You have no right—" Cassie began indignantly, finding it hard to believe he was this upset simply because she'd danced with his brother. His hands bracketed her jaw, effectively stopping her resistance. His mouth was an assault, stamping his possession on her. Her consciousness fought the realization that he was branding her as surely as he did his cattle, but finally her mind accepted the truth, and she broke his insistent hold.

"Are you satisfied?" she asked quietly, holding a narrow grip on her fury. "It's too bad you didn't have a red-hot iron handy. You could have put your mark on me and penned me up with the rest of the stock."

Shane's rage matched hers. "If that's what it takes to keep you from falling into the first set of arms that comes along . . ."

Her stinging slap split the night, and they both reeled under the impact.

His face darkened in fury while she met and held his glance. Nose to nose, they stood in electrified silence. Cassie started to step backward as Shane's arms grasped hers. She expected revenge or anger, not the overwhelming sensation of being totally consumed by his kiss.

This time his mouth claimed hers unrelentingly, but instead of the assault she expected, he once again surprised her. His tongue explored the recesses of her mouth, seeking each sensitive spot that ignited a fresh surge of desire. His tongue lapped lazily in swirls while his lips firmly molded against hers. Feeling her breasts throb in response, her loins aching, she tried to fight the sensations but found herself going limp, breathless, satiated.

Finally, when she thought she could take no more, he released her. As she rocked back on her heels, much like a rag doll, she stared at him in consternation.

His eyes were dark with desire yet laced with an uncanny, calm self-possession. *How could he look so unaffected*? "We'd best be getting inside, Cassie girl. Else people might talk."

Weak-kneed and winded, Cassie wobbled forward as he strode purposefully ahead. What kind of game was he playing? Brushing her fingers across her still-tingling lips, Cassie didn't know if she dared find out.

25

Cassie and Millicent climbed the steps of the church, trying to ignore the sudden silence that greeted them. Mr. Peabody stepped in front of them, and Cassie formed a tentative smile. His mask of disdain froze her smile, and she ducked her head, hurrying through the door. She and Millicent found a pew and sat down on the hard oak planking. The family seated next to them pointedly rose and walked away, seating themselves several rows behind. Cassie stared straight ahead, feeling the burning in her cheeks. She didn't know how much more of this ostracism she could endure.

Glancing aside briefly, she saw that Andrew had found Zack Robertson. The two of them slid into a back pew. Cassie saw a slingshot make a brief appearance and prayed fervently the two of them wouldn't act up. That was all she needed to make her welcome complete, having her brother act like a hooligan in church.

She was still puzzled by the boys' odd alliance, but Zack managed to elude his father's iron hand, and despite Jacob Robertson's threatening ways, Cassie was glad Andrew had found a friend.

The tinny-sounding piano seemed more suited to a saloon than a church, but a sober-faced woman was earnestly trying to coax "Rock of Ages" from its shallow bowels.

Cassie spared a second glance around the unadorned churchhouse and spotted Ringer, dressed neatly with his hair slicked in place, bearing down on them. Millicent's pink cheeks indicated she'd seen him too. Cassie wondered with a sigh how she could feel so incredibly lonely in such a crowd. Watching couples and families looking so solid together, Cassie ached with a sense of not belonging.

She also wished she knew to what extent these people had been hurt by her uncle. It seemed so unbelievable to her. Her father's brother had always been a kind and gentle man. The man she remembered wouldn't cut off the lifeline these people depended on. Without looking at the closed faces in the church, Cassie knew she'd get no answers from them.

Glancing around, Cassie noticed that the small, rough-hewn room was becoming uncomfortably crowded, yet her pew remained glaringly empty. Strains of "The Old Rugged Cross" spilled forth from the ancient piano. As if on cue, the congregation rose to sing. Cassie fumbled with the unfamiliar hymnal, uncomfortably aware of the scrutiny of those around her. Her back felt as though it were being drilled with a thousand holes as every eye in the place was directed toward her. Unused to such rejection, her eyes were bright with unshed tears. She remembered the closeness of her congregation back home, the welcome she'd always found at church.

Her gaze remained unfocused as she continued to fumble with the songbook, so she was doubly surprised when Shane's large hand covered hers, quickly turning to the proper page. His rich baritone filled the air while her own voice quavered a bit as she joined in. Swallowing the unreasonable feeling of gratitude that had welled up at Shane's presence, she concentrated instead on the words of the song.

Cassie glanced up at Shane, but his gaze was directed to the crude pulpit where the minister stood. When the song ended, the minister led the prayer, and Cassie issued a fervent one of her own. She couldn't bear to think of the years stretching ahead of her filled with rejection and open hostility. She'd left Boston for a fresh new start, not to take up the reins in a hate-filled vendetta she still didn't completely understand.

The puzzling paper she'd found in her desk was constantly on her mind. It was apparent from Shane's attitude that his feelings about her uncle surpassed that of all her other neighbors, and it was also apparent that nothing would stop him from trying to get back his land. If that were the case, why had his father ever deeded the land over to her uncle? It just didn't make any sense. The key to the mystery was as elusive as her neighbors' continued hatred.

Cassie listened quietly as the sermon began. She watched with well-hidden amusement as Maude's noisy brood straggled in. The way the children scattered, it appeared as though Maude had at least two dozen. The disturbance didn't seem to bother the minister, however.

He quietly continued his sermon. His gentle words washed over Cassie, soothing her frayed nerves. She listened in surprise as the minister's sermon unfolded; it seemed he was preaching the golden rule. Cassie wondered if he had chosen the topic for her benefit. Or for the good folk of Keenonburg, she thought, noticing a few people squirming uncomfortably. Glancing over at Millicent to see if she'd caught the irony of the minister's message, Cassie saw that Milly's attention was wrapped up in Ringer, as was his in her.

Shane watched the emotions flitting across Cassie's face. She wouldn't make much of a poker player; the hurt was spelled out across her face as though it had been painted there. Studying her, Shane wondered if he'd lost himself somewhere in the midst of his own manipulations.

The fierce need to reclaim his land was still strong, but now he questioned his methods. Her vulnerability rose up again to assail him, and he knew without question she was beginning to mean too much to him.

Even as he completed the thought, his hand covered her smaller one. Cassie glanced up at him, her eyes reflecting the quick pleasure he knew she felt. The look she gave him hit like a hard fist to the gut.

Shane, too, listened to the minister's words: "Do unto others . . ." His mind echoed a bitter laugh. *Before they do unto you*, he completed silently. The past had taught him to make his own rules. Rules that didn't include trusting violet eyes. Still, he didn't draw his hand away.

When the final song ended, the congregation rose and bowed their heads for the final benediction. Afterward, Cassie lagged behind the crowd as they stood talking with one another, ignoring her. Maude's and Sarah's friendly greetings warmed her heart, but the others' outright rejection tore at her sensitive nature.

Lingering inside, Cassie spoke with the Reverend Beecher while the bulk of the congregation departed. Seeing that almost everyone had left, she glanced at Shane and ended her conversation with the minister. Taking his cue, Shane shook the clergyman's hand.

"Good sermon, Reverend Beecher."

"Thank you, Shane. It seemed *timely*."

Cassie smiled fully at the minister, her face a study of gentle beauty.

"It was indeed a pleasure to meet you, Miss Dalton."

"Cassie, please."

"By all means, Cassie."

Shane didn't doubt the man would have done anything she'd asked at that moment. Taking her arm, Shane escorted Cassie out the door and to her wagon. He had an insane desire to spend the rest of his lazy Sunday afternoon with her—and an even more ridiculous wish that she wasn't a Dalton. It was a perfect day, the sky cerulean and filled with enough puffy clouds to diminish the heat. Regret tore at him as instead he lifted her up into the wagon and tipped his hat in farewell. Andrew clambered in the back, and Cassie started to flick the reins.

"Think your sister will let you get away to go fishing this week?" Shane asked Andrew. "Michael wants to get even—

says you caught twice as many as he did last time."

"Sis?" Andrew gazed at Cassie in appeal.

"If you can get Manuelo to cover—"

"I can go, Shane. When?"

Shane exchanged amused glances with Cassie. "When your sister says it's all right."

Andrew's face lit with excitement as Cassie urged the horses to start moving. " 'Bye, Shane. Thanks!"

Shane returned the boy's wave, watching the wagon move out of sight. Cassie and Millicent discussed the ups and downs of the morning as their wagon moved homeward, while Andrew contentedly aimed his slingshot at the passing scenery. Cassie couldn't resist teasing Millicent about Ringer's attention. They laughed as they rounded another bend in the road beneath a canopy of trees.

Suddenly shots rang out, seeming to explode from all around them. Terrified, Cassie snapped the reins, and the horses bolted forward. Hearing the whizzing of bullets around them, she shouted at Millicent and Andrew to stay low while she urged the horses on. Cassie continued her hell-bent pace for two more miles until she felt Millicent tugging at her arm, trying to shout above the wind.

"I think we can slow down now, Cass."

Cassie scanned the area fearfully and saw the reason in Millicent's words. Apparently no one was pursuing them. Whoever had been shooting had no doubt hidden in the protection of the trees. Waiting to ambush them.

Cassie pulled over to the side of the road, her hands trembling. Twisting around to check on Andrew, she found him frightened but unharmed.

"Would you like me to drive home, Cass?" Millicent asked, her voice steady, unlike the pounding of Cassie's heart.

"That might be best, Milly." Aware of the defeat in her own voice, Cassie held up unsteady hands, looking at them in surprise. She hadn't known she would react this way to danger, having always thought of herself as self-sufficient. What a laughable notion.

Taking a ragged breath, she handed the reins to Millicent, praying they'd be lucky enough to escape next time.

Sunshine dappled through the leaves of the surrounding trees, creating a cutwork pattern of light and dark on the sparse grass covering the ground. Strolling along, Millicent ducked to avoid a low-hanging limb just as Ringer turned to lift the obstructing branch. Self-consciously they smiled at one another as they almost collided.

Millicent's natural shyness around men had reasserted itself, and she couldn't help questioning what a handsome man like Ringer saw in an old spinster like herself. Shyly she ducked her head, feeling his gaze warm her face. She'd had countless dreams about their times together, and she shook her head at her own whimsy. Even sillier were her dreams of their future together. . . .

"Milly, it's time we talked about what happened."

She averted her face, determined to enjoy the walk instead of dwelling on the horror of being ambushed.

"No one was hurt." Millicent shrugged aside his concern, knowing where this conversation was headed, just as many others had been.

"This time." Ringer's voice sounded taut with anxiety. "Next time you might not be so lucky."

She avoided his eyes. "We don't know whether there'll be a next time."

Grasping her arms firmly, he pulled her face even with his. "Until Cassie wises up and sells the land, there'll always be a next time."

Millicent pulled away, walking beneath the shade of a live oak tree. "I don't want to fight with you about this again, Ringer. We're not giving up."

Ringer flung his hat to the ground in agitation. "If you understood what the people in this valley went through with Luke Dalton, you'd know it's not a matter of *if* you'll be run out, but *when*."

She turned a shocked face toward him, surprised at his vehemence. It wasn't a normal part of his nature.

"Ringer?" she questioned softly, knowing instinctively he'd been holding something back.

But he turned away, the muscle in his cheek twitching with an obvious effort to stay under control. Millicent had to know what was causing a gentle man like Ringer such anguish. Moving in front of him, she gently touched his arm.

"Tell me."

He hesitated, but finally the words spilled out of him like embers dredged up from the coals of a fire.

"It was so damn hot," he began. Millicent watched his face twist in agony as the tale unfolded. "What water we had dried up. I spent every day from sunup till dark riding my land, trying to keep my stock alive." Ringer laughed humorlessly. "The cattle still died. There wasn't a damned thing I could do about it. But still I kept going out every day."

He paused, recalling a past full of pain. "And Katherine was expectin'. She was only about two weeks away." His voice grew hoarse, and Millicent swallowed the growing lump in her own throat, feeling his anguish, knowing with a growing horror where his story was leading. "Only water we had left at the house was stagnant—the water was so low by then. I'd meant to ride over to the Lancers and get some drinking water for the family, but instead I went to see about the stock."

He paused again, passing a hand over his face. "Katherine drew the water that had gone bad. She and my son drank it. By the time I made it home that night, it was too late.

Katherine lasted through the night, but by morning she was gone. My boy died that afternoon."

Millicent moved close to him, taking her hand in his, barely wincing when his hand bore painfully down on hers as he tried to contain the anguish spilling forth. But she didn't mind the pain. She almost welcomed it, wishing she could absorb more of his grief.

"I wanted to kill Luke Dalton for cutting off my water."

Ringer paused, and for a moment Millicent felt the same murderous determination in her heart. Cassie's uncle must have been heartless to allow a pregnant woman and child to die from tainted water.

"Then Luke rode over and broke down. Said he'd never intended for things to go so far. Somehow, after he'd pulled himself back together, Luke and me wound up burying my wife and boy." Ringer shook his head at the strange memory. "But I knew even if he had cut off the water, it was my fault they died. I should have been with Katherine when she needed me, instead of putting the cattle first."

Millicent flinched at the bitterness in his voice and leaped to his defense.

"But you were seeing to your livelihood! It wasn't for yourself. It was for your family. You knew you couldn't lose all the cattle and still provide for them. You didn't have a choice." Millicent's voice was strident with her belief in him, and Ringer raised his troubled gaze to hers.

"I never thought of it like that."

"You never let yourself," Millicent answered softly. "Not even *you* could be in both places at once. I'm sure Katherine understood."

Millicent blinked back a tear as she thought of the pain and guilt Ringer had lived with for so long. Realizing she held his arm intimately, Millicent grew suddenly embarrassed. Moving away from him awkwardly, she leaned against a tree trunk.

If Ringer sensed her discomfort, he gave no outward sign. Since the day she'd pummeled him with her laundry, he'd been attentive, solicitous, and every inch the gentleman. Maybe that was what bothered her. She longed to feel his arms crushing her close. Glancing around at the trees swaying in the gentle wind, Milly realized this was the first time they'd been alone since he'd held her in his arms and called her beautiful.

Ringer was overwhelmingly conscious of the same thought. Since that day with Milly, he'd purposely held himself back. She'd unleashed emotions he thought had been buried so deep they had died. He'd wanted nothing more than to possess her that very day. But Millicent was no ordinary woman. Underneath her prickly humor was a sensitive, lonely woman who, he was sure, was innocent as the day she was born.

Gazing into her face, he realized she seemed softer somehow. True, her hair now fell into soft waves by her face, rather than being pulled tightly into a serviceable knot. But it was the luminescence of her smile and eyes that transformed her features—along with a belief in him that warmed his soul in a way he'd never thought possible.

It was her smile that caught him now as Milly glanced up before sinking to the ground and pulling her skirt in a circle around her knees. He'd been so worried about her since the day of the shooting. He'd wanted to take her home and protect her but knew he had no right to do so.

Sinking to the ground beside her, he carefully held himself a proper distance away. Ringer caught Millicent's eyes as they registered this deliberate action, seeing all of her uncertainty returning in full force. He nearly groaned aloud when, abashed, she cast her face downward. Unable to still the motion, he reached out to place a gentle hand beneath her chin. Cupping her face, he lifted her chin upward until her face was level with his.

"Thanks for believin' in me, Milly."

And gently Ringer tipped her face toward his, the orchestration of breeze and sunshine completing the circle of his thoughts.

26

Andrew picked his way carefully through the rocks, watching for rattlers as he climbed upward on the butte. The harsh sun glinted off the boulders, slowing his progress as he stared into the blinding light. The first pinging sound whizzed by his shoulder, and the boy stood stock-still, not certain of its source. The second *ping* struck the rock beside his hand and ricocheted away. Bullets!

Andrew flung himself to the ground, terrified to move. He saw Pepe standing guard over him and pulled the brave little dog down to the ground beside him.

Andrew lifted his head carefully to look around as Pepe growled threateningly beside him. Rolling over slightly, Andrew uncovered the rifle Michael had given him. Ducking behind the outcrop of rocks, he carefully scanned the butte and craggy hillside. Pepe started to rise, his haunches stiffened in defense. Andrew bit out a quiet, solitary command: "Stay."

The dog reluctantly dropped back, continuing to growl low in his throat as Andrew searched the brush for whoever was shooting at him. He was afraid to raise his gun, aware that the sunlight glinting off the barrel would reveal his hiding place behind the rocks.

Scouring the concealing groundcover above him, Andrew detected a quick flash just before someone's gun roared again. Andrew stared in wonder at the blood welling on his leg.

Shock forced him to keep his head down for a moment, then he drew a fortifying breath and eased his rifle from beneath its concealing cover. Knowing his shot must count, Andrew leveled his aim with great care, focused on the exact spot where he'd seen the earlier flash, and pulled the trigger. Silence greeted him. Slowly he lowered his weapon and scanned the butte for signs of life. Nothing.

He'd expected a roar of retaliating fire, and the sudden silence unnerved him. An unbidden thought leaped forward. What if he'd hit whoever was shooting at him?

Swallowing the growing lump in his throat, he slid downward as quickly as his wounded leg would allow, letting the scrubby brush hide him. He didn't know what scared him more: the prospect that whoever shot at him was alive and waiting to pick him off, or that he might have hit the other man who might be lying dead. Andrew grabbed Pepe's sturdy body and held him close. Nothing in his meager twelve years of life had prepared him for this threat to his existence.

The sound of hooves striking rock nearby penetrated his fear. Releasing Pepe, Andrew grabbed his rifle, holding it close to his body. He felt the dampness of his own sweat that beaded and clung as his fear increased, mingled with the pinpricks of thorns torturing his already shivering muscles. He swallowed convulsively as a shower of pebbles rained down the path beside him. The rider was closer!

Andrew screwed his eyes shut momentarily, praying and wishing for help. Realizing he had only himself to count on, Andrew forced himself to creep forward. To face . . .

"Andrew!" The soft call was tinged with concern, and Andrew couldn't control the sudden shaking in his body, the overwhelming desire to be protected.

"Shane?" Andrew's tentative cry reached Shane, who whipped his horse back to the ridge he'd just passed. Dismounting quickly, Shane reached the boy just as he was crawling from beneath the overhanging thorny brush.

"It's all right. I'm here now, boy. I heard shots—"

"Someone tried to kill me!"

Shane's face was as grim as Andrew's. "Are you all right?"

Andrew nodded shakily, his face pale.

Shane glanced at Andrew's leg and bent down to wrap his own bandanna around the wound. "Looks clean," he muttered. Then louder, "Let's get out of here." Shane grasped Andrew's shoulder, giving him an encouraging squeeze, while glancing at the now forbidding-looking scrub surrounding them. "Now."

When Cassie heard the news of Andrew's misadventure, she looked every bit as grim as Shane had imagined she would. Anger, fear, and frustration battled for dominance. Finally, despair won.

"Why?" she asked wearily, still not relinquishing her hold on Andrew who squirmed a bit under her close inspection. Not expecting an answer, she turned to Andrew as though seeking to reassure herself that his wound wasn't serious. Puzzlement dawned in her eyes.

"How did you know how to shoot a rifle, Andrew? We've never had weapons at home."

Andrew ducked his head and mumbled, "Shane and Michael taught me."

"What?" Her eyes widened in disbelief and burgeoning anger.

"Would you rather the boy hadn't known how to defend himself, Cassie?" Shane's quiet voice washed over her, and she blanched at the thought of the consequences had he not known how to shoot. But blast it all, she should have been consulted.

Shane continued calmly. "You won't like hearing this, but you have to admit I was right about selling out." He saw the flare of resistance in her eyes and ignored it. Deliberately he made his voice flat. "Is your pride worth Andrew's life?" The pain in her eyes triggered a flood of guilt, but he refused to succumb to it. He had to make her understand this wasn't

Boston, and people here didn't play by a prescribed set of rules. Fortunes were made or lost on a whim—and lives were sacrificed for even less. It was time she understood that.

Cassie stroked Andrew's head silently and looked at his exhausted face, realizing he'd fallen asleep, as only children can do, to escape his fear. Gently, she eased a needlepoint-covered pillow under his head and stretched his legs out on the rigid settee.

Rising, she walked into the dining room and crossed over to the window, staring sightlessly out toward the plain. She kept her voice low as she answered Shane.

"You've won."

Three long strides put Shane within inches of her.

"Don't you understand?" he questioned, grasping her elbow and turning her around to face him. "This isn't a fight—there aren't going to be any winners and losers. This is a question of your survival."

A sudden determination flared in her eyes. "It is survival, isn't it, Shane?" Without waiting for an answer, she continued. "I really thought I could make people like me simply by being a good neighbor. I've been a fool." Her tone was bitter. "I guess I'll have to use the same methods my dear neighbors have."

Shane stared at her in disbelief.

"Don't worry, Shane. I don't intend to go gunning for them. I have something even more effective to use." Crossing to the desk, she located the hidden pigeonhole and pulled out a paper. Silently she handed the document outlining her water rights to Shane.

"If you put this in force, you'll be declaring war."

She cut her eyes in Andrew's direction. "They already did that this afternoon."

Grasping her arms again, Shane brought her to within inches of his body. "You don't know what you're asking for! I won't have you risking your fool neck just to get even."

"Do you really think that's what this is all about? Revenge?"

"Well, isn't it?" he bit out, his face close to hers.

"No, it's establishing what's mine. I won't have my brother shot, my sheep slaughtered." *Or my land stolen,* she raged silently. "Your friends think they're dealing with a few weak women and a boy, but I have the law on my side. And I'm going to start damming up the water tomorrow!"

"Do you think they'll just sit back and accept that? Then they'll really have a reason to go for blood."

"Apparently they didn't even need a reason for what they did," Cassie answered, waving an angry hand toward the other room in Andrew's direction. "Perhaps if they know I mean business, they'll leave us alone."

Shane's fingers tightened around her arms, wanting to shake some sense into her. When she looked up at him, her expression showed she was wounded, hurting.

Intending to offer only a comforting embrace, he pulled her close. As he did, he tried to guess what it was about Cassie that made him toss aside a lifetime of control. Knowing he should turn his back on her unbreakable grip on his heart, instead he pulled her close. Savoring her softness, he knew she was forcing him to make a decision. Could he choose this violet-eyed sprite and turn his back on his past, on the promises he knew he had to uphold?

She was achingly beautiful, but he'd known his share of beautiful women. None had made him cast aside his natural caution. And certainly none had inspired him to want to lay the earth at her feet.

But as he held her small yet strong frame in his arms, Shane found he wanted to do that and more. He wanted to sweep her away from the ugliness she'd felt since she'd moved here. He wanted to protect and cherish her. The irony of it struck him. Astonished at the direction his thoughts moved unbidden, Shane tightened his embrace, tipping her chin up.

But Cassie stiffened as his mouth started to descend on hers, and he felt her wrench away.

"I know you think I'm a desperate female, Shane Lancer, but not this desperate. I'm lucky Andrew has only a flesh wound. But I won't forget how he came by it and I won't forget the part you've played in this whole stupid war."

Shaken, Cassie strove to catch her breath. Jim Fowler pushed the door open and came in, carrying a load of firewood. Cassie stepped across the room as he dumped the wood into the box. She wanted to be as far away from Shane as possible.

Yet as though his will alone compelled her, she found herself meeting Shane's gaze across the room. Warm fingers of desire crept up her spine as she read the promise implicit in his eyes. Her mind whirled in the crowded confusion of her own thoughts, trying to control the message he read in her own.

27

True to her word, the next morning Cassie started carrying out her plans to dam up the water. She had to coerce Manuelo, the Basque, into helping her. "Reluctant" scarcely explained his feelings. He'd been adamantly opposed to her plans.

She'd finally convinced him to help, but he made it clear by every word and action that he disapproved of her wishes. Even now, as he'd taken the wagon for another load of supplies, he'd left muttering incoherently and crossing himself at regular intervals as though hoping divine intervention might change Cassie's stubborn set of mind.

Knee deep in the mucky sludge, Cassie swiped at a scraggly lock of hair that kept falling into her eyes. Lifting her head, she gazed at the Russian mulberry and silver poplar trees flanking the low banks of the muddy river. They sprouted at odd angles from the shore as though the wind had pushed them in one direction, while the sun and water tugged them in another. Stripped of leaves, the trees shivered in naked shame as the wind snaked mournfully through the barren branches.

Shaking off the sudden oppressive feeling their image created, Cassie bent back to the task at hand. She tugged at the log she was putting into place, wishing she could hire more men to complete the job. None of the locals would be willing to dam up the water. Matt and Jim Fowler were reluctant accomplices at best.

Cassie glanced across the banks of the river, spotting riders headed her way. There were at least a dozen men in the group, she realized, her stomach lurching with her growing fear. It had been easy to sound brave when she'd stood in the comfort of her own home, resolutely planning to defy her neighbors. But now, alone on the plain, she didn't feel so brave. Her sweeping gaze raked the surrounding area, and Cassie realized with growing dread that she was undeniably alone.

Squaring her shoulders and lifting her head, Cassie unconsciously clenched the shovel held in her gloved hands. She'd made her stand and now had to abide by it. The group of men rode to the riverbank across from where she stood, pulling up their mounts and staring down at her. Their very position, from the height of the horses, lent them strength, giving them an automatic advantage. Resentfully, Cassie realized this as she searched their faces, feeling the collective anger and hate that emanated from all of them.

Recognizing Jacob Robertson's red, bull-like face, she sensed immediately that he was the leader. His first words confirmed the notion.

"You won't get away with this, missy." His face seemed to mottle even more than usual as he wagged a thick, sausagelike finger in her direction.

Before she could answer, another member of the group spoke up. "Now, Robertson, you know we decided to try and reason this out."

Cassie directed her attention to the second speaker, vaguely recognizing him from the barn dances. Yes, he was Adam Reynolds, her neighbor who owned a good-sized spread to the south of her property. He was entirely dependent on the water she was damming up.

Reynolds tipped his hat in her direction. "Ma'am."

Containing an urge to order them off her property, Cassie instead acknowledged his greeting with a cool nod.

"I guess you know why we're here. This water feeds all

the streams on our property," Reynolds stated.

Cassie intentionally made her voice expressionless. "I'm aware of that."

"Well, then you must know you can't dam it up!" the burly cowhand next to Reynolds burst out.

"I know no such thing." The steely determination in Cassie's eyes didn't falter. "I have every legal right. If you doubt it, you can see the deed I filed with the assayer."

Reynolds tried to inject a note of reason. "We don't doubt you have the paper, but there's no reason to—"

"No reason?" Cassie's voice reverberated with suppressed fury. "You call slaughtering my sheep and shooting at me and my family *no reason*?"

"Now, hold on just a minute! We didn't have nothing to do with them things!" the same burly cowhand who'd spoken before asserted.

Cassie flicked her eyes dispassionately over all of them. "Am I supposed to believe you?"

"We don't care what you believe—"

"Hold on." Once again Reynolds tried to intervene. He directed his words to Cassie. "Your uncle—"

"Didn't have a chance to dam it up again. How convenient that he was 'accidentally' killed before he could." Her words were an accusation, and Cassie was slightly satisfied by the stunned expressions on their faces. It was as though they'd taken one collective breath of disbelief and held it. As she searched each face, the telling silence lingered. Only on one face did she see a flicker of emotion other than disbelief. But Jacob Robertson quickly schooled his features to reflect no more emotion than his comrades. When her gaze returned to sweep over each in turn, she wondered if she'd imagined the difference on his face.

"Now, I suggest that you *gentlemen* get off my property."

Reynolds tried one more time. "You don't know what your uncle caused when he—"

"I know everything I need to. Now I want you to leave."

"Mighty brave words from an unarmed woman," Robertson growled.

Cassie swallowed her fear, not blinking or giving an inch.

Robertson gaited his horse backward. "We'll leave for now, but we'll be back. And when we do, we'll have the law on our side. No court's going to let a Dalton be the ruination of the territory again."

She held her silence as the group cantered away with Robertson in the lead. As Cassie watched them head north, she knew it was no coincidence that they were headed toward Shane's property.

"Damn it all to hell, Shane. We ain't gonna let her get away with this. And if you can't stop her, we will!"

Shane sighed mightily, questioning for the thousandth time how he'd gotten mixed up with the violet-eyed minx who was causing all this ruckus.

"Now, don't get riled up, boys."

"Don't get riled up . . . ?" The unanimous reaction reverberated throughout the room.

Shane held his hand up for quiet. "We'll work something out. Part of our water here at the Lazy H can be diverted until we find a permanent solution."

Muttered grumblings could be heard throughout the room at this announcement. While they welcomed his help, Shane knew they wanted him to put a stop to Cassie's threat.

Reynolds approached Michael, who was twirling a quilled fountain pen in his hand as he sat quietly behind the desk.

"What do you think about this, Michael? You're the solicitor."

"Not quite yet," Michael demurred, wishing he knew what to say to placate his lifelong friends without tossing Cassie to the wolves.

"You're the closest thing to a solicitor we have in the

territory, Michael. Can't we get some sort of court order to stop what she's doing? You know—what that lawyer from back East said we shoulda done with ol' man Dalton when he cut us off."

Michael continued to toy with the desk set, stalling for time. Given the circumstances, Michael knew it would be relatively easy to obtain a temporary restraining order preventing Cassie from damming up the water. But he also knew it wasn't a permanent solution to the problem. Feeling as he did about Cassie, Michael didn't want to be put in the position of hurting her. Even so, he knew the lifelong war between the Lancers and Daltons demanded he side with Shane and his neighbors.

Closing his conscience to his neighbors' dilemma, Michael responded without looking up. "I wouldn't know, Adam. I'm still just learning. You'd have to get yourself a full-fledged solicitor to handle this."

"But that'd mean going back East!"

"Maybe not," Shane mused, pacing the length of the long room. "You can ride to the nearest telegraph station and wire the man I use in Boston. If he can get us the restraining order, he could wire it back."

"In the meantime, you'd better do your damn best to change her mind," Jacob Robertson snarled.

"If I didn't know better, I'd think you were threatening me." Shane's voice was controlled, but a thread of steel was woven through his words.

Robertson chewed on a fingernail in an effort to control his temper. Everyone in the room knew he would depend on Shane's water until Cassie's dam came down.

"No threats, Shane. Just figured if anyone could talk her out of this damn fool plan, it's you."

"Let me do the figuring, Robertson. Too much thinking doesn't seem to agree with you." Shane turned away, but not before he saw the man's face contort angrily. Shane had more to worry about, however, than Robertson's hot temper.

It was starting all over again, but this time it wouldn't end with a Lancer licking his wounds.

Pounding hooves disturbed Cassie's reverie. Reluctantly she rose from the muddy bank and shaded her eyes against the glaring sun. The lone rider approached, and Cassie knew it was Shane. She'd been expecting him ever since the group had ridden toward his home earlier.

As he pulled up his enormous dapple-gray mount, Cassie tried to read his expression without success.

Dismounting, he strode to her side. "Well, you did it," he stated without ceremony.

"I did," she answered, equally succinct.

Shane pulled off his hat and flung it on the grass. Raking his hands through the tousled chestnut curls that framed his rugged face, he finally raised his arms upward in a shrug of disbelief.

"Why, Cassie?"

She started to answer, but he cut her off.

"I know all the reasons—but why risk your lives over this piece of dirt?"

"Oh, so now it's a piece of dirt. Is that how you feel about the Lazy H?"

"No, but that's different. I grew up on my ranch, spent all of my life there."

"But I should feel differently?"

"You weren't raised here. You weren't bred to love the land at the cost of all else."

"Maybe not, but I haven't had a home of my own to love since my parents died. That's all I've tried to do since I got here. And everyone, starting with you, has tried to stop me."

"Only for your own good."

"Well, I'm tired of you deciding what's for my own good."

"If you'd *listened,* you wouldn't be in this fix right now."

"I'm not in a fix. Your *friends* are!"

"You don't think they're just going to lay down and play dead while you cut off their lifeblood, do you?"

"What can they do?" she taunted him, her anger growing in direct proportion to his.

"You mean besides shooting you when you're all alone in the middle of nowhere?" he goaded her, gesturing to the vast, vacant range surrounding them.

Cassie refused to acknowledge the sudden burst of fear that skittered up her spine and lodged in her throat. Unconsciously, she bit down on her lip. "That would be real manly, wouldn't it?" she sneered with false bravado.

"Manly or not, it's been done," he answered, his voice suddenly quiet.

She stared at him in silence, not wanting to believe him but instinctively knowing he spoke the truth. Gazing around them, she realized with chilling clarity that he had her in just such a position. It was suddenly apparent how easy it would be for anyone with murderous intentions to do the same.

"It's time you reconsidered my offer."

Cassie jerked her face upward in disbelief. Did Shane think she could be that easily manipulated? Did he think he could warn, threaten, and bully her—and then expect her to sign away the property?

"I guess you'd like that. Then you could report to your friends you'd stopped the ferocious threat to their precious cattle and duped the spinster sheepherder all in one fell swoop." Her fury intensified until she found herself barely an arm's length away from him, shaking uncontrollably.

"What I'd like to do," he retorted, his own anger barely checked as he tried to control his rising voice, "is to save your stupid hide. Right now, I'm not certain why!"

They stood facing one another, each shaking with anger and more. Their joint knowledge of the cause of the thickening tension crackled in the air, inviting more of the same.

"You insufferable clod! I don't need you to save me. I'm not a damsel in distress and I'm just as certain you're no gentleman!"

Images of hot flesh yearning toward one goal suddenly flashed in their eyes. The suffocating cloak of unresolved desire smote the very air they breathed as each took deep, unfulfilling drags of air that did little to relieve their anxiety.

"You'd better hope I'm a gentleman," he warned in a low voice, taking a step toward her.

"Meaning?" she dared him, not retreating although she felt the heat emanating from his body as he drew even closer.

"Meaning this," he growled, grasping her arms and drawing her against him. His lips moved forcefully over hers, refusing to relinquish their hold. The unnerving invasion continued as she fought the remembered feelings of his hands covering her body, seeking her most intimate center of desire.

Then slowly he felt the unexpected surrender as she seemed to melt into his arms. And just as suddenly, he found himself under attack. Cursing, he tried to still her efforts as she kicked his booted legs and pounded furious, tiny fists against his chest. At first he thought she was just showing token resistance, but when her well-shod foot connected with his skin, he let her go to grab his injured leg.

"Damn," Shane muttered, hobbling backward.

Panting, Cassie shot him a look of triumphant fury. He'd almost done it again, she raged silently. The feel of his arms and the weakness he could unerringly create had almost done her in. But one glance at the flowing river had reinforced her strength. He probably thought he could reduce an old spinster to a whimpering state of consent with his sensual prowess, but she refused to give up that easily—even if it meant kicking him all the way to Mexico!

28

Cassie stood by the stone hearth, her feet planted firmly apart as she clenched the dreaded missive in her hand. The letter had been solicitous, but the stark finality of the action played through her mind. And enclosed was the restraining order her determined neighbors had obtained, legally banning her from withholding the water. She started to ball up the offending document, but instead she clutched it in her fist and strode out the door to the barn. Quickly, she saddled her mare and led the horse into the yard.

Concentrating on the source of her fury, Cassie mounted the animal and tore out of her pasture toward the connecting land to the north. She purposely ignored the niggling reminder that Shane had warned her the court would grant the restraining order. He'd told her he didn't expect her to win and that he hoped she wouldn't. She rode harder and faster now.

When Cassie finally reached Shane's sprawling ranch house, the horse was winded and her fury had doubled. Mindless of propriety, she pounded on the heavy oak door. Fuming, she paced the wide veranda. Not getting an answer, Cassie flung open the door and barged into the entryway. Looking from left to right, she discovered to her increasing fury that the house appeared empty. Undaunted, she strode forward and found herself in a study. Backing out, Cassie tried to determine where the parlor would be. The T-shaped hallway led in three directions. Pausing only for a moment,

Cassie stomped down one hallway.

She opened several doors down the passageway, finding only empty rooms. Frustrated, Cassie continued her search. Finding the rest of the downstairs empty, she ran quickly up the stairs, looking from left to right down a long hallway. Instinctively she turned right.

As she reached the end of the hallway, Cassie thought she heard humming. Pausing in front of the door, she cocked her ear. It *was* humming—and it sounded like Shane. She pounded impatiently on the door and heard him answer, "Come in."

Entering through the door and stalking rapidly inside, Cassie began talking. "I know you're behind this and don't deny it! I . . ." Her voice trailed off, realizing what she'd intruded upon.

Shane's gloriously naked body was submerged in a tub of sparkling water and nothing else. At first, his face registered shock. Then amusement replaced the shock as his lips curled up wickedly.

"I can guess what I'm supposed to deny, but you'll have to excuse me if I don't rise to the occasion. After all, I told you that you wouldn't win."

His amused tone threw Cassie off guard. She didn't know whether to be more mortified because she'd intruded on his bath or because she couldn't seem to tear her eyes from the magnificent picture he made. Regardless of what they'd shared, this vaulted her beyond every boundary of propriety.

"I, I . . ." Words failed her, and to her increasing embarrassment, that just seemed to amuse Shane even more.

"I guess it's not proper for me to remain seated while in the presence of a lady."

Cassie watched in fascination as he prepared to rise from the tub. When it became apparent that he was going to carry out his intention, reason penetrated her numbed senses. "You, you . . ."

Before Cassie could move, Shane rose from the tub, shaking the water from his body like a great beast. As her throat suddenly went dry, she remained still while his arms pulled her close. Feeling the moisture from his body penetrate the cotton fabric of her work shirt, Cassie sucked in her breath.

Pulling her against the undeniable evidence of his desire, she found herself arching toward him instead of backing away. When his hands cupped her bottom, molding her to him, she felt the moisture from his hands dampen her pantalets and sear her skin.

With a few easy movements, Shane unbuttoned her work shirt and unlaced the camisole. Her breasts peaked at their sudden exposure to his roaming hands. Just as abruptly, those same hands left her aching nipples, tugging impatiently at the fastenings of her breeches. Pulling them open and then peeling them off along with her pantalets, Shane grasped her close, setting her throbbing flesh over his leg. Rubbing her against the length of his muscled thigh, Cassie called out his name, begging for release. Shane lifted her, placing her on his shaft.

Gasping, Cassie slid toward him, unable to believe her actions, unable to believe the sensations Shane was creating.

Thought deserted her as she wrapped her legs around him, instinctively holding on to him for support. Lowering his head, Shane nipped at one breast, never stopping the long, piercing strokes.

Her breath coming shorter, Cassie recognized the weakness in her limbs, the drug of passion that coursed through her body.

Panting, Cassie ran her hands frantically over Shane's body, reveling in the hard muscles beneath her fingers, the soft pelt of fur covering his chest. His strokes deepened, as though he were searching for her very soul, and Cassie arched her back, unable to still the sudden cry that rose to her lips.

Shuddering, she felt Shane reach his climax. Half gasping, half panting, they drew back. Staring at one another in astonishment and incredible satiation, neither spoke.

Gently, Shane lifted her down, setting her on the chair that held his fresh denims and shirt. Breathing in shallow spurts, they continued to stare at one another without speaking. Cassie glanced at her clothing strewn about the floor, unable to believe the coupling—like that of animals in season—and unable to believe she'd wanted the sudden passion as much as Shane, savoring every moment so much she still felt a throbbing of desire.

Finally pulling her eyes away from him, Cassie glanced down at the floor and spotted the restraining order she'd ridden over to show Shane.

Sudden shame filled her. Lust for Shane had driven away all thoughts of her family's welfare. Angrily, she reached for her clothes and dressed hurriedly, fastening her breeches and buttoning her shirt with trembling fingers.

Shane's voice was tentative. "Cassie . . ."

"I'll speak to you in your parlor," she answered stiffly. He made a move to follow her. "After you're dressed," she finished icily.

Stalking from the room, Cassie moved ahead blindly. Tearing down the stairs, she reached the parlor, pacing the suddenly confining room. At the sound of Shane's approaching footsteps, Cassie froze, then slowly turned in the direction of the sound, mesmerized by the sight of him padding forward, barefoot, dressed only in his form-fitting denims and the rough cambric work shirt that hung open to the waist. She found she couldn't tear her eyes away from the chestnut hairs that swirled in a beguiling fashion from his muscled chest to the lean tapering . . .

Her response to him was automatic, and her wayward body tingled in anticipation. Turning her back on him, she hoped he would fasten the buttons on his shirt before she capitulated and threw herself at him again.

"Cassie?" Slowly she turned about, unwilling to meet his eyes. "Is this what you came to show me?" A glance at his outstretched hand showed the crumpled paper she'd planned to confront him with, which she'd apparently forgotten in her headlong flight from his room.

Cassie salvaged a bit of her pride when she remembered her original mission. "You know it is," she challenged, still not fully meeting his amused glance.

"Ah, Cassie," he sighed, raking his freshly washed hair with one hand, while further crumpling the paper in the other.

Cassie tried not to notice the droplets of moisture still clinging to the sheen of his chestnut hair. It was too easy to remember those same droplets trailing a path down his muscled torso, rivulets that caressed . . . She mentally shook herself, wishing she had a bucket of cold water with which to douse herself.

"Do you deny your part in getting the restraining order?" she demanded.

"I told you it was a fool idea and you'd be stopped."

"I suppose you had no part in it?"

"Not directly."

"Not directly! Your solicitor's signature is on the bottom of this order."

He merely shrugged his shoulders in response.

"It's certainly convenient to have a crooked solicitor on the payroll, isn't it?"

"Now that you mention it, I guess it is, especially when I have a damn fool neighbor who wants to run everyone else off the range."

Since he had drawn himself up to his full height, Cassie found that she had to tip her head back to meet his blazing look. But confront him she did. Face to face, eye to eye, breath to breath.

"Grand words from the man who wanted to run me off the range before I ever got here!"

The gauntlet was thrown, the challenge too provocative to ignore. "Maybe it would've been a hell of a lot better if I'd succeeded. I wouldn't be standing here arguing with you now . . ."

He wished they'd never met? Her face blanched at his unexpected verbal assault. While she'd mentally reminded herself at each of their encounters that his only interest was her land, to have it thrown in her face after their lovemaking was more painful than she'd realized. Her own pain was too great to see the remorse that shadowed Shane's face as soon as he'd issued the hateful words.

Cassie's huge violet eyes seemed to deepen with pain as she met his glance.

"Perhaps it would have."

Without further words she bolted from the room. Cassie scarcely heard him as he called her name and tried to run after her. Mounting her horse, she tore away before Shane could even begin to find his boots. And long after Cassie had ridden off, he stood on the wide veranda, cursing his ill-suited choice of words and kicking his bootless feet against the undeserving veranda pillars.

29

Millicent carelessly scattered feed around the yard as the worrisome chickens pecked and squawked at the hard dirt. Her mind wasn't on chores; she was thinking of Ringer and their last time together. She shivered, remembering the feelings he'd aroused. She wondered what the culmination of those feelings would have been had he not let reason intervene and stopped before they crossed that special line.

She'd lain awake at night, remembering the intensity of his eyes, the incredible feeling of his hands on her aching flesh. Millicent felt no shame, only a burning need to resolve her frustrations. Remembering Ringer's blazing eyes, she knew he was feeling a similar measure of slow torture. But, he told her, he respected her far too much to dally with her in the field. She was beginning to think that respect was greatly overrated.

Millicent glanced upward beyond the chicken yard, and a sudden frown marred her face. Cassie was crossing into the barn, her steps leaden, her face downcast. Ever since the letter from the lawyer had come, Cassie hadn't been herself. Millicent could hardly believe that Cassie had expected to win the first round so easily. No, it must be something else. But Cassie had remained stubbornly silent. Whatever was bothering her was buried too deep to be easily solved.

Millicent put the chicken feed away and pulled off her apron. She was determined to take her friend's mind off her problems, whether Cassie liked it or not.

* * *

As they pulled up to the mercantile, Cassie noticed a growing crowd gathering in the street. Plucking Millicent's sleeve to get her attention, Cassie pointed down the street. "What do you suppose that's all about?"

Millicent stared at the increasingly rowdy crowd. Cassie stood up in the box of their wagon, trying to see over the heads of the crowd. Perplexed, she turned to Millicent. "It looks like just an ordinary family."

Cassie and Millicent climbed down from their wagon and moved forward to the wooden boardwalk. Cassie, unable to conceal her curiosity, turned to one of the ladies nearby who was also trying to see past the crowd.

"Excuse me, but can you tell me what all the fuss is about?"

"Homesteaders," the woman replied briefly, obviously still trying to peer over the broad shoulders of the man in front of her.

"What does that mean?" Cassie persisted.

"They're farmers, putting claim on the range."

"But why is everyone so angry?"

The woman finally turned her full attention to Cassie. "Because they build fences!" This was said in a tone implying that Cassie was painfully ignorant and that fences were an abomination.

"Oh," Cassie murmured, automatically sympathizing with the luckless homesteaders as one underdog to another. "You mean everyone's that angry over fences?"

The woman swept a contemptuous glance over Cassie's calico-clad figure. "I'll say so. I can't think of anything that'd make a cattle rancher angrier—except maybe a Dalton."

Cassie smiled at the gleaming new fence posts with pride. Sunlight glinted off the twisting strands of barbed wire, providing her with a deep sense of satisfaction. She ignored the bothersome reminder that perhaps she was acting out of revenge—and anger at being spurned and made to feel like the spinster she was. Instead, she told herself, the fences were for her family's much-needed protection.

Ignoring her annoyingly active conscience, Cassie walked the newly blatant property line between her spread and Shane's. As though the fence posts had put out a silent beckoning call of their own, Cassie spotted the rising dust of an approaching rider. With little more than a shadowy outline in the distance, Cassie could almost guarantee who the rider would be. With a small sigh of reluctance, she squared her shoulders, preparing to meet his resistance.

Shane rode his horse dangerously close to where she stood. Unnerved, Cassie stepped back as Shane abruptly dismounted, closed the small space between them, and took her shoulders in a furious grasp.

"What the hell do you think you're doing?" His voice was low and unmistakably angry.

Cassie swallowed a suddenly large lump in her throat, trying to sound calmer than she felt. "Isn't it obvious?"

"More obvious than you realize, lady. Trying to start one war over the water wasn't enough for you. Now you've gone and put up *fences*!"

She forced herself to sound confident. "They'll keep my sheep in, and your cattle—"

"You're not fooling me for a minute, Cassandra Dalton." Cassie's head jerked upward at the use of her full name. He'd never seemed so angry before. "You're waving a red flag in front of a herd of bulls, and you damn well know it."

"I know no such thing! I'm protecting my property the only way I know how. I have every right—"

"Every right to get yourself ambushed for being such a dim-witted fool, you mean. You're not putting up protection—you're issuing an invitation to battle. I want you to tear down these fences now, Cassie." His voice softened almost imperceptibly. "For your own sake."

"And what if I refuse?"

His words hardened into shards of iron. "Then *I'll* tear them down." Just as abruptly as he'd grabbed her, Shane released his hold, leaving her swaying momentarily without his support. Dazed, she stared after him as he mounted his great sorrel. As she continued to stare, he gaited the horse backward, looking deeply into her upturned face.

"Remember, Cassie, I meant what I said."

He turned to leave, his grim words slapping backward into the mocking wind that rocked about her.

As dusk melted into darkness, Cassie rode to the barn and slowly dismounted. She noted that Ringer's horse was hitched to the rail near the front porch. *At least one of us has a gentleman caller,* she thought dispiritedly. The intensity of Shane's feelings had shaken her more than she'd thought they would. She'd meant to anger him, hoped he'd feel a fraction of the hurt she did but still she had been unprepared for his reaction.

With leaden feet she forced herself to the front door and tried to summon a cheerful face for Millicent and Ringer. One look at their serious faces told her the pretense was unneeded.

Ringer scarcely let her enter the room before he advanced on her. "I've met my share of fool-headed, stubborn women in my day, but you beat all, Miss Cassie."

Cassie opened her mouth to answer, but he didn't allow her time to interrupt.

"What could you be thinking? Putting up fences on *cattle land*!"

"Now, wait—"

"No, *you* wait. You gotta know you're fixing to start up a nasty war—and you're planning to put Milly and your brother right in the middle of it."

"I think you ought to let Millicent speak for herself."

Millicent's face mirrored her determination. "All right, I will. I told you before you put up the fences that it was foolish and I'll tell you again now: I think you're crazy for defying the entire countryside."

Cassie's face fell as Millicent echoed Shane's and Ringer's sentiments. Would no one stand loyally beside her?

Cassie's voice was heavy as she replied, "So, you've decided to stand against me too."

Millicent moved closer, her body a study of earnest persuasion. "No one's against you, Cass. We just don't want to see you or Andrew hurt."

Ringer clasped an arm about Millicent. "Or you, Milly."

Cassie watched painfully as the two gazed at one another, their love obvious and requited. It made the gaping ache in her heart seem to throb even more intensely. Was this to be her destiny—watching others fall in love and be happy while she garnered more enemies than one person need ever have?

Slowly she turned away from them, stepping quietly to the door and easing onto the porch. She doubted that Millicent and Ringer even missed her presence.

Automatically her eyes picked out the constellations she'd learned as a child. Somehow, with the vast inky darkness cloaking the seemingly endless land, the sky seemed larger and more encompassing than it ever had in Boston.

An unwelcome chill of loneliness chased up her spine, settling uncomfortably in the already aching region of her heart. How she missed Shane's strength. She had felt headstrong and brave when first confronting him, but now . . . With both Millicent and Ringer solidly lined up against her, she didn't feel nearly so brave, nor as certain she was right. She couldn't fence her entire property, and when Andrew and Manuelo had to shift the flock to a different grazing pasture, the fences would be for naught. Solitary reminders of a futile gesture.

Cassie leaned her cheek against the cool, splintered wood of the porch column. She gazed into the stars that seemed to dip in her direction and beckon in an unspoken plea, as though even the stars wanted to retain their hold over the vast, unfettered land.

All right, all right! I can't fight everyone. Cassie smiled sardonically as the stars seemed to brighten in the shrouded night.

Cassie laid down her breakfast napkin and pushed away from the table, determined to set things right and not let the gloom of the previous evening cloud her day. But still a picture of Shane's face flashed through her mind, reminding her of what she now missed.

Pausing on the front porch, she allowed herself a moment to appreciate the undisturbed beauty of the cloudless azure sky. Absently she wondered why Star wasn't nipping at her feet. She checked on the ewes in the pen and, satisfied, turned to check the shed. Seeing Millicent cross the yard with a basket of laundry, Cassie waved and sent her a large grin. Taken aback, Milly waved weakly and answered with a smile that showed her obvious surprise.

Cassie continued her early-morning inspection, thinking wryly of the still gleaming fence posts that would have to be torn down. Feeling a moment of shame, Cassie realized the only true intention behind building the fences. She had wanted to hurt Shane in the same measure as he had hurt her. Instead she had divided family and friends into enemy camps. And, Cassie realized sadly, fences were no defense against Shane's rejection. She and Shane were oil and water, and nothing would change that. Certainly not fences.

But even as her mind tried to overrule her heart, she found herself wavering. Thinking of Shane, Cassie found herself missing the strangest things. Like his eyes—the way they crinkled at the corners from years of laughter and countless days in the searing sun—and his winsome smile, the way it touched her heart with its enduring charm.

Shaking her head as though she could force such thoughts out of her mind, Cassie continued her rounds. The nip in the air reminded her that summer with its burning heat was now past. Autumn had arrived. The trees near the timber line were changing with each passing day. It seemed the seasons of her life were changing just as rapidly.

Cassie neared the shearing shed and paused as she saw what seemed to be the outline of a dog. Hesitantly she moved forward. The white shape was so terribly still. Forcing down her fear, Cassie ran forward and dropped to her knees in front of the shed. The shape was definitely canine. Oh, God, it was Star!

She gathered him in her arms. Tears ran unchecked down her cheeks as she pressed his still-warm body close. The memory of Shane bringing him home as a cuddly, wiggling puppy was painfully fresh. How could anyone kill a defenseless animal? Unaware of the keening sound she made, Cassie rocked him back and forth in her arms.

The eerie noise brought Millicent on the run. Startled, she stopped when she saw Cassie holding the dog. She approached slowly and cocked her head.

"Cassie." Cassie ignored her. Millicent listened again and grasped her shoulder. "I think I hear him, Cass. Do hush now so we can listen."

She stared at Millicent in disbelief, but quieted. At first she didn't hear anything, but then a low whine seemed to come from deep within Star's throat.

"Do you think . . . ?" Cassie couldn't complete the question.

Millicent knelt down and ran her hands gently over the dog's still body. Finally she muttered, "No wounds. Where are the bottles you used to feed that last lamb?"

"Why?"

"Just tell me, Cassie."

Cassie was torn but pointed toward the barn. "On the shelf over the shearing shed."

"I'll be right back." Millicent spoke quickly, already turning away.

"What are you going to do?"

"Just stay with him, Cass. I'll be right back."

Millicent disappeared into the house, and Cassie continued to cradle his head in her lap. Watching her dog, every memory she'd shared with Shane played through her mind. The dances, the picnics, and inevitably the lovemaking.

Suddenly she wondered how important being right had been. Shane had given her the puppy to make a new start. She'd started fresh, all right. She had started one fight over the water and one over the fences, just as Shane had accused her. And what had she won? She had infuriated Shane, alienated Millicent and Ringer, endangered Andrew, and now had probably killed an innocent dog.

"You've got to make it, Star. You're part of my bright and shining future." The futility of her words rang in the stillness of the barnyard.

Sniffing, Cassie lifted her head and saw Millicent scurrying—no—running toward her. The sight of prim Millicent running almost made her smile. But she didn't have any more smiles left. Millicent reached them and knelt on the ground beside the inert dog.

"This isn't going to be pleasant," Millicent warned.

Cassie strained closer to see what Millicent had put in the bottle. As she drew nearer, the dreadful smell of the mixture made her draw back. "What in the world . . ."

"You don't want to know."

Cassie gasped in alarm, and Millicent held up a protesting hand. "Just keep his mouth open while I get this down."

Stilling her protests, Cassie gently eased Star's mouth open. Millicent grasped the bottle with determination and started a slow trickle of the mixture into Star's mouth. Cassie massaged the dog's throat hoping to ease the vile concoction down. Star gasped and made a weak effort to keep the gruesome stuff out of his mouth, but Cassie and Millicent were determined. After almost half of the bottle was forced down his throat, Star heaved convulsively.

"He's throwing it all up!" Cassie cried.

"That's the idea," Millicent replied grimly.

An hour later, after forcing the remaining mixture into the dog and having it all come back up again, Star seemed to be resting easier.

"Do you think he'll make it, Milly?"

"It's hard to say. All of the poison should be out of his stomach. But I don't know how much of it got into the rest of his system."

"Do you think it would hurt to move him?"

"Probably not. Why don't we put him in front of the hearth?"

"I'll get some blankets, and we can make a litter to carry him in."

Hours later, as the shadows turned afternoon into dusk, Cassie paced the confines of the keeping room. She had neglected all of her chores to sit by Star, but now she feared the vigil wasn't doing much good. He was lying so still, too still.

A loud knock disturbed Cassie's grim thoughts, but she didn't move toward the door until the firm knock penetrated the stillness of the room again. Cassie hesitated. She didn't want to face anyone right now. Her mind whirled with confusing waves of anger, resentment, and despair—and she'd had little luck sorting out any of the feelings.

The knock sounded louder this time. With a sigh of resignation, Cassie reluctantly opened the door. The sight of Shane standing at her doorway left her speechless.

"Can I come in?"

Wordlessly Cassie opened the door wider as Shane entered. Raising questioning eyes to Shane, her unspoken entreaty was eloquently voiced.

"Millicent told me." Uttering that brief explanation, Shane tossed his hat on the nearest chair and walked over to the hearth, kneeling by Star. Gently running his hands over the dog's form, he paused near the abdomen.

"No bloating—that's a good sign." Cassie heard this and released her indrawn breath. Shane didn't turn around. "You could have told me, Cassie."

She blinked her eyes furiously at the sudden prickling of tears that threatened to fall. His unexpected sympathy might be more than she could bear. "I didn't think you'd want to be bothered."

Shane whirled around. "Not bothered? How can you even think such a thing?"

"It wasn't too difficult." Cassie's eyes glistened, and her lips trembled with suppressed emotion. Her teeth tugged at her bottom lip in an unconscious gesture.

Shane's long strides closed the distance between them. In a none too gentle embrace, Shane pulled her close.

"I don't know which I want to do more—shake some sense into you or kiss you senseless." Bending his lips close to hers, he made his choice.

Cassie sank into his arms as though coming home from a long and weary journey. It felt so right being held by him. Just as she felt her body lifting heavenward, Shane jolted her back down to earth.

"When are you going to stop trying to do everything for yourself and admit you need some help?"

She felt the warmth of her cocoon evaporate in a cloudless puff. "I wouldn't need help so often if I didn't have to battle the entire countryside."

"I believe I already made that point yesterday, Cass."

So he had.

"The funny part is"—Cassie's voice cracked, and she forced the strength back into it—"I'd just about decided the fences were useless. I was ready to back down."

"But nobody gave you a chance to make your decision." Shane ignored the part of him that told him to push his advantage while her defenses were down and instead gently stroked her back, brushing aside the hair that wisped around her face.

"Oh, Shane, how could anyone do such a thing? It's not as though Star was any threat to them."

"Star wasn't the point. It was the fences."

"And by putting them up I've killed him." Cassie lowered her head in defeat.

"Not so fast. He's not dead. He's mighty weak, but you can't give up on him."

"You really think he might have a chance?"

"He's got you to believe in him, doesn't he?"

Cassie nodded her head in mute agreement, and Shane tipped her chin upward, seeming to search her fathomless eyes. "I can't think of any better reason for him to get well."

Cassie lowered her lashes to hide her thoughts, but not before she saw the hunger in Shane's face. She wished water and fences had never come between them; but if they hadn't, she would probably still be in Boston instead of in the circle of his arms. And suddenly that didn't bear thinking of.

30

The explosion shattered the stillness, sending rock and debris into the air and the swirling waters of the now flowing river. Cassie watched the dam, which they'd labored so hard to erect, fall in seconds. The sheriff couldn't hide his gloating look of victory as he released the handle of the dynamite charger. Cassie still held the sheriff's court order in her hand, the one Shane's solicitor had sent to him.

Since the solicitor's first restraining order had come after she'd built the dam, they'd gotten a second order, this one commanding that the proper legal authority dismantle the dam. And the sheriff hadn't let any grass grow beneath his feet. He'd been at her house early that morning, surrounded by a group of equally smug ranchers. Jacob Robertson headed the gloating pack, his face a sneer of triumph. She'd read and digested the contents of the order and asked, "When do you plan to carry this out, Sheriff?"

"Now." His answer conveyed the importance he felt at being able to humble her.

"This order doesn't say anything about allowing all these people on my land, does it?"

The sheriff lifted his hat and scratched at the scraggly hair beneath its brim. "Well, now, I don't guess—"

"Then, as an officer of the law, I suggest you order them to leave before I charge them with trespassing."

Her neighbors' gloating faces turned resentful when the sheriff reluctantly agreed with her. But now as she stood watching the dam wash away, she didn't know if it mattered that her loss hadn't been witnessed by half the countryside.

She'd lost her bargaining card, and her family's lives were still in danger. The barely healed wound in Andrew's leg was a permanent reminder of the precariousness of their situation, and she had brought them into this mess. Her head filled with dreams of a new life, she had blindly led them into a deathtrap. That it wasn't of her own making was little comfort.

With a heavy heart, she turned and headed home, knowing that a worried Millicent would be waiting with hot tea and a thousand questions. As Cassie pulled into the yard and dismounted, she saw an unfamiliar horse tied to the hitching rail. Just what she needed, company. The last thing she wanted to do was face anyone.

She sighed deeply, resigned to putting on a confident air. Cassie didn't dare let her neighbors realize the defeat she felt. If they knew how close she was to giving up, they'd push that much harder.

Opening the door, she was surprised to see Karl Fredericks seated on the settee, sipping tea with Millicent. He rose when she came in, instantly reminding her of the breeches she wore. One hand flew to her windblown hair, trying to smooth the unruly locks. His cool elegance made her feel ridiculously ill at ease in her own home.

She took the tea Millicent offered and perched self-consciously on the chair opposite him.

"Miss Millicent was kind enough to offer me some refreshment while I waited for you. I do hope I haven't come at an inconvenient time." Fredericks's suave voice held the hint of a question combined with a knowing tone.

She demurred, sipping her tea and wishing he'd come to the point. He didn't disappoint her.

"I heard about the unfortunate business this morning," he began.

"You and the rest of Texas."

Her irony wasn't lost on him as he uttered a mirthless laugh. "Once again, my dear, the small-town mentality has struck. But I've come to assure you what happened this morning has no effect on my offer to you. I'd still like to purchase a parcel of your land. After what's happened this morning, you can see the land will be of little worth to you."

Cassie couldn't help feeling he was hiding something from her. "And why would you want to buy a worthless parcel of land, Mr. Fredericks?"

"As I said before, I'd like to help with your cash position." His eyes were lit with a familiar gleam of interest, and Cassie squirmed uncomfortably under the scrutiny. "I don't believe your uncle was given a fair deal." He shrugged his shoulders in a characteristically elegant gesture. "I wouldn't want the same thing to happen to you."

His words about Uncle Luke gave her pause. Fredericks was the first person to suggest her uncle might not be the villain Shane and his friends had depicted.

"Did you know my uncle very well?"

"To my regret, I can't say that I did. I wish now that I had. Perhaps . . ." Again he shrugged his shoulders.

"Perhaps what, Mr. Fredericks?"

"Nothing, my dear." He sipped his tea, but the seed of doubt was planted in Cassie's mind. Perhaps if her uncle had sold out he'd still be alive.

"I'll double my offer, Cassie. As a gentleman, I couldn't bear to think that you and Miss Millicent might come to harm because of a few dollars."

A few dollars! The amount he was talking about would insure winter feed and quite a surplus. But stubbornly, she refused to sell, sensing the land held the key to her uncle's death.

"Right now I don't plan to sell." Cassie saw the quick hardening of his features before he relaxed them into a smile. "But I'll let you know if I do decide to sell."

"That's all I can ask." Fredericks's voice was controlled, but Cassie detected a trace of the anger he tried to conceal.

The women watched as he rode away. "I don't know about that one," Millicent observed.

Cassie murmured in agreement, while turning his words over in her head. Perhaps. Perhaps what? Perhaps her uncle wouldn't have been killed? The suspicion that had never left her reared again as she watched Fredericks disappear over the mesa. Would she and Andrew join their uncle if she refused to give in?

31

Cassie's stomach churned in agitation as she approached the barn; she knew that what she was about to do would affect a great many lives. And one of those people might never forgive her.

When the idea had sprung to mind, she'd dismissed it as outrageous, impossible—but now it seemed to be her only option. Cassie told herself why she couldn't do this, why it wouldn't work. That the hate she'd stir up would only counterbalance what she hoped to gain. But still, as her mind turned over the limited options at hand, Cassie knew she had no choice.

She wiped sweaty hands against her trousers, knowing she was about to place all of her eggs in one basket. If Michael refused to help and then told Shane about her plan, all would be lost before it began.

Michael's face was just as confused as Cassie had imagined it might be as she outlined her idea. Having stayed up all night thinking, she knew there was only one person to turn to. Her funds were too depleted to hire a lawyer back East, and Michael was the only solicitor—or near solicitor—she knew.

"A stay countermanding their order?" Michael questioned, hunkering down near the horse as he examined the swollen tendon of the mare.

"I don't know if that's what it's called, but I want a legal document saying they didn't have the right to blow up the dam and that I have the right to do what I want with my water."

"I don't know whether it can be done," Michael answered, stalling as he picked up the mare's hoof and examined it.

"Of course it can. Otherwise, how did my uncle manage to dam up the water before?"

He glanced up in surprise. "You know about that?"

"Not all the details," she admitted, "but I know what he did caused a lot of people to lose their stock."

Michael rolled his eyes heavenward as though seeking help. "That's not the tip of what happened. Cassie, don't you see what you're asking me to do? Turn my back on my friends and family—sell them out."

"I don't have any choice. Without the law on my side, I'm defenseless. They've tried to ambush my entire family, Michael," she implored, kneeling gracefully beside him, knowing the movement enhanced her delicate beauty.

Michael saw the vulnerability in her face and was lost. He'd been lost the first time he'd gazed into those violet eyes, but only now he realized he wanted to capture them for his own. Years of trust and loyalty Michael had built with Shane rushed out to confront him. It was a hell of a way to repay that trust. His gut wrenched in two as he started to protest.

Cassie swallowed her guilt and reached out a hand to touch his cheek. "You're the only one who can help me, Michael," she said, turning the full force of her magnetic gaze on him, promises implicit in her eyes.

He stood up slowly, judging his options. Could he betray a lifetime of trust to help her? He thought of the years of unqualified love and devotion Shane had shown him. He paused, gazing into Cassie's eyes as she turned them toward him, beseeching, promising. . . . He swallowed, wondering if he could live with his choice.

"If I agree . . ."

"Oh, Michael, thank you." Guessing correctly that she had played on his need by giving him the wrong impression, Cassie still knew she'd had no other choice. Knowing she was blatantly using his crush as a weapon made her slightly sick. But she desperately believed the end would justify the means.

Michael turned back to the horse, trying to recover his composure, wondering how he'd live with the consequences of what he planned to do. He could envision his friends' anger and, more importantly, Shane's disappointment. He turned back to her, to tell her he'd changed his mind.

"But, Cassie . . ."

As though sensing his withdrawal, she placed her small hand in his, sending tingling bursts of fire through him.

"Michael, I knew I could count on you." She halted, swallowed, and then forced out the rest of her speech. "I know you're worried about what Shane will think, but this won't affect the Lazy H. It won't affect anyone if they leave me alone. I won't cut them off unless they try to hurt us. But I need that leverage." She smiled at him seductively. "And I need you, Michael." Her voice softened. "Thank you so much."

He didn't hear her thanks; only the words "I need you" reverberated through his consciousness.

"How long do you think this should take, Michael?"

"I can get the briefs ready and ride to the telegraph station. I'll wire my professor and get his help. Shouldn't take too long."

"You're a godsend, Michael." She stood on tiptoe and brushed a soft kiss across his cheek. She started to turn away when she saw the raw hunger etched across his face, but he reached for her before she could act.

Feeling his strong arms pulling her close, Cassie felt a moment of panic and wanted to flail away. Remembering the urgency of her mission, she willed her body to remain pliant, accepting his embrace. When his lips found hers, she tried to pull away, but he was insistent. In a horrifyingly detached manner, she realized how alike these brothers were, yet so incredibly different. Breathless, when he finally released her, she felt a guilt so enormous it threatened to destroy her. She only hoped her actions had been worth the deceit.

32

Cassie rechecked her ledger entries for the third time. Even with the sale of the fleece, they were still in the red. Star's moist nose nuzzled her hand, and she dropped the offending list of figures, patting the dog's head. Cassie was so glad he'd recovered that she didn't mind the interruption. Sighing aloud, she was thankful Millicent was in town; her friend worried so when Cassie worked on the books.

Cassie had spent the last three weeks waiting for the order from Michael's professor in Philadelphia—long, frustrating weeks while Shane was gone on a cattle drive. She had dreamed of the kisses and caresses they'd exchanged the night before he left.

Cassie tried to suppress her guilt, knowing how Shane would react once she obtained the order, especially when he found out she'd enlisted Michael's aid to do so. She only hoped he would never discover the method she'd used to get Michael's help. She flushed with guilt, shame washing over her.

Cassie remembered how furious she'd been with Shane before Star's poisoning, but his uncharacteristic show of concern had wiped away any trace of anger she'd felt. He had let the past lie and had comforted her, made her feel safe. And now she felt an undefinable longing, something she couldn't identify, but it stalked her thoughts and controlled her dreams.

If she closed her eyes, she could feel the roughened texture of Shane's skin as his hard fingers gently skimmed her cheeks, and the warmth of his lips against . . . No! She had to stop or she'd drive herself completely crazy. As it was, the room had suddenly become confining and unbearably warm. She had to have some fresh air.

With a start of impatience, Cassie erupted from the chair and almost ran across the room, flinging open the heavy wooden door.

She didn't know who was more startled. But Shane didn't waste any time finding out. He pulled her close before she could speak. After a long, hungry kiss he backed away slightly.

"Now, *that's* the way a man wants to be greeted when he comes home from a month on the trail."

Cassie wanted to simply melt into his arms, but her irrepressible sauciness surfaced. "How do you know I was expecting you?"

Shane's face was a comical display of mixed surprise, disappointment, and finally dawning awareness. He tweaked her nose in reply. "So, this is how you greet everybody who comes to your door, eh? I'll have to send Cookie over. I think he's been sweet on you since the day you got here."

She cocked her head in consideration. "Hmm. He's not bad-looking. He *is* an eligible bachelor—and he does have a steady job."

"But at his age, your sassy tongue would give him a heart attack."

"Says you."

"Says me. But I could think of worse ways to die." He glanced around. "Where's Millicent?"

"In town."

"Andrew?"

"In the north pasture."

"Um." His voice lowered, and he paused, loosening the pins that held her hair in an orderly chignon. As her midnight-black hair fell loose, Shane buried his hands in the shining waves. "I've dreamed of doing this for weeks," he murmured. Cassie studied his face, her breath taken away as one callused thumb swept the length of her cheek, just as she'd dreamed of.

"And this," he continued, bending down to taste her lips. Cassie's eyelids closed as her body swayed to meet his. All of her well-rehearsed plans to distance herself from him melted away. She forgot about her deception with Michael—the hurt and anger Shane would feel when he found out. No longer was she a Dalton and he a Lancer. In his arms, she was simply a woman, and he was very much a man. For now that was enough.

Shane drank from Cassie's well of sweetness, feeling he could never quench his thirst for her. She was like a wild summer rose, all prickly thorns on the outside and velvet on the inside. In his arms she unfolded like winsome petals dropping in the late-afternoon sun. Just as he'd hoped she would—just as he'd imagined she would these long, lonely weeks.

He'd missed her biting wit, remembered her hidden softness, and ached for the kisses she now gave freely. On the trail he had told himself a thousand times that he would return to his senses when he got back. No more hankering after a Dalton, no more promises pushed to the background. But even as he cursed himself, he had guided the horse to her door. Just one last time, one last taste.

His head told him to turn back, to give her the speech he'd practiced out on the trail. To tell her he had used her to try to get back the land, and that she could never mean anything to him. But as her lips gently touched his, all words, all thought was lost, and the bittersweet corner of his heart ripped even further apart.

Shane lowered them softly to the soft rug in front of the hearth. With aching slowness, he traced the contours of her face as though memorizing every detail, etching them forever in his heart.

Sighing sweetly, Cassie returned his quiet caresses. He felt the gentle tug of her small hands as her fingers slipped through his hair and over his shoulders. She seemed able to find each aching muscle, each tired, sore spot. He relaxed under her ministrations, willing her to continue.

When the buttons of his shirt slipped free, Shane pulled her closer, returning the favor. When their bare skin touched, it heated with the same slow, burning intensity their souls craved.

Yet Shane's movements were patient, controlled. Cassie sighed in satisfaction as Shane's fingers skimmed over her skin. His languorous movements mesmerized her, her limbs suddenly weightless, her skin an instrument for him to play.

And play he did as he offered her each deliberate stroke, each whisper-light kiss. When Cassie thought she could bear no more, her eyes met his. The unspoken emotions she beheld made her breath catch, her heart stop.

Still, no words were uttered as he cupped her face tenderly in his hands. But when he finally claimed her, she knew with certainty that she was his in more than body. Her soul was tagged—and the branding iron bore the Lancer mark.

33

The bell over the door tinkled out a welcome as Cassie and Millicent entered the apothecary shop. Silas Jenkins, the nearsighted proprietor, greeted them in his usual absentminded manner. Millicent took her list to the counter, while Cassie dawdled over the musty bottles.

Looking at the uneven rows of dust-covered merchandise covering the wall and then glancing up at Mr. Jenkins's clock, Cassie noted impatiently that the hour was growing late. She didn't want Millicent to know she was itching to go to the assayer's office to check the land records.

Millicent had been alarmed when Cassie confided that she planned to find out if her uncle's death had really been an accident. Millicent was opposed to borrowing trouble, so Cassie kept her suspicions to herself. But now she wanted to see those records.

Mr. Jenkins ducked behind the curtain that separated the front counter from his storage area, and Cassie caught Millicent's eye.

"You're bored, aren't you?" Millicent half asked, half stated.

"Well, I—"

"Do you have any other errands?"

"I did want to go by the post office," Cassie fibbed, her fingers crossed behind her. She would have to hurry and make it to the post office, too.

"I'll be here for a while if you want . . ."

Cassie didn't let her finish. "Whatever you say, Milly. I'll meet you in the mercantile."

Rushing out the door, Cassie barely let Millicent say good-bye. Millicent frowned as she watched Cassie fairly fly down the street.

An hour later, Cassie was bent over the ancient ledgers in the assayer's office hoping to find the evidence she sensed was just beyond her grasp. But the fragile dust-covered pages only revealed what she already knew. She sighed and turned another page. What she saw made her sit back in the chair in disbelief.

She read and reread the entry. According to the records, Shane's father had deeded the parcel of land from the Lazy H that now belonged to the Daltons for one dollar and other valuable considerations. Those would have to be some considerations, she thought with irony.

Why would Shane's father have given Uncle Luke a valuable parcel of land for virtually nothing if they were sworn enemies? Of course, she didn't know for certain they were enemies. But everything Shane did and didn't say pointed to that obvious conclusion.

Her nose wrinkled in distaste as the musty coating of dust from the page flew into the air. Before she could control herself, she erupted in a noisy sneeze.

"Bless you."

Cassie scrabbled for her hankie while she tried to speak. "Than . . . thank . . . Ka*choo*!" *How embarrassing.* Cassie glanced up and was mortified to see the calm and immaculately groomed Karl Fredericks.

"Allow me, madam." He produced a spotless linen handkerchief, which he offered to her.

"Oh, I couldn't. I'm sure I have my handkerchief here somewhere . . ."

"I insist. It's a very small gesture."

She reluctantly accepted the handkerchief. "Thank you. I

don't seem to be able to find my own."

He bowed from the waist, a courtly European gesture, Cassie was unaccustomed to. "May I ask what a lovely lady such as yourself is doing in a dusty office on such a nice day?"

Cassie scrambled for an answer. "Just checking to make sure all my deeds are filed properly. I was finishing up when you came in." Cassie rose and picked up her satchel. "It was nice seeing you, Mr. Fredericks, and thank you again for the loan of your handkerchief."

"Think nothing of it, my dear. Oh, and don't forget our discussion the other day." *As though she could.* "My offer still stands." Fredericks escorted her to the door and watched as she walked down the street to the mercantile.

Cassie forced her heart to stop its rapid tattoo as she strolled down the aisles of the store, looking for Millicent. The last thing she needed was to alert the town to the fact that she was investigating land records. She paused in front of a display of horse collars when a strong hand came down on her shoulder. Remembering her last encounter with Jacob Robertson, Cassie flung herself around in a startled motion, prepared for the worst.

"Ready to fly into my arms?" Shane's droll whisper reached only her ears. Convinced, now that the dam was blown, that it would only be a matter of time before she sold to him, Shane's humor had improved considerably. He had even casually left her papers to sign on one occasion, seeming to take for granted that she would acquiesce and sell the land. She had merely filed the papers away, allowing him to think for the moment that she might agree. But until she found out who killed her uncle, she didn't plan to budge.

Cassie's cheeks flamed in embarrassment and then drained to a pale hue in relief.

Shane noted the conflicting emotions skittering across her

face. He pulled her out of the aisle and into the relative privacy beneath an arbor created by bolts of material. "What is it?"

"Nothing, really. You just startled me."

His eyes searched hers, and he was less than satisfied when she lowered her lashes, masking her thoughts.

"The truth, Cass."

"I told you . . ."

"Nothing, as usual." He tipped her chin upward. "I believe we've had this conversation before." When she didn't answer, he eased his thumb over the satin of her cheek. "Or was that some other fella you attacked at your front door?" His comment finally nudged a smile from her reluctant lips.

"You do look familiar . . ."

He emitted a mock growl. "Be glad you had the right answer, lady."

"Hmm, I'm shaking like a leaf."

"That could be arranged too," he added with a devilish glint in his eyes.

"Promises, promises . . ."

"Lucky for you we're in the middle of a store, young lady."

Cassie cocked her head in consideration and caught his gaze with her own. "Lucky? Hmm, I think not."

Shane felt sudden heat blaze within him. What a time to be in such a public place. In another minute he wouldn't be able to walk out of the store. "I think we'd better look at those horse collars again."

"You're not afraid, are you?" Cassie teased, barely controlling her laughter.

Since his own control was almost gone, Shane pulled her from beneath the bolts of material and out into the crowded aisles.

"Terrified."

34

Cassie batted away an insistent fly as she and Sarah pored over a well-marked map.

"I don't have any idea, Cassie," Sarah replied, pushing the map across the table. "All I can tell is that it's a map of our area."

Cassie sighed. She had hoped Sarah would have a clue to the mystery she wanted to unlock. Cassie had spent a number of sleepless nights pondering why Shane's father had deeded the land to her uncle, but she still drew a blank. She knew asking Shane would be like setting a match to dry brush and watching it blaze.

"I'm really sorry." Sarah hesitated, questioning how much to tell her. Resurrecting the past wouldn't help Cassie. If anything, it would only harm her. Sarah shrugged her shoulders, deciding to let the past lie.

"Don't worry. I thought you might have some sort of hunch. I'll work it out," Cassie responded.

Sarah got to her feet. "I suppose I'll see you at the town meeting tonight."

Cassie started to demur, but Sarah interrupted. "Hiding away never helped matters."

Cassie quickly saw her point and agreed, thinking the town meeting might be the best place to start the search for her uncle's killer.

As Cassie made her way into the crowded hall, she passed neighbors who still turned away when they saw her. Ignoring them, Cassie looked about for Sarah. Spotting her, Cassie navigated toward the front, pausing along the way to greet Maude and her noisy brood.

"How ya doin', Cassie?"

"Fine, Maude." One of Maude's many children darted past, almost colliding with Cassie. A schoolteacher's natural response surfaced instantly. "Young man, walk, don't run." The phrase, uttered in her most intimidating voice, convinced the youngster to settle down while craning his head to gawk at her. "Sorry, Maude. I've done that for so many years it just popped out."

"But you don't have any young'uns."

"No, but I've been a schoolteacher most of my life."

"Well, you can set my kids straight anytime. They drive me plumb crazy. Wish you'd get rid of that ranch and be the schoolmarm. Mebbe then they'd settle down for more'n a minute at a time."

Knowing Maude meant no offense, Cassie smiled while dismissing the idea. "I don't think the town would accept me as their schoolteacher."

"Folks here'd do most anything to get a schoolmarm. Been almost three years since the last one died—can't get nobody to come out here to teach. You get tired of them sheep, you got the job."

Another of Maude's brood ran past, and Maude took off after him.

Shaking her head slightly as she thought of Maude's words, Cassie continued toward the front. Sliding onto the pine bench, Cassie felt a lithe movement beside her. Her heart quickened as she recognized the exciting familiarity of Shane's tall frame.

"Do you have room for a tired range hand, ma'am?"

Cassie searched Shane's gold-flecked eyes and seemed to consider his request. "I suppose so. Do you happen to have him with you?"

Shane tweaked an ebony curl that had escaped past her ear. "It seems I forgot him along with the sugar to sweeten that tongue of yours."

"And I was so looking forward to having some sugar with my vinegar tonight."

Shane listened absently to her banter while admiring the sparkle in her violet eyes, the faint flush to her cheeks, and the mischievous smile that danced across her face. She was like a lemon pie—tart and sweet at the same time.

Catching her eyes, he telegraphed a message of his own. Cassie's pulse seemed to quicken, and he watched in pleasure as her chest rose and fell with the increased tempo of her breathing. How well he remembered the satiny feel of the flesh beneath those constricting layers of clothing.

Watching her moisten her lips a trifle breathlessly, Shane saw the pink end of her tongue flick back across her full lower lip and remembered the pinkness of her dusky nipples when they'd begged for his touch, how they'd glistened when he'd taken them in his mouth, and the path of fire that had ensued.

"Attention, folks!" The harsh voice of the mayor boomed over the noisy, milling crowd. "We have a lot of business to get to." Shane straightened his tall frame on the pine bench, willing his thoughts to find another direction because the ones he had now were causing him considerable discomfort. When Cassie laid a smooth hand on his arm, he had to force himself not to jerk away. Slowly he eased away from her, knowing he was rock-hard. And knowing there wasn't a damn thing he could do about it.

He suffered silently while the crowd quieted and the first ten minutes of the meeting passed without consequence as some minor business was conducted.

Despite her determination not to, Cassie found herself concentrating more on Shane than on the business at hand. She tried to listen attentively, but her mind slid relentlessly back to the hard body resting on the bench beside her. When Shane's knee nudged hers, she swallowed and straightened up in her seat, trying to concentrate on the speaker. Her eyes slid sideways, resting on the chestnut sideburns that carved a path down Shane's cheeks. When he turned slightly and caught her gaze, Cassie flushed but couldn't turn away.

" . . . and right-of-way deeds." Sarah jabbed her sharply in the side, and Cassie straightened up.

"What did I miss?" Cassie whispered. Sarah rolled her eyes and mouthed, "Not much."

"The petition on water rights that we're sending to the governor is on the table at the back of the room. Everybody make sure to sign it before you leave." The mayor stared pointedly at Cassie, and she flushed under the intense regard of those surrounding her. So now they were going to petition the governor, were they?

Murmurs of agreement filled the hall, and after a few more remarks the mayor adjourned the meeting. Shane moved away to speak with friends, and Cassie stood alone.

"Think you'd better change your mind about selling out, missy?" Jacob Robertson's hissing voice came over Cassie's shoulder, and she whirled around to face him.

Cassie drew up her courage as she straightened herself to her full height. "I think not, Mr. Robertson."

"Then you'd better think again."

Cassie almost flinched at the raw hatred painted across his face.

"Wouldn't want to see you have an *accident* like your uncle's," he said with a sneer. Before she could reply, he turned and left.

"Entertaining the town's finest?" Shane asked, reappearing at her side.

Cassie tried to regain her composure. Shane had developed the most annoying habit of reading her thoughts at the most undesirable times. She pretended to dig in her reticule as she answered, "Is he part of your finest?"

Shane uttered a contemptuous laugh. "Guess every town has to have a no-account like Robertson just to kick up dust."

"Is he a troublemaker?" Cassie tried to sound casual, but Shane's perception was immediate and accurate.

"Why all the questions?"

"No reason . . ." Cassie started to mumble.

Shane left her no room to escape. He tilted up her chin and met her gaze directly. "No hidin' under the brush, Cassie. I want to know why he's bothering you."

"Just a lot of suspicions, nothing really solid."

"Like what?"

"About Uncle Luke."

"What about him?" Shane's face had taken on that hard, closed look it always did when he spoke of her uncle.

Cassie's voice was low and direct. Maybe it was time to come out in the open about her feelings. "About how he died."

"He fell—seems pretty simple and clear-cut to me."

"Does it? How do you explain why an expert horseman suddenly falls off a cliff on his own land, land he's scoured every inch of for years? And what about his dog? Isn't it terribly coincidental that a surefooted herding dog slipped at exactly the same time? Even I don't believe a dog's devotion extends to leaping to its death to join its master."

She stopped abruptly as Shane let out a long breath. "Whew. I'd say you saved that up for a while."

Cassie swallowed convulsively, nibbling on her lower lip as she did. "I have been doing some thinking about it," she hedged.

"I won't try and talk any sense into that hard head of yours." His voice turned sharp. "Plenty of people hated Luke Dalton enough to kill him, but the fact is it was an accident. Won't do any good to stir it up now. I'd say you have your hands full of your own problems." She started to protest, but he cut her off. "And now we're getting out of here." Shane took her hand in his and led her from the still milling group in the meeting hall.

She tried not to speculate about why he so readily dismissed her concerns. Was it because he had more reason to cover up her uncle's death than anyone else?

But as he tugged her forward, she loosened her grip on her fears. A reluctant smile played on Cassie's lips as she let Shane carve a path to the door. She really didn't want to battle him tonight. Her battle quota was full for the week. Once outside, he tucked her firmly at his side.

"I expect Millicent can find her own way home," Shane began.

"But . . ."

"And I imagine Ringer will thank us for not interfering."

Knowing he was right, Cassie relaxed beside Shane's sinewy frame. While independence had been a hard-fought battle, right now a lost skirmish seemed very trivial compared to the anticipation she felt merely walking down the boardwalk with Shane. Cassie knew she was a fool, but even as she completed the thought, the touch of his hand sent a path of liquid fire through her body.

They paused beneath a canopy of birch trees and then emerged under the inky stillness of the sky. As they moved forward, each star seemed to burst forth, brighter than the last.

"There's your star," Shane murmured as "Cassie's star" came into sight.

Cassie found herself melting inside bit by bit. "So it is. It seems to me we've neglected to do something."

"And what's that, Cassie girl?"

Her breath caught at the casual endearment. She moved away slightly to regain her equilibrium.

"We haven't found your star."

In spite of himself, Shane's eyes softened and he pulled her into the circle of his arms.

"So we haven't. Which one will it be?" But instead of looking at the stars, he traced a path lightly over her eyelids, her cheeks, and finally her lips. The bones in Cassie's knees seemed to have disappeared as he worked his magic. She remembered his glances during the meeting and wondered if he was thinking of their last shared caresses. The heat coiled tightly in her stomach, moving downward, making her weak.

"I kind of like that one," Shane murmured.

Cassie's mind felt like a hollow log. What was he talking about? She followed the line of his arm as it pointed skyward. The star! She was going to have to get a grip on her feelings, she chastised herself, starting to straighten up from his embrace.

"And this one," Shane continued, gently easing his lips over hers.

Cassie's thoughts swirled like leaves in a whirlpool, and getting her emotions under control no longer seemed possible or even desirable. As Shane's kiss deepened, so did his hold on her heart. For all the reasons she had decided he couldn't be hers, she wanted him still. And suddenly she wanted those barriers erased.

The hard line of his body beckoned her closer, and she found herself wanting to dissolve into him, wanting him to carry her away. . . .

As his body eased gradually away from hers, Cassie felt a sharp pang of disappointment and loss.

"We seem to have a habit of finding the darnedest places," he murmured dryly in her ear, pointing to the couple passing across the street.

Cassie immediately straightened her hat and tried to smooth down the rumpled fabric of her dress.

"It's probably a little late for that." He laughed at her horrified expression. "Don't worry, it's pretty dark out here." Cassie still looked skeptical.

Shane's disappointment matched her skepticism. "I suppose I should be taking you home."

"I suppose so," she murmured, echoing his disappointment.

"But not before you promise to go to church with me on Sunday."

"Church?"

"You do like to go to church, don't you?"

"Well, yes." She hadn't attended since the day she and Millicent had been ambushed. Millicent always invited her to go when Ringer picked her up, but Cassie had demurred. "It's just that I'm so busy . . ."

"Even God rested on the Sabbath, so no excuses. I'll pick you up early Sunday."

Cassie felt a warm glow in her heart. A man seldom escorted a woman to church unless he was proud to be seen with her. Church seemed suddenly appropriate; it would take all her prayers to win this most important battle.

35

Sunday morning dawned sun-drenched and clear. Gazing into the impossibly lapis blue sky, Cassie couldn't see anything to mar what she hoped would be a perfect day. She smoothed the already flawless line of her skirt for the hundredth time that morning, but she wanted to look special.

The lavender taffeta had always enhanced her unusual eye color, and so she saved it for special occasions. Like today. Her eyes softened as she thought of Shane. And she pushed aside her notions from the night before. Just because Shane wanted her land didn't mean he'd go so far as to murder for it. But, her subconscious reminded her, someone had.

As if in response to her thoughts, she spotted Shane's buggy on the road, a wake of dust following its progress. Quickly she adjusted her hat, taking another peek in the mirror as she inserted the pearl-tipped hatpin that had been her mother's. After a final searching look in the mirror, she was ready.

She could scarcely wait until he reached the hitching rail. Then propriety alone kept her from flinging open the door and running to greet him. The seconds seemed excruciatingly long as he climbed down from the buggy, hitched the horse, and walked across the porch. Surprise lit his face when she opened the door the moment he knocked on it.

"Prompt as always, I see," Cassie began, a light dusting of pink staining her cheeks, revealing her embarrassment at seeming so eager.

"No more than you," he responded with a touch of irony, enjoying the telltale blush.

"I wouldn't want us to be late for the services."

"Nor I," he replied in the same serious tone, his eyes alone showing his humor.

Completely flustered, Cassie gathered up her reticule and parasol. "I'm ready."

Shane's lips twitched slightly at this unnecessary statement, and he bowed toward the door.

"After you."

Cassie allowed Shane to help her into the buggy and then felt the vehicle lurch sideways as Shane climbed in. Glancing up at him beneath the brim of her hat, Cassie saw the amusement still flickering across his face. She started to give him a chastising glare when the humor of the situation struck her. *She must have looked as if she'd been shot out of a cannon!* Cassie ducked her head slightly to hide her sudden smile. She was surprised he wasn't laughing out loud.

The husky note in his voice when he did speak took her aback. "I don't suppose it's proper to kiss you before church."

"I don't suppose so," Cassie whispered in reply, feeling her body tingle all the way to her toes in anticipation.

"A highly improper way to start the Sabbath," Shane murmured.

"Highly," she echoed as the buggy seat suddenly seemed very small, and Shane's body suddenly seemed terribly close.

"We'd be the talk of the town," Shane continued, his head tilting closer to hers.

"The talk," Cassie replied, feeling Shane's breath dance across her cheek.

"We'd probably never hear the end of it," Shane continued, as his lips hovered a fraction from hers.

"Never," Cassie replied, not caring if her neighbors shouted the news from the rooftops.

"In that case," Shane said, straightening suddenly, "we'd best be on our way."

She blinked, and tried to get her bearings. Shane flicked

the whip and started the horses off at a trot. Barely catching the edge of the buggy as they took off, Cassie shakily tried to straighten up, and instead nearly lost her seating again.

"Better hang on tight. We don't want to be late."

Cassie could have cheerfully choked him. If he weren't whistling happily, she might have thought he'd been equally affected. Instead she felt like a rag doll on a bucking bronco, while he was as confident as a Boston banker.

When they pulled into the churchyard, Cassie saw several heads turn in their direction in surprise. Firming her chin, Cassie hoped the meaning of the Sabbath would sink into her neighbors' hearts.

Shane helped her out of the buggy, and they started toward the door as Shane's friends and neighbors greeted him. Nearing the entrance, Cassie felt someone tug hesitantly on her sleeve. She turned around and faced a woman whose four young children clung to her calico skirt.

"Miz Dalton?" the woman questioned hesitantly.

"Yes, I'm Cassandra Dalton."

"I'm Nellie Porter. My husband's one of Mr. Lancer's hands."

"Yes?" Cassie encouraged her, wondering what the woman wanted.

"I hear tell you're a schoolmarm."

"I was." Cassie could feel the collective turning of heads nearby as people digested this information. "In Boston. But I'm not teaching now."

"I want for my young'uns to learn. Would you teach 'em?"

The request flabbergasted Cassie. "You know I run a sheep ranch now?" The woman nodded her head. "I'd be more than happy to lend you some primers for your children, but I'm afraid I don't have time to teach them myself. You could—"

"I can't read, Miz Dalton." The woman's voice was flat and expressionless, but Cassie could see the flicker of regret and embarrassment in her proud, lined face. "But I want my young'uns to have better. I want 'em to read and write and figger. We don't have no school here 'cause we can't get no schoolmarm to come and teach 'em."

Cassie felt her heart constrict with pity and admiration for the brave woman who stood in front of her, willing to confess her own lack of education if it meant bettering the lot of her children.

"Perhaps once or twice a week after suppertime," Cassie began hesitantly, wondering how she'd fit this into her already full days.

"That's right decent of you, ma'am. My Henry'll work off what it costs at your place." Cassie could almost feel the stir of disbelief in the crowd around them.

"I'd not planned to charge you anything, Mrs. Porter . . ."

"We don't take no charity. From what I hear, you can use another man round the place." The woman swallowed, fighting back a tear, Cassie suspected, but still the pride in her face was clear. "I'm mighty obliged to you. You need anything, you come to Nellie."

Before Cassie could respond, the woman turned and melted into the crowd that was entering the church.

"That was a nice thing you did, Cassie girl." Shane squeezed her hand and offered his arm. They made their way up the steps and into the church. Cassie wondered if she imagined a new dawning respect on the faces of her neighbors.

They entered a pew and picked up hymnals to join in the song already in progress. As the strains of "Amazing Grace" filtered over her, Cassie's eyes roved around the one-room building. She realized again how much she missed the camaraderie and fellowship of neighbors and friends, something she had taken for granted all her life.

The song ended, and Cassie sank into the rock-hard pew. Shane slid a trifle closer than was entirely proper. Cassie stared at her own small ivory hand engulfed in his large tanned one. The tingle of his fingers warmed hers in a new and wonderful way. She felt protected, cosseted, and wanted. Strangely, she needed all three. For the moment she needed to forget all that was not right between them.

The first part of the sermon seemed to pass quickly, although Cassie didn't hear much of what the Reverend Beecher said. As the moments slid by, she became increasingly aware of Shane's lean length pressed close to her side.

As the preacher droned on, Shane casually picked up her hand. He drew a path over her thumb, along her knuckles, and then over her palm. Each movement set off a series of minor explosions. Cassie wondered if he knew what he was doing to her as he continued the slow swirling motions.

When the piano started playing "Nearer My God to Thee," she jerked her hand away with a start. Her cheeks flaming, Cassie tried to concentrate on the words of the song. Without thinking, she raised her eyes to Shane's and saw the desire lurking there.

Cassie's back was ramrod straight, her posture impeccable, her behavior beyond reproach. If not for the smile twitching at the corners of Shane's lips, she would have been in control.

When the closing prayer ended the service, everyone broke into the socializing that was as much a part of Sunday as the sermon. Cassie looked for renewed hostility and was surprised by tentative greetings from those who had snubbed her before. Could it be the news of her teaching credentials?

One of the ladies she remembered from the engagement dance approached. "Potluck on the lawn at two o'clock, Miss Dalton."

The imperious tone made the words sound more like an order than an invitation, but at least it was an overture.

Cassie stuttered, "Why, why . . . thank you."

The woman nodded her feathered hat and walked on. Cassie stared after her in amazement.

"Dinner on the lawn, eh?" Shane's voice lilted in her ear.

"Fancy name for a piece of dirt with a few sprigs of grass on it," he continued.

"Right now it sounds heavenly." Cassie didn't see the amazement on Shane's face as she responded to a few more greetings. *Just heavenly.*

Millicent breathed a sigh of relief as she slipped off her corset and pulled on a cotton wrapper, knotting its sash around her waist. Ringer had left a few hours earlier, and she finally had some time to herself. They had agreed to meet at around four o'clock for a picnic dinner instead of going to the church potluck. Millicent hoped that meant Ringer wanted what she did: privacy.

With the chicken fried to a golden brown, and the wicker basket packed, Millicent looked forward to her time alone.

Picking up the hand mirror, she critically examined her face from all angles. Her eyes were reasonably attractive, and her face was shaped in an acceptable fashion, she decided. She failed to see the depth of her moss-green eyes or the exquisite bone structure she possessed. But what she did see were those blasted freckles that stared at her relentlessly. Millicent took a deep breath. Desperate times called for desperate measures. If she wanted romance, she needed clear ivory skin instead of splotches.

Millicent stared at the newly gathered basket of strawberries at her side. She'd had a whale of a time keeping Cassie and Andrew out of the strawberry patch while they were growing, but now she had an important use for them.

Her resolve hardening, she patiently sliced each strawberry in half lengthwise and laid them in a bowl of lemon juice. After they were all prepared, she poured fresh buttermilk from a pitcher into a separate bowl containing honey. Making a paste of the honey and buttermilk, she then smeared the concoction all over her face. While the mixture was still wet, she placed the strawberries, cut side down, all over her face.

Remembering the instructions in the beauty book, she generously applied the fruit, covering all the skin containing freckles—which was every square inch of her face. The book had guaranteed that the mixture would remove even the most stubborn freckles.

She sat perfectly still as the mixture attached itself to her face. Picking up the hand mirror, Millicent had to restrain a gasp as she eyed herself in the glass. What a ghastly mess! *This had better work*, she thought with a shiver of distaste. If men only knew what women went through. . . .

Millicent cocked her ear. She could have sworn she heard a light knock on the front door. But who could be out on a Sunday afternoon when everyone was at the potluck? She picked up her watch fob on the dresser. It was only two o'clock. Ringer wasn't due for two more hours.

Opening the bedroom door, she peered out into the keeping room. Not seeing anything, she moved to the window. Pulling back the curtain, she collided eye to eye with Ringer. It was hard to say who was more shocked.

Horrified, she dropped the curtain, rushed over to the pump, and started furiously cranking the handle. Grabbing a towel, she scrubbed frantically at her face, dislodging most of the telling evidence.

Hearing the door being flung open, she cringed and darted into the corner.

"Millicent, my God! What happened?" Ringer closed the distance between them, and she felt his hands on her shoulders, trying to turn her around. She clung more fiercely to the corner cabinet, twisting her face so he couldn't see it.

"I can't help you if you don't let me see, Milly. What is it—a burn? Don't turn away."

Twisting further away, she gulped for air and wondered if a person could truly die of embarrassment—suddenly hoping she could.

"Milly, turn around so I can help you."

She shook her head stubbornly, refusing to speak.

"You mean you *won't* turn around?"

She nodded her head.

"Dad blast it! You turn around, Millicent Groden, before I turn you around! If you need help, you'll not refuse while I'm here."

Millicent's head slumped forward in defeat. Eventually she would have to turn around; she couldn't sit in the corner until he left. Slowly she twisted around until she stood face-to-face with him.

Staring into his shocked eyes, Millicent prayed again for instant death. Instead Ringer held out a hesitant hand, touching her face in wonder.

"Strawberries?" The incredulousness in his voice was matched only by the amazement in his eyes.

"Yes, strawberries. Are you satisfied?" Millicent flushed under the awful mask and wanted to choke on her anger. She started to move away when Ringer stopped her.

"It really is . . . I thought you were hurt . . ."

"Instead of crazy."

"Now, I didn't say crazy. I just can't say that I've ever seen anyone put strawberries on her face," he replied cautiously, licking his finger and tasting the honey-coated fruit.

"You've obviously never known anyone with this many freckles," she retorted, then clapped her hand over her mouth. Why did she have to blurt out the truth?

"Freckles, Milly. Did you say freckles?"

She saw that he was fighting laughter and wanted to smash him. How dare he make fun of her shortcomings?

"Yes, freckles, dammit!"

Ringer took in this unexpected swear word with a chuckle.

"It's easy enough for you to laugh," she raged, feeling hopelessly unattractive and foolish. "The horrible, ugly things aren't spread out all over *your* face."

"Oh, Milly." Ringer pulled her close, and she could feel him still trembling with restrained laughter. "My beautiful Milly. I'll not have you calling them ugly. They're God's drops of sunshine, spread out on the loveliest landscape in creation."

"You're just saying that." Millicent wanted to believe his blarney, but she knew what she looked like.

"I'm saying it because I believe it." His laughter seemed to die down as he lowered his face close to hers, licking a strawberry on her forehead. "You're tasty, too."

If possible, she flushed to an even deeper hue of rosy red.

"I know how awful I look," she protested.

Without answering, Ringer scooped her up and carried her toward the settee. "I think I'm ready for my picnic right now," he stated, nuzzling her lips and retrieving another strawberry.

Millicent flailed her arms and legs wildly. She'd never had a man pick her up bodily like that—not that it didn't feel wonderful, but still . . .

Feeling a bit light-headed, she protested, "I have a basket all packed. If you'll put me down and let me get cleaned up . . ."

Millicent shivered deliciously at the devilish twinkle in his eye as he bent to taste the nectar on her face.

"What? And waste the best part?"

Ringer bent to place a gentle kiss on her lips. The kiss, intended to be butterfly quick, deepened, and as he felt Millicent respond, a deep shudder of desire shook him.

One by one, he licked the few remaining strawberries from her face, each time swooping closer to her mouth as she made tiny sounds of pleasure. As her hands fastened first in his hair and then roamed over his shoulders, he found the last of his control slipping away. Urgently he gathered her trembling body to his. Instead of pulling away, Millicent merely sighed his name and melted even closer.

She was lost in the heady sensation of being held once again in Ringer's arms. Feeling the shudder of his desire, Millicent reveled in the unexpected power she'd only now discovered she possessed. His lips brandished a fiery trail of kisses over her waiting mouth and down the sensitive hollows of her throat. When his mouth descended to the discreet vee of her wrapper, she arched closer.

His fingers closed around the sash that held her wrapper together and slowly untied it. As the material slipped free, Millicent curved her neck back in delight when he untied the top lacing of her chemise. The air nipped at her almost bared skin, and Millicent gasped aloud when Ringer traced the outline of first one aroused nipple and then the next.

His gaze fastened on Millicent's flushed face, noting the passion darkening her features. He knew, despite her innocence, that she was ready for him. And, just as certainly, he knew he would have to control the inferno they'd ignited.

Desire battled with the urge to protect her, to take her away from the ugly fight she'd been unwittingly placed in the middle of. Unable to resist, Ringer scooped her off the settee and placed her on the soft rug in front of the hearth. Shifting closer, he grasped her cascading hair. His lips closed over hers as he pulled out the confining pins that entrapped her hair. It spilled out, the blazing red strands washing over her gloriously naked shoulders, illuminating all the fantasies he'd had about her. And, as the leaves on a tree tremble in the shifting breeze, so did Ringer's heart.

One strong hand gently stroked her satiny cheek. The other arm brought her into an embrace, his fingers kneading the skin at the back of her neck. It took only moments for their accelerated awareness of one another to skyrocket.

Steel-blue eyes captured moss-green ones. Their breathing quickened and each ragged gasp penetrated the stillness of the day. This time, when Millicent swallowed the lump in her throat, it wasn't from fear, it was from anticipation—hungry, long-denied, overwhelming anticipation. And this time she didn't back down from the hunger in Ringer's eyes, for it matched her own intense need.

At the sudden change in Ringer's breathing, Millicent felt a heady sense of power. She watched in suspended wonder as his lips moved closer, and felt her chest swell with excitement, her knees weaken at the destiny she saw written in Ringer's face.

She knew without a moment's hesitation that this was a destiny she'd craved for a lifetime. Slowly, ever so slowly, his lips descended on hers, and she savored the sweetness of the moment. Millicent sensed suddenly that she was nearing the end of a long journey, one that had taken a magical turn not of her own making. But one she wouldn't change for all the cattle in Texas.

Millicent drew a quick breath as Ringer's mouth moved over hers insistently, demanding a response. Her eyelids flickered shut briefly, translucent coverings over her turbulent emotions.

She felt the gentle butterfly kisses Ringer rained across the milky expanse of her neck. She sucked in her breath as one gentle kiss found her sensitized nipple separated only by the thin material of her chemise. Linking her hands together in his hair, she relished the texture as it teased her fingertips.

Once again their lips met, and Millicent's eyes fluttered shut briefly as their bodies touched. Each kiss that descended across her throat and over her bodice shook her from deep inside. She wondered if she'd ever imagined the dormant volcano that had lain inside her until this moment.

Ringer lifted his head, searching her eyes, his hands resting on her lace-trimmed chemise now held together with only a few ivory buttons. Millicent's eyes blazed with pride and desire as she met his look. One by one, the buttons eased open, and only the lacy fastenings of her camisole separated reality from fantasy, desire from fulfillment.

And in one breathtaking step, she knew fantasy would no longer suffice, and with her eyes told Ringer her decision. She reveled in the feel of his strong hands as her camisole disappeared and the cool breeze from the window tantalized her bare skin. Caught in an incredible onslaught of sensation, she was dimly aware that her other clothing had disappeared until only her pantalets remained.

Suddenly she wanted to see and know Ringer in the same fashion. Her hands were clumsy and impatient as she tore at the buttons on his shirt. His eyes widened a bit in surprise and pleasure at her eagerness. But when his shirt was gone, Millicent stared at his pants and grew suddenly shy. Sensing her awkwardness, Ringer dispensed with his other clothing and turned to her again. Millicent felt an incredible heat burning in her stomach and moving downward as she stared at his perfectly formed body.

Years of outdoor labor had honed his body to sleek perfection, and Millicent hesitantly reached out to touch the rippling muscles that had always been hidden by work shirts and denims. The springy hair beneath her fingers curled damply as she traced a path to the dark, pebbly nipples on his chest. When her fingers grazed the distended nubs, he groaned aloud.

He held her against the length of his body, and Millicent wanted to feel him—all of him—against her. As though reading her thoughts, Ringer gently eased the remaining garment from her, revealing her milky white body in all its glory. When their eyes met, all the promises of the past months melded into a desire that shook them both.

As though every nerve and feeling she possessed had been set on fire, Millicent strained even closer against him. When she felt the evidence of his desire, she paused in a moment of panic and then almost cried aloud when Ringer parted her legs with his knee.

But even as she wondered, she reached out to run her hands over the rippling muscles of Ringer's back and chest. Each curve, each plane promised another tantalizing mystery she wanted to unravel.

As the afternoon sun teased the dark locks of hair across Ringer's forehead, Millicent questioned suddenly if she was indeed the same lonely spinster who'd come from Boston. Even as the thought danced through her mind, Ringer's eyes feasted on her body, and the darkening flush of desire on his face denied she'd ever been an undesirable old maid.

Ringer's voice washed over her pleasure-driven senses. "You know we can't turn back now, don't you, darlin'?"

Millicent managed to nod her agreement, wondering if he knew she was helpless to stop her own actions, much less his.

She felt his weight settling more firmly, as though every cell of his body now merged with hers. When he searched her eyes for some unspoken answer, Millicent wasn't sure what was expected of her and so instead uttered the words she wanted most to say.

"I love you, Ringer."

He briefly captured her lips before replying, "And I love you, Milly. More than you'll ever know."

With those words, he brought his hips against hers, urging her legs apart. She felt another sudden ripple of fear at the unexpected pain, but before she could withdraw, Ringer pulled her to him and deepened his strokes. She felt her breath catch at the unfamiliar but pleasurable sensations he was creating. With an abandon she'd not known she possessed, Millicent matched his movements, searching . . . seeking . . . and finding. As the bursting crescendo shattered the stillness of the afternoon, she wondered if heaven could in any way compare with Ringer on earth.

36

Cassie glanced over at her friend, noting again the smile that seemed to constantly hover on Millicent's lips. Alternately she'd been dreamy, preoccupied, and bursting with happiness. Cassie suspected a wedding date was not far off.

When a knock sounded on the door, she stared at the wooden barrier, a slight knot of apprehension starting to build. The day had begun with more threats, this time in the form of a strangled chicken with a nasty letter attached to it. By now Cassie had almost hardened herself to the threats. Almost.

She opened the door and on the threshold stood Nellie Porter and her children.

"Evenin', Miz Dalton. My young'uns are ready to learn, if'n you're ready to have 'em."

Cassie tried to contain her feelings of dismay, but watching the proud tilt to Nellie Porter's work-lined face, she knew she couldn't refuse.

"Fine, Mrs. Porter. Let's plan on about two hours this evening. If you'd care to wait here, that would be all right, or you can come back . . ."

"I'll jest help Henry this evenin'. Next time he'll bring the young'uns. What you be wanting us to do?"

Cassie had no intention of putting the woman to work on outside chores, no matter how willing she was. "Why don't you help Millicent, Nellie? And I'll direct Henry with some outside chores."

Nellie nodded and waited for directions from Millicent. After Cassie had sent Henry to shovel out the pens, she directed her attention to the children. Four fresh-scrubbed faces stared as she got out books, tablets, and pencils.

When their session came to a close, Cassie had to admit the children were quick learners and hard workers, much like their mother, who had scrubbed and cleaned the entire two hours.

As Cassie and Millicent waved good-bye to the sober-faced children, they each sighed aloud in relief.

"She made me tired just watching her," Millicent commented. "I'll be about six hours ahead of schedule tomorrow because of what she accomplished."

"I can't say I'm sorry I don't have to muck out the shed tomorrow, but I don't imagine they'll come back after that chore," Cassie replied. "I wish Andrew was as eager about his lessons."

But the Porters did return, and it seemed that every day the number of children she tutored grew. Cassie hated to say no, and the children appeared so painfully eager for their lessons. She was stretched so thin at times that she doubted her own abilities. But as one after another of the families brought their youngsters to her for lessons, Cassie couldn't find the heart to refuse. True, it was the women who brought their children, since most of the men still kept away. Except for Henry Porter, whose able assistance was a godsend.

If only she was accepted as a person as well as a schoolteacher, she might learn to like living in the harsh land. With a sigh, Cassie realized that once she learned the identity of her uncle's killer, any tranquillity she had would be destroyed.

"A poetry reading?" Cassie questioned in disbelief, bending over to drive a nail into the flagging corral gate.

"Can you imagine anything so exciting out here? An actual poetry reading? The whole town will be there. We can't miss an opportunity like this. What do you think we should wear? And our hair? Would hats be appropriate? Maybe our Sunday silk . . ."

Cassie smiled in spite of her weariness. If anyone had told her back in Boston that Millicent would be acting like a nervous schoolgirl, she would never have believed it.

But Millicent was right: the whole town did turn out for the reading. As they made their way through the crowd and started toward a pew, Shane materialized beside Cassie. Her pulse quickened at the sight of him, looking tall, lean, and hungry. The expression in his eyes told Cassie that he'd like for her to be the main course.

"Evenin', Cassie." His voice washed over Cassie like warm water in a river bed. Before she could reply, they were separated by a rush of people coming down the aisle.

As soon as they passed, Shane tucked her arm firmly under his. "Don't want to take a chance on that happening again," he said, guiding her to one of the back rows.

While the babble of voices around them continued to rise and fill the room, Cassie and Shane sat side by side, the heat from their bodies radiating toward one another.

Cassie let her eyes roam over him, pausing at the pulse point in his throat, watching its tempo increase when he laid one hand over her leg. When his fingers unobtrusively closed over her knee, she sucked in her breath, feeling the warmth of his skin through the layers of her clothes.

Risking another glance, she saw that his eyes had darkened, and his full lips were moist. Remembering those lips on her own, his hands moving over her body, Cassie tried to control the erratic beating of her heart, which she felt must surely be visible.

She was relieved to turn her attention to the traveling circuit actor who announced his selections for the evening, Whitman and sonnets by Shakespeare. During the polite clapping that erupted in the room, Cassie straightened up a bit. Whitman?

Some of his selections were so, well, risqué that they'd been omitted at the readings in Boston. Despite her uneasiness, a wicked smile played about her lips as she glanced around at her neighbors eagerly awaiting the cultural evening. Their excitement showed they were starved for anything from back East, since the West was at least ten years behind their seaboard contemporaries. Well, they were in for some enlightenment tonight.

Cassie schooled her features into a mask of composure as she awaited the selection. Glancing at Shane, she wondered if their proximity to each other affected him as it had her. She met his eyes—smoky and probing—and immediately knew that it had.

Deliberately he allowed his gaze to lower, pausing lingeringly at the curve of her breast, the vee of her dress that hinted at the flesh he knew so well. She met his gaze. The slow smoldering heat she found there made her believe he did know. She flushed, not from embarrassment but from desire.

Cassie tore her gaze from Shane's when the actor began to speak, reciting a Shakespearean sonnet. The townspeople applauded enthusiastically when he reached the end of the first reading.

While the actor recited the second selection, Cassie looked around the room at all the intent faces, then glanced up at Shane, who also seemed absorbed in the actor's words. She couldn't quash the smile that hovered on her lips as the actor got closer to the portions of the poem she knew so well.

" ' . . . This is the press of a bashful hand . . . ' "

She placed her hand softly in Shane's. He glanced down at her, eyes darkening further in pleasure as the actor continued. Cassie's tongue slowly traced a path around her lips while Shane watched in fascination.

" ' . . . Press close bare-bosom'd night . . . ' "

Knowing she was playing with fire but unable to resist the temptation, Cassie flicked a long raven curl over her full bosom as Shane's eyes followed her every movement. He swallowed and straightened up a bit on the pew.

"'... O unspeakable passionate love.... We must have a turn together, I undress, hurry...'"

Refusing to dwell on where her actions might take her, Cassie languidly unfastened the button on her cuff as Shane's eyes widened, and his breathing visibly changed. Holding his gaze, she ran her finger lightly up his arm and watched him turn an unhealthy shade of red.

"'... the hand roaming all over the body, the bashful drawing of flesh...'"

Cassie raked her nails lightly across Shane's thigh, then met his tortured eyes. Wrapping a strand of hair around her finger, she twirled it slowly while Shane fidgeted on the hard planking. She wondered suddenly if his discomfort was physical and possibly visible. Allowing her eyes to drift downward, they fell on the straining cloth of his Levi's. Raising her eyes, she saw the muscle in his cheek twitch nervously.

"'... takes his will of her, and holds himself tight till he is satisfied...'"

She drew a tantalizing finger across Shane's palm. He jumped slightly and picked up his hat, fanning himself with the Stetson. Smothering her grin, she noticed that the room was aflutter with fans and handkerchiefs. Woe to the good people of Keenonburg!

Cassie tapped her fingernails lightly against Shane's knee, and he jerked sideways. She smiled into his eyes, doubting he could take much more. Was that a nervous tic he was developing?

"'... winds whose soft-tickling genitals rub against me it shall be you!...'"

Bending her head to control her smile, she then slowly flicked her tongue around her lips again. Shane's eyes bugged a bit more. When she heard the next words, she almost wished she hadn't.

" ' . . . phallic thumb of love, breasts of love, bellies pres'd and glued together with love . . . ' "

Unable to resist, Cassie dropped a deliberate wink at Shane, who in turn, dropped his hat on the floor. As he bent to retrieve it, Cassie bent over, too, her breath brushing close to his. When their eyes met, Shane looked like a condemned man. Finally, taking pity on him, Cassie retreated a bit and only held his perspiring hand, sitting sedately through the last few stanzas.

When the actor finished, an uncertain spattering of applause was heard throughout the room. Most of the townspeople weren't sure if they'd been culturally enriched or morally outraged. Uncertain, they simply smiled weakly at one another as they headed outdoors. When they reached the boardwalk, Shane drew Cassie aside.

He pulled her down the walk before she could utter a word of protest or agreement. "You trying to make me crazy?"

"Did it work?" she asked, remembering how he'd set her astir in church and in the buggy.

"You're a pip, Cassie girl, a real pip." Shane raked his hands through his hair, a sure sign of his agitation.

She smiled slowly, seductively, and he almost dropped his hat again. He wondered if Cassie could possibly know the effect she was having on him. He wanted nothing more than to drag her off into the night, the consequences be damned.

Still she didn't speak, instead swaying close to him. Not touching him, just tantalizing him with her nearness.

To hell with it, he *was* going to drag her off! Before Cassie could offer more than a moue of surprise, Shane swept her off the boardwalk and through the dark alleys.

"Shane, where . . . ?"

He didn't answer, instead walking so quickly down the alleyway they were almost running. Just as abruptly, he stopped. Having found his destination, Shane opened the wide double doors of the livery. Cassie stared with wide eyes as Shane flung the doors open. Standing stock-still, she moved forward with a jerk when Shane pulled her inside. He released her long enough to set the heavy wooden board in place, effectively locking out any intruders.

Cassie's eyes strained in the darkness as she heard the clanking of a lantern and smelled the quick flare of sulphur when Shane struck a match against the sole of his boot. The soft glow of the lantern cast a golden aura over the shadowed corners of the livery.

Her breath grew ragged when Shane's eyes lit on hers. There was no threat in his expression, only a promise that her teasing had heightened his desire, fired his determination.

Involuntarily she stepped backward as Shane advanced. Each long, muscular stride brought him closer. When he was within inches, she stopped suddenly, finding she no longer wanted to back away. The heat that always curled within her at Shane's touch now ignited with the mere expression on his face.

His grasp pulled her firmly against him, and it took less than a second to feel the evidence of his intent. Heated by the fire in his eyes, Cassie felt her own blood thunder through her veins. Suddenly reckless, she wanted him now. Not after gentle strokes of love, but now.

Boldly she reached downward, her small hand cupping the hard bulk that strained against his denims. Hearing his sudden hiss of indrawn breath, Cassie ran her hands up over his lean hips. Restless, her hands continued their journey until she eased them between the buttons of his shirt.

Smiling devilishly, she ripped the buttons loose. Before she could finish shredding his shirt, Shane shifted. With swift, sure movements he tugged her skirt and petticoat out of the way, then began untying her pantalets. Cassie felt her undergarments drop to her feet and she kicked them away impatiently. Her hands flew to the fastenings on his denims, but Shane's hands were there first.

Her breath grew even more ragged when Shane bunched her skirts upward around her waist, pulling her forward with an impatient tug. Feeling herself being lifted, Cassie was scarcely ready when Shane impaled her on his waiting shaft. But it took only seconds to fit her moist warmth around him.

Shane's strong hands massaged her buttocks as Cassie milked the strength of his manhood, thrilling as the tip of his shaft seemed to penetrate to the center of her being. Each forceful stroke thrilled her anew.

Scarcely noticing the rough bark of the wall behind her, Cassie clung to Shane's shoulders, riding the crest of his powerful strokes with a frenzy she could scarcely believe was her own.

Rotating her hips in an ancient ritual, she heard Shane moan aloud in pleasure. Feeling an equal measure of heightened sensation, Cassie again milked her own warmth against him, sending showers of fire through her body. Sensing the bursting crescendo she rocketed toward, she again ground her hips against Shane's.

Shane grasped her buttocks tighter, emptying himself into her waiting womb. The massive shudders eventually trickled into a thousand tiny shivers.

Still holding their bodies intimately together, Shane reached for her lips, telling her without words the marvel of their shared exchange.

Cassie looped her arms around his neck as Shane gently lifted her and laid her down amidst the fresh hay of the stable.

With tender hands he smoothed her skirts and reached for her pantalets, easing them up her shaking legs. When his hands found the juncture of her thighs, his long fingers teased the curls. She gazed at him in surprise.

"We have a lot to share, Cassie girl." And then he brought the pantalets up to her waist, tying them carefully. After smoothing her skirts once again, Shane refastened his own clothes.

He lifted one side of his mouth in a sardonic grin as he gazed at his ruined shirt. Plucking a wayward piece of hay from Cassie's hair, he smiled at her.

"No doubt about it, woman. The townsfolk will know for sure you've had your way with me."

Cassie frowned in mock protest. "Me?"

"You." Shane fingered the rent material of his shirt and then growled deeply as she shivered in delight. "I still have three buttons left. Do you want to make a complete disgrace of me?"

The soft glow of the lantern beckoned in the stable as their laughs grew into gasps. The chestnut bay stood in a stall, contentedly munching his oats while the man and woman across the stable satisfied a more intense hunger.

37

Cassie stood, hands on hips, as she watched the men hauling the heavy boulders into place. The horses provided the strength, but the job still took a lot of labor. Cassie resented having to rebuild the dam. But with Michael's court order resting happily in her pocket, she felt confident again.

It seemed that her neighbors' court order, causing her dam to be blown apart, had been the catalyst for even more maliciousness. She had hoped the teaching would thaw her neighbors. But rather than backing down and leaving the Dalton ranch alone once the water had been freed, the attacks had been escalated. More sheep had been slaughtered. Someone had taken a shot at Millicent on her way home from town. And the poison pen letters arrived in droves.

Cassie knew, of course, that she could sell either parcel at any time and end her problems. Shane continued his offers, each time more heatedly than the last. And Karl Fredericks had intensified his campaign to "help" her. But now she was determined to hang on. The only way to prove that her uncle's death was not accidental was to stay in place until whoever killed Uncle Luke made his move.

And hope she was prepared when he did. Her heart tightened at the thought that the mysterious "whoever" could be Shane. Cassie refused to accept that fact. Even so, she couldn't discount the evidence: so far, he apparently had more reason to hate her uncle than anyone else. But why?

As though in answer to her unspoken question, Cassie spotted Shane riding over the mesa. She quelled the smile that rose automatically to her lips. Shane was going to be furious when he saw that the dam was going back up.

She was right. As his horse thundered to a stop, Shane jumped off. "What the hell do you think you're doin'? This one'll be blown too!"

"I don't think so, Shane." Cassie's voice was controlled even if her emotions weren't.

His face was livid as he moved closer.

"What do you mean?"

"I have a court order, overthrowing the original restraining order and staying anyone from a repeat performance."

"And so now you're gonna step into your uncle's boots and ruin the whole territory."

"There's no need to ruin anyone. I'm rebuilding the dam so I can release *or* stop the water anytime I want. If I'm left alone, the water will be too. If I'm not, the water'll be stopped up."

Shane raked an impatient hand through unruly hair as he stalked away and then just as quickly closed the distance between them again, his eyes narrowed.

"Why should I believe you have a court order?"

"Because I have the document," she answered, not wanting to produce the paper and have him see the incriminating signature.

"Then where is it?"

"I have it," she returned, trying to sound confident and in control.

"And I'm supposed to take your word for it?"

"I have it in my pocket," she blurted without thinking. She followed his eyes as they traveled to the small pocket over her breast where the folded paper was resting. She moistened her lips and backed away. "There's no need for you to see it. It's perfectly legal."

"Then why don't you want me to see it?" Shane advanced on her as she continued to back away, stumbling over rocks in her haste.

"There's no reason at all," she replied huffily, trying to command some force into her voice. "I simply don't like my honesty questioned." The last word came out as a squeak when she nearly tumbled backward over a large cactus.

"You think your neighbors are gonna take your word for it, Cassie?"

"That's not the point. I don't like your tone," she accused, trying to keep moving away with a semblance of dignity.

"Hell, I don't like what you've got to say. Now, let me see that paper!"

Cassie decided to stand her ground, convinced he was only bluffing. "I don't think so."

"I do." Shane reached into her pocket, his intimate touch searing her through the shirt. She blushed mightily, feeling like a fool. Despite what they'd shared in the past, she hadn't expected him to be so boldly callous in broad daylight with workers nearby.

But after a moment her embarrassment was forgotten as she watched his expression move rapidly between disbelief and anger.

"What the hell does this mean, Cassie?"

"It means that I have the right to—"

"That's not what I'm talking about." His voice was a feral growl, and Cassie felt the hackles on the back of her neck rise. "What did you do to make Michael help you?"

"I didn't *make* Michael help me," she replied indignantly.

"Then what did you do to convince him?" Shane's implication was clear and insulting.

"I didn't *do* anything."

"What did you promise him, Cassie? God, you must have thought we were fools, playing us both like fuzzy-cheeked boys who couldn't figure out why you were so eager to share your favors."

Her slap split the morning air, but Shane grabbed her arm before she could connect a second time.

"Don't give me a reason to get even," he warned.

"You'd like that, wouldn't you?" she taunted him, not sure why, but still reeling under his insults.

He dropped her hand suddenly. Regret and sadness warred with the anger on his face. "If I were the man my father hoped I'd be, I'd say yes. Hope you get a good laugh out of this, Cassie. Because the answer is no—I wouldn't like that."

Cassie felt bands of pain digging into her heart. The love for him she'd denied stung painfully. Regardless of her suspicions, she could no longer delude herself. She loved him.

Unable to stand his condemnation, she protested. "It wasn't like you think, Shane."

His face was still and closed, but she could see the pain he tried so hard to control. "I've heard all I have to."

Cassie tried to take his arm, but he shrugged it off. She stared after him as he rode away, until only the wind remained where he'd ridden.

"I told you why I did it!" Michael's voice began to hold more anger than frustration.

"What about your sense of family, Michael? Doesn't that mean anything to you?"

"Of course it does, but what I feel for Cassie means something to me too."

Shane shuddered beneath the iciness that reached into his heart and then wrapped around his throat, strangling him. His voice was low as he questioned his younger brother. "And just how much is that, Michael?"

"I don't know, dammit, I just know I care about her."

"Have you slept with her?"

"What?" Michael's face contorted with anger.

"You heard me!"

"I heard you, but I don't believe you." Michael clenched and unclenched his fist. "I wouldn't take that from any other living human being, and if you say it again, I'll forget how much I respect you. You've been a fool about Cassie from the start. And it doesn't look like you're ever going to wise up."

Michael stomped away, and Shane stared after him. Watching Michael's retreating back, Shane realized bitterly that a Dalton had once again ruined another precious relationship in his life.

38

Cassie picked her way through the rocks on the cliff, her surefooted mare finding a path through the crevices that lined the mesa. She wasn't sure what she was seeking. But since Shane's visit the day before, she'd felt compelled to look for some evidence of her uncle's death. She needed to prove to Shane that her actions were based on more than a scattering of suspicion, that she'd had good reason to ask for Michael's help.

Skirting the big boulders, she searched the ground for something, anything that would give her a clue.

The sun, despite autumn's encroachment, beat down relentlessly. Feeling uncomfortably warm on the Indian summer day, and knowing she had neglected chores to come on a wild-goose chase, Cassie started to head back. Just then she spotted a flash of gold amidst the rocks lining the cliff.

Her curiosity aroused, Cassie headed toward the shiny nugget. Just as she neared the top of the cliff and bent over, she heard the distinctive sound of hooves. Before she could retrieve the elusive piece of gold, she straightened up and glanced down the narrow path.

The sight of Jacob Robertson's sneering face sent shivers of fear skittering up her spine. Her stomach suddenly felt like yesterday morning's mush, while her breathing became labored and uneven. She couldn't have picked a worse place to encounter him. Looking around wildly, Cassie saw that his horse blocked the path, and the only other way out was off the edge.

Remembering her uncle's fatal plunge from the same spot, Cassie gulped convulsively and tried frantically to think of another way out before he got any closer.

Catching sight of her, Robertson paused midway up the path. "Well, well, missy. What do we have here?"

"You *don't* have another victim. You'll not get rid of me like you did my uncle."

Her mind whirling, Cassie barely registered the surprise on Jacob's face as she plunged forward on the same path, urging her horse on as it approached the boulder veering off in the other direction. Holding on tightly and praying fiercely, Cassie guided the horse in a wide leap over the protruding rock. Taking a moment to look back at Robertson, who stared slack-jawed at her feat, it was hard to say who was more surprised that she'd succeeded.

Not taking time to applaud her success, Cassie spurred her horse on down the mesa. As she neared the base of the cliff, Jacob Robertson bent down and picked up the discarded object. Pocketing it, he stared after Cassie, his face a study of conflicting emotions.

She reached the safety of her corral and slid off the horse in a relieved slump. Shane's unexpected voice coming from directly behind her frightened her so badly she nearly knocked him over as she jumped back.

He didn't seem to notice as he stared at her coldly.

What now? she thought wearily, still shaken after her encounter with Robertson.

"Where the hell have you been? I've been waiting for over an hour for you to get home."

"Well, isn't that just too bad," she snapped, grateful to be latching onto anger rather than fear.

"I want you to stop seeing Michael."

"Seeing Michael?" She raised her eyebrows in disbelief, her eyes widening with the same emotion.

"That's right. I won't have it."

"*You* won't have it?" He'd thrown out the challenge, and she saw red. That morning's encounter with Jacob Robertson had sent her flying in an emotional tailspin. Everything seemed radically out of proportion, including her reaction to Shane's words. "If I *wanted* to see Michael, you couldn't stop me."

"Don't bet on it, Cassie. I've had all I'm going to take from you Daltons."

"You keep saying that. What does it mean?"

"It means you'd better watch your step. And if you have half a brain, you'll sell me your land and get out while you still can!"

Cassie swallowed the fear rising in her throat, his last few words dancing through her brain. Did that mean that Shane was the one?

Before she could complete the thought, he continued in an almost silky voice, "You're to be congratulated, Cassie. Your charm is working very well on Michael."

"And what's that supposed to mean?"

"I think you know what it means. How far were you willing to go to convince Michael to help you?"

The revealing flush in her cheeks was a dead giveaway. Her implicit promises to Michael haunted her, knowing she'd led him on. Guilt now made her flush heatedly.

The flexing of tense muscles in Shane's cheek was the only sign of his anger. When his arms reached toward her, there was little gentleness in his touch.

Even as she willed herself to deny him access, her body responded to the fire he was creating. He massaged her breasts beneath the rough work shirt she wore, shooting a path of pure fire to her loins. The aching intensified as his lips replaced his fingers, and unwittingly she ground her pelvis against his.

Cassie moaned when Shane picked her up, carrying her the short distance to the barn and then dropping with her to the hay. His hands never left her. She gasped aloud when he molded his hands to her womanhood, leaving her hot and damp. And ready.

Shane rolled on top of her, his body automatically fitting to the contours he'd grown to cherish, to love.

As abruptly as he'd touched her, Shane released her. What had come over him? He'd fully intended to show her how little she meant to him, that he could take what she offered and walk away.

Instead he'd made it painfully clear to himself just how much he cared for her. Not cared—loved. He loved her enough to throw away his pride and the promises he'd held sacred for a lifetime.

When he suddenly stood up, she stared at him in disbelief, trying to gather the shards of her shattered dignity.

He forced himself to turn away, remembering what she must have shared with Michael. Stopping for a moment, he turned back. "And after today, I'll make sure Michael isn't deceived either. I wouldn't count on him being your lap dog anymore."

"But I thought you . . . and I . . ."

"You thought wrong."

Shane forced himself to look away from the shimmer of tears and pain in Cassie's violet eyes—eyes that had no doubt sucked Michael into their depths. Realizing a Dalton had caused him to turn his back on a lifetime of commitment tortured Shane almost as much as the realization that he still loved her. His heart aching with the knowledge that Cassie had played him for a fool, he stalked away.

Only the haze of the suddenly empty barn remained. Sitting up, Cassie closed her shirt and gave in to the tears that had haunted her since the day she'd arrived. But as she cried, she knew no amount of tears would wash away the humiliation. And worse, they wouldn't erase the love she felt for the man who thought she had betrayed him.

39

Shane galloped across the connecting land, the demons that had been pursuing him for days intensifying. He tossed his Stetson on the oak hall tree where it rested on a peg. What the hell was he going to do? He needed to show Michael once and for all that he didn't have a chance with Cassie.

Maybe he should plan a romantic dinner at the Lazy H, he thought with a sigh. He refused to dwell on the regret that the dinner couldn't take place solely to romance Cassie, to see her eyes light up with pleasure, her sensuous lips curve with delight. He shook his head to clear the thoughts.

'Course he'd have a hell of a time convincing her to come to dinner. Pouring a tumbler of whiskey, he downed the fiery liquid in one gulp. He'd make her accept his invitation if he had to tie her to her horse. Regret tore at him like a cancer. He had to place Michael's welfare ahead of everything because first he was a Lancer, then a man.

Settling in at his desk, Shane opened the heavy leather cover of his journal just as he heard Cookie's raspy voice.

"Thought that was you," Cookie stated, clumping into the study. Without waiting for an invitation, he sat down in the leather winged chair closest to Shane. "So, how's the little filly?"

Shane merely cocked his eyebrows at Cookie's question.

"Don't play dumb with me, boy. I seen the two of you together enough to know what's going on."

"Nothing's going on." *Anymore.*

"I 'spect that's what's bothering you, son."

Shane avoided Cookie's gaze. "I 'spect you're right, Cookie."

"Them's the kind you don't let get away, boy."

Shane steeled himself against Cookie's insight. "You're right again, Cookie. How 'bout fixing up something real fancy for dinner tomorrow night?"

Cookie looked suspicious. "Fancy how?"

Shane pushed himself back in the chair. "Not stew."

"Since when don't you like my stew?" Cookie's face reddened, starting to puff up.

"I like your stew. I was just thinking of something more suited to dinner for a lady."

"Don't know what she'd have against my stew either," Cookie muttered.

Shane sighed. This was going to be harder than he'd thought. "Whatever you cook will be all right. Cassie's not too hard to please."

"Well, I do know how to make a mighty fine duck, if I can bag one."

Shane shot a surprised glance at Cookie. He must really like Cassie to make an offer like that. Cookie believed in putting beef on the table every night.

"Whatever you think."

Cookie kept muttering, more to himself than to Shane. "Got that special stuffing for it too."

Shane returned his attention to the journal as Cookie wandered out of the study, still muttering about what to serve. After Cookie left, Shane pushed his face into his hands, wondering what a truly intimate romantic dinner with Cassie might have been like. But now, with Michael involved, that wasn't possible.

Jacob Robertson pushed away from the saloon table in disgust. Ever since the Dalton woman had agreed to tear down her fences and free up the water, the men in town acted as though she'd grown wings. Sure, she was teaching half their young'uns by now, so some of 'em probably felt obligated to back off. But, by God, he didn't. Just 'cause the Dalton woman was mixed up with the Lancers, she thought she was uppity. It was time to take her down a peg. His pa hadn't raised no weak-kneed sissy. Hell, she was lucky she still had her land to sell.

Jacob thought of the day his pa had died, a broken man since Luke Dalton had dammed up the water. His pa should have been living easy, too, but they'd lost most of their stock, and things had never been the same.

The Dalton woman might have fooled his neighbors, but not him. Robertson slammed his mug of beer against the splintery grain of the bar and watched as it sloshed onto the counter. It didn't matter that she had torn down her fences and let up on the creek; he wouldn't rest until all the Daltons were gone.

40

The candlelight surprised Cassie. She'd expected a kerosene lamp, not soft candles flickering in silver holders. When Shane's invitation to dinner had arrived, Cassie had torn it into tiny bits and then stomped it under the heel of her boot. Then one by one, she had picked up the torn pieces, rereading the words: *I deeply regret my actions . . .*

Knowing that pride was a huge piece of the puzzle that made up Shane's character, Cassie realized this was Shane's way of apologizing. She fingered the bouquet of wildflowers that had accompanied the note, and smiled slowly, remembering the abashed cowhand who'd awkwardly delivered both the note and the flowers.

Using one of her few remaining pieces of decent stationery, Cassie replied formally that she would be delighted to attend. Jim Fowler had taken her missive to Lancer as though she were crazy. Darn fool notion, carrying mail to your next door neighbor, he'd muttered. But Cassie hadn't minded.

The day of the dinner, she thought of nothing but the evening to come. She had to know why Shane had invited her to a formal dinner after the way he had spoken to her that day. Was he planning to accuse her again of consorting with his brother?

Cassie cursed her abundance of curiosity. She should have declined. Determined to set him on his heels and make him regret what he had missed, instead she had fussed and primped, trying on every dress she owned.

Millicent swept her hair up in a flattering cascade of curls, and Cassie wore her mother's pearl and diamond earrings. The blush in her cheeks was her own, and the lilac scent she had dabbed on wafted gently in the air.

Sitting across the table from him, Cassie swallowed nervously, wondering what was to come.

But he surprised her. The hard, angry expression was gone, replaced by the charm that had captivated her from the first. In place of his usual denims, Shane wore an elegant gray worsted suit and starched white shirt that emphasized his bronzed skin and broad shoulders.

Cassie swallowed almost painfully as she studied the strong lines of his face that commanded attention. She swept her eyes away from his face, and they rested on his hands, strong, virile, and restless. Pulling her gaze upward, she stared at the broad expanse of his well-muscled chest, remembering the silky tufts of chestnut hair that rested beneath the confines of his dress shirt.

Picking up her wineglass with shaking hands, Cassie smiled weakly, hoping for once he hadn't read her thoughts. When his lips curved up slowly, devilishly, she knew her wish hadn't been granted. Instead of commenting on her distress, however, he occupied her with polite dinner conversation, skirting artfully around the tension that was ripe in the air.

While she enjoyed his attention, she kept waiting for the other side of him to emerge, the part of him that had cast her aside. Instead he was everything she had wished for since she had first met him. But oddly enough she missed their sparring. It was like having dinner with a polite stranger. After a delectable meal that amazed Cassie, Shane escorted her to the front room, opening the wide window and allowing a refreshing breeze to enter. Uncapping a decanter of sherry, Shane poured a glassful and handed it to Cassie.

When he turned back to her, Cassie caught a look of surprise on Shane's face that was quickly replaced by determination. Without preamble, Shane crossed over to her and abruptly pulled her into his arms, kissing her thoroughly. Even though his kiss ignited a familiar fire, she felt a prickling on her neck that warned all was not right.

As Shane released her, she looked over his shoulder into Michael's furious face. Her mouth dropped open in surprise.

"Michael!" she called out after him, but he'd stomped through the massive double doors, slamming them loudly. She turned furiously to Shane. "You did that on purpose!"

He moved to the sideboard, coolly uncorking a crystal decanter and pouring a shot of whiskey. Only the slight tremor of his hand revealed that anything was amiss. Throwing his head back, Shane downed the drink before turning to her. "And if I did?"

Her contempt rose. "I knew you'd stoop to anything to get your way, but I didn't think it included a display like this."

"What's the matter?" Shane shoved aside his regret. Michael's interest in Cassie had to be stopped. Shane knew he was goading her but couldn't stop. A hard knot of jealousy ate at him. "Afraid Michael won't be at your beck and call anymore?"

"You're despicable!"

"You didn't think so a minute ago when you were melting in my arms."

She threw the remainder of her drink in his face, but he refused to flinch. "I told you I'd stop whatever was between you and Michael and I meant it."

"What's the matter?" she taunted in return. "Afraid of a little competition?"

He wiped the drink from his face. "You don't know anything about it."

"Then try telling me!"

Instead he pulled Cassie into another embrace, as demanding as the first. Only this time there was no audience, and they were both electrifying aware of that fact.

She saw the haunted agony in his eyes before he shut them. Regretting her involvement with Michael, she evaded Shane's caresses. She moved aside to avoid him, inadvertently throwing herself even closer. Cassie realized her mistake when she felt his hot flesh through her clothes, burning a path to her heart.

His hands moved over her impatiently. When he didn't release her, Cassie cried out involuntarily in protest. He stood perfectly still at the sound. She finally raised tearful eyes to his, and he dropped both hands, moving away from her. She heard him take a ragged breath as he turned away. Cassie saw the convulsive movement as she stared at his back, but he said only, "You're going to tell Michael it was your plan all along to use him."

"I will not!"

Shane whirled about, and Cassie took a stumbling step backward.

"You'll tell him you were using us both to get what you wanted, and when I found out, you admitted it."

"You're crazy. I'll do no such thing. Michael's my friend—or he was."

"You're playing with fire, and I'm not going to let Michael get burned." Shane's voice was harsh in the dim light.

"Why? Why would Michael get burned? I'm not as heartless as you think. I wouldn't—"

"I can't take that chance."

"But why not?" Cassie cried.

"Because Michael's your cousin," he finally ground out, releasing his grip on her and turning away. He stopped near the window, raking his hands through his hair.

Cassie's face was a kaleidoscope of emotions. Disbelief, misunderstanding, and finally a dawning awareness rushed over her. "Then your mother . . ." she began softly.

"And your uncle," he finished, the fire in him extinguished.

Cassie moved beside him, reaching out and then pulling her hand back, uncertain of what to do. She fiercely wanted to offer comfort but didn't want him to pull away. She settled for standing close, facing him as he continued to stare out the window. "Why didn't you tell me, Shane?"

He laughed mirthlessly. "Even I wasn't supposed to know. It's not the kind of secret you trust many people with."

That he had, even in the convoluted way it had happened, touched her. "But it could have saved so much misunderstanding. I see now why you were so worried about Michael."

Shane only nodded in agreement, accepting her hesitant touch as she placed a hand on his arm. "But, Shane, there's never been anything between Michael and me. I've tried to make you understand that."

He gazed at last into those eyes that in the past had been flushed with desire and darkened with fury. But all he saw now was trust and truth. Still, the past gnawed at him. "That's not how he reacted when he saw you in my arms."

"He's had a crush, Shane." It was her turn to move away. "And if I were entirely truthful, I'd admit I used him because of it." Her eyes were downcast for a moment. "But I didn't think I had a choice. I was fighting for my life."

Regret chiseled his features and coated his voice. "I trusted before. I won't make that mistake again."

Knowing he referred to his mother, Cassie placed her hand tentatively on his arm. "Shane, forget for a moment that she was your mother. Think of them simply as a man and a woman in love, with the same feelings anyone in love would have."

He hesitated, the words seeming to be dredged up from the depths of his soul. "I knew my father and Luke Dalton fought over my mother when they were all young, but she made her choice when she got married. Your uncle knew how vulnerable she was. He took advantage of the fact that my father was gone." Shane paused as though the words were more painful than he could bear. "It was during the Indian raids. Pa had been missing almost a year." His voice closed again, waves of memories assailing him. "We thought he was dead—but he escaped. And came home to find my mother carrying Luke Dalton's bastard."

"But you learned to love Michael anyway, didn't you?"

Shane raked an impatient hand through his hair again. "Of course I did. That's never been an issue."

"But if you love someone as my uncle loved your mother, don't you always try to get that person back?" she asked, thinking of the twisted man Luke had become because of his love for Shane's mother.

Shane's face hardened. "She was already married, she'd made her choice."

"And maybe Luke couldn't live with that choice. He never married. It's apparent he always loved your mother. Not that I'm saying what happened was right, but she thought your father was dead. Love changes the rules."

Shane glanced away, clinging stubbornly to the outraged beliefs he'd held since he was fourteen years old. "Not all the rules."

Her voice was soft, almost a whisper. "Did your father know?"

Shane passed a hand over his face. "Michael was born a little more than eight months after he returned. I think he always suspected, but he never knew for sure. After my mother died and the drought came, Luke held the water rights over my father's head like an ax waiting to fall. Pa watched his friends and neighbors suffer and die, and then he gave in and deeded part of the Lazy H to your uncle. And gave up. He couldn't live with the knowledge that Luke had bested him again. It wasn't long after that he died."

"But Luke had to hurt, too, don't you see? He'd been denied not only the love of your mother, but his own son, too. That must have ripped him into tiny shreds every moment of his life."

Shane's face remained closed. "He wasn't alone then, was he?"

"They were a man and a woman just like you and me, can't you see that?" she finally cried.

He looked at her regretfully. "No, not like you and me."

Her tears flowed as she realized how much this man meant to her. It had been difficult to see beyond just his strength. But now she saw what lay beneath the complicated layers of his soul. She accepted the strength the way she'd desired the sensitivity, knowing he was a complex mixture of both.

Cassie watched him struggle against his feelings, but even while denying her words he pulled her into a crushing embrace. She accepted this as she accepted his words. Even as his lips ground against hers in a desperate effort to erase the past, she wondered if the hate Shane had carried for her uncle since he was a boy had finally pushed him to the brink. Was the man whose arms promised her heaven in fact her uncle's killer?

Resolutely, she closed her eyes to the possibility as he scooped her up in his arms. If that was the truth she'd been seeking, she wanted this night to remember, for the future would be a cold companion.

41

Shane knocked tentatively at Michael's bedroom door. Not getting an answer, he cautiously pulled it open. Michael didn't acknowledge his presence. Striding to the chifforobe, Michael pulled the clothes from it, stuffing them unceremoniously into the bag that lay open on his bed. Shane took in the scene, swallowing as he did so.

"You change your mind about law school?"

Not getting an answer, Shane wandered over to the dresser. He picked up the daguerreotype picture of their mother. Studying her likeness, he wondered suddenly which parent he was disappointing.

Replacing the picture, he turned again to Michael, noticing that he hadn't yet packed his suits.

"You're planning to go back East, I take it?"

"What difference does it make? You got what you wanted."

"Of course it makes a difference. I want—"

"I don't care anymore what you want, big brother. It's time I started watching out for me."

The irony of his words struck Shane like a blow.

"I know you won't believe me, but that's what I've been doing all your life."

Michael paused for a moment, but then he started packing again. "You have a hell of a way of showing it."

"Maybe you're right. I seem to have a hell of a way of showing a lot of things."

Michael threw down the pile of clothes, not caring that they landed in a heap. "Why'd you do it, Shane?"

Shane shrugged, unable to tell him the truth, unable to live with the lies of the past.

"Will you stay for a while, boy?"

Michael flung the bag across the room, where it landed against his dresser. "I'll stay until it's time for school to start. But that's all. And don't expect it ever to be the same, Shane, because it won't be."

Shane watched Michael continue to ravage the clothes in the chifforobe and then walked over to the dresser, picking up the picture of their mother that Michael's bag had knocked to the floor. *It won't ever be the same.* The words mocked him as they had so many years ago.

Slowly Shane sat down on the edge of the bed, remembering in despair the first time he'd heard those words replayed in his head, like a bad dream he couldn't shake. He'd been fourteen when he'd heard the words that changed his life forever.

"It won't ever be the same, Luke."

"Lily, we have to talk about this."

"There's nothing to talk about, Luke. It was a mistake. A dreadful mistake. I thought John was dead. I was scared and lonely."

"I've always loved you, Lily, even when you picked him over me. I've never stopped loving you."

"Luke, it's over. It won't ever happen again."

"But the boy—Michael."

"As far as I'm concerned, Michael is John's. And nothing you can say will ever change that. John is my husband, and he'll always believe that Michael's his."

"Do you expect me to walk away from my own son?"

"If you love me like you say you do, you'll leave and forget what was between us."

The silence stretched between them. Fourteen-year-old Shane swallowed the tears in his throat and the hurt slicing his heart as he listened to his mother and Luke Dalton from the hayloft.

"I'll leave, Lily, because I love you. But don't expect me to forget. I'll never forget."

And Shane had never forgotten, either. He could never see his mother again without picturing her in Luke Dalton's arms. And when she died, he cried not only because she was gone, but because she had been lost to him since that day.

After her death, and the drought had come, Luke Dalton held the water rights over his father's head, forcing him to sign over a portion of the Lazy H rather than see his neighbors starve and die. But by the time the paper was signed, the damage was done.

And Shane knew. He knew why Luke Dalton had forced his father to lose that showdown. Because of his mother, the woman both men had loved. Deep down, Shane felt that his father knew too. His deathbed request convinced Shane that his father knew—perhaps even about Michael—because he'd made Shane promise to get back that part of the Lazy H from Luke Dalton and to make sure no other Dalton ever laid claim to another acre.

Shane passed a weary hand over his face. The time had come for him to tell Michael the truth, the truth he was afraid would rip them apart. Glancing up, he saw that Michael had stopped his frantic packing and was staring aimlessly out the window at the gathering storm clouds.

"Michael, what I have to tell you . . ." Shane paused, not knowing how to continue. It was so damnably hard to shatter someone's life, violate his past, rob him of his parentage.

"What is it, Shane? I don't imagine anything's worse than what I already saw tonight."

Looking into Michael's wounded eyes, Shane knew this hurt would be deeper, more lasting, and infinitely more difficult to impart. Shane glanced away, cursing his mother and

Luke Dalton. "But there is, little brother." His voice almost broke on that last word. After tonight Michael would know they were only half brothers, not that Shane could have ever loved him more. Shane bent his head, intently studying the intricate pattern on the rug that covered the gleaming wooden floor.

It seemed he now had Michael's attention. "What are you trying to get at?" Michael's earlier belligerence was toned down but still evident in his voice.

"It has to do with what happened tonight."

Michael turned back to the bag resting on the bed. "I don't think there's anything else I need to know about tonight."

Shane momentarily rested his head against steepled fingers, wishing he didn't have to go through with telling him, dreading Michael's reaction. "I'm afraid there is, Michael." Shane raised his head, then abruptly rose and walked over to the window, wishing he could escape into the overcast night, escape what he had dreaded having happen for as long as he could remember.

"Well, what is it?" Michael's voice was impatient, unconcerned.

"It's about Cassie." The words were drawn out of Shane as was Excalibur from its stone sheath.

"You want to tell me how good it is between you two, big brother? Don't bother—I saw, remember?"

The old hurt surfaced, like hot lava through his midsection. Shane didn't answer, not knowing how to form the words.

"Or were you planning to tell me I could have my turn with Cassie when you're through with her?"

"Cassie's not like that," Shane burst out, realizing for the first time the utter truth in those words. There was no one like Cassie. And he loved her. Every irreverent, impossible thing about her.

"Maybe she'll decide she wants me after *she's* through with *you*." Michael's voice was taut with undisguised hurt.

"It's not ever going to be like that, Michael."

"Don't think I can win her back, big brother? Don't think I've got what it takes? I—"

"Stop it, Michael! For God's sake, it's nothing like that." He paused.

"Then what the hell is it?" Michael asked, his belligerence rising again.

"Cassie's your cousin!" Shane blurted out. Then his voice softened as he finally imparted the truth. "That's why I had to stop you from falling in love with her."

"But that can't be." Michael stared at Shane in bewilderment. "Hell, if she's my cousin, she's yours, too."

"No, Michael, she's not."

"But that doesn't make any sense. The only way I can be related to her if you're not is if—" He stopped abruptly, panic and disbelief chasing across his face.

"We're still brothers, Michael."

"Then how the hell am I related to Cassie?"

"Luke Dalton was your natural father." The words seemed to reverberate around the room. Michael's face went slack with shock. Then anger spewed forth like a broken fountain. "I don't believe you. You're lying so I'll leave Cassie alone."

Shane turned to Michael, his face a mask of anguish and regret. "I wish I were, Michael. I wish to God I were."

Michael's anger gradually disappeared, and the uncertainty returned in full force. "But how?"

Shane explained as gently as he could what he had overheard twenty years earlier and the anguish he had lived with in keeping that secret. Finally Michael sagged into a prickly horsehair chair, his face reflecting his confusion.

"I don't know what to make of this, Shane."

"I know you don't, boy. I expect it'll take you a while to get used to the idea. Just don't forget what I said. You're my brother—nothing will ever change that. And Pa loved you, Michael. He'd be mighty proud of how you grew up."

Shane placed a heavy hand on Michael's shoulder. Then lifting it, Shane slowly moved to the door. As he walked out, Michael's voice stopped him. His words were hesitant, his voice soft. "What *are* you going to do about Cassie, Shane?"

Shane bowed his head for a moment. "I don't know, Michael. I just don't know." The door thudded softly as it closed, the sound echoing with the vortex of emotions that seeped in the air.

42

Rain fell in great splashing torrents as Cassie peered through the blurry windows. Each blast of heavy rain seemed too painful for the earth to bear. She refolded the last letter she had read, turned, and replaced it in the cupboard.

She hadn't thought about the letters Millicent had found when they first moved in until now. They had lain untouched while she questioned and worried over the key to her troubles. Only after last night's startling revelations had she remembered them and then wondered if the letters her uncle had so carefully saved could have given her the answer. And they had.

The sweet gentle man she remembered had been twisted by his love for Shane's mother. Love that had been rejected. The final rejection, in the form of a son he promised never to recognize, had pushed him to disregard his neighbors' plight in his need to punish Shane's father.

Turning back to the window, Cassie shivered as the distorted silhouette of a rider appeared. She watched mesmerized as the man struggled against the sheets of water that poured over him. When he pounded harshly against the door, Cassie jumped in spite of herself. Millicent was trapped in town, having gone there before the storm had begun. Cassie knew the time of reckoning had come. Knowing she was alone in all ways, Cassie closed her eyes for a moment, wishing for fortification, wishing she could leave him standing on the porch.

But the pounding continued, louder now, more insistent. Fighting the buffeting wind, Cassie cautiously opened the door. Without waiting for an invitation, Jacob Robertson burst through the door and looked wildly around her neat keeping room. She stilled her pounding heart. It wasn't Shane beating down her door.

"Is my boy here?" Robertson demanded without preamble.

"You can see he's not." Cassie didn't know whether to be relieved or alarmed, but her reply was civil. Barely.

"Is he still with that brother of yours? I saw Fredericks trying to get home. He said they were together a couple of hours ago when he saw them."

Cassie peered more closely at Jacob's face. It wasn't anger she saw there, but fear. "Why do you want to know?"

"You've got two eyes in your head. Take a look."

"You mean the rain?"

"And the floods."

"What floods?"

"Flash floods, if you're in the wrong place when it's coming down. Now, are you gonna tell me where my boy is—or do you just want to let him drown?"

"Michael took Zack and Andrew down the arroyo to—"

Jacob blanched, his ruddy face suddenly pale, his eyes fearful, his voice a mere whisper. "The arroyo?"

Cassie felt fear burn in her belly as she sensed Jacob's sudden terror. "What?" When he didn't answer, she shook him. "What about the arroyo?"

"Come a flash flood, the arroyo fills up like a river. And with that dam of yours, it'll come up twice as fast with nowhere to run off. It's a deathtrap."

"But the dam's letting water through," she protested.

"Not enough. With the rain comin' down like this, that dinky pass hole won't be worth nothin'."

Cassie's heart nearly stopped as her terror mounted. "What can we do?"

" 'We'? There's no 'we,' lady. My kid's out there, and I've got to save him."

"I wouldn't give you a plug nickel for your life after you killed my uncle, but your son's not to blame. I'll do whatever I can to save him."

Robertson's eyes seemed to assess her while her mind whirled, looking for an answer.

"What if we blow the dam?" Cassie asked, the thought unbidden but welcome.

"You'd blow the dam?" Jacob's disbelief lingered in the air.

"I'm not sacrificing the lives of innocent children for a dam," she cried out, unable to believe the man's denseness.

Jacob's gaze rolled over her slowly, then he nodded and spoke. "You'll have to get the dynamite."

Cassie looked at him questioningly.

"Closest, fastest way is Lancer. He'll have what you need. I'll see if I can get to the boys before the water does." Robertson tugged at the brim of his hat as he moved to the door, preparing to face the raging storm. He hesitated a moment and then turned back.

"I hated your uncle enough to kill him, but I didn't lay a finger on him."

Cassie was suddenly still, her heart caught in her throat.

"But I know who did." Robertson searched Cassie's face as though he expected her to beg for a name. Her still countenance was more overpowering than anything she could have said. "Fredericks."

Cassie remembered the uncanny feelings she had for Fredericks and shivered in the cold night air. She'd wondered for so long how she would react to knowing the truth, but now that the moment had arrived she felt strangely calm. "Why?"

Robertson rapidly scanned the cabin, his eyes settling on a coil of rope near the pantry. Quickly moving over to pick it up, he answered, "Money. He never figured on Luke having an heir. He was trying to scare the old man into selling when he went off the ledge. Don't think even Fredericks planned on him dying, but the ledge gave way." Robertson shrugged hurriedly. "Fredericks had it in mind to charge everyone a king's ransom for the water. Then he'd have his own empire."

"How do you know this?"

"Fredericks figured I was the man for the job. Didn't think it'd matter to me if I killed Luke to pay back what he'd done to my family."

Robertson tossed a heavy gold cuff link on the kitchen table. It landed with a thud, reflecting dully off the flickering lantern light. "That's what you saw that day up in the hills where your uncle died. It's Fredericks's—has his initials."

"But why didn't anyone ever search there before?"

" 'Cause no one cared what happened to Luke Dalton. Most folks were glad he was dead."

"How did you identify Fredericks as the murderer just by this cuff link?"

"You suppose anybody'd dress in duds like that to climb in scrub brush? You don't wear cuff links with Levi's and a work shirt."

Cassie was silent as she stared at the square piece of gold.

"You ever see him get dirty?" Robertson asked, looping the rope around his bulging arm.

"No."

Robertson continued. "Because that was one job he couldn't hire out and be sure it stayed a secret."

"But if he tried to get you to . . ."

"I didn't have a reason to stop him neither."

Slowly Cassie picked up the incriminating evidence. Turning it in the light, she saw the engraved initials. Her voice was low as she glanced up. "But why didn't you at least tell the sheriff when you found it? Especially if Fredericks wanted you to—"

"Like I said, I didn't have no use for your uncle. I couldn't kill him, but I was glad he was dead."

She shook her head sadly—so much hatred and deceit. And what had any of them gained?

Jacob opened the door and peered at the water sluicing in wind-blown sheets against the timbers of the porch.

"Move fast, lady. In better'n an hour, nothin'll be left of that canyon." *Or the boys.*

"I could send Fowler—" she began.

"Who the hell do you think's been doin' Fredericks's dirty work?" Robertson stared at her as if she were crazy.

Cassie swallowed convulsively. So Shane had been right about him, too. She rushed to change from her dress into breeches as soon as she heard Jacob slam the door shut. Pulling on a poncho and hat, she wondered which was worse, facing the raging storm or looking into Shane's face knowing she'd wrongly accused him.

She found Shane in the Lazy H stable, quickly readying his mount. The rain dripped from her poncho and pooled around her as she stood in the shadows of the barn. Hearing her, Shane whirled around, his face a perplexed mask of relief and disappointment.

"I thought you were Michael." He turned back to the horse and continued saddling it.

"I wish I were right now." Her voice sounded soft, but it betrayed the myriad emotions she tried to stem.

He turned around slowly. "Meaning?"

"Meaning Michael took Andrew and Zack down the arroyo."

Shane's lips formed a word, but no sound emerged.

"We have to blow the dam, Shane." His head snapped up, and his eyes narrowed. "And I'll need your help."

"Now's a hell of a time to admit that."

"I'd say now's a hell of a time, no matter what I admit."

Shane's flinty eyes challenged her statement, but he quickly finished saddling the stallion. Without further words he gathered up the blasting materials, tucking them into his saddlebags.

"Stay in the house and get dried off. I'll be back when I find the boys."

"I said 'we,' Shane."

"You gonna argue now? Doesn't anything ever slow you down?"

"Can't say as you ever will. Are you going to waste time arguing, or are we going to blow a dam?"

Shane could hardly believe he was still standing there, arguing with her while the storm raged in fury around them.

"Well, if you're coming, let's go," he finally muttered, leading his horse to the big double doors.

The rain hitting their faces stung painfully. Lowering the brim of her hat, Cassie hung on tightly as they rode quickly toward the dam. Great whorls of water cascaded over the low-lying creek banks, creating a frightening panorama of land and sea. The jarring reality that this sea of water should all be flat, dry ground hit them both as they turned toward one another. A new sense of urgency propelled them forward.

Approaching the path to the dam, Shane reached out to grab the reins of her horse. Shouting to be heard above the rain, he stilled the mare. "We need to find a place to cross or we'll have to ride all the way up and around."

Cassie nodded to show him she understood, doubting he could hear a reply in the overpowering din. They picked their way carefully along the sodden banks of the swollen creek. Shane still held her reins and started to cross. Just as abruptly he pulled back, taking Cassie with him. He pointed into the roiling water, and Cassie's eyes followed the direction of his arm. Floating quickly down the muddy rapids was a hat—a black bowler—the distinctive hat that Fredericks sported.

They immediately looked across the bank. Fredericks's palomino was struggling to climb up the bank. They watched in horrified fascination as the great beast's flanks heaved with exertion as it finally conquered the fast-disappearing bank.

Feeling sick, Cassie felt Shane's hand close around her arm as they watched Fredericks bob to the surface, struggling against the treacherous current. Shane handed her the reins to both horses and dismounted quickly, grabbing the rope from the pommel of the saddle. Forming a quick loop, he threw the lasso toward the river.

Cassie watched in terror as Shane almost slipped into the water. But he backed away and ran along the bank, throwing the rope in for another try. Once again the rope floated uselessly in the water. Cassie pressed her knuckles to her mouth. She saw Shane's lips moving and guessed he was shouting to Fredericks to grab the line. But since the rain obliterated any other sound, she doubted that Fredericks could hear Shane's voice.

Fredericks went under, and Cassie held her breath as he struggled frantically to surface. Fredericks continued to struggle, but as Cassie watched, he flailed more weakly, finally going limp. Just as he did, Shane tossed the rope for the third time and it connected, but Fredericks remained still. Shane tried to reel the rope in, but as he did it caught on the roots of an upended tree trunk. He struggled fiercely with the snagged rope. Cassie counted the minutes as they dragged by, watching Shane's exertion, almost feeling his pain as the rope dug into his hands. The tree trunk finally burst loose as a large wall of water rushed by. Pulling against the fast-moving current, Shane hoisted Fredericks's inert body up the bank.

Cassie dismounted, leading the horses behind her. When she reached Shane, he didn't have to tell her. The frustration in his eyes spoke for him. It was too late—Fredericks was dead. She felt no taste of victory in knowing her uncle's killer was dead. Just another useless death, she thought, shaking her head. Her fear for the boys' safety, however, now overshadowed any other feelings. The horrible image of pulling three other bodies out of the water spurred her into action.

Swiftly they mounted and rode at a hard pace, without caution, because now they knew they had to take the long way around. Trying to cross the swollen river wouldn't save the boys; if Shane and Cassie didn't make it, the boys would lose their only hope of rescue.

Frantically they fought the driving rain that threatened to make them lose their course or plunge them off the ever-changing banks of the creek. Cassie could feel the exertion of her horse beneath her: white flecks of spittle formed around the mare's mouth and was lost in the never-ending flow of water that poured around them. Holding on tightly, Cassie prayed the horses wouldn't lose their footing.

When she sighted the dam, Cassie could have cried aloud in relief. Instead she glanced at Shane. His face reflected determination and, as he turned to her, a measure of hope she shared.

When Shane reined in, she instantly took charge of the horses while he unpacked the blasting equipment. The rain plastered her sodden poncho to her body as Cassie searched for a place to hobble the horses. Finding a tree, she tied both horses and then ran after Shane. Shouting to be heard, she tugged at his arm.

"I want to help!"

He shook his head, but she tugged relentlessly on his arm. They could blow the dam faster if she helped.

"All right," he shouted in return. "But don't get the charges too big." He showed her how to set the charges, and she nodded in agreement as the rain bit into her face, carefully accepting the dynamite and blasting wire. They separated and started placing the charges. Each moment that ticked away reminded them of Michael and Andrew.

Perversely, each moment seemed intolerably long yet sped by unbearably fast. When they neared the middle of the dam, they met. Swallowing the fear that constricted her throat, Cassie stepped back as Shane placed the final bundle. Making their way quickly to the edge, Cassie felt herself slipping. She gasped in relief as Shane's strong arms held her steady until they reached the end.

Shane picked up the charger and prepared to push the lever down. Cassie's fearful eyes met his, and he shot her a look of encouragement. She nodded and closed her eyes.

The blast sounded incredibly loud, horrifyingly close, and even seemed to make her feel as though she were floating in the air. But when her body hit the cold shock of icy water, Cassie realized it was more than just a feeling. The blast had thrown her into the vortex of the river that was quickly being filled with the debris from the dam.

Struggling against the current that sucked at her and threatened to pull her beneath its deadly surface, Cassie grabbed at a limb that sped past. Frantically trying to kick toward the bank, she found herself swirling instead with the current. Fighting the fear that she knew could immobilize her, she hugged the limb closer and fought to keep her head above water.

The current was strong—and deadly. Cassie gasped and spit out a mouthful of water as she surfaced again. The heavy poncho was now dead weight that dragged her down along with the relentless current. Each breath she took burned a ragged path to her lungs, and the muscles in her arms and legs burned with equal intensity. The chilling water numbed her body, turning her skin blue and engulfing her in waves of shattering chills. The bank seemed to flash by as though she were being propelled faster than even the debris that threatened to cover her.

Thinking it would be a relief to close her eyes and stop the awful cold and fear, Cassie was jolted when she felt something thump her head none too gently. As she tried to focus on what it was, she felt it again. Staring up through the rain continuing to pelt her face and arms, Cassie saw that it was a rope. Fighting certain death in the river, Cassie panicked as she reached out to grab it, but the elusive cord disappeared.

Her fragile store of strength was almost spent when she saw the rope again. This time she willed a burst of energy and grabbed for it again, but her numb fingers refused to take hold. Feeling the heat of her own tears coupled with the water that sucked at her, Cassie fought the sobs of fear that threatened to drown her as surely as the rushing water. When the rope appeared again, she reached out, fingers outstretched, arms taut and extended. She had it!

Grappling until she had a firm grip, she hung on to the rope. A swift strong tug on the other end started pulling her toward the bank. When Shane's strong arms lifted Cassie toward him, she clung to him with the last of her ebbing strength. She needed to feel his control, his aliveness. The specter of death was too recent a visitor to be forgotten. Still sobbing, she vaguely felt him pull his poncho around them both.

Tenderly his hand traced the contours of Cassie's face. With each touch Shane felt the love that was so difficult for him to express, but the rain didn't allow him the words he wanted to say. Instead he scooped her up and rapidly carried her over to the horses.

Knowing the urgency of finding Michael and the boys, Shane fought his emotions, unable to resist holding her a moment longer than was necessary. Almost losing her had dissolved the dregs of the past he had clung to. Shane could no more stop his love for her than he could the water rushing by—water that gave life and now almost caused her death. His lips touched hers gently, almost reverently.

"You're safe now, Cassie girl, and I won't ever let you come to harm again. You're mine, and nothing's ever going to keep us apart. Can you ever forgive me?" he whispered into her ear. He felt her weakly lace her fingers around his rain-slick neck.

As the rain poured over their faces and carved its path over eyes, cheeks, and lips, Cassie's face told him all he needed to hear. He could see the exhaustion overtaking her as she buried her face in his neck, her soft lips nuzzling the roughness of his stubble. When she raised her pain-filled, trusting eyes to his, he felt his heart being branded for all time.

Shane quickly pulled a soggy blanket from his saddle and wrapped it around her, deeply worried as he saw the blueness of her limbs. Her eyelids drooped closed, and he knew she'd fainted. He held her fragile body close, willing his body heat to warm her frozen limbs.

Torn, he knew he should take her home, make sure she was safe and warm, but the fates of their brothers were still undecided. He shook his head a moment as though to clear it. He could have sworn he heard shouting. Glancing across the river, he spotted three horses, and one was Michael's! He uttered a quick but fervent prayer of thanks.

Judging from their waving and shouting, he could see that the two boys and Michael looked safe—and that they were stuck on the other side of the river. Andrew and Zack kept pointing toward the Dalton spread. Apparently they intended to head toward Cassie's place to wait out the storm. Grateful to see them safe, Shane waved back to show them he understood. Looking back at Cassie's still shape, he was relieved his choice had been made for him.

43

Shane climbed the back stairs and pushed the door of the guest room open with his foot, balancing the tray of hot soup and tea as he did so. When the door swung open, he nearly dropped everything. The bed was empty, and Cassie was nowhere to be seen. Leaving the tray on the dresser top, he ran down the front staircase, taking the stairs two at a time, shouting for her as he ran. He reached the end of the stairs and saw that the great double doors had been flung open, and the pounding wind was driving sheets of rain into the hall.

Startled, Shane saw Cassie as she ran toward the corral, looking like an apparition in the fulminating storm. Running to Cassie, he grabbed her and whirled her about. The terror in her face was painful to watch. He scooped her into his arms as she fought him, but her panicky struggles were no match for his strength as he brought her back to the house, pushing the doors closed behind him.

"I found Andrew," he kept saying over and over as she pounded her hands against his chest, fighting to be released.

"But he might drown!" she cried out, unable to believe he had given up the search for the boys.

"Not at your house he won't," Shane answered, gently peeling her fingers away from his Adam's apple.

"My house? Andrew's at my house?" His words seemed to penetrate at about the same time she realized she was trying to choke him. All of the emotions of the past twenty-four hours erupted with as much force as her dam had.

"It's all right, Cass. They're alive and safe," he said, tenderly stroking her rain-soaked hair.

"Why do you think I'm crying, you big lout?" She sniffled into his chest as his hands rubbed comfortingly across her back.

"Damned if I know, woman. Nearly getting blown to death with you didn't make me understand you any better."

"What a surprise," she retorted, regaining her equilibrium yet leaning closer into his embrace, savoring his strength.

"With you everything's a surprise."

"Keeps you on your toes."

"Lucky I have any toes left after the way the dam blew. I just can't understand why it blew that hard."

Cassie raised her head and looked at him questioningly. "Shouldn't it have?"

"Hell, no. Small charges—"

"Small?"

"Sure, several small charges should have made it blow easily, but it blew like we'd set out to take half the countryside with it."

Cassie gulped, not knowing whether to be amused or horrified as he continued.

"I know the charges I set were small, and I told you not to make yours too big."

Cassie's voice was suddenly quiet as she answered, but her meekness was tinged with restrained humor now that she knew Andrew was safe. "I thought you said to make them big."

"You what?"

She hurried to explain. "What with the rain coming down so hard, I could hardly hear. I thought you said to make them big."

"I said don't make them *too* big."

"Details."

Shane didn't know whether to strangle her or kiss her, but

the latter was more appealing. "That settles it, Cassie girl. I'm marrying you for your own protection."

"You are, are you?"

He started carrying her up the stairs, their sodden clothes dripping on the carpet beneath them.

"Don't you think you ought to ask me if I want to marry you?"

"And start another fight? Nope. I haven't got enough energy left to fight *and* make love to you. And I sure as hell plan to make love to you."

Her eyes twinkled as she gazed at the man she loved. "You do?"

He answered in a mock growl. "Yeah, you got something to say about that, lady?"

She smiled mysteriously as she twined her fingers through his hair. "For once I don't think I'm itching for a fight."

Cassie's mouth grew suddenly dry when she saw Shane's amusement fade to be replaced by a steadily growing flame of desire. The heat blazed in her cheeks. Pent-up tension hung between them.

"Shane, this gown—how . . . ?"

"You had to have warm clothes. I couldn't let you stay in yours. The gown was my mother's."

She lowered her eyes, suddenly unreasonably shy.

"I want to ask you one thing, Cassie."

She swallowed and nodded.

"Are you all right? I mean with the storm and all . . ."

Her eyes deepened and widened, knowing what he was asking.

Her voice was husky as she answered, "I'm perfectly fine, Shane."

Without further conversation Shane carried her quickly up the stairway, his torso gleaming with droplets of moisture.

He pushed open the door to the great bedroom and then kicked it closed behind them. He laid Cassie down none too gently on the bed and stripped away his sodden clothes. Then he shook the remaining moisture from his firmly muscled body.

Cassie met his eyes, her invitation painted in the recesses of her soul. It no longer mattered that he was a Lancer and she a Dalton. In that instant they became simply man and woman, a man and woman who'd fought frustration and desire. It was time now for the reckoning.

Unable to tear her eyes away, Cassie watched in fascination as Shane moved forward, each sculpted thigh rippling as he walked. As he neared the bed, she let her bold gaze travel slowly downward. The remaining droplets of water trickled over his body and rested in the springy hair that revealed as much of his firm manhood as it covered.

He closed the distance between them and grasped her now trembling body next to his. Cassie gulped, trying to swallow the impossibly large lump that surfaced in her throat. She felt the moisture from his chest dampen her cambric gown and sear her awakening breasts.

Shane boldly lowered his mouth to lap at her nipples through the gown. He took first one and then the other as though they were a feast too rich to choose from. The unbelievable sensations of his tongue's mastery, coupled with the touch of the fabric as it rubbed her skin, tantalized her nipples until they were begging for his attention. Roughly he released the buttons on her gown, pulling it free, feasting his eyes on her proud breasts, pointing upward, begging to be touched. Cassie heard his indrawn breath and reveled in the power that was hers. His mouth sought out hers—tongues questing, battling, seducing.

Through her passion-clouded senses, Cassie felt his hands searching and arousing her with his touch. Dimly she felt his hands gently grasping the fastenings of her gown. Only the singular garment remained, and suddenly she couldn't wait for it to be removed so that she could feel the hard length of

Shane next to her, his drenched, naked skin upon hers. As though he'd read her mind, he eased off the gown.

Cassie's hands roamed over his hard, rippling muscles. Feeling the full length of him against her, she marveled at the instant heat that ignited between them. Boldly she caressed the firm flesh covering his wide shoulders and lean hips. It was as though she could never get enough of him.

Gasping, she abandoned herself to the sensations his hands caused as they skimmed over her flesh. He trailed his fingers lightly up her inner thigh. He paused, for the barest instant. Then he moved to caress the other leg. The whisper of his fingertips made her body tremble, her legs suddenly weak, fluid. When his touch reached the tousled curls covering the center of her desire, she arched upward, eager for release.

As he stroked the tender flesh, Cassie sighed aloud, burying her face in his neck. When he took his hands away, it was to put them on her hips and pull her closer. Fitting herself to Shane's lean contours, Cassie wanted to scream with pleasure when he finally filled her. The long, slow strokes seemed to penetrate to her womb. Each was a slow torture of the finest kind.

When he increased the thrust of his movements, she found her legs moving of their own accord to wrap themselves around his buttocks. She knew in that instant she never wanted to be separated from him. And with her body she conveyed the urgency of her message.

In the aftermath, Cassie heard the words she'd longed to hear . . . dreamed of hearing. . . .

44

"I love you." His words drifted through the room, shimmered in the moisture that covered them, and danced in the breeze that skimmed over their bodies.

Her eyes closed briefly, and a single tear cascaded from each violet pool, tracing a path over her ivory cheeks.

"What? Tears?" Shane's incredibly gentle touch wiped away each drop, and his kiss dissolved their tasty reminder.

Cassie moved her head lightly to the side, unable to speak.

"Regrets?" The disappointment in Shane's voice wounded her to the core, and she turned toward him, drawing her hands lightly over the chiseled cheekbones and strong contours of his face.

"Never." Cassie's eyes searched his. "Never," she repeated softly. "I love you, Shane."

Whatever Shane could have imagined wouldn't have prepared him for her response. A mental dam of reserve melted with her words. It was too late for regrets, and with Cassie curved in his arms, it was hard to remember there should be any. Now he could put the past where it belonged. Forever.

Millicent walked slowly beneath the canopy of willow trees, content simply to rest her hand in Ringer's, to gain comfort from his presence.

"It seems like weeks have gone by since the flood, instead of hours," Millicent murmured. "So much has happened."

Ringer was unusually quiet as they paused beneath the endless sky. "I don't think I can go on this way anymore, Milly."

Her stomach plummeted to some distant region while her heart beat painfully against the sudden constriction of her rib cage. Could he mean . . . ?

She tried to swallow past the tears that clogged her throat, wishing she could turn back the clock, undo whatever she had done wrong.

He moved her toward him, his clear blue eyes deep and troubled. Millicent started to turn away from the painful truth she was afraid she'd see there. Instead Ringer gently grasped her chin and turned her face toward his.

"Meant what I said, Milly. Couldn't stand another day like yesterday during the storm. Wondering, thinking the worst." Abruptly he dropped her hand, turning away and shoving his hands deep in the pockets of his denims. "When my wife and young'un died, I thought I'd died, too. Maybe for the last ten years I *have* been more dead than alive." Ringer dug his boot into the muddy sledge of the field and turned his face upward, as though seeking answers that lurked beyond his ken.

Millicent felt her heart constrict even tighter than before. If he meant to say good-bye . . . The anguish spilled across the planes of her face.

Suddenly Ringer turned to her and grasped both arms. "Until I met you, Milly. I wasn't alive until I met you."

As he pulled her close in his embrace, Millicent felt a fragment of hope come alive in the aching regions of her heart.

"When I couldn't find you in the storm last night, I thought you'd drowned and I'd lost you. Can't let you go back again, Milly. Give me your answer *now*."

She tilted her head back a bit. Had there been a question? Could it be—*that* question? She shook her head a bit, hoping to regain some of the sense that had taken wing and left her.

"Well," he demanded, "will you marry me?"

Millicent couldn't restrain the sudden tears that sprang to her eyes, blurring her vision, choking off her voice. She tried to bury her head in his strong shoulder to muffle the sniffling that threatened to overcome her. Instead he pulled back to see her face.

"Oh, my God. Does marriage to me make you want to cry?" The consternation in Ringer's voice was clear and very real. His need brought Millicent out of her own reverie.

She laid her hand gently against the tanned skin of his cheek and slid it down over the beginnings of stubble on his chin. "Only for joy," she managed to say between gulps, hoping her nose hadn't turned bright red from crying.

It took a moment for the words to sink in, and then Ringer whooped for joy, grabbing her and whirling her around the meadow. When he finally set her down, he was suddenly struck still with the fullness of the moment. Holding Millicent close in his arms, Ringer rested his face in the soft fullness of her hair, breathing in the scent that was only hers, thankful she was only his.

45

The ivory lace netting settled lightly over the long raven curls and then cascaded over Cassie's shoulders and down the satin bodice. A matching veil, held on her brow with a garland of orange blossoms, hid her creamy face, but even the veil couldn't hide her startling eyes.

Clasping her bouquet of flowers close in her moist hands, she strained to hear the music. The large puffed sleeves of her gown tapered into close-fitting cuffs near her wrists. It was a good thing her silk gloves hid the evidence of her nerves: damp palms didn't befit a bride, she mused.

When a small hand tugged at the tulle train that trailed past her wide satin skirt, Cassie looked down and broke into a smile.

Bending over, she spoke close to the little girl's ear. "Sadie, aren't you supposed to be sitting with your mother?"

"Yes, Miz Dalton. But I gots to know sumpin' first."

"What's that, Sadie?"

"Are you gonna be my schoolmarm for real?"

"For real, Sadie."

"I mean in a real schoolhouse, Miz Dalton, during the day, when we get a *whole hour* for recess?"

"As soon as the schoolhouse is built, Sadie. Until then, it'll be a real school, only we'll meet in the church house."

The child eyed her suspiciously for another moment. "You're sure you're not gonna go back to sheep ranchin'?"

"I'm very sure, Sadie. When Andrew's old enough, the

ranch is for him. Right now it'll be part of Mr. Lancer's grazing land."

The child brightened then and gave Cassie a toothy grin. "I'm awful glad, Miz Dalton."

"I'm awful glad, too, Sadie." Cassie glanced over at Millicent who was decked out in a beautiful silk gown of her own design with white gauze trimming. She wore a becoming headdress fashioned of oyster satin, ribbons, and white lace. Millicent appeared serene and not a bit anxious. Cassie clutched her own bouquet with renewed nervousness.

As the organist played the familiar wedding march, Cassie turned to Millicent and found to her surprise that a tear sparkled in her lashes. It was the end of an era. She and Millicent had shared so much, and now they were going their separate ways with the men they loved.

As though sensing Cassie's distress, Millicent winked at her and linked her arm through her friend's. "This is it, Cass. Now don't get all maudlin on me. You know I look just dreadful when I cry. My nose gets all red, my freckles stand out . . ."

Cassie laughed in spite of herself. She shook her head a bit as she watched her friend. Millicent's soft glow bespoke a natural beauty she had kept hidden for too long. Ringer was a very lucky man. Watching him nervously pull at the cravat that seemed to be choking him, however, Cassie didn't think he believed he was lucky. The next moment he lifted his head, sought out Millicent, and the love brightened his face like sunshine after rain. Cassie's smile softened. They would be happy together. As happy as she hoped to be with Shane.

While the brides moved together down the aisle, Cassie sought out Shane's chestnut head. His flawless attire was a stark statement of his striking handsomeness, and Cassie almost pinched herself to see if this was real. The man with the heart-stopping looks and the tender, loving heart was standing at the altar, ready to pledge his troth forever.

As they glided forward, Cassie's eyes sought out Shane's. The love she saw blazing there propelled her forward.

The minister's words flowed over her like the silk on corn, fluttering, unobtrusive, but wonderfully real. When she finally uttered "I do," she knew her heart was now whole, her life complete. Cassie's eyes brimmed with tears a moment later when she heard her best friend pledge those same words to her new husband. Clasping Shane's hand, Cassie watched as Millicent and Ringer reverently exchanged vows, their faces transfigured with love.

The rest of the minister's words—with the exception of "I now pronounce you man and wife"—flowed over her. The serenity she had been searching for settled in her heart. The reception was perfect, the people kind and welcoming, as they had been since she had agreed to abandon the land and become their full-time schoolteacher. It seemed she had gained their respect by blowing her own dam to save the boys. But it wouldn't have mattered because she was encased in a bubble of happiness that wouldn't burst.

When Michael approached her, Cassie felt a moment of trepidation. Shane confided that he'd finally told Michael the truth, but instead of the hurt and anger Shane was afraid Michael would feel, Michael had accepted the truth and realized why Shane had acted as he had. Still Michael had managed to keep his distance all during the wedding preparations, and Cassie fretted that he was nursing bitter feelings. She wanted to be a family, a whole family.

"Michael." Her voice was soft, laced with worry.

"You make a beautiful bride, Cassie."

She smiled. "Thank you. You made a handsome best man."

He returned her smile and then placed a perfectly proper kiss on her cheek. "If I couldn't have you for my girl, I'm glad to have you for my cousin and sister." He paused for a moment. "It's all right, Cassie. Everything's forgotten. This is a new start for all of us."

Cassie swallowed the lump in her throat, feeling a familiar prickling behind her eyelids.

"Don't go all emotional on me," he groaned. "I'm counting on you to be the calm one."

Thinking of the past few weeks, Cassie laughed aloud. "Calm might be a tall order to fill."

"If anyone can fill it, it's you."

She smiled again as Michael winked and moved away. It truly seemed that the alliance of the Lancers and Daltons would forever erase the blot on her uncle's name. Cassie was overwhelmed by her good fortune. If she had thought she'd not deserved the poor treatment she had received in the past months, now she felt equally undeserving of so much happiness. But Shane held none of her reservations. A generation of hate had been buried, and he felt they deserved their ration of happiness and then some.

When Cassie finally threw her bouquet into waiting, upraised arms, she laughed in relief. Her own home with the man she loved awaited her. As Shane flicked the reins of the buggy, Cassie glanced back once more, waving at Andrew and Michael. This was no dream; reality proved more incredible than any dream.

The soft glow of the oil lamps lit the corners of the huge master bedroom suite. The mahogany four-poster bed was laid with a fresh coverlet over the goosedown tick. Lace-edged pillowcases had been retrieved from Cassie's hope chest and now covered the plump pillows that rested invitingly against the massive headboard.

The flicker of the freshly lit fire in the fireplace cast an intimate aura over the room. Cassie paused at the cheval glass, seeing her own happiness reflected in the floor-length mirror. Shane stepped up behind her, his hands on her shoulders as he, too, looked at their images.

"It's really us," she said softly.

"I hope so."

She laughed quietly against his chest as she turned toward him.

"Much as I like Millicent, I'm glad I went home with the right bride."

"I imagine Ringer's glad you did too."

"There's my girl. I was beginning to think getting married might have taken away your lovely vinegar."

But instead of laughing, Cassie merely buried her head deep in his shoulder.

"What's this? Cassie . . ."

"I'm just so happy," she finally muttered. "And I'm afraid it can't be real."

Shane tipped her chin upward. "It is real, Cassie girl. And make no mistake, I'll always feel for you what I do today. I'm not saying we won't have our share of worries—but I'll always love you."

A single tear escaped down Cassie's cheek, and Shane wiped it away tenderly with a callused thumb. She closed her eyes briefly, her dark lashes hiding her tears. When she glanced up, her eyes were bright. "My love for you won't ever change, Shane. Today, tomorrow, always."

With a groan he caught her close, and Cassie felt him shudder against her. Suddenly she felt a new fever, one that only he could cure. Shane lifted the veil away from her face, and soon the intricate satin and lace gown joined the veil on the thick rug carpeting the floor.

Impatiently Shane shed his clothes and joined Cassie on the huge bed that had bred generations of Lancers. The blue ribbons entwined on the silk camisole slipped away under Shane's strong hands. His breath caught when he recognized the satin garter with rose-colored ribbons and pearl beading that he had given Cassie at the barn dance so many months ago. Reverently he slipped it from her leg, kissing the back of her knee and the soft flesh of her inner thigh. She shuddered at the feelings he created as he slowly unrolled the delicate silk stockings with their embroidered clocking of ivy and roses.

Remembered sensations collided with heart-stopping memories. When the stockings finally joined her camisole and gown, Shane lifted her ankle and kissed the sensitive instep. As he released her ankle, he slid his hands over her calves, up her thighs, teasing the raven hair at the juncture of her legs.

Cassie wondered if she could die of ecstasy. She was suddenly impatient for him—all of him. Her hands roamed greedily over the silky hair on his chest, the muscles that rippled in his back, and the firm tautness of his buttocks. Feeling his response, she grew bolder and grasped the shaft of his manhood. At his groan of pleasure, she allowed her hands to continue their exploration. She gasped aloud when his hands joined her search and sought out her secrets.

As Cassie writhed in pleasure on the fragrant sheets, she ached for the fullness of him. At that moment he rolled over and Cassie felt his full weight. One hand tenderly stroked her hair while his lips descended on hers. His tongue's mastery was second only to the fire his body created when he joined her. Each thrust brought her closer to the brink she'd visited with him that first special day.

Just when she thought the pleasure would overwhelm her, Cassie heard Shane's voice rasp in her ear, "I love you, Cassie girl."

Suddenly the world exploded once more. The dim light of the fire continued to flicker, outlining Shane's heaving chest, reflecting in the sheen that coated their bodies. As his strong arm encircled her in a close embrace, Cassie felt her heart soar.

She turned toward him, memorizing every detail of his face—each handsomely carved plane, each endearing crinkle around his eyes that told of smiles that had stayed with him. She closed her eyes briefly, remembering for a moment a lonely life before she found him, a regrettable past, and then opened her eyes wide. The alliance between the Lancers and the Daltons had forever altered those regrets. The light that now shone promised a new life, a new legacy.

"Yep, I brought home the right bride, Cassie girl."

"Today, tomorrow . . ."

"And always."

The author welcomes mail from her readers, and you can write to her c/o the Publicity Dept., The Berkley Publishing Group, 200 Madison Avenue, New York, NY 10016.

If you enjoyed SUMMER ROSE by Bonnie K. Winn, you'll want to look for a new *Diamond Wildflower Romance* every month . . .

OUTLAW HEART

Noah was fighting for his dream to build his own cattle ranch in a lawless land. Isobel was searching for the truth behind her father's murder. But together they found more than they were looking for—more passion than any man could tame . . . more ecstasy than any woman could resist.

Turn the page for an exciting preview of the newest *Diamond Wildflower Romance*, OUTLAW HEART by Catherine Palmer. Available now from Diamond Books.

Glancing behind, Isobel scanned the scrub-oak and twisted-pine woods. The small party of travelers who had accompanied her from Texas to New Mexico—the itinerant priest, the missionary doctor and his family, the school-teacher—rested from the journey. Their horses grazed, tethered in a clearing a safe distance from the trail.

The delay would put them in Lincoln Town after dark—too late for her to speak to the sheriff. She chose not to tarry and drink coffee. Instead she walked alone through the forest, back toward the trail, thinking.

If only her father hadn't come to the New Mexico Territory. He'd still be alive, his golden hair shining in the sunlight, his deep laughter echoing over the rolling hills of Catalonia.

Hoofbeats thudded across the damp snow, up the trail. Highwaymen? *Bandidos*, such as the men who had murdered her father?

Her eyes darted to the trail. Alarm froze her breath. Her traveling companions were too far away to be of help, and she had left her pistol in her saddlebag.

With instinct born of terror, she melted into the gray shadows of a huge alligator juniper tree. She pulled the silk gathers of her skirt close against her thighs. Her heart beat with every thud of the horses' hooves. She leaned against the rough trunk and peered through the lacy folds of her *mantilla* down the light-dappled trail.

"Things are looking ugly indeed in Lincoln Town, Noah." A young voice. English—not American.

She cocked her head out. Three riders, faces half-hidden under red scarves. Several unmounted horses and mules behind. Other men at the rear of the party, barely visible.

"You should be glad you've been away on the trail, Noah. Mr. Chisum's a good man. You'll stay out of the worst of the trouble if you continue in his employ."

"Chisum keeps to himself, all right. Lets me run the cattle the way I see fit. But with Dolan stirring things up and conniving to land Chisum in jail, there may be a few changes around South Spring River Ranch."

The second man—the one called Noah—rode tall on his black horse. Dressed in dark leather from his muddy boots and heavy chaps to his long coat, he wore a thick beard and a black felt cowboy hat. His blue eyes darted back and forth . . . watchful, alert, missing nothing. This man—and not the other—knew of life.

"You don't suppose Mr. Chisum would take my side against Dolan, do you?" The Englishman's voice held a note of hope. "Assuming he's released soon?" Sandy hair, a porcelain-smooth face, and side whiskers lent an almost fragile appearance to the young man, who could not have been more than twenty-five years old. Isobel found herself wishing him the aid he desired.

Noah shrugged. "Chisum stays out of a fight until it touches his own back door."

He studied the trail as he rode. Isobel stared with alarm at the freshly trampled snow.

"Don't worry," the third rider put in—a slender man, with the classically handsome eyes and curly hair of picture books and statues. "Just some trumped-up charges, I reckon. John Chisum can't be pinned down for long, and it's my guess he'll come out fighting mad against Dolan."

"I expect so—" the Englishman began. A loud squawk just yards from Isobel shattered the stillness. She whirled, dropped her muff, and clutched the rugged tree trunk.

"Turkeys." Noah rose in his stirrups and searched the gathering dusk. "I had a feeling we'd run across some. How about it? You want to see if we can bag one?"

"Sure!" The slender man slid his rifle from his saddle scabbard and spurred his horse. "Coming, Tunstall?"

"No, thank you." The Englishman beckoned the three riders behind the stock. "But go on—all of you. Perhaps McSween's wife will cook it up for us when we get to Lincoln."

As the men set off through the trees toward the nearby ridge, Noah glanced aside. His gaze fell upon Isobel. He blinked once. Reining his horse, he let his unknowing companions ride on. His eyes narrowed. He raked them up and down the young woman. Emerald gown, red ruffles, lace *mantilla*, ermine cape. Then he focused on her face.

Her breath went shallow. His bright blue gaze memorized her hazel eyes, her nose, the high curve of her Spanish cheekbones, and her lips . . . he lingered on her lips.

"What have you there, Buchanan?" the Englishman's voice rang out.

Noah looked at Isobel an instant longer, as if to confirm the strange apparition in the woods. She straightened, trying to swallow the dry knot in her throat.

This rough man might do anything. Yet there was something in the way he looked at her. Or perhaps it was the way he held the reins in his hands . . . gently, expertly, as if he were an *artista* and not a cowboy. She had seen the hands of a poet, and this man's hands—though large and strong—showed no malice.

He turned in his saddle. "I thought I saw something in the brush," he called to the Englishman. "There's nothing here."

Glancing at her one more time, his eyes flashed with . . . what was it—warning? Then he spurred his horse and thundered through the woods and was gone.

Isobel licked her wind-parched lips. Her eyes focused on the nearby ridgetop. At that moment she saw what the others had *not* seen. Armed horsemen—forty or fifty of them, she calculated quickly—guided their horses down onto the trail from the ridge.

"Tunstall!" A shout rang out to the lone Englishman not far from the tree where Isobel hid. "That you, Tunstall?"

"It is I." He reined his horse. "Who's there?"

"It's me, Jesse Evans, and Rattlesnake Jim Jackson—and a whole posse Jimmie Dolan sent to round you up. He's made us deputies." The riders advanced to within twenty yards of Tunstall, filing down the trail. Isobel saw they would meet directly in front of the big juniper tree.

"Come ahead, Tunstall," the man called Rattlesnake commanded. His heavy jaw and wide nose were coated with the blue light of the setting sun. "We ain't gonna hurt you."

"What is it you want, Snake?" Tunstall kept riding, even though the men facing him threw up their rifles so the stocks rested on their knees. Isobel shook her head, willing the Englishman to stop and draw his own rifle. Didn't he see that these men meant to harm him?

Snake urged his horse forward. "Not now," Isobel heard him mutter to Evans. "Let's wait until he gets nearer."

She clutched the tree trunk. Her *mantilla* buffeted her face. She must warn the Englishman! At that moment Tunstall's companions burst among the unmounted horses. They whinnied. Scattered.

"Take cover, Tunstall!" Noah shouted. "Head for the trees!"

"Now!" Snake swiftly raised his rifle-sight to his eye and fired. The bullet slammed into Tunstall's chest. He jerked backward and dropped from his horse to the frozen ground.

Evans leapt from his own horse and ran to where Tunstall lay in a heap. Men cheered. Evans jerked Tunstall's revolver from its holster and shot the Englishman in the back of the head. Then he turned the gun on the dead man's horse and pulled the trigger.

The other men in the posse crowded forward, a mixture of triumph and horror written on their faces. Evans cocked back his head and looked from Snake to the men around him. "With the two empty chambers in Tunstall's gun, the judge'll think he fired first."

Snake smiled, his heavy jaw jutting forward. "Good idea, Evans."

"Let's go round up the rest of Tunstall's men and give them the same medicine!"

Trembling, Isobel watched as Evans remounted and rode away. Four men—including Snake—remained. They stretched out the Englishman's body and wrapped it in blankets. Chuckling as if it were a joke, Snake pillowed Tunstall's head on a folded overcoat. Then he laid the horse's head on the Englishman's hat.

"This is—" Isobel whispered, icy fear melting before crackling rage. "This is abominable." And suddenly she saw her father—lying just as Tunstall now lay—murdered. Golden hair matted with his own crimson blood. His laughing mouth transformed into a grimace of horror. Slain with no one to defend him.

As she raised her head, the wind caught her lace *mantilla*, tugged it from the comb, and whipped it across the trail like a dancing white butterfly. She caught her breath. Snake's pale eyes darted up, then narrowed. A frown creased his face. He straightened, spat, and stepped over the body of Tunstall.

"Don't move, señorita." His voice dripped with contempt. "Hey, fellers. Looks like we got us a Mexican. There—behind that juniper tree."

Isobel swallowed the last of her fear and touched again the raw, stabbing wound of her father's death. As if on cue, the familiar anger flowed through her. If she, too, must die, she would die bravely. Lifting her chin, she stepped from behind the tree and moved out onto the shadowed trail.

"*Yo—*" She stopped as the men turned to her, their eyes wide. Forcing herself to think in English, she opened her lips. "I have seen the murder. I curse you—*asesinos*—assassins!"

"I'll be damned!" Snake whisked his rifle to his shoulder. Before he could pull the trigger, a horse thundered across the trail. Its rider swept Isobel from the path of a bullet.

"You're dead, you Mexican bitch!" Snake's voice rang out. "I swear I'll kill you!"

"Get down, get down!" Noah Buchanan rode through the trees, his head low against raking pine branches. Isobel crouched in front, barely able to breathe for the steel band of his arm around her waist. "Keep your head down. We'll ride till we lose them."

She twisted in his arms. His mouth was hidden by the red scarf, but his blue eyes burned in the darkness. "Who was the Englishman?"

"Damn." The man's breath was hot against her ear. "They got Tunstall, didn't they?"

"Rattlesnake killed him," Isobel hissed over her shoulder, her anger returning.

"Quiet!" Noah's leather-gloved hand clamped across her mouth. "Didn't you see how many were in that posse? Are you crazy, ma'am? They're all over these woods now."

She shook her head free from his hand. She, crazy? This man was *loco* the way he rode his horse through the forest as though he were possessed of sight in the darkness.

"There were two who did it—Rattlesnake and Evans," she said. "Snake rode forward first and shot your Englishman. Give me your rifle and horse. I saw the man—I shall make him pay!"

"Whoa, there." Noah reined his horse to a halt in the shadow of an overhanging sandstone lip. He sat breathing heavily for a moment, then lowered the bandanna to his neck. "Give you what?"

"Your horse—your rifle." She turned in his arms and stared at the bearded face beneath the black hat. "For revenge."

His eyes went deep, searching her face, denying the final word from her mouth. She saw concern written across them—a gentleness that should have been embarrassing to a man of such immense size and power.

"Revenge," she repeated. "It is what I seek."

He didn't answer. But the softness in his eyes seemed to grow.

The man was a contradiction. Raw male strength and an undeniably ruthless self-confidence emanated from every pore. Yet his eyes held the tenderness of a child.

As if words were not necessary between them, she could feel a deep pain that rose out of him and mingled with her own. She sensed that he understood what witnessing the murder had done to her. Unspeaking, he beckoned the ache in her heart, called it out of hiding.

Around her all was suddenly calm—the wind, the horse, the trees, her pounding heart. And the man, gently summoning her hurt . . . the brutality she had witnessed, the blood, the utter emptiness in her heart . . . her father. She fought to keep her anger burning.

Without a word he stripped away the protective layers she had built so carefully. His blue eyes laid her anger to waste, and all he left her was the raw pain.

Covering her face with her hands, she folded inward. Tears ran down hot cheeks, ran between her fingers, soaked through her gloves. Her stomach muscles tightened. She pressed a knotted fist against trembling lips.

Then warm arms came around her, drawing her into a dark cocoon. A place with the scent of worn leather, dust . . . and the trace of something undefined . . . a muskiness that hinted of bare male skin beneath the rough flannel shirt against her cheek.

"Now there, little lady." His voice was low, murmuring against her ear. "Revenge never did a lick of good. Those men are going to pay for what they did one way or another. You put everything you saw right out of your head, hear?"

He stopped and lifted his head, listening. "The woods are clear. The posse's gone to Lincoln to tell Dolan they've done his dirty work. . . . Listen, I rode past your people. I'll take you back. You'll be safe."

He turned his horse in the direction of the trail. The rhythmic gait eased the tension in her shoulders. Brushing fingertips across her eyes, she focused on the silhouettes above. Piñon, cedar, juniper. A hawk drifting overhead. The trace of a cloud.

The horrors of the evening began to drain away. Her numbed senses came to life. There was a velvet silkiness about the darkness that enfolded the horse and its two riders. She drank in the stillness, the quiet.

Noah's arm shifted, still tight around her. His thumb pressed just beneath her breast. A swift and unfamiliar sensation coursed through her. Instantly alert again, she saw herself draped against the warm man, this stranger. She was conscious of his thighs, lean and hard, against her own; his broad chest, solid as granite against her cheek; his heart, beating strong in her ear.

She recognized with a start this highly improper—highly dangerous—situation for a woman of her position. The man had rescued her and now—by all that was right for one of his lower station—he should remove his hand from her waist. He should stop . . .

She closed her eyes. His breath stirred the hair on her neck where her *mantilla* normally would have lain. His hand . . . each individual finger . . . warmed the skin beneath her breast. . . .

Her head snapped forward. She straightened away from him. Clearing her mind of the unfamiliar thoughts that had usurped it, she forced logic to reassert itself. She must get back to her horse, her rifle. The lawmen of Lincoln County had failed to bring her father's killer to justice. Now she had seen some of them—men who claimed to be deputies of the law—ruthlessly murder another man.

Something must be done.

The horse picked its way up the hill. Noah watched the moon rise over the ridge above the pines. He had to take the woman back to her party and rejoin the men. No doubt they would have regrouped after Dolan's posse cleared out.

Damn Dolan and his lawless ways. John Henry Tunstall had been a good man. And young, barely over twenty. Now all hell would break loose. No doubt the lawyer Alexander McSween would go after Tunstall's killers.

He shifted in the saddle and let his arm relax around the woman's slender waist. She held herself on the horse pretty well, he thought with mild surprise. Her straight back and raised head indicated years of training. That strange accent . . . Spanish. But her hair was golden in the moonlight. It didn't fit with his image of a señorita.

Of course, she looked the part of a rich Spanish doña—shiny green dress all ruffled with red lace, red button-boots, jeweled tortoiseshell comb keeping her dark blond hair in place. Proud and noble.

There was something about the way her long neck curved into her shoulders. He gazed at the moonlight silvering the silken gold ringlet that curled down her back. If he took out her comb, the whole mass of hair would come tumbling down. Its mysterious, spicy scent would waft out into the air. . . .

* * *

Noah sat on a three-legged wooden stool before the fire and warmed his hands. The second pot of water had just begun to boil. He thought of the woman in the next room. She'd probably crawled into bed by now. She had to be tired, no matter how wild and hotheaded she talked.

He smiled and shook his head as he poured a large basin full of hot water and set to shaving his whiskers off with Dick Brewer's straight razor.

Good old Dick. He hoped his friend could stay out of the worst of the trouble. Of course, being Tunstall's foreman, Dick was bound to get into the thick of things. Noah peered into the cracked mirror by the iron cookstove. If Dick got hurt, he couldn't stand by, no matter what promises he'd given the señorita.

Of course, the way she acted today, he'd probably have trouble keeping *her* out of it.

He dipped his head into a second bowl of fresh water and scrubbed his scalp. She'd said her father had been murdered in Lincoln County. Who could have killed him? She was crazy to come after the killer all by herself.

Of course, Noah thought, *he* was crazy to have done what he did. Marry her? John Chisum would take some fancy convincing to swallow that one. But it had seemed like a good idea at the time. Billy the Kid's idea, he remembered wryly . . . *loco.*

It seemed with the shedding of their clothes that all boundaries and reservations had fallen away. After their loving, Isobel lay in Noah's arms, her cheek on his chest, her dark gold hair soft against his shoulders. Their legs twined, toes nestled, hips pressed flush. She gazed at the tangle of dark chest hair growing around his brown nipples. Sunlight sifted through the coarse curls and blended them into mist. Despite their springy texture, they felt soft against her ear.

"Noah." Her breath stirred his skin. "The first day we met, you went searching Dick Brewer's cabin for paper."

She sensed the slightest tension ripple through the muscles in his chest. "Yeah . . . I did."

"What do you write, Noah?"

His fingers laced through her hair, weaving among the golden waves as he pondered her question. Finally he let out a breath. "Not much yet," he said.

She lifted her head and studied the uneven, sun-hardened planes of his face. "The moment I first saw your hands—when you saved me from the bullet's path that day on the trail—I knew," she said.

"What did you know?"

"I knew you were more than a cowboy. I knew you were an artist. Your hands are those of a poet."

He smiled a lazy grin, his eyes never leaving her face. "I'm no poet, Isobel."

"Then tell me what it is you write. Please, Noah."

After a moment's hesitation he shrugged. "Aw, stories mainly. They're all up here. In my head. Not a one of them's written down on paper yet. So I can't call myself a writer. Not really. I just have patches of ideas floating around. Stories about life on the trail. About things that can happen to a man when he's living off the land, when he and God and the lowing of the cattle are his whole world. Yarns the men spin while they're sitting around the fire after a long day." He paused and laughed. "It's probably a crazy notion."

She regarded the cowboy with his blue eyes focused somewhere far above on things she couldn't see. And she began to understand that what to her was a rough, untamed land was to this man a place of dreams. As his poet's hands slipped up and down her back, her heart grew and opened toward him.

"It would be crazier *not* to write down your stories, Noah," she said softly.

"Maybe so, Isobel. Maybe so."

A white butterfly drifted over their heads. Noah watched, wondering how it had emerged from its cocoon so soon. Too soon. A frost would no doubt end the fragile creature's life before summer. The white wings trembled, and the butterfly alighted on the creamy round swell of Isobel's bottom. She didn't notice. Noah smiled.

He liked Isobel this way, he mused. Of course, not many men wouldn't. She was soft, feminine, delicate. She was fleshly and giving in a delicious way that made him want to do things he'd tried to put clean out of his mind. Things like protect, honor, and provide for her. He wanted to keep her at hand so he could touch her hair and run his lips across her open mouth. He'd like to know her sweet thighs were waiting for him at the end of a day.

If he could keep her just like this . . .